The Saturday Treat

Catherine Clifton Clark

PIATKUS

For more information on
other books published by
Piatkus, visit our website
at www.piatkus.co.uk

First published in Great Britain in 1993 by
Judy Piatkus (Publishers) Ltd of
5 Windmill Street, London W1T 2JA
email: info@piatkus.co.uk

First paperback edition 2000

*A catalogue record for this book is available
from the British Library*

ISBN 0 7499 3250 3

Set by
Action Typesetting Limited, Gloucester

Printed and bound in Great Britain by
Cox & Wyman Ltd, Reading, Berkshire

Remembering Samarès and everyone who lived there and *M.Y. Marise* and all who sailed in her.

Not long before the outbreak of the second world war in 1939 the Sheridan family moved into The Chestnuts, one of the three houses in The Clearing, so called because that is exactly what it was — a clearing at the end of a lane that had wild balsam, cow parsley and elderberry bushes growing on either side.

Someone had thoughtfully painted the words 'Cul-de-Sac' in thick black letters on a white board under the place name so it was seldom approached except by residents and anyone who had business there.

It was an uncommonly secluded place although within easy reach of shops, transport, libraries and churches of most denominations.

On that warm Whit Saturday when the Sheridans came there was just enough room for the pantechnicon bringing their furniture to inch up the lane although it broke off quite a few twigs on the way. The noise of its approach brought Kate Hope running to the window of The Limes which stood directly opposite The Chestnuts, a gloomy-looking house that had been unoccupied since the Munich Conference as its elderly owners, the Wilsons, believing war to be inevitable, had put it up for sale and taken themselves off to live with their grown-up children in Canada.

Kate was eleven and a half years old and, like everyone else in The Clearing, was burning to know what the newcomers were like. She hoped there would be children. There were none of her own age nearby — the Lambert boys at The Walnuts were both too old to be companions for her; they

1

were practically young men, at least Tom was. But Guy! Oh, she went dreamy at the thought of him.

The Council member responsible for designating the houses in The Clearing had said it was dishonest to call a house The Chestnuts or The Limes or The Walnuts when there was only one of each tree in the respective front gardens. There had been a heated debate about it in the Council Chamber, letters appeared in the local press and it became quite an issue. He was eventually overruled and retired in high dudgeon. But that was way back in the 1880s when the houses were new and the trees mere saplings. Now they were fully grown. Today the chestnut was laden with blossom, and the buzzing of almost every bee in the locality filled the air.

It was afternoon when the pantechnicon drew up outside The Walnuts so as to allow room for the following taxi to stop outside the new owners' front door.

Kate, at the window opposite, held her breath. The great moment had come. At last she was to see the Sheridans. But not until the taxi drew away. Ah, but the offside door was opening and a girl was getting out. She stood in the middle of the road and looked directly across at Kate. She was small, square, in a gym slip and a school hat with a large hard brim, just like Kate's.

She breathed out. Should she wave? Tentatively she raised her hand. She waved and the girl waved back.

'Mummy, quick! The Sheridans are here!' she shouted, running to the door.

Mary Hope had given up watching for the pantechnicon half an hour earlier but she came scurrying in just as the taxi chugged away and saw the three Sheridans standing in the road obviously admiring the huge chestnut tree which was at the peak of perfection, the candle-like flowers glowing white and the leaves not yet darkened by the heat of summer.

'Let's go over,' she said. She was not one to stand on ceremony and crossed the road with outstretched hands saying. 'Welcome to The Clearing. I'm Mary Hope and this is my daughter, Kate.'

'How lovely to be welcomed!' It was Mrs Sheridan who spoke and the first things Kate noticed were her sweet

2

expression and soft voice. There was no need to know more for the time being; it was enough for Kate to take an instant liking to her, and Mrs Sheridan seemed to encompass her in a special look that surely meant she had recognised a kindred spirit.

Hester Sheridan saw in Kate the schoolgirl she once had been. She had no idea what sparked off this flash of recognition unless it was seeing a mother and daughter so obviously in tune with each other as she had been with her own mother before outside influences jangled the harmony. 'George,' she said, turning to her husband, her hand on his arm, 'I think we've fallen on our feet.'

'I'm sure we have.' Mr Sheridan, with his arm round his daughter, peered down at Kate over his spectacles, reminding her of a benevolent giraffe.

'Well, well, I should say you're about the same age as Sally,' he said.

'I'm eleven and a half,' said Kate.

'So am I,' said Sally.

'Twins!' they cried, linking little fingers and beginning to fire questions at each other: what, when, which, why, where, who?

The pantechnicon was backing cautiously into position. The removal men got out and opened the rear doors while Mr Sheridan, key in hand, went to let them in.

Mary Hope had already discovered the Sheridans were complete strangers to the district and was offering to show them round. She knew all the best shops and amenities that made their London village quite the most attractive place to live. 'And do let me give you some tea before you tackle your unpacking,' she said.

'That would be heaven. I'm gasping,' Mrs Sheridan said, and threw open her coat and patted her face with a little lace handkerchief.

Mr Sheridan had the move well organised with each piece of furniture and its position clearly marked but he knew it would be hours before they could get any tea themselves so he was glad of Mary's offer and soon followed his wife and daughter into her house. This was similar in design and layout to The Chestnuts but it was rather like walking into a fine art dealer's as the front sitting room where they had tea – 'So you can see how the men are getting on,' Mary had said – had several items of furniture and ornaments of a kind not generally seen in suburban houses and he had passed others in the hall. That grandfather clock could only be a Tompion, couldn't it? Natural good manners forbade him to stare.

He sipped his tea and hoped this would not be one of those spontaneous friendships regretted on further acquaintance. From the conversation going on between the two women he gathered that Mary's husband was the Orlando Hope who had a fine art shop in the exclusive area that lies between Pall Mall and Jermyn Street. That, of course, accounted for the furniture he could not help noticing. It probably *was* a Tompion. Mrs Hope referred to her husband as 'Ollie' and said he was having the cellar reinforced for themselves and their treasures in case war broke out and there were air raids.

'It's lucky these houses have such good cellars,' she said. 'I was sorry for people digging trenches in their gardens last September. It was so hot.'

'You don't really think there'll be a war, do you?' Hester Sheridan's father had been killed in the 1914 war and it upset her to hear people speaking of another as inevitable.

'Well, it looks like it, doesn't it?' said Mary. 'Ollie joined the A.R.P. ages ago and he always seems to be on duty. It disrupts meals. But what a mercy we've had a respite. At least it's given us time to breathe.'

They went on talking about that critical September of 1938 when Mr Chamberlain flew back and forth to Germany. Mary had watched his plane go over, such a little, lonely plane in the morning sky, and then she saw it come back. She wondered how he felt, an elderly man with greying hair and a black moustache going to meet another man with a black moustache. A lonely old man, his hand clasped by the younger one, the smiles, the greetings, his hope that all might yet be well. And that piece of paper. Peace in our time. How could they honestly believe it? Not when they heard that ranting voice, saw that upraised arm and the countless crowds responding – the ranks of uniformed

4

men, the dreaded *Zieg Heil*. There were so many Germans in Danzig by now – a city they had scarcely known existed before.

A fool's paradise ... They were living in a fool's paradise. Who had said that? Could it have been Mr Sheridan? Mary realised her attention had wandered and gathered it was he who'd said it for Mrs Sheridan declared if that were so she liked it and went on to talk about the problem of her husband's books. The flat they had left in South Kensington was too small to accommodate them all.

'It was the weight. We were afraid the floors would give way,' she said.

Mr Sheridan agreed the weight was a problem but didn't tell them he had rented two empty rooms to take the surplus. He glanced out of the window at the crates on the pavement. The men were scratching their heads. Should he go out? Another cup of tea was offered. Best not to interfere. They knew what they were doing.

Guy Lambert from The Walnuts came skimming up the lane on his bicycle and Kate's heart did a funny little loop. He slowed down and stared at the pantechnicon. He looked like a late teenager to Sally and she asked who he was.

'Guy Lambert.' Kate tried to sound casual. 'He lives next door to you.'

Sally took a long look at him. He had alighted and was walking the length of the pantechnicon, obviously noting the name and address. He took his time about it. Then he got on his bicycle and began trick-riding round the space in front of the houses. He jerked the bike backwards and went round with the front wheel off the ground. Then he swung it down, put his feet on the handlebars, leaned back in the saddle and went round again. He performed several other feats and ended up sitting on the handlebars pedalling slowly backwards round and round with both arms extended. Kate held her breath. He performed his tricks every afternoon and she hoped he would fall off one day and give her the chance to run out and help him up. Not today. He got off, took another look at the pantechnicon and strolled off, wheeling his bike to his own house.

Kate expected Sally to be thrilled by his daring but to her

5

intense disappointment all she said was: 'Pooh! Doesn't he fancy himself!'

'Fancy himself! Wouldn't *you* if you could do tricks like that?' demanded Kate.

'I could if I wanted to,' said Sally. 'You can do anything if you want to hard enough. Didn't you know?'

'No,' said Kate, but she was interested.

'You have to want to really hard,' said Sally. 'It's no good being wishy washy.'

'What do *you* want?' asked Kate.

'To go to Oxford. And I shall. St Hilda's. That's where I'm going.' Sally had a slipaway chin. She had heard it was a sign of a weak character and was always trying to thrust it out. She did so now. Kate was fascinated by the effect. 'I *will*,' said Sally. 'I will go to Oxford. What about you?'

'That's my secret,' said Kate.

'Tell me.'

'It wouldn't be a secret if I did.' She wanted Guy Lambert to be her special friend but she wasn't going to tell anyone. 'I shall go into Daddy's shop when I leave school.'

'What sort of shop? Grocer? I'd like that. You could pinch the raisins and sultanas.'

'Daddy is a fine art dealer,' said Kate.

'Oooh. Far superior.'

'Would you like to see my jade animals? I'm collecting them. I've got a rabbit, a fox and a fieldmouse so far. What do you collect?'

'Nothing. Dad collects books and Mum says one collector in the family is one too many.'

They went out of the room chattering and Mary said Kate had been hoping there would be children at The Chestnuts.

'Only one,' said Hester, 'and we can't quite make out where that one came from, can we, George?'

He agreed. His theory was that children were not so much the creations of their parents as reincarnated ancestors — often most unpleasant ones. As a university lecturer he came in contact with a great many young people and was often staggered when he met their parents who, for the most part, were mild, inoffensive people and often quite frightened of

6

their demanding, belligerent children. His own Sally, he liked to think, was a new-minted soul, a loving child, though a very bossy one. It was a pity about her looks, or was it? She didn't favour her beautiful mother and his own features were fairly regular, whereas Sally's ... 'Dad,' he remembered her saying after a rare but prolonged look in the glass, 'why is my face a smudge?' 'If more smudges were like your face I should be all the better pleased,' he had replied.

And here she came, back into the room with Kate. She took the scone Mrs Hope offered, the last one on the plate. 'Half each,' she said to Kate with the smile that did wonders for her: crinkly, comical, sweet. Sally was lovely when she smiled.

As soon as the Sheridans left, Kate and her mother agreed they were going to like them. They would be an asset to The Clearing. Mrs Sheridan was lovely to look at. 'And she looks so young, Mummy. Like a girl,' said Kate.

'I daresay she is very young, dear. Much younger than her husband.'

Mr Sheridan, though rather dry, had a benevolent expression and a remarkably pleasant voice. And as for Sally — she was just great.

The Chestnuts' gloomy look would soon disappear for it was to be redecorated inside and out and Mrs Sheridan meant to get rid of the blinds and replace them with curtains.

'And I shall have someone to go to school with,' said Kate for Sally had been enrolled and was already wearing the uniform. They were friends from the first and would continue so. 'All our lives', they very soon said.

And yet they could not have differed more, both in appearance and character. Kate had even features, large eyes and upturned lips. Her head was well set, her neck graceful. Her hair was straight but it was thick and manageable. She had a serious expression but was quick to see the funny side of things and would hurry home from school to tell her mother anything comical she had seen or heard. She was quite a good mimic and would amuse her parents by apeing the idiosyncrasies of the teachers — the way Miss Hunter, the headmistress, pursed her lips when she rang the handbell at prayers or Miss Carey, the history mistress, of the peculiar walk, rolled along with her legs wide apart — 'just as though she's wet her knickers, Mum.'

Mary spluttered with suppressed laughter. 'You mustn't. It's disrespectful. Now get on with your homework.'

Kate did not want to do homework. It was bad enough having to go to school at all, especially in summer, and she was forever being called to attention in class and reproved for daydreaming, but the school orchard was so much more interesting to look at than the blackboard. Very often she was busy arranging tunes in her head, selecting, discarding, extemporising for she had a small gift. She could play the piano by ear and delighted everyone who heard her. When she first began to pick out tunes her parents sent her for lessons thinking she would learn easily. She refused to be taught and when entreaties, threats and even bribes failed, she got her own way. Instead, she listened to the wireless and to gramophone records and surprised everyone by playing whichever song happened to be all the rage in fair imitation of a concert piece.

Sally had no particular gifts but paid close attention in class, her hand always first to shoot up when questions were asked. She had powers of concentration and a photographic memory so always excelled at examinations. Very often, on the way home, she would tell Kate things she had missed in class and explain points she didn't understand. She often seemed much older than her age and had already decided she would never marry. 'Much too dicey,' she said, and laughed when other girls talked of romance. 'There's no place like home,' she would say, 'I like being with Mum and Dad.'

George Sheridan never regretted the friendship that developed between his family and the Hopes. He especially liked Orlando Hope, Ollie, as everyone called him, but was not enamoured of his other next-door neighbours, the Lamberts. Unfortunately Hester got off on the wrong foot with them the very day she moved in. She was walking round the garden that evening when the young fellow who had been showing off on his bicycle when they were at the Hopes looked over the fence that divided their gardens.

8

'Good evening,' she said.

'Your name's Sheridan, isn't it?' he asked without returning her greeting.

Slightly taken aback, she replied that it was.

'Lady or Mrs?'

In the ordinary way she would have been amused but there was something in the boy's manner she found offensive. 'Plain Mrs. Mr, Mrs and Miss. I hope you're not disappointed.'

'My mother's been worried in case you might not be our sort,' he said.

'Indeed. And what sort are you?' she asked, bristling.

'We're the Lamberts and we don't want the tone of The Clearing to go down.'

Later on she thought of what she should have said: 'If you are an example it can hardly sink much lower.' But she didn't think of it till later. As it was she said nothing and a querulous female voice called out, 'Guy, dear. Guy, I want you.' The youth disappeared from view.

'Not worth your notice, my dear,' George said when she told him.

After this Hester did not entirely trust the hand of friendship Ella Lambert extended a few days later and guessed it was prompted by curiosity. A year earlier George had inherited Heron House from his father. It was situated on the river bank between Marlow and Henley. With it went *Corsair*, old Robert Sheridan's forty-foot cruiser, his paid hand Sam Sharkey, and his housekeeper Mrs Sharkey, mother of Sam. Ella gained this information from her husband who had extracted it from George when they went up to town together on the eight-thirty. She concluded the Sheridans must be pretty well-off if they could keep two houses going. In order to learn more she invited Hester in for coffee and was able to inspect her at close range.

She was not pleased with what she saw. The looks that had enslaved George had not faded in the fourteen years of the Sheridans' marriage. The hair colour was undeniably natural – Ella's was tinted – and the make-up almost invisible. Which foundation did she use, if any? Ella could not deny that Hester Sheridan was most attractive and she

9

was jealous of her. Yet she was intrigued and wanted to know what had brought George and Hester together – he was so much older and, she guessed, came from a far superior background. It could hardly have been a love match. Perhaps he got her into trouble and did the honourable thing?

She was a long way from the truth. Hester seldom spoke of her early life and felt Ella Lambert would probably sniff at her family and its background so didn't tell her that her father had been killed at the end of the Great War and that her mother worked in the bank that had employed him before he was called up. Their little semi-detached house, their annual holiday at Herne Bay, their pleasures, their happiness and contentment, were not things Ella would appreciate.

Hester saw Ella as a spoiled petulant woman whose main interest was the latest fashion, no matter how ill it became her. That and gossip. She became absorbed in the gossip columns and behaved as though she featured in them herself. She could not claim to be a bright young thing but she saw herself as the aunt or favoured friend of those whose antics were reported in the Sunday papers. 'Knocking a policeman's helmet off,' she would exclaim. 'I shall reprove Lady Eleanor next time I see her. *Not* the way for a peer's daughter to behave.'

Hester took this for gospel as she sipped her coffee in Ella's sumptuously furnished drawingroom in which the armchairs and sofas were so deep and soft that once down it took an effort to get up. And the chests – two of them – so much red and gold.

'And do you think you'll enjoy living in The Clearing?' Ella asked.

'Oh, yes. Far more than in South Kensington, although that had its advantages.'

'Do you often go down to Henley?'

'As often as we can. Since my father-in-law died there are a great many things for George to see to.'

'You're very lucky to have a country house to escape to,' Ella said.

'Indeed we are, and it's so nice for Sally.'

Ella offered the biscuits once more. She had taken a dislike to Hester's plain, bumptious little girl. And why, she asked herself, should this young woman have so much? She was so consumed with curiosity that she managed to work in quite a few questions. She simply had to know where Hester had met her husand. 'I'm such a romantic,' she cooed.

'I was one of his students,' Hester said.

'Oh, you were at University?'

'Not for long,' said Hester. Why should she tell this old parker they'd met at an evening institute? Especially as George had taken the course there out of pure generosity of heart? She turned the conversation by saying she had heard Ella's son was going up to Cambridge, and soon was on much more comfortable ground.

Ella was devoted to her younger son, Guy. She regaled Hester with tales of his exploits from the cradle up and produced photographs of him from infancy onwards. He had an arrogant expression even as a baby. Further acquaintance with this young man, slight though it was, did not incline Hester to like him any better. He seemed to look down on her and she always felt at a disadvantage in the few meetings they had.

There were not many fine days in that summer of 1939 and when one came George said it was a special blessing and it behoved everyone to make the most of it for the world would not be at peace much longer.

'We're only enjoying a respite,' he said.

'Oh, you old misery! If you keep prophesying war you'll bring it on us,' Hester said. 'Still, you're right about making the most of the weather. Ollie's asked us if we'd like to go to Eastbourne on Sunday if it's fine.'

The two families had been on several expeditions together and the girls adored running down to the coast in Ollie's open tourer. It was a special treat for Kate because she could look for wild flowers on the downs. She had an ambitious scheme in mind. Ollie had bought six dining room chairs which he'd seen standing outside a shop in the High Road. They were unusual as the backs of each one had a different picture on its carved oak panels. The upholstered seats were in a bad condition with the horsehair stuffing coming out and were far beyond repair, but the backs took his eye so he bought

11

the chairs for a song. Now they were in the cellar. When Kate saw them she said she would like to embroider covers for the seats and floated the idea of making a different design of wild flowers for each one. She thought small flowers like pheasant's eye, buttercups and veronica would be better than large garden flowers and talked of the gleaming pink, red, blue and green silks she could buy.

Ollie told her such intricate work would take a very long time, years perhaps, but she refused to be put off. She knew she would need help with the designs and began taking measurements and asking for graph paper. Before long she was bringing home specimens of wild flowers and making careful, detailed drawings. Her parents were impressed and encouraged her, especially as Miss Bush, who taught needlework at school, thought highly of her skill as an embroideress and told Mary she had a flair for it.

With a great deal of help from Ollie, Kate drew the first of the designs and it was painstakingly transferred on to the canvas. Then she began the stitching and spent half an hour on it each morning before going to school and the same in the afternoons when she came home. She glowed with pleasure as a leaf or flower emerged from the background and would call Sally in to look, but Sally only showed a polite interest. 'It's very nice but it won't show when you're sitting on it,' she said. Kate thought this a very limited way of looking at things, but there was no need to dwell on such shortcomings today as she had found several flowers and grasses that were new to her. Sally had found a grass tussock to sit on. She had taken her glasses off and closed her eyes. Kate sat on the grass beside her. 'What are you thinking of?' she asked.

'Being Chancellor of the Exchequer,' Sally said.

'Oh, shucks. On a day like this?'

Sally laughed but she was half serious. She thought about her future a good deal. She was not as light-hearted as Kate because in a strange half-understood way she felt it was her place to take care of her parents. They were not practical people, both living in other worlds much of the time, and yet as a family, a trio, they were absolutely united. She loved her mother dearly but there was an added depth in her affection for George. It was rather like a touch of pity, and just as the merest pinch of salt can alter the taste of a dish, so her feeling for her father had an almost imperceptible difference.

War was imminent. People clutched at fragile straws of hope; holiday makers back from Germany could not believe it possible after the welcome they had received there.

Kate and Sally had other things to think of. Their walk home from school in the afternoons was a long drawn out process as Kate always tried to dawdle in the hope of running into Guy Lambert. Sometimes he would cycle past them in the lane, furiously ringing his bell. 'Out of my way, little girls,' he once said. 'Oaf!' shouted Sally.

Once he accidentally dropped a cigarette card and Kate picked it up and used it as a bookmark.

'I believe you've got a crush on him,' Sally said.

Kate blushed crimson. 'I have not!' she declared.

'Yes, you have. You're blushing.'

'I am not. It's the heat. You look like a turkey cock yourself.'

Sally made gobbling noises, she crowed, she laughed. 'Kate's cracked on Guy,' she sang.

Kate fetched her a biff with her satchel. 'Shut up!' she shouted. 'Shut up! Shut up!'

Ernest Lambert bought Guy a motorbike for his eighteenth birthday and he streaked along the lane at a terrifying speed. Oh, if he'd only take me on the pillion, Kate thought.

His mind was on other things. When he went up to Cambridge in the autumn he meant to join the University Air Squadron and then he would be in the front line for a commission. He did not intend to tell his parents.

Hester often saw Kate going along the lane to the street market with her mother on Saturdays. They went arm in arm, talking their heads off, and the sight of them, so happy in each other's company, reminded her of her close relationship with her own mother. They too had been attracted to street markets and when she happened to mention it, Mary Hope asked her if she would like to go with them.

The three of them spent an hour or so wandering round the stalls but she found it all vastly different from the market she remembered. There was a teashop on the pavement behind the stalls and pleading tiredness she excused herself and went in.

'We'll only be a few minutes now,' said Mary.

'I'll order when you come,' Hester said.

She sat down and past scenes crowded into her mind. Of course she had been very young, only about four years old, when she first went to the market with her mother and father, but how brilliant those mental pictures were, brighter by far than those outside the teashop window, and the noise, the stall-holders' cries, the buzz and bustle of the crowd, were not like those of long ago. The thing that had impressed her most at the time was the man with the tame white rats that walked up his arms and crossed each other on the crown of his head. She was frightened of rats but fascinated by these tame ones with their sleek white fur and pink twitching noses. She held tight to her father's hand and when he searched in his pocket for a penny to put in the man's cap, she clutched his trouser leg. The man came round the crowd, collecting. One of the rats sat in his cap washing its whiskers, the other sat on his shoulder. 'Stroke him. He won't bite you,' the man said, holding the cap under her nose. She retreated behind her father and was glad to move away. And there, to her dismay, was a fierce-looking man trussing up another in a strait waistcoat and fettering him with chains. He looked so angry, so threatening, and he threw the captive to the ground and laughed to see him struggling to get free. She hoped the police would come and arrest the torturer. Why did no one go to the victim's aid? She was so sorry for him she started to cry but the crowd jeered and laughed and told him to try biting through his chains while he heaved and writhed and groaned helplessly, and then with one miraculous twist and turn burst out of his fetters and punched his tormentor on the jaw.

'It's all a trick,' her mother said, and she took Hester's hand and said, 'Let's buy some shrimps for tea,' and they went on to the fish stall and the array of food from the sea was enough to dazzle the eye: winkles, whelks, mussels, cockles, crabs, lobsters, bloaters, kippers and buckling. The lobsters were navy blue.

'Dad, aren't lobsters red?' she asked.

'Not till you boil them.'

'They're alive. Look, they're moving!'

'So they are.'

'We're not going to boil one, are we?'

'I should say not. They shriek when you throw them in.'

It was her mother's turn to be served. 'A pint of shrimps,' she said, and the man shovelled them up in a mug and tipped them into a paper bag. His hands were deadly white for he had been descaling fish in the ice cold water, chopping off their heads to order, and cutting up eels which still went on wriggling after they were in pieces.

Hester had an unfading picture of that market in her mind and could still see herself as a child walking between her father and mother with each of them holding a hand on their way home to enjoy their tea.

Then she saw another picture: the same child with only her mother, for England was at war with Germany and her father was in the army.

It was strange without him at home. There was an emptiness in their little house, and quietness too, for her father made a lot of noise singing in the mornings. He sang 'D'ye Ken John Peel' and when it came to the View Halloo, flung her bedroom door open and sang it again. Next he was whisking her out of bed and carrying her into her mother's room where he threw her down on the big double bed and her mother kept saying, 'Oh, Andy, do be careful.'

One morning when they were all three sitting up in the big bed drinking their tea they heard the postman pushing letters through the door. 'It'll only be bills,' her father said.

'You never know. It might be a windfall,' said her mother. Laughing, she ran downstairs to see and came back with a brown envelope addressed to Andrew Field. It was odd how the temperature fell, how the laughter stopped.

'It's my call-up papers,' he said, and Hester, without understanding what it was all about, began to cry.

Kate and her mother came back very soon. Kate stopped short in the doorway. 'Doesn't Mrs Sheridan look sad?' she whispered.

Hester looked up at that moment. Her eyes were glittering with tears but she blinked them away and smiled. 'They have some lovely-looking pastries,' she said. 'Shall we go and choose?'

Her strange reverie seemed to have lasted for hours although it had all taken place in a few minutes and now they were pondering over the cakes. 'I'm going to have a cream bun,' she said. Kate decided to have the same but Mary chose a mille feuille.

In the middle of August the unsettled weather changed and a succession of fine sunny days set in but there was no escaping the threat of war that darkened everything. Vague talk about a blackout became urgent; Hester and Mary bought acres of black sateen and Kate and Sally were conscripted to help with the curtain making. They hated it. They liked rambling about the meadows at the back of The Clearing, talking endlessly and arguing over their holiday tasks.

Their English teacher had read them a lecture that set out to prove Falstaff was not a coward and they had been told to write an essay on the subject. Sally got through hers quickly. Kate read it and accused her of being a hypocrite. 'You know jolly well he was a coward,' she said.

'Of course he was,' agreed Sally.

'You've said he wasn't.'

'Of course I have.'

'Why?'

'Because that's what Miss Fowler wants, of course. She was smitten by all that old tripe and she wants us to agree with it.'

'How can you if you don't believe it?'

'You can if you want top marks, soppy.'

'Sally Sheridan, I'm disgusted with you!'

'Lawks a' mussy,' teased Sally. 'Shall I do penance?'

'I hope you come out bottom!'

'I'll be top. You'll see.'

Kate, nose in air, kept a dignified silence. They had been sent out to buy more cotton for the curtains and Sally said they had better buck up about it or they'd be in hot water. She skipped on ahead. Kate trailed behind. Sally nearly

16

always came top of the class while she had a struggle to get halfway. Anyhow, it would be daft to quarrel over an essay. She quickened her pace. 'Race you to the shop,' she shouted. When it came to running or tennis or swimming she had Sally beaten hollow.

While the world hovered on the brink of war Ella Lambert dropped her rather superior attitude and was glad of company to tide her through the day so she joined Mary and Hester and even sewed a hem. 'We're having frames made to fit our windows,' she said. 'Costly, but more effective than curtains, Ernest says.'

'You'll have to put them up every evening and take them down in the mornings. I'd go for curtains every time,' said Hester.

'Frames are more satisfactory,' Ella said.

'And much stuffier. You'll all suffocate.'

Mrs Lambert turned her attention to Kate who was trying to thread a needle. She could thread her embroidery silks with ease but black on black was something different.

'Hold it against something white, dear,' Ella advised. She was rather fond of Kate, a pleasant well-behaved girl, not at all like that nasty little Sally Sheridan who was not the right kind of friend for her at all. Should she warn Mary about this friendship? Perhaps not. The two families were thick as thieves. Always in and out of each other's houses. That funny old Mr Sheridan in a hat that looked like a bit of old suit. And always reading, even as he walked along the road. And that wife of his! Just look at her sitting there preening. Hester's very presence irritated Ella so much that she had to say something to divert her mind from the face, the figure, the air the woman had.

'You want to get in a good stock of soap,' she said. 'It's one of the first things to disappear in war time.'

'Do you think we should be stocking up?' asked Mary.

'With soap. And sugar.'

'None of us take it,' Hester said.

'And corned beef. And sardines.'

'What about pepper?' queried Hester.

Is the woman laughing at me? Ella wondered. 'Certainly pepper,' she said.

17

The B.B.C. news was due. Mary turned on the wireless and they listened to the calm, measured tones of Stuart Hibberd reading a bulletin that gave even graver news than the previous ones. Thousands of children were being evacuated from towns and cities.

'Just fancy, all those children being evacuated,' Ella said, her voice more quavery than ever. 'Poor little things. What an experience for them.'

'And what a mess,' Sally whispered to Kate.

'Ollie and I will stay where we are, and Kate will stay with us,' Mary said. 'We've talked it over.'

Hester and George had reached the same decision about Sally.

'We wouldn't go even if you tried to send us, would we, Kate?' said Sally. 'We'd camp out in a field. We refuse to be evacuated. Evacuated! Sounds like a dose of salts.'

Ella's face expressed disgust but a few minutes later she said: 'I can't help but think we'll be as safe here as anywhere, tucked away in The Clearing. And I still hope it won't happen.'

'So do we,' they chorused, and went on stitching away at their black sateen.

'Dear Sybil doesn't believe Hitler will go to war with us,' Ella said.

'Sybil?' Hester had yet to learn that Ella imagined herself on intimate terms with all kinds of people she had never met.

'Sybil Thorndike, my dear. We were talking only the other day. She told me we should trust the Füherer, and her opinion should be respected.'

Mary managed to give Hester a wink. She didn't believe Ella had ever exchanged a word with the actress, and anyway she had read Miss Thorndike's plea in the newspaper.

'Don't any of you think war can be averted?' asked Ella.

'George doesn't,' said Hester.

'Neither does Ollie.'

Ella put down her work. 'I'm almost glad Tom's delicate,' she said. 'He won't be called up. But there'll be no holding Guy if war comes.'

As she spoke Guy came whirling up the lane on his new motorbike.

'He's just eighteen,' his mother said.

Kate was frightened of thunder and the storm that night was the worst she had ever experienced. She sat by the window with her mother waiting for Ollie to come home. The storm seemed to come nearer by the second. Lightning illuminated the room, and then came the crash almost directly overhead. And the torrents of rain driving hard against the windows, the noise of it all, the tumult. Would guns sound worse than this? And bombs? They would be safe in the cellar, her mother said, but Kate hated the idea of going underground. 'I'd feel safer in the open,' she said. 'I'd rather be in a field.'

'We're lucky to have a cellar,' said Mary. 'Lots of people will have to take cover under the stairs. Think how cramped. We've plenty of room to move about.'

Ollie was doing his turn at the A.R.P. post. He came home very late that night and got soaked to the skin on the way.

'What a rotten Saturday,' he said.

Next day a strange, unreal atmosphere prevailed. It was such a beautiful Sunday morning, people were going to church, working in their gardens. There was to be an announcement on the wireless, Mr Chamberlain was to speak to the nation, and the Sheridans came across to the Hopes so they could hear him together.

At eleven o'clock they edged forward on their seats and listened to the Prime Minister's words: 'We are at war with Germany.'

How could they be on such a lovely day? Mary had just been going to light the gas oven. Should she still do it?

'It is evil things that we shall be fighting.'

Not one of them grasped the full meaning of those words.

A terrible wailing filled the air. It was a noise that turned the stomach. An air raid already? That was certainly the warning. Each one of them carried a gas mask.

'We'd better put them on,' said Ollie uncertainly. 'You never know.'

So they did. The six of them sat in a circle feeling self-conscious in their gas masks. Kate pointed at the window. Mr Lambert had come to his front gate and was scanning the heavens. He glanced over and was met by the curious sight of six people gathered at a window wearing gas masks.

'It's a false alarm!' he shouted.

'How does *he* know?' demanded Ollie, voice muffled.

'He doesn't,' said George.

'Clever cock,' Ollie said.

But that time Ernest Lambert was right. Twenty minutes later the All Clear sounded and later they heard that the warning had heralded a friendly plane approaching.

How could Kate and Sally believe a state of war existed when the violent eruption they had been led to expect did not happen? The weather was maliciously lovely with long sunny days and unclouded skies when they could lie on the grass talking and dreaming of what they would do when the war ended. Sally had ideas that never entered Kate's head. 'Perhaps I'll stand for parliament,' she said.

'How dull. Ugly old men making long speeches,' Kate objected.

'I'd soon liven them up,' declared Sally, chin well out. 'Anyway, I've got to get through school and then Oxford, and by that time the war might be over.'

'But that's years. It won't last all that time,' said Kate.

'Dad says it will.'

'Oh, don't let's think of it. Just listen to the sparrows.'

In that first week of the war the noise the sparrows made held a disturbing element. It happened every afternoon. Flocks of them gathered in the trees and chirped and chirruped in a loud, tuneless chorus.

'It makes you think they can sense something we know nothing about,' said Mary. 'I never remember them kicking up such a din before.' Neither did anyone else.

The shops in the High Road had a neglected look. Several had closed down and dead bluebottles and the odd tin or packet lay gathering dust between the window and drawn blind. Hester bought wool and a book of instructions and

20

began to make socks. 'Women always knit in wartime,' she said.

'It's soothing,' said Mary.

'Not when you're trying to turn a heel,' Hester said.

'You'll have plenty of time to improve, Mum,' said Sally.

So many residents in neighbouring roads had taken themselves off to safe areas that an air of desolation prevailed. It was like living in a deserted village and the sound of Guy's motorbike was heard no more. He had enlisted in the R.A.F. and was training to be a pilot.

Ella Lambert managed to keep a brave face on the day he left. She smiled and waved as he sat beside his father in the car and listened to it drive away. She compressed her lips and stifled her sobs, holding on to the banisters, feeling the pain of parting mount in waves. When it subsided she went to his room and took his two good suits from the wardrobe. She brushed them thoroughly, then pressed them, put protective dust covers over and returned them to their places. Next she took his shoes down to the scullery and polished them; one pair needed to have the heels set up so she put them aside to take to the mender when next she went out. She shook out all his underwear, refolded it and replaced it in the chest of drawers with tissue paper in between the layers and little bags of dried lavender dispersed among them.

All this took some time. When she could find no more to do she called on Mary Hope, struggling not to cry because of ruining her make-up. There was nothing worse than a mascara-streaked face. Mary welcomed her in, knowing this was a difficult day for her.

'I'm so frightened of aeroplanes,' Ella said. 'The very thought of Guy flying one makes me shake like a jelly. You've no idea how I'm suffering.'

Mary did not like Ella much and didn't care for Guy either but that did not prevent her from sympathising. She could put herself in Ella's place and feel for her with all the depth her imagination gave her. Her heart ached for this woman who was obviously exerting iron control but still could not keep her hands from trembling.

And this is just one mother out of millions, she thought,

as she made coffee and tipped a measure of whisky in to each cup. All over England, all over the continent, everywhere, mothers are parting from their sons, wives from their husbands, children from fathers. And just look. She can hardly hold her cup steady.

Ella was sipping the coffee. 'I'm freezing though it's hot out,' she said.

'It's a mockery having this fine weather now,' Mary said.

'I'd almost feel better if something happened. It's all so stupid. All this build-up, expecting air raids, invasion, enemy landings. Ernest keeps saying it may never happen. But it will and I fear the worst, especially for Guy. I love Tom dearly but there has always been a special bond between Guy and me. We get on so well together and he's so considerate and kind to me.'

Mary encouraged her to go on talking as it was obviously doing her good, though she found it trying to hear Guy's praises sung at such a pitch. To her mind his brother was far preferable in every way. He was twenty-three and had been working for a chemical company in the Midlands ever since he got his BSc. He was in a reserved occupation so Ella could not be expected to feel the same concern for him as she did for Guy, but he was by far the better character of the two, Mary thought. He was unassuming and not above chatting to Kate and Sally whereas Guy ignored them. He was not handsome but she liked his face although he was so thin and delicate-looking. A bout of pneumonia and pleurisy in late boyhood had undermined his health and, had he been her son, she would have worried about him far more than Ella did.

'I've a good mind to go and stay with my sister in Bath,' she was saying. 'Now both my boys are away there's nothing much to keep me here.'

'What about Ernest?'

'He'd like me to go. He's been working late hours for months so I hardly see him. He can stay at his club and come home at weekends.' Ella had no idea that Ernest's club was a comfortable little flat with only one other member — an equally comfortable and unfashionable little woman.

'I should certainly go if I were in your place, Ella,' Mary said.

'To think it should come to this!'

Mary saw she would have to resign herself to comforting Ella for the rest of the day and was thankful to see Kate and Sally coming along with George Sheridan. They stopped outside his gate and seemed to have a great deal to say. Still arguing about the Falstaff question, she supposed.

'One wonders why Mrs Sheridan doesn't persuade her husband to buy a respectable hat,' remarked Ella. 'That and the half moon glasses. He must be years older. Old enough to be her father, I should think. What do you suppose she sees in him? Or he in her, for that matter?'

'That's a riddle with so many couples,' Mary said. 'I like those two individually and together.'

'They managed to produce a very unpleasant child between them,' said Ella, with a sniff.

'Sally? Don't you like her?'

'I think she's a horror.'

'She's down to earth and practical. We think she's good for Kate. I'm sure there's a lot of good in her.'

'She needs it to make up for that face.'

'Oh, Ella! It's quite a nice little face,' Mary said, and looking across the road to where the three were standing she was afraid Kate would not stand up to the inescapable trials of life with anything like Sally's strength.

Ella was still droning on about the Sheridans. 'Is it true he's working at the Foreign Office now?' she asked. 'I thought he taught at some university.' She spoke in an aggrieved tone as though someone should have told her.

'He does. Or did. A great many people like George are working in the Civil Service now,' said Mary.

'Oh.' So the Hopes and the Sheridans were on Christian name terms. That made them allies. Ella had no wish to be a member of their little club and yet she felt excluded. She was sorry the Sheridans had come to The Clearing. Far better when the Wilsons lived next door and everyone kept their distance.

The peculiar situation of being at war but not under attack

continued. After a while people began to leave their gas masks at home, then those who had tin hats left those at home, too. Gradually evacuees drifted back home. The Air Raid Wardens frittered the days away and spent the nights spying out chinks of light in houses with faulty blackouts.

Mary was reprimanded several times. Her black sateen curtains hungs from rings and little areas of light appeared all along the tops. It was the same with Hester's. They had to remove the rings and make wide hems to accommodate the rods. But this made them short at the bottom. They had to lengthen them with more sateen and grew very ill-tempered doing so.

'It's not as though we ever have a raid,' said Hester. 'I suppose I shall have to make sure the curtains at Heron House are all right too, though I expect Mrs Sharkey's made a good job of them.'

'Do you ever think of living there now the war's on?' Mary asked.

'George threatens to banish Sally and me there if the raids get bad,' said Hester. 'I'm torn between London and the country, you know.' She loved the countryside, and the villages and towns of Buckinghamshire. Marlow and Henley were especially dear to her and when George's old father died and left him his house with its extensive walled garden, a large field, a barn and some outhouses, she'd thought it would be very pleasant to live there.

There were no neighbours to speak of; the nearest was the farmer whose land adjoined theirs. Alfred Ford grew vegetables and fruit and kept a small herd of cows. Some of his land was let out for grazing and Hester enjoyed the sound of sheep bleating. She liked the farmyard sounds and thought it fun to be woken by the cock's crow. She said one could always drop off to sleep again and the animal noises were far preferable to traffic.

On the other hand there were no theatres or cinemas to speak of. Repertory companies were not the same as star-studded West End productions. There was nothing to match the excitement of Shaftesbury Avenue in the modest local theatres. George enjoyed a good play and Sally was theatre-mad. Hester liked modern plays, Shakespeare was out, so while George and Sally hied themselves off to The Old Vic on Saturday afternoons she went to the cinema for the latest Gloria Swanson or Bette Davis. But best of all was Garbo, especially in Camille. She would go home, her heart and head full of tragic love, to find Sally spouting Shakespeare at the top of her voice, and George too. They enacted bits of the play they had just seen and upset her own remembrances. 'Oh, dry up, you two,' she would say.

'Mum's in one of her moods,' Sally would observe.

'I don't have moods. I've just seen something very beautiful and moving and I don't want it driven out by the ravings of King Lear.'

A bit later when they were having supper Hester supposed they would have to get used to doing without plays and films if they went to Heron House.

George was attached to his old home and would have enjoyed living there permanently but he did not relish the prospect of travelling up and down to town every day. It had been Hester's idea to find somewhere to live on the outskirts of London and keep Heron House for weekends and holidays. That would be nice for Sally. The Clearing offered the solution. 'Bags of room for all those old books of yours,' she told George.

'That's true. But won't Heron House be a bit of a white elephant?'

'You'll kill Mrs Sharkey if you get rid of it,' she said.

He had been heard to say in an unguarded moment that he worshipped the ground Hester walked on and apart from his wish to indulge her every whim there was the question of safety. If air raids proved as disastrous as he feared she would surely be safer in the country with Sally.

'We'll see how things go,' he said. 'It isn't a good time to sell anyway.'

'Bless you, my darling old codger, don't let's ever sell,' she said, and she sat on his knee and stroked his thinning hair.

He had still not got over the wonder of having her. He had never deceived himself into thinking she was in love with him, but she was sincerely fond of him and with her cheerful disposition and generous heart, was a joy to live with.

He remembered noticing her when she came to his lectures. She was unusually lovely to look at and he had the greatest difficulty keeping his eyes off her. She did quite well in that first autumn term. It was after Christmas that things changed. Her work deteriorated and he wondered why. When she came for a tutorial he said bluntly: 'You're not the least bit interested in eighteenth-century history, are you?'

'Oh,' she stammered, and her lip trembled.

'Perhaps you'd be happier if you took some other course? What sort of career are you thinking about?'

'I thought I might teach,' she said.

'Do you think you could?'

'I must earn my living.'

'What about secretarial work? Shorthand and typing?'

'I'd rather go charring.'

'Oh, don't say that.'

'I do say it. But you don't know — and how could you? You don't know what it's like.'

To his acute discomfiture she began to cry. He had no idea what to do but before he could do anything at all she got up and dived for the door. In her anxiety to get away she turned the handle the wrong way so it failed to open. She twisted it desperately as he put his hand on her shoulder. Gently he touched her and fire ran through him.

'What's the matter?' he asked. 'Won't you tell me?'

She was looking up at him and seemed no more than a child and yet so much more. He would do anything to help her, to save her from whatever threatened. He led her to the hard, shiny horsehair sofa and asked her again to tell him. 'You'll feel much better if you tell me what's troubling you,' he said, and his voice was so kind that she poured the whole thing out right from the time her father joined the army and went away. After that, she said, she slept with her mother in the big bed except when he came home on leave. Each time he came he was more handsome than the last for he was an officer and the uniform, the peaked cap, the little cane he twirled, the moustache he grew, all helped to turn him into a hero. They had a photograph of him on the piano and another in the bedroom.

His leaves were interludes of sheer delight. They went to

the music hall in the evenings and women patted him on the back and wished him well. There were such splendid turns on the stage. They roared with laughter at the comics, and listened attentively when De Groot played the violin, and there was a lady with a deep bass voice like a man's who sang 'The Lost Chord'. At the end all the performers came on to the stage and sang 'Keep The Home Fires Burning' and the audience joined in. Her father sang lustily but her mother kept dabbing her eyes and Hester wondered why she was crying.

Sometimes, when her father was on leave, a new friend of his, a Canadian officer, came with him. His name was Edward Lane. Hester looked forward to his visits; he made a great fuss of her and she was enthralled by the tales of his boyhood in Prince Edward Island which sounded so beautiful she longed to see it.

'When the war's over you must all come and stay with me,' he said.

It was something to dream about, but her father shook his head after Captain Lane rejoined his unit and said they would never have enough money for the fares to Canada just for a holiday. Their fortnight at Herne Bay every summer was as much as he could manage.

'And, besides, the bank would never give me all that time off,' he said. He was a clerk, and although his prospects were good every penny of his salary had to be carefully budgeted.

The years went by. It was 1918 and Hester was nine. People were saying the war must be over soon but it seemed it had been going on for ever. Men came back from the front caked with mud. The wounded wore hospital blue. She would see them when she was on her way to school.

Each afternoon when she came home she wanted to know if Dad had written, and if there was a letter she would sit at the kitchen table and they would read it together. He must have been safe when he wrote it but was he safe now? And where was Captain Lane?

Her mother made valiant attempts to be cheerful. Her father's bank was so short staffed they offered jobs to the wives of the men who were in the forces and Molly Field was glad to accept the offer. They made her a cashier, a thing unheard of before the war. She was glad of the money. Andrew still received his salary so between them there was more coming in than ever before. 'We'll have a lovely big nest egg when Dad comes home,' she told Hester.

Hester was at school when the maroons sounded the Armistice at eleven o'clock on a cold foggy November morning. The children were marched into the assembly room to be told the war was over and the rest of the day was a holiday. They sang two hymns, prayers of thanksgiving were offered, it was all bewildering. Several girls whose fathers had been killed at the front burst into tears. The thought of rejoicing was too much for them and Hester was thankful she was not one of them.

She remembered going into the street with her friends and seeing the crowds all rejoicing. The fog had not yet thickened and open topped buses went by with people waving flags from the top decks. Soldiers on leave climbed up the sides and the crowds cheered them. Rattles sounded. There were no strangers, everyone was a friend and they were laughing, shouting, their relief expressed in noise. In a doorway a woman turned her face away and wept. Tears poured down her white face. Her hair was escaping from its pins. She was bedraggled, desperate. Other women stopped their rejoicing to comfort her. Hester was frightened. She did not want to go near the woman. She went to the bus stop with the others. It was a penny ride home.

Her father had been on leave only a fortnight earlier. Now he would be home for good and everything would be different, just as it used to be.

She let herself in with her latchkey. It was early afternoon and the house seemed even emptier. And cold. There was a bundle of firewood in the hearth so she lit the fire but it did not want to go so she had to draw it up with newspaper. It took a long time to ignite properly. As soon as it did she went into the kitchen and made a cheese sandwich which she ate standing up. Then she had the idea of going to the bank to wait for her mother. It was not far away but by the time she arrived there the fog was really thick.

'Why, what are you doing here, Hester?' asked her mother when she went up to the counter.

'They let us out of school,' she said. 'Isn't it wonderful? I've got the fire alight at home.'

'Good. As soon as I've finished cashing up I can go. Shan't be long. Sit over there and wait for me.'

Hester sat on a bench against the wall. The staff were leaving, one by one, and several of them stopped to say how glad they were her father would soon be home now.

At last her mother came out in her hat and coat with the fox fur her father had bought on his last leave clasped round her shoulders. They walked close together, cuddling up to each other, not talking much, just feeling wonderful.

'We'll have a nice cup of tea the minute we get in,' her mother said.

The fire had burned up well and was glowing red. Hester warmed her hands at it; she heard the water running into the kettle and her mother singing softly in the kitchen.

The double knock at the front door was so loud it made her jump. Could it be Dad home already? Her heart was pounding.

She opened the front door and the cold fog came choking in. She scarcely saw the boy on the step. She only saw the telegram he held out. Her mother was there now. There was no colour in her face as she opened the envelope. 'There's no answer,' she said. She closed the door and the telegram fluttered to the floor. Hester picked it up.

Andrew Field had been killed in action.

It was a relief to tell Professor Sheridan all this, just to put it into words, no matter how badly, and she never paused to wonder what he thought of people who had shrimps for tea. But the telegram. The never-neverness of it. She didn't notice her hands were in his, that he was trying to comfort her, saying there were sure to be good things ahead and what had happened to distress her so now?

'My mother's getting married again. She's going to live in Canada with Edward Lane. He was Dad's friend. In the war.'

She had not known it was coming, had no idea of what her mother planned, and it had come as a shock. It meant

29

her home would go and she would have to find a bedsit and earn enough to keep herself. Oh, yes, they wanted her to go to Canada with them but she simply could not. Kind and considerate though they were she would be an encumbrance, a hanger-on.

'So,' she said in a strong voice, 'I must be independent. I simply must. I'm going to look at a room this very evening.'

'I'll come with you,' he said. 'May I?'

'Would you?'

'After we've had dinner. I'm hungry. Aren't you?'

He could hardly believe they were walking along the road together, entering a restaurant he knew and liked, and their argument because she only wanted Welsh rarebit. 'This is on me,' he said when it dawned on him that she expected to pay her share. He adored the way she went pink, and looked down and then up, and said how silly she had been to give way as she did.

He told her he was sure she had nothing to worry about; before long she would be married because there must be at least a hundred men in love with her.

'Not one,' she said.

'Surely there's one at least?'

'I've never even been taken out.'

'You're out now.'

'Oh, but that's different. You're a professor and you're so very kind and it's wonderful how you've made me feel so much better. I never thought I'd have dinner with someone distinguished like you. This is an occasion and I shall never forget it.'

She enchanted him with her smile. 'I shan't either,' he said.

She became very serious. 'It's getting late. I must go and look at this room,' she said.

They were out in the street. She checked the address under a lamp post.

'If you married me you wouldn't have to bother,' he said.

'You're teasing.'

'I'm asking.'

It was an old-fashioned lamp post and it cast a gentle light. She liked him so much. More, much more, than any of the young men she'd ever met. More than anyone she knew outside the family. She told him so.

'Honestly?'

'Honestly,' she said.

George Sheridan was forty, more than twenty years older than Hester. At the time of their marriage she preferred older men and it never occurred to her that he was a substitute father. All she knew was that she liked him immensely, wanted to be with him, and found the love and security he gave her more than enough to compensate for all she had lost. After the shock of her mother's decision and the imminent loss of her home, a new life with a man of George Sheridan's standing was beyond her dreams.

He took her to meet his father and she marvelled at the beautiful house by the river, so different from her modest semi in the suburbs. Old Mr Sheridan gave her the warmest welcome; his sister, George's Aunt Josephine, liked her on sight, and Mrs Sharkey the housekeeper was practically enamoured. 'Oh, Master George,' she kept saying, 'whoever would a thought it eh? I hope as Mrs Hester's going to spend a lot of time here.'

George was so proud of her, so much in love. The advent of their daughter, Sally, a year later, would have completed their joy if it had not almost cost Hester her life. Many years later when they lived in The Clearing and she was having a long, confidential talk with Mary Hope as they sewed the blackout curtains, she said she would have dearly loved more children but having one had nearly killed her.

'George said he would never let me go through that again even if it meant he had to live like a monk.'

'And does he?' Mary asked.

'He does not,' said Hester, 'but I really believe he would have done. He's wonderful, Mary. Much too good for me.'

'Here he comes, up the lane with Ollie,' Mary said.

The two men were walking side by side. Ollie was young-looking and most attractive. George did not make the most of himself, never had. His tie was no better than a length of string, his coat sagged with the books in its pockets and he hadn't cleaned his shoes for weeks. Hester felt the slightest twinge of annoyance. There was such a contrast between the two men, and although she would never have admitted it there were times when she would have liked George to have more romantic looks.

'I simply must buy him a tie. Several, in fact. Come with me tomorrow, Mary.'

Next morning Ella Lambert saw Hester and Mary leaving home together and wondered where they were going.

Off again, she thought. It was never like this when the Wilsons were at The Chestnuts. We all kept ourselves to ourselves then, and quite right too.

The weather had turned cold and damp and the dread of things to come was unnerving. If they were invaded how would the Nazis behave towards civilians? Mary could not help dwelling on the possibilities. She and Hester talked about them and both recalled words they had read and never considered. Rape and pillage.

'They just go over your head when there's no fear of them,' said Mary. 'But now, I worry about the girls.'

'Yes. It's terrible to think of them being slit up the middle with a knife.'

'Slit up the middle? Whatever do you mean?'

'Rape, of course. That's what they do to you.'

'Hester! You're not telling me that's what you think rape is?'

'It's what I've always understood.'

'My dear! What a sheltered life you must have led!' Mary told Hester just what the word meant and saw the shock, disbelief and disgust register on her face.

'I didn't know my life was as sheltered as all that,' she said, 'but why should we know about these disgusting things?'

'There was no need when we were young and lived at home with our parents,' Mary said.

'My childhood came to an end when I was ten,' Hester said.

'Hester! Do you mean it was just cut off?'

'My father was killed the day before the armistice so all

the dreams my mother and I had about what we'd do when he came home vanished.'

'Oh, my dear, that's terrible.' Mary dropped her work. 'To be deprived of a father so young.'

The numbing pain of loss was there again in Hester's heart, recollected as she sat there with Mary and found herself talking about it, about the way the smallest pleasures were diminished. Fruit drops didn't taste the same because it was not Dad who handed them to her. She was journeying through her own mind. Her mother was invited to stay on at the bank after her husband's death but she was not a cashier any more. As men came back from the front or young ones were recruited, the female staff was relegated to less responsible duties. In peacetime it seemed women were incapable of doing the work they had carried out successfully during the war. This was galling but Molly, and many like her, were thankful to have jobs. It meant she could keep the home going though she had to economise more so that Hester would not be deprived of things more fortunate children took for granted.

Hester had her own ideas. She wanted to help. 'As soon as I leave school I'll get a job and earn some money. Only another three years,' she said.

'Thirteen's much too young to leave,' said Molly.

'I could do a paper round now. Then you wouldn't have to give me pocket money.'

'Hester, I won't hear of it. We manage quite well enough.'

'With you taking in sewing?'

Molly reddened. She had begun to take in needlework after a chance meeting with Mrs Taylor, the mother of one of Hester's friends. The weather had been unseasonably cold and miserable when they met. 'I hope it won't be like this on Thursday,' Mrs Taylor had said.

'Why Thursday in particular?' Molly asked.

'The school trip to Oxford, of course. Had you forgotten?'

'I had for the moment,' lied Molly. 'Still, there's time for it to clear up.'

She went home puzzled and worried. 'Hester,' she said, 'what's all this about a school outing?'

33

'Nothing,' said Hester, looking away.

'Come along. I met Mrs Taylor just now and she spoke of a trip to Oxford. What's it all about?'

'It's only a coach trip and it's not the whole school. Just three classes. You don't have to go.'

'You should have told me. I felt very awkward hearing about it from Mrs Taylor and not knowing what she was talking about. What made you keep it dark?'

'Because it costs seven and six and I know you can't afford it. I wish you hadn't found out. And I don't want to go anyway.'

'Are all your class going?'

'Yes.'

'Then you're going too.'

They were staring at each other, eyes full of unshed tears, frustration, anger, concern for each other in their hearts. And love. Then they were hugging, holding close, saying, 'Never mind, don't let's have secrets.'

But after that Molly began to take in sewing and mending and Hester was more determined than ever to make it up to her. She found ways to earn small sums: old Mrs Parsons who lived over the baker's shop paid her sixpence a week to sponge the leaves of her aspidestras and another fourpence to dust the sides of the stairs. On Saturday afternoons she spent two hours wheeling the Hastings twins round the green so their mother could go shopping. She got one and sixpence for that. And on Thursday evenings she kept Mrs Williams company so that her son Nigel and his wife could go to the first house at the music hall. They paid her half a crown so altogether she earned four shillings and tenpence a week. She made a point of saving most of it but always spent tenpence on chocolate as a special treat for Saturday evenings when they put on gramophone records and listened while they ate it.

There was another great treat: the letters from Captain Lane who was back in Canada. He had been to see them at the end of the war before he returned home, and as a friend of Andrew's he became theirs too. He wrote a long, newsy letter once a month and Molly kept a journal to send to him. At Christmas and Easter he sent money for gifts which he could not send in kind because of the duty. Sometimes they bought shoes or cardigans, dress lengths, gloves, and always new hats for Easter. Consequently they were always well turned out and everyone thought they were prosperous.

At fourteen Hester left school and got a job serving in the dress department of a large store. The pay was small but she enjoyed the work and as time went on the manageress recognised her natural flair for clothes. Hester could be depended upon to show customers with awkward figures just what would suit them.

By the time she was seventeen she was so pretty people always looked twice; she had a musical voice and a gentle manner so customers liked having her to serve them. She was completely oblivious of her charm and this added to her attractiveness. And she was happy. Her one aim in life was to make things easy for her mother.

One day the history mistress from her old school came in to buy a dress. Miss Trelawney had always liked Hester and expected her to do well so she was disappointed to find her serving in a shop. In the fitting room she asked what her prospects were.

'We get our salary and a percentage of our sales on top but there's scarcely any chance of promotion,' Hester told her. 'Of course, the best job is as a buyer.'

'Does that mean a long wait?'

'Years. It's dead women's shoes. Still, I'm lucky to have a job at all.'

'Have you thought of any other career? Teaching, for instance?'

'It's outside my range, Miss Trelawney. I couldn't go to college, not even if I got a place.'

Miss Trelawney recalled that Hester's father had been killed in the war and knew things were hard for the families of such men.

'There are other ways of entering the profession,' she said. 'You could get a diploma and then take a teacher training course. It can all be done at evening classes, you know.'

'Could I? Could I really?'

'You should go along to the Evening Institute. No, wait

a moment, I have their prospectus here. Yes, here it is. What about a course in eighteenth-century history? You like history, don't you? And the tutor is Professor Sheridan. I'd go anywhere to hear him lecture – it's the most wonderful piece of luck getting him. Interested?'

'Yes. Oh, yes, I am.'

'Then go along and enrol. Don't waste any time. And let me know how you get on.'

Hester went the same evening and joined a long queue. There were more applicants than places and she was told she must attend the following evening for an interview. She called on Miss Trelawney with this piece of news. 'I'll give you a letter to take,' the teacher said.

Armed with this Hester joined another queue, and after a long wait it was her turn to go in. Professor Sheridan sat behind a desk with a pile of forms in front of him. He had a half-smoked cigarette behind one ear, the straggliest tie she had ever seen, and his tweed jacket bulged in all directions. But when he looked at her – and it was a long look – she noticed the quirky humour lines at the corners of his mouth and the kindly eyes, and knew she was going to like him very much indeed. He read Miss Trelawney's letter and looked at her again.

'Well, Miss Field, so you serve in a shop and my old friend Miss Trelawney thinks there are better things in store for you? What do you say?'

'I say the same though I love the shop,' Hester said. 'It's handling clothes made of such gorgeous materials and matching them up with people. You'd be surprised the way women always want dresses they look simply dreadful in because they've seen them worn by a sylph at least twenty years younger. The trick is to persuade them differently. There's so much fun in it.'

'Is there indeed? Then why change?'

'To better myself.'

'Miss Trelawney tells me you'd like to teach. Why?'

'I have to think of the future and teachers get a pension. That's very important.'

He tipped his chair back, looked at the ceiling and roared with laughter. 'You're not even twenty,' he said at last.

'You're only seventeen. You'll be married before I can say knife.'

'That I will not,' she declared. 'I've too many responsibilities for that.'

He did not laugh now. 'I see,' he said. 'Yes, I understand.' He glanced at Miss Trelawney's letter again and she guessed there was something about her circumstances in it.

'If you seriously mean to study for this diploma there will be a place for you,' he said. 'You'll have to do a great deal of reading. Do you think you can manage it?'

She was sure she could.

'And write essays?'

'I'll do my best,' she said.

He began to fill out a form, thinking all the time of what Miss Trelawney had told him. This girl's father had been shot dead in the trenches the day before the Armistice. Her mother was a bank clerk and her chief aim in life was to help at home.

He stood up and gave her the form for the office. 'I'll see you in class,' he said, and to her surprise shook hands and opened the door for her to go out.

She did well that autumn term. Christmas promised to be better than usual that year for Captain Lane was coming to England for a month and wrote to ask if he might spend Christmas Day with them. It was an exciting prospect and they enjoyed putting up the decorations, buying a little tree and making the house look really festive.

He called on Christmas Eve laden with presents and a large sprig of mistletoe under which he kissed them both, holding it aloft over their heads. He looked older but more distinguished and extremely prosperous. He called them his two dears.

'I'm booked in at the local hotel but I want to spend as much time as I can with you two,' he said when the first greetings were over.

'We're both working women, you know,' Molly told him.

'Can't you get time off? I'm depending on you to show me round,' he said. 'Come on, Molly, swing the lead, can't you?'

37

'I might take three days,' she supposed.

He had brought wine, chocolates, candied fruit. There was never a lull in the talk and Hester realised how good it was to hear a man's voice in the house and smell the smoke of an expensive Havana. He took them to the theatre and to supper at Rule's afterwards. He hired a car and drove them down to Brighton for Sunday lunch at The Old Ship. Molly took three days of her annual leave and went out with him every day. They explored the shops in Oxford and Regent Streets and came home laden with parcels dangling from every finger. Nothing was too good for Molly. He insisted she have new shoes, hats, scarves. Hester had never seen her sparkle so.

'It will be ever so flat when you go home,' she told him the day before he left.

'I shall have to come back at Easter then,' he said.

'Good. I like having something to look forward to.'

'And you must come and stay with me.'

'That's just a dream. We get such short holidays.'

There was a long pause before he responded. He was looking at her thoughtfully, mulling something over. At last he said: 'Then I shall have to see what can be done about it. You'd like things to be easier, wouldn't you?'

The atmosphere had changed; she was on her guard. 'What do you mean?' she asked.

'Only that I want you both,' he said, with so much meaning in the simple words that she drew away inwardly. She was not clear what he meant and did not want him to be more explicit. She shied away from being wanted. Having Edward to visit them was one thing; going to him was quite another. It would have been entirely different if Dad had been alive and they could have gone as a family.

He said no more but there was an almost imperceptible sense of strain between them now and she did not feel comfortable until he left.

Molly talked of him a great deal and liked to recall the good times they'd had, but she noticed Hester's reticence and one day said: 'You don't seem very fond of Eddy these days, Hester. Is there anything wrong?'

'It's just that I don't want him taking us over.'

38

'As if he would. The idea!' Molly's face had gone quite red.

'Look at all the things he gave us. He must have spent a fortune. Men don't do things like that for nothing.'

'I don't like to hear you talk in that cynical way, Hester. It's most unpleasant. Eddy is very generous. Remember how much your father thought of him. Anyway, I hope you're going to change your opinion because he's asked me to marry him.'

Hester gasped. 'Mum! You wouldn't!' she exclaimed.

'Why not?' Molly demanded.

Why not indeed? Hester looked round the room and saw every object separately and as though magnified. Dad's photograph on the piano, the cherished ornaments they had gazed at in shop windows for years while they saved up to buy them, the firescreen they had embroidered between them — it was all more than precious to her. It was the whole of her life and she could not endure to be wrenched from it.

'Hester dear, I'm very fond of Eddy. I thought you liked him too. He certainly likes you and I'm positive we'll have a good life with him in Canada.'

'We?' queried Hester. 'I'm not going to Canada.'

'But of course you are. We want you.'

'Want, want, want! Well, I don't want. I don't want any part of it.'

'Why not? It would be a much better life for you, from all Eddy tells me.'

'I'm not interested. This is where I belong.'

'Hester dear!' Molly was stricken. She knew she had handled the situation badly and so had Eddy. They had talked the matter over between them for hours, wondering how best to win Hester's approval of their plan. Now she saw they had failed miserably.

'She'll understand, Molly,' Eddie had said. 'You're young now but life won't get easier as you get older. She'll see that. And it won't be long before she'll be wanting to marry herself. Do you suppose she'll think of you then?'

'I don't know. All I know is that she's thrown her heart and soul into helping me from the moment that awful telegram came.'

'I realise that. But I can give you both so much. It's a wonderful life where I come from. And besides, I love you, Molly. I've been thinking of you all these years, hoping I'd be able to persuade you to share my life. You know I have. I'd have taken you back with me right after the war if I'd had the nerve to ask you. You know that, don't you? Come on. Admit it.'

Molly knew only too well. It would not have done then but now – now was the right time. 'Why does there have to be a fly in every pot of ointment?' she asked. 'And why does it have to be my own daughter?'

'I'll be back at Easter and we'll get married no matter what. O.K.?' he said.

'O.K.'

Hester had friends at the shop and at the evening class. She asked them in turn how they would react if t!.eir mothers were to remarry and they all said they'd hate it. They couldn't bear to think of another man stepping into their father's shoes and, even more unbearable, his bed.

And yet ... If your mother is still young? If your father died a long time ago? And when you marry yourself? Think, Hester. Think.

And he wants to take you to Canada? Whoopee! Lovely country, kind people, horses, boating, climbing. And what have you got here, Hester love? Grind, grind, grind.

She thought long and hard and tried to put reason first, emotions second. She recognised the benefits of this marriage but the thought of Eddy in her father's place was unendurable. It hurt to see her mother in love with him and she knew she could not live with them.

There was a wretched atmosphere at home. Hester was dull in the shop and could not concentrate on her class work. This development in their lives meant their home would go. The house was rented and she could not possibly keep it on by herself. She would have to get a room somewhere – be a boarder. Horrors!

She made herself face it and one day screwed up her courage and told Molly what she had decided. There were arguments, tears, persuasive talk, but having made up her

40

mind, she was determined not to change it. In the end Molly unwillingly accepted her decision and when Eddy came back he had to agree too, but it marred their happiness.

That was when George Sheridan came in and his intervention changed the whole picture.

'So you see how lucky I am,' Hester said, for she had told Mary so much as they sat there together, their work suspended. 'I doubt if I'd have done very well if I'd been left to my own devices. As it is I have George and Sally and so much besides, and now we're settled here I simply love it.'

'And we're glad you're here,' Mary said. 'Two trios. It couldn't be better, could it?'

Hester thought it would be a good idea to invite the Hopes to Henley while the fine weather lasted and before the girls went back to school. She had been wanting to share her pleasure in the country and the river with them for some time.

She suggested it to George. 'Let's go on Sunday,' she said. 'Who knows what will have happened by this time next year? We could take them on a little river trip. The girls would love it.'

'Do you think Ollie would mind driving?'

'Of course he wouldn't. I'll put it to Mary when I pop in for coffee.'

'That's another thing. Coffee may get scarce.'

'Oh, George! You really do make the most miserable predictions.'

'Don't you ever stop to think where all these things come from?' He gave her an extra special hug and kiss, took his hat from the hall stand and went off to work.

Ella Lambert, from the vantage point of her bedroom window, remarked for the hundredth time that she just could not understand Hester allowing her husband to go about in a hat that looked like a piece of old suit. Ernest always wore an Anthony Eden and looked very smart. She saw to that. Before she left the window she was in time to see Hester going across to the Hopes and in at the open front door. Always in and out, she thought. It won't last.

Mary jumped at Hester's invitation – 'just the thing

before the winter sets in, and why not enjoy ourselves while the going's good,' she said. So early on Sunday morning they all piled into Ollie's open tourer and set off for Heron House. They would have coffee when they arrived and then go on board *Corsair* for a cruise upstream and lunch in the saloon, after which they could either cruise further on or tie up and lounge on deck as the mood took them.

The cool air of early morning was refreshing and their route took them through long wooded lanes where the sun glanced through. There was no traffic to speak of and no sign posts either. These had all been removed to hamper the Germans if they invaded. Ollie depended on George for directions.

The leaves were beginning to turn colour. There was peace and stillness everywhere. Cows grazed in the meadows, poppies grew profusely by the roadside. Poppies – a reminder of blood. Blood pouring into the soil of France and Belgium. Only twenty-five years since that other war began, Hester thought. She remembered it clearly. She was proud of her father in his Army uniform. When they walked along the road together all the privates saluted him and this made her think he must be very important but he told her, no, he just held a commission and the men were saluting the King's uniform, not the man inside it.

And then he went away and never came back. He was awarded the Military Cross posthumously. She shivered.

'Cold?' George put his arm round her.

'No, I'm not cold. It's heavenly, isn't it?'

Some children playing in a field looked up and waved to them. One little girl held a bunch of poppies, another had poppies in her hair. 'Something to remember,' George said.

She shook off her nostalgic mood. They had crossed the suspension bridge at Marlow and George was leaning forward to give Ollie directions. There were several turnings before Sally said: 'You'll see the house in a minute. Look, Kate. On the right.'

And there, standing back and above the level of the road, was Heron House. Ollie drove slowly in and drew to a halt

42

outside the massive front door which was immediately flung open as though someone had been waiting on the other side with a hand on the latch.

And so someone had. Mrs Sharkey, mother of Sam, was the Sheridan's housekeeper and caretaker. She had the appearance of a woman with a rolling pin concealed behind her back and George had often remarked that he would not care to offend her. This was not without reason for she had a poor opinion of men and an enormous admiration for women. She adored Hester. Hester could do no wrong in her eyes, and she was very fond of Sally who rushed up the two shallow steps to the front door and clasped her round the middle. Mrs Sharkey had long given up any pretensions to a waist.

'Oh, you dear old Shark, what a one you are, flinging the door open like that!' cried Sally. 'See who I've brought with me – my best friend, Kate, and her mum and dad.'

'Sally, Sally,' expostulated George. 'Let us have a more dignified introduction, if you please.' And with that he presented Mrs Sharkey to the Hopes and saw she approved of them.

'You'll find all in apple pie order,' said Mrs Sharkey when they were settled in the drawing room. 'I've sent Sam down to *Corsair* with the hampers. Everything you ordered, Mrs Hester. The deck shoes are ranged on the pontoon, a pair to fit everyone.'

'Lovely,' said Hester. She poured coffee into delicate porcelain cups.

The drawingroom was large with long windows overlooking a lawn that swept down to the river. Midway between the house and river was an ancient cedar tree. The lower branches touched the ground.

'When you lie underneath it's like looking at the sky through black lace,' Sally told Kate.

'Will we have time?' asked Kate.

'Not today. Sam will be shouting for us to go on board any minute.'

Mary said: 'I don't know how you can tear yourself away from this, Hester.'

'It can be gloomy in the winter,' she said, 'but I really

43

love it. I don't ever want to have to choose between this and The Clearing.'

'Perhaps you won't have to,' said Ollie. 'You should learn to drive and then you could potter up and down between the two.'

'Petrol will be rationed. There won't be much joy-riding soon,' said George.

'Oh, really!' exclaimed Hester. 'On such a lovely day you have to drag in rationing. I think we should forget the war for today. Don't you all agree?'

There were no dissenters and as they had finished their coffee and Sam, in Wellingtons, was plodding his way to the house, it was clearly time to go.

Sam was gnarled and weather-beaten with countless lines, grooves and wrinkles etched into his face. He had thick wiry grey hair stained yellow in front by the smoke from his home-made cigarettes. In the usual way he wore tobacco-coloured corduroys with straps below the knee, a moleskin jacket and a bright red scarf. Today, in honour of the occasion, he had on a reefer jacket that had belonged to his master. It was well cut and had dark buttons embossed with anchors. It was rather on the large side for Sam's spare frame and yet it seemed right for him.

'All ship shape?' asked George.

'Aye, aye,'

They walked across the smooth weed-free lawn, catching glimpses of the rose garden on the other side of a bilberry hedge. It was past its prime but Mary wished they had time to go round it. All she saw surpassed her expectations. It was so lovely it made her throat ache.

What could be more entrancing than a lawn sloping down to the water's edge and a cruiser moored to its own landing stage? Kate had expected to see a rowing boat or a punt. She was not prepared for an eight-berth cabin cruiser with decks like a ballroom floor, life belts neatly stacked, a dinghy hoisted on davits astern – it was beyond her most extravagant dreams. Deck shoes of all sizes were set out in a row and her first sight of the deck told her they were necessary. No heeled shoes had ever stepped on board.

'You never told me you had a boat like this, you mean thing,' she accused Sally.

Sally loved *Corsair* but she was accustomed to it so it held no surprises for her. 'It was Grandpa's. He always called it a neat little craft.'

'Little? It's huge. I bet you could go to sea in it.'

'Grandpa did. So did Dad when he was young. They went foreign.'

Kate thought this a very odd way to talk but she didn't query it for fear of betraying ignorance. They went on board and Hester led the way into the saloon which was the size of a moderate drawing room and closely resembled one. The floor was thickly carpeted, the seats were upholstered in soft leather, and there were printed linen curtains at the portholes. At one end there was a dining area with a table large enough to seat six and beyond it the galley with every fitting and device the galley slave could desire.

'You're a dark horse, George,' Ollie said. 'We had no idea you were a boating man.'

'Not now. I was in my old man's time. This is all his. Sam looks after it and lives on it most of the time. I'd never have the heart to part with it.'

The engine had begun to throb gently. Sam, with a battered yachting cap on his head, was in the wheelhouse and George, obeying instructions, let go the ropes. *Corsair* swam smoothly away and into midstream. Mrs Sharkey had come down to the pontoon and stood there waving a large handkerchief as though she was seeing them off on an ocean voyage.

They all sat on deck luxuriating in the sunshine, seeing the glitter on the water, looking back at their wake. How magical it was, how calm and peaceful, and yet it caused such stirrings of the heart. Swans glided by, ducks scurried out of their way. And everything was gold: the trees along the banks, the fields, the hills, were all touched with it, sometimes light, sometimes deep and rich as though the sunlight of summer was locked into them. There even seemed to be gold dust on the water, and gold sparkled in the air. Dragonflies darted, glinting like jewels.

Afterwards, when she looked back, Kate saw it as a day in a million. It was just as though it had been plucked out of the sky and laid at their feet. Surely there could be no river in the world to match this? And to think they could sit at a table and eat the superb salmon trout Mrs Sharkey had prepared, drink a little glass of white wine and then go on deck again and lazily watch for a fish to leap out of the water. It was a new experience for her, one she would never forget.

Just before dusk fell they turned to go back. Hester and Mary, side by side in deck chairs, were indulging in one of their confidential chats, just desultory remarks which they followed up or dropped as the mood took them.

'Do you ever,' asked Hester in her soft voice, 'feel you've missed something in life? Do you feel there's something mightily important which you've passed without even noticing and then, when you realise, you can't go back?'

'I suppose you could say a day like this. Though if you'd never had it you wouldn't exactly miss it, would you? It could be something you'd missed out on altogether – like never going to India.'

'Or never being able to play the violin. But that's not quite what I meant.'

'On an evening as romantic as this it would be awful to realise you'd never fallen in love. I think it's romance we miss – and our youth, of course.'

'But don't you ever get a kind of longing – and you don't know what for?'

'Oh, that's adolescence. We're long past that.'

She heard the men's voices and stirred lazily. Two cigarettes glowed in the half light.

'Who's Ollie talking to?' she asked.

'George.' said Hester.

Mary could see Ollie now she looked but the other man – surely it wasn't George?

'Yes, it is.' Hester followed her gaze. 'He's put his father's yachting cap on.'

'Hester! It makes him look like Clive Brook. Don't you think so?'

'I suppose it does in this light.'

'I used to have a crush on Clive Brook. I waited at a stage door for his autograph once.'

'Did you get it?'

'Yes. On the programme.'

'Were you thrilled?'

'I was as he walked towards me. He looked wonderful. He said, "Good evening," and raised his hat and, oh dear, his hair had receded to the back of his head. It was such a shock. He wore a toupee on stage.'

'That's rather endearing, isn't it? I'd have liked him all the more.'

'It completely cured my crush,' said Mary.

One morning Kate and Sally set off to spend a day picnicking in Kew Gardens. When they reached the end of the lane and crossed the road for a bus they were stopped by an Air Raid Warden.

'You girls shouldn't be out. There's a raid on,' he said.

'That's the first we've heard of it.'

'You heard the warning?'

'Ages ago.'

'At six-fifty precisely. The All Clear's not been sounded. Go down the shelter opposite and don't hang about.'

They obeyed unwillingly because the sky was so clear and there were no ominous sounds. The shelter had a clammy atmosphere. The air was stale and decidedly smelly. 'It's just as though men come down here to pee,' said Sally, sniffing ostentatiously. 'I bet they do,' she added.

Kate shushed her.

'Pooh,' said Sally.

There were a dozen or so people in the shelter sitting on wooden benches and looking blank as though they were in a doctor's waiting room. Most of them had been caught on their way to or from work. There were several women with large shopping baskets − office cleaners, probably. They talked among themselves in loud unlovely voices, repeating words and phrases as though at the behest of an unseen prompter.

'My Bill −'

'Where is he?'

'Dunno.'

'Don't they tell you?'

'Somewhere in England.'

'Aaah.'

An old woman had a cocker spaniel on a lead. He shivered uncontrollably and someone said: 'He knows. Poor thing.'

'Ought to be put down,' said a man with pinched nostrils and rimless spectacles. 'Ought to be muzzled. He could bite someone.'

'So could I,' said his owner, glaring at the speaker.

'Animals aren't allowed in shelters,' he said.

'Then what are you doing here?'

'Get stuffed.'

These words, uttered in a very small clear voice, startled everyone. They had been uttered by a budgerigar no one had noticed as his owner had pushed his cage under the seat so it was concealed by her legs.

'Get stuffed. Boil your head,' said the budgerigar.

His owner, a little woman with a headscarf over her hair curlers, tried to quieten him. 'Night, night, Nathaniel. Beddy byes,' she said.

'My name is Nathaniel,' announced the budgerigar. 'I live at number 68 Terminus Buildings. I'm a budgerigar. Boil your head.'

'Beddy byes, Nathaniel.'

'Bum,' said Nathaniel.

The welcome note of the All Clear sounded so no one heard the rest of the bird's repertoire. They all scuttled for the exit and the girls spent the rest of the day exploring Kew Gardens and talking about the flat they had decided to share when they left school.

The weather was maliciously lovely. Long sunny days and cloudless skies gave the illusion of peace.

'And an illusion is all it is,' said George Sheridan.

'You're a pessimist, George,' declared Hester.

'On the contrary. But we have a long way to go,' he said.

Despite the quiet at home the news from abroad grew worse every day with Hitler's relentless advance on Poland. On the very day the girls went back to school they heard Warsaw had fallen.

The first day of term began as usual with assembly in the

48

big hall. There were many empty seats: some girls had been sent into the country for safety, several even to Canada and America. There were anxious faces. Fathers and brothers were with the forces and their families did not know where they were stationed or where they might be sent.

Erica Helberg's parents were German and they were interned. Erica had been boarded out with friends for the duration. Her great friend, Zara Karminski, was absent. They always sat together but now there was a vacant chair on either side of Erica.

The clamour of excited talk stopped abruptly when Miss Hunter, the headmistress, entered the hall and took her place at the lectern from which she was accustomed to deliver her opening address. This morning she seemed hesitant and after the preliminary 'Good morning, girls' and their chorused response she did not announce the hymn with which the proceedings always began. Instead she cleared her throat and said: 'I have very sad news for you today, girls.' There was a heightening of attention, an even deeper quiet.

'It is about Zara Karminski,' she went on. 'She is Polish, as I expect most of you know. This summer her father went to Warsaw because he was worried about his parents, who live there. Very little is known about his movements after he arrived, but one fact is certain. A few days ago Mr Karminski was executed by the Nazis.'

A gasp went round the hall. Every vestige of colour left Erica Helberg's face. She clutched the back of the chair in front of her. She had always boasted about her admiration for Hitler, hero-worshipped him, had his photograph pasted inside the lid of her desk. She made a little whimpering noise.

'There is nothing more I can tell you about this terrible happening at present,' Miss Hunter went on. 'Zara will be rejoining us in a few days' time and I know I can trust every one of you to show your sympathy in your own individual ways. Zara is a very strong-minded, admirable girl but her shock and distress must be far deeper than if her father had died a natural death. We will stand in silent prayer for one minute.'

The interminable seconds crept by. There were stifled sobs.

As the minute ended rustling ensued and Erica Helberg went down in a dead faint. Two teachers ran to help and she was carried from the hall. This caused a diversion of another kind. The girls began talking, turning to one another for comfort. Some were seething with indignation and hatred for Erica, saying she should be sent to Coventry.

Miss Hunter rang a small hand bell and ordered silence. 'I trust each and every one of you not to be unkind to Erica,' she said. 'There must be no talk of Coventry or any other sort of retaliation. Is that understood?'

There was a murmured, 'Yes, Miss Hunter.'

'And now it is the Upper Third's privilege to choose the hymn for today. Sally Sheridan, will you announce it?'

Sally stood. 'We have chosen "Oh God, our help in ages past",' she said, her voice not much more than a whisper.

They all rose. An opening chord was struck on the paino and the two hundred girls sang uncertainly at first, but gradually gaining power so that the last verse rang out with strength and determination.

Kate could not join in. Her voice seemed to have gone and all she could produce was a husky whisper. She admired Zara Karminski and continually sang her praises. Zara was the tops at netball, it was hinted her tennis was nearly good enough to take her to Wimbledon, she could play the piano and she could act. Her performance as Orlando in As You Like It at the end of the summer term won a great deal of praise.

Outside the big hall Kate clutched Sally's hand. 'Suppose it happened to us?' she whispered — talking in corridors was forbidden.

'I can't bear to think.'

'I'd die if it was Daddy.'

'You wouldn't. You'd just carry on.'

'Executed.'

'Murdered!'

'Do you think he was shot?'

'Hope so. It's better than hanging.'

'Hanging! They wouldn't!'

'They'd do worse.'

The first day of term always ended at noon and was taken up with registers, getting accustomed to new class rooms and to the timetable. The whole of Kate and Sally's class had gone up. They were now in the Upper Third. They were twelve years old. As a rule this first day was fun but today the kind of gloom none of them had ever felt before invaded the classroom. And there were two empty desks — Zara's and Erica's.

Sally had a nightmare after she went to sleep that night. She dreamed she was sentenced to be hanged and woke up screaming. George and Hester rushed into her room and there she was, her face almost green, mouth wide open, eyes staring. 'What is it?' they said, 'What's wrong?'

Hester held the trembling child. 'What frightened you, darling? Tell us,' she said gently.

'I can't. I can't,' gasped Sally.

'Much better tell us, little one,' coaxed George. He was stroking her hair, holding her hand. 'Get it off your chest. Come on. You can tell your old dad.'

'I can't. It was awful. The waiting. Knowing ...'

'Knowing what, sweetheart?' he asked.

But Sally would not say. She could not put the terrifying sensations she had felt into words. The horror of those dreadful moments were not to be described.

It was a long time before the spasmodic trembling ceased. George held her close while Hester went down to the kitchen for warm milk. What on earth could Sally have dreamt about? Hester could not recall anything in her short life to cause such terror. Of course the war, the tales of Nazi atrocities, of Jews being sent to concentration camps, perhaps these had triggered it off, but there was no way of protecting anyone from the news. And then poor Mr Karminski. The girls had been so distressed about it when they came home from school. Sally had been even more upset than Kate which was surprising. Hester was troubled. It must have been Mr Karminski. She had met him several times at school functions and to think ...

She sat with Sally, waiting for her to fall asleep and for a long time after that. George was beside her.

'Why don't you go to bed?' she whispered.

'I'd rather wait for you.'

*

The atmosphere at school was one of trepidation. In spite of their strongly held disparate beliefs Zara and Erica were friends. They talked, argued, debated, but that did not allow their differences to destroy the affection they had for each other. They had never parted in acrimony, but now the fate of Mr Karminski was bound to come between them. Zara always sat next to Erica in class, they came to school together, walked home together afterwards. There would be no coming and going now: it would not be possible because they were not neighbours any more. Erica was living in a different part of the town now her parents were interned.

Zara came back on the Monday following Miss Hunter's announcement. She did not come into assembly but everyone knew she had arrived. Erica, who looked ill, still sat with an empty chair on either side of her. Afterwards she filed out with the others and walked along the corridor to the classroom. She did not go in. She stopped at the door and held on to the doorpost. Miss Hunter, accompanying Zara, appeared at the other end of the corridor.

Kate had a clear view of all that went on because it was her duty to wait in the corridor with the register till the form mistress arrived, then follow her in, place the register on the desk and close the classroom door. There was no sign of the form mistress yet.

Erica was shaking. Her teeth were chattering and Kate felt almost sorry for her. She must have been aware of the general feeling in the class. They all thought she should have been withdrawn from the school and sent somewhere else, preferably to the Isle of Man with her parents. None of them could stomach the thought of her being in the same room as Zara. Not even in the same world, some of them said.

But now Zara was approaching. She saw Erica and stepped ahead of Miss Hunter. She was hurrying. Kate told the others afterwards that she almost ran and put her hands on Erica's shoulders. 'Oh, Erica, aren't you pleased to see me?' she said, and Erica broke down, stared at Zara with tears spilling down her face and then almost collapsed, hiding her face against the wall and sobbing. Zara put her arms round her. It was she who did the comforting.

Miss Hunter signed to Kate to go inside the room so she did not see any more, but other girls, moving from one class to another, reported they had seen Miss Hunter going towards her study with an arm round each girl. It was also said that a member of the kitchen staff had been sent to the study with a pot of coffee and three cups.

At mid-morning Zara and Erica came into the playground. Erica looked dreadful. Her face was disfigured with the tears she had shed. They walked round the perimeter of the netball court. The Games Mistress, Miss Seymour, joined them. She was carrying a netball. It was the turn of their class to play at the next session and when the bell rang at the end of break the classes lined up in double file and returned to school, class after class.

The Upper Third remained standing. Miss Seymour blew her whistle and they all took their places on the court. The game began. It was a crisp, rather cold day, just right for a brisk game. Neither Kate nor Sally were good players but Zara was at the top of her form. When it was over and they all went back to their classroom it was as though a threat had been lifted.

Kate was not the only one to notice that Hitler's photograph had been removed from the inside lid of Erica's desk. In its place was a large coloured photogravure of the King and Queen.

As the winter threatened to be severe and there were all the hazards of hard weather to consider George went down to Heron House to make sure the pipes were lagged and was pleased to find a cellar full of coal.

'And that's not all,' said Mrs Sharkey. 'It takes a deal more fuel than that to heat a house this size so I've got Sam sawing logs. It's them pipes I worry about.'

'So do I,' said George.

'If you ask me — all right, Mr George — I know as you don't ask me but I'm telling you just the same, our government's harder on us than on the Jerries. First they declare war and then they sit on their behinds and do nothing about it. Got plenty of time to make silly little rules though. Thumb twiddling lot.'

'I daresay there's plenty going on we don't hear about,' he said. 'Anyway, Mrs Sharkey, we shan't be coming down during the winter so I'm relying on you and Sam to do the best you can here.'

They were sitting in the kitchen which was warm and comfortable with a log fire burning in the open grate and a very old black kettle steaming away on the hob. Mrs Sharkey set about making cocoa. Much better for warming you up than tea, she said.

Sam came in at the back door, beating his arms across his chest after crunching across the frosty grass from *Corsair*. George had already been down to look at the boat which Sam had laid up for the winter. He had drained the engine and sheeted over decks and wheelhouse with tarpaulin. Now his mind was on other things.

'We ought to keep chickens, Mr George,' he said, resuming the conversation they had begun on the towpath. 'We'll be rationed afore we know where we are. Mum can tell you what it was like in the 'fourteen war.'

''Orrible,' said Mrs Sharkey.

'You'll be glad of a few eggs, Mr George. Nothing like a couple to start the day. A rasher or two helps.'

'We're not keeping pigs, if that's what you're thinking,' said George. 'I leave it to you to get some chicks, Sam.'

'And what about all this land? Ought to be cultivated. Taties. There's nothing worse than mouldy taties. Mum says that's what we'll be getting afore we're much older.'

'Nineteen-fourteen war they called 'em chats,' said Mrs Sharkey. ''Orrible, they were.'

'A very good idea to grow some potatoes. I leave it to you, Sam.'

'And what about a goat?'

'Don't goats stink?'

'Only when they want a billy.'

Mrs Sharkey reared herself up in her chair. 'We're not having any of that, thank you!'

'A donkey. Save you cutting the grass. A nice little donkey and a goat.'

'Now, look. I don't want any harm to come to the lawn, Sam. It's taken years to get it to its present state and I won't have animals tramping over it. Is that clear?'

'Perfickly.'

George hated mispronunciations and shrugged impatiently.

'A goose. Let's have a goose!'

'Stoopid!' shouted Mrs Sharkey.

'Nark it, Mum. A goose'll protect you better than a dog. A goose'd see a German parachutist off better than a wolfhound. What about a goose, Mr George?'

'Ignore him,' said Mrs Sharkey. 'He's got overenthoosiasm again. Pay no attention.'

'If we go on like this we'll have a menagerie. It's no to the goose and the donkey and the goat. Chickens and potatoes are quite enough to be going on with.' George drained his mug of cocoa. 'Now I'll be getting back to town,' he said.

It was the cruellest of winters: the relentless cold, the cheerlessness of the dark streets, blacked out windows, sandbags. Air raid shelters that were never needed. No one could remember a worse time.

Kate and Sally trudged down the lane to school muffled up to their eyes, their breath making their scarves wet. It was too cold to talk, too cold to hurry. It hurt to breathe. At school it sometimes seemed colder in than out and Miss Seymour exhorted them to exercise. 'Exercise, girls. Trot. Smartly there. Come along now. No slacking.' How Sally hated that bright, high-pitched voice as she panted round the perimeter of the netball court. Skipping ropes were encouraged in the playground.

'It's the coldest winter in living memory,' a girl in their class announced one morning. 'I heard it on the wireless. It's official.'

'And to think we're living through it,' said Sally dolefully.

Miss Seymour, overhearing, exclaimed: 'Well! Isn't that exciting? It's a record!'

Her enthusiasm was not catching. No one cared about

records. All they wanted was relief from the chilblains on their hands and feet.

On the way home Kate saw a blackbird on its back in the lane. She picked it up. The sight of the stiff fragile legs and half-open eyes distressed her.

'It's dead,' said Sally, peering.

'Perhaps it's only unconscious.' Kate wrapped it in the end of her scarf and held it under her coat. She had listened to the blackbird's song in the spring and summer of the year. Perhaps not that particular blackbird but one of its family. It had sung till late in the evenings, every evening. She could not bear to think it was dead. Perhaps it would revive in the warmth of the kitchen.

It was a vain hope. 'It's frozen,' her mother said. 'Frozen to death, poor thing. It must have fallen out of the tree. Better put it under the hedge, Kate.'

'Couldn't we bury it?'

'The ground's too hard to dig a hole.'

'Oh, Mummy. How awful.'

Kate laid the blackbird down gently and scraped up some frosty leaves to cover it. She hated leaving it out there in the wicked cold and felt mean as she toasted her feet by the fire and drank the soup her mother had made.

Mrs Sharkey sent the Sheridans a large Christmas cake, three Christmas puddings and three dozen mince pies.

She had hoped they would spend Christmas at Heron House as usual but quite understood how little time Mr George had to spare and had heard the inclement weather was causing delays on the railways. She was glad to assure them there had not been a freeze up so far and Sam had made the promised chicken run.

Hester read between the lines. The poor old girl was disappointed they would not be going down; there was nothing she enjoyed more than a Dickensian Christmas with holly, ivy, port wine, and far too much to eat. A Christmas without a bilious attack was a failure in her eyes. Still, there was no help for it. George would only be able to take the one day off and then there was fire watching. He would never miss his turn on the rota.

She packed up the scarf she had knitted for Sam and a soft fleecy bed jacket for Mrs Sharkey and sent them off with affectionate messages.

This was going to be a strange Christmas, the first and the last in this war, she hoped. There was something contradictory in enemies celebrating the same season of peace, going to church in Germany, going to church in England, praying for victory over each other. Poor old God, she thought. Let's hope he's deaf.

To make what she could of the occasion she invited the Hopes to dinner which they had midday as Ollie would be on duty at the Warden's post in the evening.

Sally insisted on decorations, and a tree, and whatever happened they must have crackers. As yet there were no shortages to speak of so on the day the two families enjoyed an old-fashioned dinner with excellent claret and good port wine. When they had pulled the crackers and read the mottoes and put on their paper hats they all felt comfortably replete and in the mood for a few toasts.

'Not quite Dingley Dell but I'll take wine with Ollie,' said George.

They all began toasting one another, swapping hats, tucking in to yet another mince pie, a walnut, a chocolate. It had grown quiet. 'Angel passing,' someone said.

'Oh, look at the time! It'll be the King,' exclaimed Hester, switching on the wireless.

They had forgotten all about the King's traditional broadcast and were only just in time to catch the end of it. The deep, halting voice, impressive in its measured tones filled the room with words they would always remember: 'I said to the man who stood at the gate of the Year, "Give me a light that I may tread safely into the unknown." And he replied, "Go out into the darkness and put your hand into the hand of God. That shall be to you better than light and safer than a known way."'

But the spring! How ravishing it was in its intensity. And the brilliance of the flowers. It seemed to be striving to redress the bitterness of winter with an added depth of colour in everything that grew. The grass, renewed and cleansed by the snow, almost glittered. There was more than pink in the cherry trees, than ice in the white of the pear blossom, than molten gold in the laburnam — there was radiance as well. The flowers seemed to shed light, to glow as though this spring was unlike any that had gone before.

And the war that had smouldered through the autumn and winter leapt with the ferocity of a starving tiger and devoured Norway and Denmark. Even then ordinary people went on leading their ordinary lives. Girls bought pretty material and paper patterns to make summer dresses. They played tennis. Men awaiting call-up put on their white flannels and played cricket. They hoped the weather would hold over Whitsun.

On Friday Mary went shopping with an extra long list for the weekend. At the dairy the manageress was on the telephone. Mary waited with other customers rather impatiently. The young assistant had gone off to join the Land Army so the manageress had no help and ran the shop alone. Mary saw her replace the receiver. She came to the counter, looked round at the assembled customers and said in a blank tone of voice: 'No need to buy for Monday. Bank Holiday's been cancelled.'

There was a general exclamation of incredulity. This was ridiculous. It was not possible. Cancelled? Bank Holiday! Whoever heard of such a thing? It must be a rumour.

The news spread fast. In the street people spoke to strangers. They gathered in groups to discuss it. Mary saw Ella Lambert coming out of the bank and hurried to join her. 'Is it true?' she asked.

'Indeed it is. The first cashier isn't at all pleased. He was going to play golf on Monday. They say it's because of the French. They insisted on us cancelling it.'

'The French? Are we to be dictated to by the French?'

'It looks like it,' Ella said.

'I don't see how it's going to help them,' said Mary. 'And it's such lovely weather, too. It would have done people good to have a day off.' Inwardly she feared it meant the outlook was far darker than they had yet been able to realise. The glorious days of May and the freedom from attack had deceived them all.

58

Ella asked Mary to go home with her. She was finding it hard to be alone, worrying constantly about Guy and dreading the time when he would be in combat. 'Let's have a sherry to cheer ourselves up,' she said.

They each had a glass and turned on the wireless for the latest bulletin. The news was grim. Holland and Belgium were invaded; the German armies were moving towards France. They looked at each other in consternation, scarcely able to credit it.

'It's getting so near.' Ella had to put her glass down because her hand was shaking. 'What shall we hear next? I dread air raids. I'm such a coward.'

'No more than the rest of us,' Mary said. The wireless was still on but they were no longer listening and missed an item requesting owners of mobile pleasure craft to send details of their boats to the Admiralty.

'And I'm in such a ferment over Guy all the time. Sometimes I get so strung up it would almost be a relief if he got killed before it all starts.'

'Ella! How can you say such a thing? You know you don't mean it.'

'I do in a way.'

There was a silence. Then Mary said: 'I think you ought to get a job, Ella.'

'Me? Whatever next? I've never had a job in my life.'

'Then it's high time you started. Join the W.V.S. or go and help at the hospital. There are a thousand things you can do. Anything's better than sitting here moping and harbouring such dreadful thoughts about your own son.'

'How dare you?' croaked Ella. 'How dare you speak to me like that? You can see the state I'm in. I don't know how you can be so heartless.'

'You drove me to speak plainly,' Mary said. 'I'm sorry I've offended you but anyone would say the same. We'd be fools to fall out now of all times, wouldn't we?'

Ella was snivelling and Mary considered putting an arm round her and decided against it. She drank the rest of her sherry, stood up and said: 'I'm down at W.V.S. headquarters this afternoon so I must go.'

Ella tottered to the front door with her and picked up a

59

postcard from the mat. It was a very saucy one depicting an irate red-faced woman of enormous size comfronting a thin giggling one over a fence. Behind the fat woman an outsize pair of shocking-pink knickers billowed from a clothes line and out of her angry mouth came the words: 'I *will* have respect.'

The card was from Guy 'somewhere in England'. It was addressed to his father. 'Dear Dad, Tell Mum to dry hers indoors,' was what it said.

Ella looked at the picture frowning. She handed it to Mary who took one look and laughed.

'Not funny,' Ella said.

'It's only harmless fun,' said Mary.

'He could at least have put it in an envelope. The postman must have seen it.'

'Well, that's not the end of the world.'

'The R.A.F. isn't doing my boy one bit of good. He would never have done a thing like this before he joined up.'

'Oh, don't make such a mountain out of it, Ella.'

'I shall speak to him very strongly,' she said with such a grim expression on her face that Mary thought she really meant to.

One night at Heron House Mrs Sharkey heard *Corsair*'s engine start up and went hurrying down to the landing stage expecting to confront a thief. Sam stepped off the boat, leaving the engine running just as she arrived.

'Oh, so it's you,' she said. 'And what might you be up to?'

'Just turning her over,' he said. 'Matter of fact, I'm going for a bit of a run.'

'This time of night?'

''sright.'

'You'll do no such thing, young Sam. You can stop that engine right away.'

Sam, who was over forty, set off back to the house without a word. She followed, firing questions at him all the way, none of which he answered. In the kitchen he hacked two doorsteps off the loaf and took all that was left of the cheese.

'What are you up to?' she demanded. 'I thought you was on Home Guard.'

'Going down to Teddington. Now don't ask any more questions, Mum. I wouldn't know the answers anyway.'

'Does Master George know what you're up to?'

'Yep.'

'Well, I don't like it.'

'Then you'll have to lump it. I'm going there and back. Home tomorrow.'

She knew very well there was more to this and he knew she knew. At last she said: 'I'm not stoopid, Sam. You wouldn't be going through all them locks, there and back, just for the ride.' She began to count on her fingers. 'Fourteen locks. Good many miles. It don't make any sense to me but I reckon it does to someone.'

'Yes, I reckon it does,' he said.

He had on his thick fisherman's jersey and oiled wool socks turned down over his tall boots.

'What am I to say when people notice *Corsair*'s missing?' she asked.

'Say she's gone for a refit.'

She had been on the point of going to bed and was wearing a plaid dressing gown and carpet slippers. Her hair was in two very thin plaits tied at the ends with bootlaces. 'I believe you'd have gone off without telling me,' she accused.

'Go on up to bed, Mum, and go to sleep. I'll be home soon.'

'You said tomorrow.'

'Or the next day.'

Or the day after that, she thought.

''Night,' he said.'

''Night, son.'

She bolted the door behind him. There was a sense of impending danger in the air she breathed. She felt menaced. The news had been getting worse for days. It seemed nothing could stop the German advance. They were already in France now and the B.E.F was retreating to the coast. So were the French. And what was to become of them all? All those thousands and thousands. Would they be driven into the sea to drown? Or would they all surrender?

And then what? Invasion? Nazis conquering England and goose-stepping down Whitehall? Glad we never got a goose, she thought. And her Sam, was he off to take part in some kind of action?

It was too dark to see *Corsair* from the window but presently she heard it go chug, chug, chugging downstream, and listened till the sound died away.

Kneeling was uncomfortable. She squatted by the side of her bed and prayed. 'Oh God – you up there. I know Sam's going into danger. Don't let any harm come to him. Goodnight, dear God. Amen.'

Corsair was clocking up a steady six knots and Sam felt the tiller under his hands and revelled in the propellor's response to his lightest touch, but he was impatient to reach Teddington where Mr George would be waiting for him. Unknown to Mrs Sharkey the two had spoken at length on the telephone and although Sam was not entirely clear about the reason for the trip he knew they were going to sea and wished he could fly over the locks. In the ordinary way he took the delays in his stride but other craft were on their way too so there was always a queue for the locks, all fourteen of them, as his mother had reminded him.

He was bound in the first place for Tough's Boatyard, and as he knew the Tough family well and they knew him he did not expect to be held up for longer than it took to refuel and fill the water tanks. *Corsair* was seaworthy and always maintained in the pink of condition – ready for a force nine gale anytime, as he said. He had never reckoned on bombs or bullets.

At last he arrived but the noise from the yard reached him long before that. George was there waiting and came on board to don his seagoing gear which was stored in a locker. Oiled wool pullover, sealskin donkey jacket, long boots. Sam was glad to see he had brought some provisions and while he attended to the refuelling George had the kettle on and was making instant coffee and opening a pack of sandwiches which, as he told Sam, he had scrounged from his department's canteen as there had not been time to go home when the signal for action came.

'We're to make for Sheerness,' he told Sam. 'You'd better snatch some sleep. You've been at the wheel all night. Better let me take over.'

Sam groaned. Sleep meant he would miss his favourite reaches – Syon, Strand on the Green, Hammersmith Bridge – but as he didn't mean to forego the excitement of the Pool and the ever broadening stream he reluctantly agreed. 'So long as you wake me soon as you taste salt on your lips,' he bargained, half asleep as he spoke.

George took over the wheel. It was great to be out in the open and once clear of the half-tide lock at Richmond he went at full throttle, nine knots: at that rate they should reach Greenwich in three hours. It was strange to pass the familiar landmarks in different circumstances from those he'd known in his father's day. Richmond to Calais in twelve hours, and the thrill of entering a French harbour, climbing a slithery iron ladder and standing on alien soil for the first time in his life. Now he had no doubt they were making for danger. It was a rescue operation although he had no idea of the scale of it and guessed it must be the first of its kind for pleasure craft to be called on to help.

The barrage balloons were in place and spoilt the skyline – snoozing elephants as Hester called them. He imagined her sitting in the garden as it was warm and fine and was sorry he had only been able to speak to her briefly on the telephone. She would be worried, but he mustn't think of that. Salt on his lips from the spray at Tower Bridge. Let Sam sleep a little longer.

At home Hester had gone over to tell Mary about the cryptic message she'd had from George. 'He only said he'd been called away on business and might be gone a day or so. It's never happened before. I don't know what to make of it.'

'Probably some kind of conference in a secret location,' Mary said.

Hester looked doubtful. The news was growing worse day by day, even hour by hour, and gloom was in the very air they breathed. Whenever she went out she saw groups of people talking and they were all shaking their heads. The German army was advancing on all fronts and she shuddered at the thought of the allies' resistance breaking down, of refugees from France, Belgium and Holland trudging the roads with their miserable possessions, and going where? Where was there any place to go? They would come to the sea.

She chewed it over with Mary. Would the next thing be an invasion? They both went back to The Chestnuts because she wanted to be there in case George should ring again. As they entered the house the telephone was ringing. It was Mrs Sharkey.

'I thought as I'd better tell you Sam went off in *Corsair* night afore last, Mrs Hester,' she said. 'Told me he'd be back in a day or two but he ain't and I'm worried. Does Mr George know anything about it?'

'He's not at home, Shark dear. He said he'd been called away on business.'

'I'll wager they're together.' Mrs Sharkey sounded angry. 'Slyboots the pair of 'em,' she said. 'Ought to a told us. Ought to trust us. Know us well enough by now.'

Hester tried to soothe her. The poor old girl must be worried stiff. She was raging on about duty. 'Time he knew his dooty to his mother,' she said.

'Shark, dear, I'm quite sure he does,' said Hester. 'Now try not to worry. We've just got to sit tight, you and me. The minute I get some news I'll ring you, you may be sure of that.'

Mrs Sharkey was far from satisfied but she grumbled her way off the line and Hester returned to the sock she was knitting. She kept the wireless on in case there should be unscheduled bulletins and Mary went down to the W.V.S. office and was told to stand by as help was wanted at reception centres where troops were arriving. She volunteered at once and went home to collect a few things and ask Hester to look after Kate and Ollie as she did not know how long she would be away.

Hester was thankful to help. At least I shall be doing something useful, she thought.

Corsair had made good time on the journey to Sheerness where she was provisioned with food and blankets. The authorities there were desperately short of crew and reluctant to allow ships to proceed without at least one professional sailor on board, but as Sam was able to quote his long experience of seagoing *Corsair* was allowed to go on and told to make for Ramsgate.

Sam loved the mouth of the river. It could be hazardous for small craft but he enjoyed the pitch and toss and the waves breaking over the deck. Soon they would be out in the Channel on their way to Calais as they had been so many times before, but at Ramsgate they were told Calais was occupied so now their destination was Dunkirk. They would be towed over by a Dutch skoot along with other small ships. Furthermore they could not go till dark.

'Remember how we used to look out for white horses, Mr George?' Sam said.

'There aren't any now,' said George, and indeed the sea was remarkably calm though the air was not. It was full of the sound of gunfire, the shriek and thud of bombs, the drone of aeroplanes. He was not so much apprehensive as anxious to be on their way. Large numbers of men had already been brought home but more and more were approaching Dunkirk, mostly on foot, a harbour official told them. Things were grim now but they would get worse and the sole object was to bring the troops home though God only knew the state they were in.

As dusk fell they set off on the six-hour crossing, taking it in turns to snatch some sleep for there would be no rest once they neared Dunkirk. Their orders were to get in as close to the beaches as possible, pick up as many soldiers as the boat could hold, and ferry them back to the larger ships moored offshore.

At first light George looked out on a scene he could never have imagined. The sky was blood red because the whole of Dunkirk seemed to be on fire and out of this inferno columns of dense black smoke rose from the millions of gallons of burning oil. The sun rose and soon he could see the beaches, mile on mile of drab sands with countless dark mounds which he did not at first identify as men huddled together. They were sitting, lying, kneeling, all waiting to take their turn in the columns walking into the sea. A fighter skimmed overhead firing into the crowds; he saw a great cloud of sand rise and scatter as a bomb fell among them. Was that a greatcoat falling as the sand settled or was it a man blown to pieces? He munched a dry biscuit in an effort to keep his stomach from turning.

The captain of the skoot was casting them off, they were in action now, and Sam was at the wheel going in as close as the keel would allow. But it was not close enough. A whaler crowded with men drew alongside and George saw their white faces and soaking clothes and began to help them on board. The steps were already lowered and up they came, grasping his hands while those who had managed to swim out were attempting to scramble up the sides and were more in need of his help. Most of the swimmers wore nothing but their underpants and were thankful for the blankets. Those already on board helped the others. Some were wounded, bleeding, hardly able to walk. They crowded down into the saloon, packing every inch of the interior and the decks. Fifty men. *Corsair* could not take any more.

He took the wheel from Sam, turned to the nearest skoot and helped the men on board. Some shouted their thanks, patted his shoulder. He turned shoreward again; a German fighter sprayed the deck with bullets and one pierced Sam's cap which he had just taken off to scratch his head. He looked at it in a bemused way, looked at George and remarked his head could have been it.

Again they collected their complement of men, and again and again, but still the crowds on the beaches increased and so did the numbers of small ships plying back and forth from the beaches to the big ships. Bombers disgorged their load, attempting to sink the battleships with their cargoes of rescued men. Sometimes they succeeded and George tried to shut his ears to the screams of hundreds of men pitched into the sea, clutching at pieces of wreckage, drowning, drowning. He saw bobbing heads, sink, rise, sink again. There was the constant threat of machine gun fire from the fighters, but there was no time for fear, no time for anything but saving as many as they could. He lost count of the number of trips *Corsair* made from the whalers to the skoot.

Night fell, but it was not the first night or the second. Could it be the third? Daylight must come and they would start again and there would be more small ships arriving to help. By now George and Sam were on their knees with exhaustion. On the beaches men still waited in long lines or waded into the sea up to their necks. The water was filthy; oil spilling into it created whirls of gleaming colours, wood from the wrecks and dead bodies floating threatened to foul up propellors. He saw it all in a mad jumbled picture. Horses let loose charged crazily up and down the sands till a merciful bullet killed them. Faithful dogs, shot by the men they had followed, floated in the shallows. The dead were everywhere, on land, in the sea, on the ships. They were cast overboard to make room for the living.

On the last of their trips back to the skoot they were told their men were to stay on board. *Corsair* was to be towed back to Dover.

Mary was at a reception centre with other helpers. Their task was to tend to the feet of soldiers who had marched mile after mile just ahead of the enemy. They had come through deserted villages or ones where only the old and lame remained. Sometimes the villagers gave them food, sometimes there was none to give. On this long trek their boots had worn through to the uppers but still they went on.

Now they were home and their spirits had revived. It was luxury to have their cut and blistered feet washed, their sores dressed, and to be given new socks and boots that fitted by motherly ladies from the W.V.S.

At first Mary quailed at the sight of these damaged feet but she quickly overcame her repulsion, inspired by the men's courage. They could laugh and joke and bless her for helping them.

When her two-day stint was over she went home to find Mrs Sharkey was staying with Hester and they were both wondering if they would ever see their men again. Sally was so worried about her father she couldn't concentrate on lessons and ran home at lunch time in the hope of hearing good news, but it grew worse with every bulletin. Rescued troops were landing at Dover but many battleships had been lost off Dunkirk, sunk by enemy bombs. And what of the little ships? Most of these were manned by naval personnel, only a few by their owners, so what of *Corsair*? That Sam! Mrs Sharkey was either saying what she'd do to him when she got him home or telling everyone what a beautiful baby he'd been. 'Image of his father,' she said. 'We was only married a fortnight. Don't remember him much. Told me I snored. If it wasn't for that and for Sam I'd think I'd dreamt him.'

Hester was glad to have Kate staying with them and Ollie dropping in for a meal while Mary was away. The more people she could gather round her the better, and even Ella Lambert came in to draw what comfort she could from company. She was worried about Guy, knowing full well he was in action. In her heart Kate thought of him too but she couldn't say so.

They were giving way to depression and to a very real fear of invasion until Mr Churchill spoke on the wireless and dispelled the gloom, not with vain promises but with words that filled the nation with courage and cast out the prevailing despondency. The mood changed. Shoulders were squared, heads held high. There would be no defeat. Kate played popular songs on the piano, merging them into a concert piece with her own trills and arpeggios. She played patriotic songs in the manner of various composers.

And at last George rang up from Dover. He and Sam were safe and on their way home. The relief after the tension almost hurt. 'Now everything will be all right!' cried Sally, and she raced round kissing and hugging everyone.

But it was not all right. In no time at all the bombing started and went on night after night, day after day, and George sent Hester and Sally to Heron House for the duration.

It was a tremendous wrench. Hester hated to leave The Clearing and Mary and Ollie. Kate and Sally were inconsolable.

'You can write to each other,' George said.

And write they did.

Heron House had six evacuees – 'horrible people', as Sally described them. Two mothers with two children apiece. The children might become house-trained given time and patience, she told Kate, but it was the mothers! She could imagine the ding-dongs in the kitchen between two East Enders and dear old Sharkey. They stood opposite her, hands on hips, and breathed fire. She breathed back brimstone. No need to light the gas stove, Mum says!

Kate's news was milder. It was horrid to see The Chestnuts looking so empty. Uncle George spent the nights with them in their cellar when the raids were on. 'He is an absolute darling. He may be your father, Sally, but he's my uncle,' Kate wrote. Senior schoolgirls went into the Services when they left. Zara wanted to be a Wren so the juniors, who all adored her, couldn't wait to be old enough to join the Wrens, too.

Later on, to the intense relief of Hester and Mrs Sharkey, the evacuees all packed up and went home. They much preferred the blitz to living in the country under the forbidding eye of Mrs Sharkey. 'And you can keep your bloody eggs!' they said as they departed.

In their teens boths girls began to feel new and exciting emotions. Kate was overwhelmed by the magic of ordinary experiences and described them to Sally, daring her to laugh. She would catch her breath at the sight of lilac lolloping over a wall as though she had never seen it before.

Once she saw an old man sitting on a bench feeding scraps to an ancient dog, and she came to an abrupt stop. Her eyes filled with tears, she was full of longing, she wanted to embrace the scene, to preserve it forever. It was so strange to feel her heart almost bursting with joy and yet to be sad and then to feel a great surge of love encompassing all she saw, all those who comprised her world.

'I'm so happy,' she would say.

That year the scent of the lilacs was achingly sweet. Sally said it was because of the war. This might be the last time they would ever smell lilacs. Danger made colours more brilliant, flowers larger, people kinder, love deeper.

They reached the age of sixteen in 1944 and by then it was thought the war would soon be over. There had been a desperate spate of air raids but in late summer it became quiet. Mary thought it would be good for Kate to stay at Heron House for a few days.

'I wish you could come, too,' Kate said.

'Perhaps we will,' her mother replied.

George went down occasionally, when he could get away from work, and on one unforgettable day he arrived unexpectedly bringing Mary and Ollie with him. That day stood out from all the other days in Kate's life. She had walked on the towing path beside the river with her mother and father; she remembered looking back at Henley bridge and seeing the church and then looking ahead and saying no place in all the world could be so lovely.

There were several skiffs on the river and one solitary eight with a coach who rode past them on a bicycle shouting commands and encouragement through a megaphone. The sound of oars, plash, plash, the amplified, encouraging voice – these sounds were to remain with her.

And so back to the house and a special dinner – Hester had procured an illicit leg of lamb, and how they enjoyed it! Afterwards they all went to the station to see George, Ollie and Mary off home. Kate had to fight back her tears as the train drew away. She hated to see them go, even though the war would soon be over. But it felt lonely; the stroll back to the house arm-in-arm, with Hester in the middle. And the smells of that late summer night, wood smoke, trodden grass, tobacco flowers glimmering in front gardens, a chink of light from a window where the blackout curtains had not been properly drawn – all these things became clear in retrospect.

Late the following night Kate woke to hear voices coming from downstairs. One of them sounded like Uncle George's but she knew he wasn't there. She turned over in bed, snuggled down and went to sleep again. She woke feeling happy. The sun was out, it would be a glorious day. After breakfast she would persuade Sally to come out in the dinghy. It was much too fine to stay indoors swotting and she could bring her precious books with her.

Then she heard Uncle George again and it sounded as though he was at the front door. She went to the window and saw him walking to the gate and turning back to wave. So he must have been home overnight which was unusual.

Presently Hester came in with two cups of tea on a tray.

70

'I just saw Uncle George leaving,' Kate said. 'Did he come for something special?'

'Yes, dear, he did. Let's drink our tea.' Hester sat on the side of the bed. Kate sipped her tea. 'I'd like to go on the river,' she said.

Hester's cup rattled against the saucer. Kate saw how pale she was. 'Aunt Hester — you've been crying. What's the matter? Did Uncle George bring bad news?'

Hester put down her cup. 'Kate, dear, this is going to be hard,' she began, but Kate was staring at her, eyes wide in alarm, knowing, knowing before ever a word was spoken, and when Hester began to speak the dumb animal look on the girl's face struck her to the heart for she had to tell her that a new and terrible weapon had fallen on The Clearing the night before. It had fallen at six o'clock in the evening and that was why Uncle George had come.

The Clearing was no longer there. Her mother and father were not there. An enormous crater had engulfed the three houses, not a stick of furniture, not a brick or a slate was left whole. And the families? The Lamberts were away, Uncle George had been at work, only Orlando and Mary Hope had been there when the V2 struck.

It was impossible. They had all been together, they had walked to the station. Kate, disbelieving, got out of bed. 'I must go home. I must go,' she said, her voice high and shaking.

And yet she knew.

Utterly bereft, groping as though her sight had gone, her mouth open in a despairing cry with no sound coming, Kate clutched at Hester and was held in her strong arms. Not only in that first excess of anguish, but afterwards. Hester comforted her, sheltered her, drew her close into her own family. Hester was the one who understood Kate's terrible awakenings from her own experience. Sometimes when they were sitting quietly together Kate would start up to go in search of something. She had remembered something she meant to do — it was a book she had promised to lend Sally and it was in the bookcase in her father's study. She must get it now, before she forgot. Then the shock. There was no study, no house, no anyone. The unique sense of

71

belonging, of being and having and giving, was no more. She would stop, hands pressed to her forehead, and Hester would be there, gently leading her back to her chair, understanding the wrenching pain of that terrible moment when past and present resumed their proper places.

Yet even when she realised the truth she could not shake off the conviction that there had been a mistake, that she must go on searching till somewhere she would find. Her life was a quest.

Once someone told her, in a tone of gentle admiration, that she had taken her loss nobly. She stared at the speaker, mute, disarmed, but it was all she could do not to cry out, 'You don't know! You don't know!' for inside there was this bleak desolation, this feeling that nothing would ever be worthwhile again.

Hester and George had decided to live at Heron House permanently. 'And we want you with us, Kate,' George told her. 'You belong with us now.'

They treated her as their own child.

Sometimes it was hard to believe a war was still being waged. George took a room in town to be near his work and only came home at weekends so Kate, Hester, and Sally were left to themselves. Sally was studying hard. Kate couldn't concentrate. She had no ambition. If the war ever ended Orlando Hope's would reopen and Mr Proctor, her father's junior partner, would run the shop so she might work there but that was way off in the future. Meanwhile she helped Sam Sharkey weed the garden and cut down the perennials to get it clear for spring.

One day in late autumn George came home with a great bag full of bulbs. Mostly narcissi, he said. Narcissi! To her the most poignant of flowers for they were her mother's favourite. At home they came up year after year under the apple tree. When they were over her father would grow tired of waiting for the leaves to die down because he wanted to cut the grass, and every year her mother protested. 'You don't give them a chance,' she would say. 'They'll survive, you'll see,' was his answer and he was right.

Now the very name of the flower brought all this back to

her and set off an inward trembling, just as though Uncle George had plucked a harp string and set it vibrating. She mastered it, stilled it.

'What about helping me plant them?' he asked.

He was not to know the effort it cost her to speak cheerfully, to jump up as though she was eager to help and go out with him to the garden. Once there the thought that this was something she could do for her mother came to her. It was a way of perpetuating a thing her mother loved and she would be foolish to shut it out. It hurt to remember. Well, let it hurt. She would never forget those flowers with their ice white petals and golden eyes growing under the apple tree and her mother's delight when she gathered some to bring into the house. Next spring she would see them again, growing again in this garden.

George came out of the tool shed with trowels, dibbers, hand forks. 'I think they'd look good on this bank, don't you?' he said. 'Sam dug it over last week so all we have to do is to put them in. Shall we plant them in rows?'

'Oh, no! Throw a handful and plant them as they fall. Rows are so military-looking.'

'I see. Well, let's both throw some.'

It was quite fun throwing but making the holes was not so easy. 'They mustn't be too near the surface,' she said, keeping her eye on him. 'You're not pushing the dibber in deep enough, Uncle George. 'Four inches at least. And make sure you get the earth well round them. You must make them feel comfortable, just as though they're tucked up in bed.'

'My knees are getting cramped,' he complained a little later.

'That's no excuse. A young man like you.'

'I wish I hadn't bought so many. Where's Sally?'

'Swotting.'

George growled something about Sally knowing when to make herself scarce.

'It's just the two of us,' Kate said.

He was thankful to see her brightening up, teasing him, just as she had done before her world caved in. It was worth an aching back.

At last all the bulbs were in and they returned to the house to be greeted by Hester who had not known what they were doing.

'We've been planting narcissi. Come and look out of the breakfast room window. On the bank over there. See?'

Hester saw more than the bank which would be covered with flowers in the spring. She saw signs of revival in Kate. The overwhelming sorrow which was bound to persist would be gradually lightened by everyday occurrences, by the kindness of friends, by the natural wish to help others, and the re-awakening of interest in Sally's affairs and in the events her old school fellows wrote about. Now that she would not be returning to her old school she received letters from Zara Karminski and another from Erica, a joint effort from her old class and thoughtful messages from the teachers. A first reading brought tears, a second gave cheer. Above all they helped to strengthen her.

Kate had heard a good deal about Uncle George's aunt. Miss Sheridan's visits to Heron House were always preceded by a telephone call which gave them little time to prepare and when Mrs Sharkey took it she invariably confused the message and would give Hester a jumbled version.

'What she said and what she meant's two different things. Something about rations and something about beds. The rest of it's elsewhere,' she said, so no one knew exactly what to expect until an Austin 7 came jerking and leaping up to the front door and stopped with a horrible grinding of brakes.

It was hard to believe that such a stately lady would step out of such a small car, but so it was and Kate had to agree that Aunt Josephine bore a remarkable resemblance to Queen Mary as Sally kept telling her while trying to suppress a fit of the giggles.

Miss Sheridan straightened her back and gave the hastily assembled welcoming group a gracious wave. Her eyes were very blue, her face very pink, her feet very large and planted at ten to two.

'I have brought a friend to stay,' she announced in a voice that was pitched very deep, and she reached into the car with

74

one hand and dragged out a small weasel-eyed girl of about nine years old wearing an extra short gym slip and a grubby blouse. Her gas mask in its cardboard box was slung round her neck on a piece of narrow white tape.

'She's an evacuee,' Aunt Josephine explained. 'You're an evacuee, aren't you, Puss?' she went on as she moved towards the front door. Aunt Josephine did not walk. In the manner of royalty she moved, or progressed, or made her way. Puss shuffled along beside her, sniffing. She managed to twist her nose up to the left and down to the right in a circular movement as though she was performing facial gymnastics.

'Well, Aunt Josephine, it's very good to see you,' Hester said, kissing her.

'And Puss, too, I hope. Give Puss a kiss or she'll feel left out.'

Hester, George and Sally obeyed the order. Kate hung back till introduced and then was included in the kissing and hugging.

'Puss is *my* evacuee,' Aunt Josephine informed them as Hester shepherded them into the drawingroom. 'Not officially, let me add, but very agreeably. Poor Widow Mutton, my neighbour – name of Lamb but always called Mutton round our way – poor Mutton, as I was saying, has more evacuees than she can manage so I took Puss. And we get on very well together, don't we, Puss?' She gave the child a dig in the middle with a long nicotine-stained forefinger. 'Speak up, Puss, or they'll think you're ill-treated.'

'Is Puss your real name?' asked Uncle George kindly.

'Nope.'

'Say, "nope, Mr Sheridan",' corrected Aunt Josephine.

'And what is your real name?' he asked.

'Jack-qwee-lyne.'

'You see why I call her Puss,' said Aunt Josephine. 'Now, listen. I doubt if Sharkey gathered that Puss was coming to stay with you?'

'I don't think she did,' replied Hester.

'Never mind. I'm sure you can accommodate her for a night or two, can't you, Hester? Don't say no or I shall hate you.'

'Yes,' said Hester.

'Yes you can or yes you can't?'

'I'll arrange things,' said Hester.

'I have to trot up to London for a few days and Puss must be properly looked after while I'm away. You two girls, Sally and Kate, can I leave her safely in your hands for a little entertainment?'

'I have to study,' Sally said.

'Trust you.'

'I'll look after her,' offered Kate, 'I'd like to. There's lots to see.'

'Good girl. You have a kind face. So that's settled. And now what about tea? I've brought a quarter of a pound for you, Hester. And some plum jam. Last year's and a bit crystallised on top but eatable. George, have you got that kettle on?'

'Right away, Aunt.'

'No. On second thoughts you can bring in Puss's luggage and you, Kate, shall put the kettle on.'

Kate withdrew to the kitchen, giving Aunt Josephine the opportunity to enquire if she was the poor girl who had lost parents and home in that terrible V2 attack?

'You hear that, Puss?' said Aunt Josephine on being told this was so.

'Gossocks,' said Puss.

'Puss said God's socks. It's an expression of sympathy,' Aunt Josephine explained.

Kate returned to say the tea was ready and they all adjourned to the diningroom to eat bread and margarine and jam and some astonishingly yellow rock cakes made with dried egg.

'We call them Chinese buns these days, or else Chink cakes because they're yellow,' Sally said.

'Puss and I rather gathered that, didn't we, Puss?'

'Yep,' said Puss.

After tea George offered to show Aunt round the garden while Hester hastily made up a bed for the child in Kate's room. Entertaining an unexpected guest, even such a small one, was not easy, especially as all the current week's coupons in her ration book had been used. Mrs Sharkey did not view this with favour but there was nothing she

76

could do about it beyond bringing her influence to bear on the local shopkeepers, which she did with gusto whenever she had the chance.

'Poor you. I don't envy you your evacuee,' Sally remarked to Kate after Aunt Josephine had left.

'You've had your share of them. It will be an experience for me. I shall enjoy it,' said Kate.

Puss was a slum dweller so the country was another world to her and she liked it. Her family home, or rather hovel, had been blitzed and she told Kate she wished her dad had been in it but he was away at sea. She hated him and hoped he'd be drowned, though drowning was too good for him the way he took the strap to her mum. 'Drop o' salt water won't do 'im no 'arm,' she said. 'Guzzler, that's what 'e is.'

Kate was thunderstruck. She had never met a child who hated its father.

'If 'e does come 'ome, Mum and me's goin' to scarper,' she informed Kate. Mum, it seemed, was always having miscarriages. 'Drunk every Sat'day night 'e is. First 'e gives 'er an 'iding and then 'e gives 'er one in the oven.'

Kate learned a great deal during the week Puss spent at Heron House, far more than Puss learned from her, she often said. They went for long walks, talking all the time; Puss sat entranced when Kate played the piano and was overcome when Hester found some material in a drawer and ran up a dress for her.

'Don't know meself,' she crowed, standing in front of the glass. 'Wish me mum could see me now.'

'What would you like to do when the war's over?' Hester asked her.

'I'd like a little 'ouse wiv a barf in it and I'd live there wiv me mum. We'd 'ave a garden and we'd live there ever so 'appy, 'er an' me.'

'That would be wonderful, Puss dear,' Hester said, and she had to get up and look out of the window because this was so like her own wish after her father was killed.

'The poor little thing,' she said after Puss was collected and driven away by Aunt Josephine. 'I don't think she's nearly as tough as she pretends.'

'Who is, my dear?' asked George.

In her way Puss had stirred them all up. Tough, loving, totally without self-pity, she went out of their lives though not out of their thoughts, and Kate told Sally she was very glad she had met a genuine evacuee. 'She wasn't a bit like those little horrors you used to write to me about,' she said. 'I wouldn't mind helping in an orphanage when I leave school.'

'I thought you were going to work in your father's shop?'

'I might. I'm not sure what I want to do.'

'I am,' said Sally. 'I'm going to be the first woman Chancellor of the Exchequer, but I'll get a job at the Treasury first.'

One day there was an unexpected visit from Mrs Lambert. She felt she had to come to see Kate who had always been a favourite with her and on this occasion she showed genuine sympathy. It was not long before the talk turned to her sons, more especially to Guy who had been awarded the DFC after his outstanding courage during the Battle of Britain.

'It's very strange to be the mother of a hero,' she said. 'Thrilling in a way but also frightening. I live with my heart in my mouth, Kate, but I manage by helping at the local hospital. I couldn't just sit at home.'

'Where do you live now?' asked Kate.

'Well, dear, we're at The Lancer's Hotel – the one near the station, you know. It's well enough for the time being. Once all this trouble is over we shall have to look for another house and then you must come to see us.'

'I'd like that,' said Kate, thinking of Guy. But by now he seemed even further away from her than when he showed off on his bike. He was someone to be adored from a distance and she could not imagine him coming down to her level.

That spring a contingent of Italian prisoners of war came to work on local farms, some on the land next-door to Heron House. They were all young and some felt sorry for them being so far from home. Their arrival caused a diversion: Sally was intrigued by their dark good looks, and so was Kate. Hester was glad to see the way she brightened up.

78

'I wish we could see them properly,' Sally said. 'That wall's much too high.'

'I'll give you a boost and you can look over,' Kate offered.

The ancient wall they complained of separated their garden from Alfred Ward's land. Old Robert Sheridan had planted a row of fast growing cypressus on his side of the wall because he didn't care for the look of bare earth in winter and rows of potatoes in spring and summer. He would have preferred pastures with Jersey cows. The sight of men with bent backs and spades put him in mind of Van Gogh and he much preferred gentler scenes. However, it was not for him to complain as the Wards always gave him liberal gifts of potatoes and, as he said, he could hear the lowing of the Jerseys from the meadows beyond.

Now the older generations of Wards and Sheridans were no more. Young Alfred Ward had succeeded his father but, due to the war, was always short of hands. He had two elderly men, a boy, and his wife, Lorna. She milked the cows, fed the hens, collected the eggs and looked after the dairy. She also looked after her children, twins Baba and Roy, who were three years old and into everything. 'They're no trouble. Good as gold,' she said as she piggy-backed one or other of them round the henhouses.

An old woman with rheumatic knees did three hours housework in the mornings and complained bitterly if she had to bend, stretch or kneel. 'It's me knees, Mrs Ward,' she would groan, so most of the time Lorna did her work for her.

Lorna was very young, very pretty, and very much in love with Alfred who was equally in love with her. It worried him to see her so overworked and he mentioned his concern to Hester. 'She wasn't born to be a slave,' he said.

'Hark at Mr Pot talking about Miss Kettle,' said Lorna.

'Listen, Miss Kettle. You don't get any time off at all and you'll be old before your time at this rate.'

'Shucks,' she said.

'How would it be if I came over to mind the twins

sometimes?' offered Hester. 'It would give Lorna a bit of a break, wouldn't it?'

'Brilliant. You're a peach,' said Alfred.

They arranged for Hester to go on Wednesdays after lunch. The twins loved her. She played with them, told them a story and had no trouble settling them down for their afternoon rest. Once they were alseep she could read or knit or quite often just sit and dream.

Being alone in the comfortable farmhouse kitchen with the clock on the wall ticking loudly had a rather disturbing effect on her. Alfred and Lorna had gone but the air was charged with their youth, their gaiety, their love. It roused strong emotions in her. They ragged each other, shared jokes, and were in such accord they could exchange a look and burst out laughing because each knew what the other was thinking.

'We communicate by telepathy,' Lorna said. 'It's very odd. I suppose you and Mr Sheridan are the same?'

'Oh, yes,' said Hester for she couldn't have borne to say no. The truth was she had never experienced any such phenonomen with George. She had a cheerful temperament and warm heart and was very happy to be married to him, especially at first when she transformed his gloomy South Kensington flat that smelled of old books. Before long all the furniture was polished till it gleamed, there were rugs on the floors, cushions in the deep leather armchairs, new curtains at the windows and a notable absence of dust. How marvellous to have money to spend!

George smiled benevolently and admired the alterations. He was deeply in love with this beautiful undemanding girl and thought himself the luckiest man alive. It was paradise to look up from his book and see her puzzling over the pattern of a pullover she was knitting for the old codger, as he had christened himself.

'Just do one plain, one purl,' he said.

'Oh, you silly old codger, I must do it right! And what do you know about plain and purl?'

'As much as you know about Homer, I daresay.'

'You could teach me about him.'

'That would spoil it. I like you as you are.'

'Ignorant?'

'Never that, darling. That's the last thing. Come on, let's go to bed.'

When Sally was born Hester knew unbounded delight. She was truly contented in her little world. It was a very long time before she experienced a slight sense of dissatisfaction. She loved romantic films but left the cinema with a sense of loss, and when she saw young lovers strolling hand in hand or going to half-crown hops in church halls she could not help wishing she was among them.

George often had friends home and they talked endlessly of books. They were like so many kindly uncles and she half-expected them to pat her on the head. She only listened with half an ear to their talk but there was one time when a chance remark registered. Someone was talking about the laughing part of youth. It seemed that somebody had missed it.

The laughing part of youth, she thought. When they were alone she asked George what it was all about.

'Oh, that was Byron. He complained he'd missed it,' George told her. 'Why do you ask?'

'No reason. It just struck me.'

George, hands deep in his pockets, strolled over to the window. After a bit he came back and said, 'Do you think you've missed it, Hester?'

'No, of course I don't,' she said. But she was lying. Byron had expressed her feelings exactly.

Although the Wards were only allowed one Italian prisoner to help on the farm, they counted themselves lucky to get him. Hester was not particularly interested but Sally and Kate were bursting with curiosity. One day when she set off to mind the children, the two girls accompanied her. 'Just for the walk,' they said.

'Are you sure that's all?' she asked suspiciously.

'Truth to tell, darling mum, we want to take a peep at the Ward's Eytie. We can't see him over the wall.'

'So that's it. Well, I'm not having you gawping at him. He's not an exhibit in a zoo, you know.'

'Oh, you *are* mean. Have *you* seen him?'

'No, and I don't suppose I shall. He'll be out working somewhere.'

'Mustn't he feel lost and lonely?' remarked Kate.

'Don't waste your pity on him. There are plenty of our men feeling lost and lonely, so pity for him is out,' said Sally.

'All right then. Compassion. I suppose I'm allowed a little compassion?'

'Don't quibble,' Sally said.

'I shall if I want to.'

Hester laughed to hear them squabbling with each other and leaving her at the Wards' gate to go back home. She went round to the kitchen door which was wide open; there was laughter from within. Lorna and Alfred were at the table finishing their lunch. A young dark-haired man was with them. He had just pushed back his chair and Roy and Baba were perched one on each of his knees.

'Hester, come in and meet our treasure,' Lorna said. 'Gianni is here to help Alfred.'

Gianni stood. He bowed. '*Signorina*,' he said.

Alfred interposed. 'Mrs Sheridan is *signora*, not *signorina*' he said.

Gianno bowed again and looked puzzled. 'Not *signorina*?' he queried.

Lorna said, 'No. *Si*. I don't know how to say it. Hester, meet Signor Giovanni Morelli. He's teaching us Italian and we're doing ever so well with nouns. Point, Gianni.'

Gianni pointed at a loaf on the table.

'*Panna*,' Lorna said.

'Wrong. *Pane*,' he said.

'Gianni is quite good at English,' Lorna told Hester, speaking as though he was not there. 'He learnt it at school and has kept it up. Something like me with my French, I don't think! Come on, Alf, or we'll miss Donald Duck.' She whirled out of the door, kissing the twins on the way. Alfred followed her and Hester went out to see them off on their motorbike. 'Your new help looks all right,' she said. 'Does he have meals with you?'

'Of course. He can't just nip off home like our other helpers.'

'You didn't expect us to give him a crust on the mat, did you?' quipped Alfred.

'I just wondered if they have their own arrangements,' said Hester.

'Not for midday. He's a jolly hard worker and deserves plenty to eat,' he told her. 'We like him very much and so do the kids. It's just a pity he's not on our side.'

They were ready to go. Alfred put his foot down, the bike spluttered, back-fired, and went off in a cloud of smoke.

Hester returned to the kitchen to find the children had followed Gianni outside and were coaxing him to play with them. He was pulling his heavy boots on and telling them no.

She called them in. 'You mustn't bother Signor Morelli,' she told them.

He looked up. 'No bother, *signora*,' he said, and shepherded them to the door.

He had been laughing with the Wards. Now he was serious, his face calm and composed. She did not know how to behave with an enemy now she was at close quarters with one. 'Thank you,' she said, and closed the door.

Wednesdays followed the same pattern but Hester found herself looking forward to them with a strange flutter of excitement. There was a different atmosphere in the Wards' kitchen now; she tried to think of a word to describe it and could only come up with camaraderie. Alfred, Lorna and Gianni got on so well together. They were young and full of life and made her feel staid and middle-aged. I must be ten years older than Gianni, she thought. But why should she mind? And why did she take to getting there earlier and earlier? She told herself it was because she wanted to be with Lorna and Alfred but she knew it was because Gianni was there.

Sometimes when she was in the village collecting the rations she would meet Lorna out on the same errand. They always stopped for a chat and sometimes Gianni's name came into the conversation. His English, already quite good, was improving every day and he came out with colloquialisms which made them laugh. 'Just as well he's so good at it. Alf and I are hopeless at Italian,' Lorna said. 'Incidentally, he's living with us now. The authorities find all this collecting and putting down of prisoners isn't necessary as they can be trusted. They go back to camp at weekends. So we'll be a threesome all the week.'

'Do you mind?' Hester asked.

'Not a bit. Why don't you stay later on Wednesdays and make a foursome? Gianni could do spaghetti. He's an absolute ace at it.'

'Lorna, I don't want to be paired off with an Eyetie,' Hester said.

'No? Well, perhaps I shouldn't say but he's fallen for you. Can't take his eyes off you. Haven't you noticed?'

'What nonsense!'

'And he's always asking questions. It's a real case, I tell you.'

'Look, it's nearly lunch time and George is home. I simply must go.'

'Ta-ta for now then. Try to come in time for lunch Wednesday.'

Hester wished they hadn't met. It was true Gianni was always looking at her and she was finding it more and more difficult to avoid his eyes. Worse still, she was weaving fantasies round them both. She must, decidedly and resolutely *must*, stop thinking about him. Each time her thoughts returned to him she must cast them out, set her mind on something else, read something aloud, learn a poem and keep repeating it.

On those all-too-short Wednesday afternoons she was never alone with Gianni but she learned a good deal about him in general conversation. His parents owned a hotel at Santa Carlotta on the Ligurian coast and that was where he worked. He spoke French and had been learning English so he could speak with English visitors. He was glad of the chance to practice with the Wards. He was one of a large family, brothers, nephews, nieces.

'You have brothers and sisters, *signora*?' he asked Hester on one of the rare occasions he addressed her.

'No. I was an only child,' she said.

'Then you are lonely?'

'Not at all. I have my husband and family.'

'Ah!'

Lorna and Alfred had gone and the children were playing outside. She had never been alone with Gianni before and it was time for him to go back to work. He looked back at her from the doorway and seemed on the point of saying something, hesitating as he stood there.

It was a moment in which the world could have turned the other way but it was shattered by a child's cry. Baba was howling. Hester rushed out but Gianni was ahead of her. The sacks of potatoes had not been tied and the children had pulled one of them over. Baba had fallen, the potatoes were rolling out of the sack as Roy tried to pull it back and only succeeded in tipping it further forward. They both knew they should not have gone near the sacks and their howls were more of fear than pain.

Hester picked Baba up. 'There. You're not hurt at all,' she said.

Gianni hauled Roy to his feet and carried him indoors. There was a lobby just inside and he set about scrubbing the boy's knees while Hester continued to soothe Baba who gradually stopped snivelling. 'You were very naughty to play with the sacks,' she said, whereupon Baba started to snivel again. 'Want to wee-wee,' she said, wriggling in Hester's arms.

Gianni moved aside. 'Quick, quick, wee-wee,' cried Baba.

Hester hauled the child's pants down, sat her on the pan and was rewarded by an urgent piddling sound.

'Coo! She *did* want to go,' said Roy smugly.

'You next,' Gianni told him.

Hester turned and met his eye. He had a broad grin on his face. She began to laugh. 'Oh, Gianni, aren't we awful?' she said, and the constraint between them wasn't there any more. He leant against the doorpost laughing. She laughed, too. So did the children. All pretence was over. Gianni was the first young man she had ever been in love with and it was the most exciting, wonderful, dangerous and inescapable thing she had ever experienced. She was sure it was not her voice that said: 'We'd better pick up the potatoes,' but then it was not his. And they were picking up the potatoes, their hands were touching, he was holding hers and the children were over on the grass making a daisy chain.

They began to talk, the two of them, easily, eagerly; they laughed about the inauspicious setting for the flash that illuminated each of them to the other. It was as though they emerged from bas relief and became fully rounded figures.

It was not difficult for them to meet. Gianni had to stay within the bounds of the farm but there were ways she could get in as darkness fell and find him waiting for her. They exchanged confidences: her life, his life, his hopes and ambitions, his certainty that she would always be with him. After the war. After the war. She listened and allowed herself to be carried away into the life he promised her. It was so tempting. The Hotel Villa Laura at Santa Carlotta. That's where they would live.

She had to stop him. This was an interlude, an idyll, and it must be set apart from everyday life.

'No. It's true,' he said. 'Everyday life can hop it.' His earnest face, the way he picked up inappropriate phrases, made her smile, but he meant it.

'In your heart you know we can't be together,' she said.

'We can, damn it! We will. You'll see.' And he held her so close and kissed her so passionately she could scarcely breathe.

She hated the weekends because he was back in camp and they couldn't meet, but he told her the prisoners had a choir and sang at High Mass at St Michael's, a nearby church. 'If you come, at least I can see you,' he said.

At home she mentioned the choir casually and the girls jumped at the opportunity so on Sunday they all trooped off.

They had not attended a Roman Catholic church before and found the mass an unexpectedly moving experience. The rich vestments, the incense, the tinkling sound of the bell at the consecration, and the rhythm of the Latin verses were new to them.

Hester read the translation: 'I will go unto the altar of

God, to God who giveth joy to my youth.' She went into a daydream. Youth. Joy. She glanced at Sally and Kate. They had youth and would surely have joy. And George? Had she given him joy? She had given him her youth.

The choir was singing the *Kyrie Eleison*. She had never heard the music but found it beautiful. She hardly dared look for Gianni. She went back into her dream. They were both in this church, profoundly in love, and no one knew it but the two of them.

She did not see him move a pace forward. She simply knew a glorious voice was singing *Panis Angelicus*. She drew in her breath and glanced up. He had not told her he was a soloist or that she was to hear a hymn that would stay with her through all the days of her life. Her heart swelled with emotion, with love and gratitude. To think he loved her, wanted her. Wasn't that enough?

She knew he was looking at her and for a fraction of a second their eyes met. The organ pealed out, the congregation stirred, shifted, knelt, stood. The mass ended and the people shuffled their way to the doors, talking as they went, surprised by the excellence of the choir, praising or blaming Father Keith for encouraging it, gossiping, greeting, pushing, anxious to get home in time to make the most of the rationed meat they had saved up for Sunday.

The music, the singing, the sadness of these young men being prisoners, touched Kate's heart. She could talk of nothing else. Surely that soloist must be a famous opera singer in his own country? She had *Panis Angelicus* on the brain. So had Sally. They whistled it, sang it, heard it in their heads.

'Oh, stop it,' said Hester, impatiently for her.

'Don't you like it?'

'Not when you two murder it.'

'I hope he'll sing it again,' said Sally. Hester was looking out of the window and appeared to take no more interest.

Now the girls had seen the prisoners they each had a special favourite and indulged in fantasies about them. They might princes, they must be nobles from ancient families, perhaps the Black Aristocracy. They would fall in love with the two English girls and come back after the war to declare their undying fidelity. Oh, those romantic nights in gondolas gliding through the canals of Venice or attending magnificient balls in palazzos where the guests, clustering in the light of glittering chandeliers, would try to discover their identity and ask was it true that Prince O was in love with the fair one and Prince Y with the dark?

Kate was sure the prisoner who had enchanted them with his solo in church never took his eyes off Sally, but she thought he was looking at Kate.

'It's you he's looking at,' said Kate.

'Don't be daft. Who'd look at me?'

'He would.'

'With my phiz?'

'Distance lends enchantment to the view,' teased Kate.

Gianni, the prisoner in question, was working in a field that ran beside their garden wall and he had certainly stopped to look up at the windows. 'Let's wave,' Sally said. They did and he waved back.

'See, he *is* looking at us,' said Kate. They were unaware of Hester at an upper window and knew nothing of the turmoil in her heart.

Sally found an Italian phrase book among some old holiday brochures and dared Kate to go and greet the prisoners over the wall. The wall was too high for them to see over but they found footholds where the mortar had crumbled away, enough to be able to get their heads over the top. The solo singer was hoeing up a long line of potatoes.

'*Buon giorno, signor*,' shouted Sally, so loudly she startled him.

'Good morning, Miss,' he said.

'Oh, you can speak English!'

'Very little.' He spoke more English than he was going to admit until he knew their motives.

'We heard you singing in church. Are you an opera singer?'

This did not amuse him. 'In my family we all sing,' he said stiffly.

'Are you famous?' asked Kate.

'*Non comprendo.*'

'Dad says you're as good as Gigli,' said Sally.

'*Non comprendo,*' he said again, though he understood perfectly well.

Sally tried saying it in French. '*Mon père dit que vous chant comme Gigli,*' she said.

'Gigli? You tease me,' he said, and began hoeing again.

Sally had collected her sweet ration that morning and she held her open bag of fruit drops towards him. He stepped over the furrowed ground and took one. This gave her the chance to have a good look at him and she liked what she saw. He had the classic Italian good looks, but so much more. 'It's such a *good* face,' she said later when comparing notes with Kate.

'Where do you come from?' she asked him.

'Santa Carlotta Ligure.'

'Liggery?' she queried. Light dawned. 'Oh, you mean Liguria. What a funny way to say it!'

'It is you, *signorina*, who say it funny,' he said, on his dignity again.

'But you mean you actually live by the Ligurian Sea? Kate, do you hear that? It's the sea Shelley drowned in!'

She turned her attention to Gianni again for this made him all the more intriguing in her eyes. 'You must have trodden on those very sands where they built a funeral pyre and burnt his body,' she said. 'Doesn't it give you a thrill every time you put your foot on those sands?'

'Miss, *mademoiselle, signorina*, I live at Santa Carlotta Ligure, and now I must get on with my work.'

Sally was disappointed. She and Kate had only just discovered Shelley and were fascinated by his life and the lives of his friends. They did not take the trouble to read his poetry because the man and his romantic attachments were so much more exciting than anything he wrote, in their eyes. They pored over all the biographies Uncle George could find for them, followed in his footsteps to Italy, were bewitched by the glamour of his elopement − Shelley and Mary, both so young. 'Not much older than us,' they said. And then the meeting with other expatriates, Byron and that fantastic, swashbuckling Trelawney − just to think of them all meeting and talking in the long warm summer evenings with bottles of wine on the table, crusts of bread and cheese. 'Chianti in those straw-covered bottles that never stand quite straight,' Sally said.

And to think this prisoner, who had told them his name was Gianni Morelli when they asked, came from that very shore! It gave him a special interest in their eyes. They longed to ask him more, to be able to have endless talks, but these were ruled out for Mrs Sharkey told Uncle George the girls had been talking to a prisoner over the wall.

'Fratterising, that's what it is. Our girls fratting with an Eyetie. Scum!' she said in a tone of hearty disapproval.

Whether she meant the girls or the Eyetie was not clear but whichever way it was George told them they had better keep away from the wall.

'You wouldn't want to get the young man into trouble,' he said.

'But he's so nice, Dad,' protested Sally.

'I don't doubt it,' he said. 'Still, I think you'd better do as I say for all our sakes.'

They agreed but it was hard to resist the lure of the young men on the wrong side of the wall and sometimes, when they knew Mrs Sharkey was safely out of the way, they would creep over to say hallo to Giovanni, and in church, if they managed to catch his eye, they winked.

George was well aware of their deceit and amused by it.

'High time they had some boy friends,' he remarked to Hester. 'We don't want them getting enamoured of the Italians, but they are a nice-looking crowd and they certainly seem to turn their eyes on the girls in church. Haven't you noticed?'

'I can't say I have,' said Hester in an off-hand way.

'Well, I have. Perhaps it's you they're admiring, my darling, and not the girls at all.'

'Oh, George, how can you be so ridiculous? It will be a mercy when the war's over and they all go home.'

In spite of what she said Hester dreaded the thought of Giovanni Morelli going home. Yet how could his stay in the vicinity help her? She was suffering torments from this inexplicable thing that had happened to her, this thing people called falling in love, for she had fallen deeply in love with Gianni and he with her. The looks that passed between them in church, the signals he sent as she gazed from an upper window, led to more clandestine meetings, managed she scarcely knew how. She experienced feelings she never knew existed and they shocked and frightened her. In Gianni she found what she had been missing in life and knew it was the passionate love she had never felt for anyone else.

Once, long ago, on a delicious evening when she was on board *Corsair* with Mary Hope, she had tried to tell her she felt she had missed something, somewhere, and they had made a joke of it. Now she thought Mary was the one person she could have confided in, and perhaps Mary would have stopped her from doing anything rash. She longed to tell someone what had happened but it was not easy to translate her feelings into words, and even if she found a way to do that who could she spill them out to? George was her best, her truest friend, but how could she ask him to save her from this overwhelming torrent of love she was drowning in? It had always been easy to talk to him but not of a thing like this. There had never been the need. She liked him more than anyone she had ever known and this consuming passion did not diminish her affection for him. She had enjoyed many years of easy, loving companionship but had never been in love with him, yet if Gianni had not crossed her path she would have gone on in the same comfortable way.

So surely it would be a blessing when Gianni went home? So far they had resisted the ultimate but his embraces, the things he said, his lips on hers, the certainty that he felt for her as she did for him, bound her to him. Deferring the final union held them closer, made the bond more secure than if they had succumbed.

She grew thin as passion ravaged her and George noticed and was anxious. He confided in the doctor who told him it was the early onset of the menopause and not to take too much account of it. Consequently he was even more attentive than usual.

'After the war we'll have a car and go about a bit,' he

91

told her. 'It's dull for you down here with just the girls for company.'

'I like it. It's not a bit dull,' she said.

'Come up to town with me for a few days and we'll do some shows.'

That meant she wouldn't see Gianni and she could hardly bear to lose a moment, but she had to go though it was misery to sit through a play knowing he was waiting to catch a glimpse of her. Worse than that were the nights, trying to respond to her husband who had lost none of his early ardour. To whom was she a traitor — to George or to Gianni? It was an impossible situation.

And then, unbelievably, her problem was solved. The war ended.

She had always known her strange affair of the heart would end when this happened. Those last meetings with Gianni were almost unbearable because soon they would part and she would never see him again, never feel the touch of his hand or listen to him telling her of the change she had made in his life. He talked of his home, his family, the place where he lived, and how he longed to take her there. He said she would love the Hotel Villa Laura where he lived with his parents and which was to be his when they retired. There was a large peach orchard behind the hotel and in spring the sea of blossom stretched right away up the hill. Santa Carlotta was not a fashionable resort but the Villa Laura attracted a special kind of clientèle; discriminating people chose it for its tranquil atmosphere, its delightful grounds, its excellent service. And Santa Carlotta itself with its maze of little streets, its gleaming white church and the piazza where all the local festivities took place — that was where he wanted to be seen with her. He talked of it more and more in their last snatched meetings.

'You'll forget me when you go home,' she said.

He swore he would not.

'You must.'

She told him this part of their lives was an interlude. It was precious and they must be grateful for it, but it was a thing apart. When peace separated them they would each resume their ordinary lives.

'This is no interlude,' he said. 'I shall come back for you. You will see.'

When the trucks bearing the prisoners away rolled past Heron House Kate and Sally ran down to the gate to see them go and to wave goodbye while Hester, with a splitting headache, stopped up her ears so as not to hear the noise of the convoy. She felt used up, burnt out. She looked out of her window at the empty fields with a sort of despair. She woke every morning in a state of bewildered misery and it was a moment or so before she realised the cause of it. Gianni had gone, she would not see him any more, and life was meaningless without him. She had to will herself to appear natural, to be interested in what was going on around her.

Sally would soon be taking up the place she had won at Oxford. Kate was wondering what to do when she left school. Orlando Hope's shop would reopen and she could work there with Mr Proctor to teach her. It would mean living in London and this appealed to her.

'But you'll come home at weekends, Kate,' Hester said when they talked it over. They were in the kitchen having coffee and Mrs Sharkey, at the sink, kept chipping in.

'All very nice, I'm sure, but I don't like to think of a young thing like you living alone in London,' she said. 'It ain't right or proper and you should put your foot down, Mrs Hester.'

'Well, there isn't much scope down here and I think it would be splendid to work in her father's shop and deal with beautiful things. I'm sure we'll find her a nice place to live, Mrs Sharkey.'

'Oughta get married and have a fambly,' muttered Mrs Sharkey.

'All in good time,' said Hester. 'Anyway, Kate darling, no matter what you decide, this is always home.'

'It's wonderful knowing that,' said Kate. 'I shan't think about it till after the summer holidays. We'll all be here, won't we? Or are you and Uncle George going away, Hester?'

'We shall be here,' she said, thinking of Italy and wondering just what Gianni was doing at that very moment. Welcoming guests? Supervising the dining

93

room? Or perhaps snatching time for a dip in the sea?

'I do miss Gianni and the boys,' said Kate. 'I miss their singing.'

Hester shivered. It was as though Kate had lifted the feelings from her heart. Were they so strong that they could be sensed by others, shared by others? She would have to quench them, stifle them, but how when she could not expel Gianni from her very being?

He was everywhere. She imagined him standing in that desolate field, felt his presence in the church. She looked from her window in vain whenever an army truck went along the road.

And there was no one to whom she could talk of this overwhelming love that had caught her up and swept her along, changing everything she saw, everything she did, even changing people and making them seem remote. George, Sally, Kate − it was as though they were in another room, as though they were just out of earshot, just disappearing through one door as she entered by another. Oh, but she still loved them, cherished them almost more than she had before Gianni came.

I must get over it, I must, I must, she told herself. And although the strength of her emotions sapped her energy she forced herself to do hard physical work. She washed paint, polished floors, and took long solitary walks.

'You'll kill yourself,' said Mrs Sharkey anxiously. 'Why don't you sit quiet?'

Hester tried to reassure Mrs Sharkey; she did not want to draw attention to herself by too much unwonted activity.

One afternoon, just as she was going out, she had an unexpected visit from Father Keith, the priest from the Catholic church. He was in his forties, with dark hair just greying and a pale, well-featured face. She had often thought he would make a good husband and it was a shame he had to stay single, but that, as he once told her, was his choice.

'I've come begging,' he said as she showed him into the drawing room.

'I don't suppose you like that very much,' she said, 'but I expect it's for a special cause.'

'It is. It's the church floor and it's going to cost thousands. We have several projects on hand for raising funds and that's why I've come to see you. I know you're not of our persuasion but I'm sure you enjoyed the singing when the Italians were here.'

'Yes, I certainly did,' she said, beginning to feel very strange inside.

'So I just wondered if you would consider lending your garden for a fête to raise funds?'

He would have gone on but she agreed without hesitation. It would please her very much to help and she was sure George would agree. 'You can count on us,' she said.

'Splendid. The idea is to have stalls, a raffle or two, refreshments. Of course there's no need for you to be involved in any of this. We have an organising committee of very enthusiastic ladies.'

'I'd like to help if I can,' she said. 'I expect the girls would, too.'

'Your daughters? That would be fine. Sally, isn't it?'

'And Kate. Kate isn't our daughter but George and I are as fond of her as if she were. Her parents were dear friends. They were killed almost at the end of the war. The V2.'

'Ah!'

Hester found herself telling him the whole story, right from when they first met and the spontaneous friendship that sprang up between her family and the Hopes. She told him about The Clearing and the Lamberts and he listened, taking it all in, watching her, assessing her.

'Lambert?' he said. 'The name rings a bell. Is that the Guy Lambert —'

'DFC and bar,' she said. 'Yes, that's the one. Do you know him?'

'If you'll do me another favour, I might get to know him. I was wondering if you could ask him to open our fête? He'd be a tremendous draw.'

'There's no doubt of that. I don't know where he is just now but I can get in touch with his mother.'

'Would you?'

'I can't promise anything.'

'Of course not. It's a liberty to ask.'

'Not a bit. I'll write to Mrs Lambert straight away,' she said.

He accepted her offer of tea and they went on talking easily. Like old friends, she thought. Before he left she took him on a tour of the garden and he declared it to be much larger and more beautiful than he had imagined. Just as he was leaving he stopped short and said: 'Goodness me, I clean forgot,' and took a letter out of his breast pocket. She saw the foreign stamp.

'I've heard from one of the ex-prisoners,' he said. 'Giovanni Morelli. The one with the splendid tenor voice.'

She was glad her hand was on the gate. She needed something to hold on to. 'I hope they are all happily settled back at home,' she said, and her voice sounded tinny and thin in her ears.

'They are. Would you like to see the letter? Gianni sends kind remembrances to all those who were good to them. He mentions you by name, Mrs Sheridan – and the *signorinas*.'

She took the letter he held out to her. 'May I show it to the girls? I'll let you have it back.'

'Of course. No hurry.'

She held the letter against a heart that was beating much too fast. She watched Father Keith till he rounded the bend in the road. Then she went down to the barn where she and Gianni had met when they were able. She looked at the spiky writing, read the carefully composed phrases, and they conveyed nothing of the real Gianni to her. 'Please convey my duty to the Signora S.,' he wrote. She was hurt. It would have been better if he hadn't mentioned her, but then she imagined him writing the letter, puzzling to know how he could put something down on paper that would not betray his true feelings to Father Keith. Further on there was something more. 'My parents would be happy to welcome those of you who did not regard us as enemies at the Hotel Villa Laura as their honoured guests.' Surely that was meant for her? It was the nearest he could get to a direct approach. Oh, Gianni, Gianni, you seem so much further away than the miles between us. We are separated forever and it's more than I can endure.

She was sorry she had seen the letter and giving it to Kate and Sally made her feel worse than ever. How they pored over it, chuckling at the stilted sentences and wondering if they would ever go to Santa Carlotta.

'Please take it back to Father Keith,' she said.

Then she remembered why he had called and told them about the projected fête. Outwardly she was composed and she tried hard to find inner calm. Through attending the church she had several prayers by heart and she recited the Hail Mary over and over again. She even bought a little rosary and kept it in her pocket, fingering the beads and the crucifix. Gianni had a rosary – he wore it wound round his wrist. Thinking of that gave her some comfort.

A few days after Father Keith's call the committee members from the church came to see her with the object of telling her their ideas and how they wanted to organise the event. The fête would be declared open at 3 p.m. on the chosen Saturday. They would set up stalls in the morning – soft toys, home made cakes, jams and chutneys, hand-made children's clothes, hand-knitted garments, potted plants, pottery and ornaments. Refreshments would consist of tea, coffee, lemonade and ices, and there would be a set tea of scones, Devonshire cream and cake at a fixed price. Wine would be available by the glass.

Hester listened with a sinking heart. It was the old familiar garden fête all over again, and she thought of the tatty tray cloths, embroidered pillow cases and fancy aprons she had seen at so many similar events. Still, she was committed to help and so wrote off to Ella Lambert, half-hoping for a refusal. The reply came almost by return. Wing Commander Lambert, DFC and bar, would be delighted to open the fête on the day and at the time requested.

After that preparations went ahead with almost relentless enthusiasm and the great day dawned overcast but mild, and gave way to blue skies and warm sunshine as the morning raced on.

Kate had lost most of her possessions when the V2 fell on The Clearing but she still had the scrap book she had started at the outbreak of war. It was almost entirely devoted to the exploits of Guy Lambert and she admitted, if only to herself, that she was more interested in him than anyone else. She pasted in all the magazine and newspaper cuttings that mentioned him. There were a good many press photographs for he had caught the imagination of the public with his good looks and daring.

Sally teased Kate good-naturedly and declared she must still have a crush on him. 'Have you still got that cigarette card you picked up?' she asked.

'As a matter of fact I have − and it's as good as new. You must give me credit for being discerning,' Kate said, and added, 'None of us knew he would be a hero then.'

'Did you ever have a conversation with him?' Sally asked.

'No. Scarcely a good morning. I didn't have your nerve,' said Kate.

'I had several chats.'

'You never told me.'

'Didn't want to put your nose out of joint. Anyway, he was just too, too condescending and an awful prig into the bargain. Let's hope the RAF has knocked all that nonsense out of him.'

'We'll see what he's like now,' Kate said. She rather dreaded meeting him, partly because of her shyness, partly because she didn't want to be disillusioned. She was to help serve lemonade at the fête so she would have to stay at her post and wouldn't be noticed in the crowd.

And there was a crowd. People began to arrive long before 3 p.m. and wandered round previewing the stalls. Hester's misgivings disappeared when she saw what was for sale and she was glad to own she had misjudged the organisers.

'You needn't have worried, Mum,' said Sally. 'The things on the needlework stall beat Bond Street. I'm going to buy some handkerchiefs for Dad. Look, rolled edges.'

'And monograms. Have they got a G?' They had. The other stalls displayed goods of equally high standard: beautifully smocked and honey-combed children's clothes; tablecloths with intricate drawn-thread work designs; several evening handbags of petit-point that must have been years in the making − it was all far and away above average.

Kate knew the Lamberts had arrived when the crowd

converged on a small dais that had been set up. She stood on tiptoe at the back but could not get a clear view. She could just about hear Father Keith making his introductory remarks, and judging by the ripples of laughter they were going down well. Then came the great moment. Wing Commander Guy Lambert was introduced amid applause. He spoke. He had a good clear voice but she did not hear one word because Mrs Sharkey was close by her side with a running commentary. Mrs Sharkey wanted to get a good look, and why did all these people in front of have such big heads? She even prodded a woman in the back and requested her to remove her hat.

'Saved us, he did. Him and his like. And I can't see him because of your hat,' she complained. 'One of the Few, he is. Think of that!'

'Oh, please! I want to listen,' said Kate.

But the chance had gone. By the cheer that went up Guy had declared the fête open and that meant hurrying back to her lemonade stall.

The Lamberts, Ella, Ernest and Guy, were making a tour of the stalls escorted by Father Keith and a gaggle of committee ladies. They were in no hurry; there were introductions, compliments, mild jokes. Ella was obviously buying.

Kate's table with its glasses and jugs all set out on a white cloth was the last on the round but it seemed they were passing it by for Ella had seen the little tables set out for tea on the other side of the lawn and she did not notice Kate. She went on ahead with Ernest. Guy was a few steps behind but instead of catching up with them he made for her stall. She saw him for the first time in five years and his uniform made him look even more striking than he actually was, and that was something. He was right in front of her.

She heard him say: 'I must have some lemonade. I'm parched.' Could he be addressing her? He smiled. He held out sixpence. She gave him twopence change. He did not know her from Adam.

'What a beautiful day. I hope you'll do well,' he said.

'Thank you.' She held his sixpence. She would keep it

99

and substitute one of her own. Could he be lingering? Was he on the point of saying something else? If so he lost his chance for he was surrounded by at least eight girls who bore him off and away out of sight.

There was a brisk demand for lemonade so Kate was kept busy. Buyers formed an orderly queue. She filled glasses, took money and gave change without noticing who she served until Guy appeared again.

'Oh,' she said. 'Another?'

'Please.' He did not move away this time but stood near the table, drank a little and then said: 'May I have some more sugar?'

'I'm afraid there's none here,' she said. 'I could get some from the house if you like.'

'Wizard!'

But before she could move another helper arrived to take over and by the time she had explained the procedure Guy had put his empty glass down and was moving off towards the lawn. She wondered whether to catch him up when she saw Sally coming, and what did Sally do but grab his arm and say: 'Hi, big shot. Here's Kate!'

The idea — calling him big shot! He looked round.

'You can't have forgotten her?' said Sally.

'Kate?'

'Do you mean to tell me you've been buying her lemonade without recognising her? Come off it.'

'I had no idea — honestly.' There was no mistaking the look of admiration on his face now. 'Why, Kate,' he said, and took her hands in his. She thought he was going to say something about her parents, her loss, for he hesitated for what seemed an age and then he did the most extraordinary thing. He kissed her on the forehead. She knew this was his way of expressing his sympathy.

She could hardly believe they were really there together. Not in the most far-fetched of her dreams had she ever imagined anything approaching this. It was not because of the light brush of his lips on her forehead or his undisguised admiration, it was because he was seeing her true self, a girl alone, a girl who had nothing to do with the schoolgirl who had admired him from a distance, a girl who could look

100

back into his eyes, meet his gaze and know he had found her, in one of those extraordinary flashes that change a whole existence.

There they were, the two of them, in this familiar garden with people all around, with the sound of voices, conversation, greetings, laughter, the chink of china and clink of glass, yet they were apart from it all. She was aware of all this in the moment that was eternity and, like eternity, had nothing to do with time. She was aware of individuals, of Mrs Sharkey gathering up glasses on a tray and wearing an enormous white apron. Hester, nearby, was in earnest conversation with Father Keith, Sally — where was Sally? She was walking away, making a tactful retreat.

Guy linked his arm through hers. 'You've grown up,' he said.

'Five years make a difference,' she said. She knew he had survived encounters with the enemy, been close to extinction many times, lost comrades, waited for them to return from missions in the hostile sky, counted the planes as they came back and hoped against hope that one, two, even three missing had landed somewhere else. And then, in the bar, jugging up, blotting out the memory of those who were there last night and would never be there again. She knew all this and wondered it did not show in his face. He talked lightly, inconsequentially. Perhaps there were times when he talked of deeper things, but not now, not today.

'So all this is in aid of the church,' he remarked, as they strolled across the lawn towards the river. 'How did you get involved?'

'I live here now — with the Sheridans,' she said.

'Really? I didn't know.'

She knew so much about him and he knew nothing of her. It was strange and in a way hurtful to realise it. After the tragedy of The Clearing surely the Lamberts would have talked of the lost ones amongst themselves? And there was so much about it in the papers. Mr Churchill himself had visited the scene the morning after the disaster and talked to Ernest Lambert who had been on his way to the railway station the night before when the explosion occurred. There was an air of mystery about it for secrecy surrounded the cause and it was widely reported that a gas main had exploded. No one believed this for long and it soon became known that the weapon was a rocket, the V2, Hitler's latest and deadliest.

There were articles in the papers about the three families who had lived in The Clearing and the miracle that only two of them had been killed. The greatest interest centred on the Lamberts because of Guy who had spent a few days leave at home and rejoined his unit that very morning. At the same time his mother returned to her sister in Bath and his father had left work and was on his way to his 'club'. George Sheridan, too, had had a hair's breadth escape.

Far more interest centred on those who had escaped than on Orlando and Mary Hope. Reporters sought interviews with the survivors and asked the usual insensitive questions — 'How did you feel when you saw the crater?' 'Did you lose much?'

One had even arrived on the doorstep of Heron House to interview Kate and had been sent about his business by Mrs Sharkey at her most formidable. 'Be off with you, you young scallywag,' she shouted when he announced his errand. She said a lot more that he didn't wait to hear.

And to think that with all the publicity and his own involvement in it Guy didn't even know she had escaped because she was with the Sheridans at the time. He had not given her a single thought. Yet surely the way he had taken her hand and planted that brief kiss on her brow meant something? It was his way of saying he knew everything so it was stupid to think him unfeeling.

'Yes, I live here now,' she repeated, 'with the Sheridans, and I can't tell you how super they are.'

'Are they really? I don't know them very well.'

Although she could never bring herself to speak of the V2 she could talk of Hester and George and Sally and how they had adopted her and of her life with them at Heron House. 'I'm so lucky,' she said. 'It's glorious here — well, you can see. And the Sheridans are such a kind family.'

'It's a bit quiet here, isn't it?'

'Oh, we have all kinds of diversions. There were a lot of

Italian P.O.W.s working on the farms round about not so long ago.'

'I hope you didn't fraternise with them?'

'Mrs Sharkey thought we did. She's our housekeeper. More than that — she's our everything. She keeps us all in order. She put her foot down because Sally and I used to call out *'Giorno'* to them, so of course we did it all the more. You're not shocked, are you?'

'A bit surprised, but tell me more.'

So she told him about the prisoners' choir and how they had all gone to church on Sundays to hear them sing. 'We didn't go for the right reasons at all,' she said. 'At least, I didn't. I only went for the singing. But we got to know Father Keith and he's a dear. Hester says it's wicked he's out of the marriage market. We're having the fête here today to help him.'

He wanted to know what she did with herself. Did she go dancing, for instance. No. She loved swimming, swam in the river, went for long walks. She was trying to decide whether to work in her father's shop which would mean living in London.

'Sally and I used to dream of having a flat of our own when we were at school,' she said. 'We imagined bottle parties and going for midnight swims in the Serpentine minus our clothes.'

'Very cold, the Serpentine.' How like Noel Coward, she thought.

He kept looking at her as though he had never seen her before, and neither had he. She was a butterfly emerging from the chrysalis and spreading painted wings. Delicate, fluttering wings with fabulous markings in resplendent colours. Wait till they're properly dry, just wait and see how entrancing I am, she seemed to promise.

'We were going to explore London, the whole of it, strange places with stranger inhabitants, especially Soho. We really meant to go to town there. Italian waiters and spaghetti. We're both mad about Italy. We're going there the first chance we have and we might get a whiff of it in Soho, don't you think? Only now that Sally's going to Oxford I shall have to explore it alone.'

'You must never go to Soho alone,' he said quickly.

'Why not?'

'It's no place for a girl like you.'

'Aren't there lots of little restaurants and shops that sell garlic sausage and loads of cheese and pastas and olives?'

'There are, but you mustn't go there. Not alone.'

'Then I shall ask Uncle George to come with me.'

'Why not ask me?'

Could this be real? It was like one of her fantasy conversations. 'Ask *you*?' she said.

'Let me take you to dinner at a very special restaurant I know. It's right in the heart of Soho. The proprietor will kiss your hand and give you a red rose. How about that?'

'I'd love it!'

'Wizzo!'

Wizzo indeed. The ridiculous word opened the door to a new world. She was stepping into it and at first it was like entering an enormous soap bubble full of shimmering light with more colours than she could have imagined merging together. Soon it would float away, carrying them both inside it, and they would see the garden and the people through its transparency.

But no, this was solid. She was strolling towards the cedar and into its shade with Guy, feeling the ground where no grass grew under her feet, noticing the bark, the low branches. He was lifting one up so they could both pass under it together and step back on to the springy turf where a few daisies were opening again though all their heads had been mown off that morning.

They were almost at the river bank and there were two women standing together talking. Hester and Ella. They both wore dresses saved from before the war, of the kind seen at Ascot or the Regatta. Ella's was a gentle shade of grey with an unobtrusive design, probably pink roses if the material were spread out but now gathered in, just lending subtle colour in the folds. Hester wore almond green silk. It brought back a picture to Kate's mind. She saw her mother and Hester home from a trip to the West End. They were opening a brown paper parcel and taking out a pattern and a length of silk that was to become this dress. They unfolded

104

it and Hester draped it over herself, standing before the long mirror in the hall and gathering it this way and that while her mother asked should they cut it out now or wait till tomorrow?

Seeing this picture in her mind's eye and hearing the echo of voices did not disturb Kate today. Not long ago reminders of the past had hurt almost beyond bearing – not so now. And it was odd she had not even remembered the dress when Hester put it on today. Now she saw it without the shock of remembrance. It brought the pleasure of the past without the pain. And no wonder, for she was walking hand in hand with Guy and it was really happening. Her life was happening!

Ella turned as they approached. So did Hester.

'Kate, my dear, where have you been hiding the whole afternoon?' cried Ella, feigning surprise at seeing her. She knew perfectly well that Kate had been serving lemonade but she was adept at only seeing people when it suited her. She had been basking in her son's reflected glory when she passed the lemonade stall in search of tea and cakes.

'How noble of you to run a stall,' she went on. 'And how well you are looking. No wonder, living in a beautiful place like this. I quite envy you. And this garden, Hester. It's simply divine. Don't you agree, Guy dear?'

She rambled on, turning from one to the other, including them all in her eulogies, and although she mentioned envy she kept it out of her voice with an effort. It was really not fair to discover that Hester was mistress of all this. She had been to see Kate in the winter after the tragedy but then she had not noticed the extent of the grounds nor the desirable situation. All her attention had been fixed on Kate and her tragic plight. She had always liked the girl and had much preferred the Hopes to the Sheridans whom she had never felt fitted in. They did not conform to her idea of what a solid middle-class family like her own should be. And now, if you please, they might almost be classed as landed gentry. The very words 'landed gentry' made her smoulder inside. How many cuts above the Lamberts might that be? Well, she could put up with George Sheridan – he might well qualify – but his wife could have been a barmaid or a chorus girl and was probably no better than she ought to be. George had lifted her from the gutter and she had no rightful place here at all.

With these thoughts in her mind Ella addressed Hester with a sugary smile. 'So that's the boat – the one that went to Dunkirk?' she enquired.

'That's *Corsair*,' said Hester. 'She was a spanking craft when she went to France but just look at her now.'

The yacht had been badly damaged on its mission. The decks were smashed in and all the portholes broken but the damage was not irreparable and Sam Sharkey had begun the task of putting her to rights. There was a pile of planks on deck with which he would replace broken floor boards.

'And Mr Sheridan actually sailed there and brought back seventy men, I've heard.'

'That's perfectly true.'

'Just fancy that!'

Ella could only picture George wearing a peculiar hat and reading a book as he walked swiftly home to his house in The Clearing, the house that was no longer there. She listened to Hester's account of what the family called George's escapade with surprise. She knew he was an authority on eighteenth-century history; now he was a hero as well. Ernest had accompanied him to town on the 8.30 for months on end and although he had discovered George had inherited a house by the river, it had gone no further than that. Or if it had Ernest had never told her. Just like him. He read the *Financial Times* on the way up and George read a book when they could have spent the time better in getting to know each other. They had never even asked the Sheridans in for a drink. What an opportunity lost! And now, only today, she had discovered quite by chance that George owned one of the little ships that brought 'our boys', as she called the troops, back from the beaches of Dunkirk. And Ernest, on those trips to town, hadn't even discovered that. Oh, she would have something to say to him this evening, and if it turned out he knew about the Dunkirk episode and had kept it from her she would be very, very angry.

They were going on board *Corsair* now to inspect the damage. Ella, following Hester, noticed how slim she was.

Nothing on the hips, long slender legs. Most women had put on weight during the war but Hester had actually lost it. How annoying. She was only too conscious of her own expanding waist line and dieting made her go thin in the face and thick everywhere else.

Kate was following her up the gangplank. Ella looked over her shoulder and was cheered by the sight of the girl's eager young face. And there was dear Guy bringing up the rear, holding both rails so that Kate was practically in his arms. How splendid he looked. What a nice couple they would make, she thought. Such a pleasant, healthy girl. She had never been ill as far as Ella knew. And probably quite well off as she must have inherited Orlando Hope's. Her spirits rose.

Down in the saloon they all marvelled that so many men had been packed in, and Sam Sharkey, who was snatching a nap in his bunk, rolled out to tell them how fraught with danger those trips had been with Heinkels dive bombing to say nothing of the horror of the blood, vomit and worse.

'But *Corsair* pulled through, Missis,' he declared, directing the information at Ella. 'A game old girl, that's what she is. Time I've finished with her she'll be better than new, what with the plaque to show she done it. She done it, eh, Mrs Hester?

'She did indeed, thanks to you, Sam.'

'Not forgetting Master George?'

'Not forgetting him, of course.'

'We were shipmates, him and me.'

'You still are, Sam.'

'Give me another year, and we'll be off up to Wallingford like we did in 'thirty-nine. Remember that run, Kate?'

'I shall never forget it,' said Kate, for then her father and mother had been there and they had all talked about the trip for days afterwards.

Hester, too, was thinking of that day and of how she had tried to tell Mary of her inner feelings and the vague sense of a lack in her life. She had felt then that there was still something to come. Now she knew what it was. Gianni. Oh, Gianni, your hands smoothing my hair, the violets you gathered for me. They are pressed between the pages of a book. The phrase book! Remember how we laughed?

Sam was talking to Guy, showing him his cap with the bullet hole. 'Lucky it weren't on me 'ead, Mister!' General interest in the cap gave Hester the chance to recollect herself. Thank goodness no one had noticed her drifting off. She said it was time they were getting back to the house and they all followed her down the gangplank.

The stalls were packing up. Everything was sold and Father Keith and his organisers were delighted with the results. They had done far better than expected, partly because all the items for sale were gifts of such high quality that buyers had paid far above the prices asked, and partly because raffle winners had given their prizes back to be offered over and over again. The takings were still being counted.

In the house Mrs Sharkey had taken enormous pains to produce a buffet for the visitors.

'I can't undertake to dish up a dinner for all that lot, willing as I am, Mrs Hester. There's the rationing,' she had said when the question of feeding the parting guests had been discussed.

'They will only have had tea,' Hester pointed out. 'We must be grateful to them for coming so we'll have to serve up something. They won't expect dinner.'

'I should think not,' said Mrs Sharkey, 'rationing being what it is. They won't expect nothing much.'

'No, Shark dear, but I can trust you to cook up nothing much, can't I?' wheedled Hester.

'Seeing as how one of the Few's coming I suppose you can,' Mrs Sharkey conceded. 'How many's expected?'

'There'll be the Lamberts. That's three. Father Keith and four of his committee and ourselves. Say twelve in all.'

Mrs Sharkey shook her head, not because she couldn't do it but because she wondered how. 'Keeping us on short commons all this time after the war's over! And to think we won it,' she complained to Sam.

'Don't worry, Mum,' he said.

'I won't. You can do the worrying about what's to be got from the garden,' she said. 'That's what we'll have to rely on.'

Tomatoes. Asparagus. Mushrooms. He rubbed the knees of his corduroy trousers and grinned. 'Make us a cup of tea, Mum.'

There were a few eggs from their own hens and she did not ask where the rest of the two dozen had come from, neither did she ask about the rabbits. No one would know rabbit from chicken when she had dealt with it. Gently cooked, diced and incorporated in a creamy sauce with a bit of parsley, she could use it as a filling for her mouthwatering vols-au-vents. The eggs, hard boiled, halved, and stuffed with their own yolks mashed up with some pulverised anchovies, would go down well. And what about some paper thin pancakes with a spoonful of sliced mushrooms done in a little butter and well seasoned? Just gather up the corners so they looked like little sacks. Very tasty. Tomatoes ... Now what could she stuff those with? Cream cheese? Not bad with a few chives scissored up. And in case this was all too light and fancy she'd boost it up with open sandwiches. Better boil the ham they'd been saving. A few bowls of lettuce and cucumber salad perhaps with her home-made dressing. But, oh, for some good old olive oil and some butter!

Down in the village shop she glared at Mr Parsons as she demanded extra butter. 'It's for a good cause,' she said. 'Come along. Cough up. Don't give me none of that rationing nonsense.' He gave her half a pound over the family allowance. Withered by the look she cast on him he produced another quarter. 'I should think so, too,' she said.

'You'd better get the silver cleaned, Sam,' she shouted at her son as he passed the kitchen window with a laden trug of produce from the garden.

And now, after all her hard work and to her great satisfaction, Mrs Sharkey, aided by a girl from the village, had just finished setting out the feast on the sideboard in the diningroom, and very fine it looked. The sideboard took up almost one wall of the room. It was oak, highly polished with a handsome backboard, but it was the carving on its three doors that arrested people when they came in. Cornucopias of fruit, swathes of flowers and birds, stood out a whole inch or more and were the very devil to keep free from dust in the cracks and creases, but there was never a speck to be seen. The wood gleamed, bunched grapes shone golden, all the colours of the carved oak were there from ebony to a deep shining tan to the colour that was almost gold in the fruit.

She saw the invited party come straggling across the lawn and noticed Kate was walking with the young airman. Then Mr and Mrs Lambert, him very portly with jowls and her looking as though everything she had on hurt. Sally was skipping along beside Father Keith, such a catch but for the impediment of that collar. And Master George was surrounded by the committee ladies, single every one of them and all devoted to Father Keith. Ah, well. Things could be worse. Mrs Hester walked alone. How thoughtful she looked. Tired out more than likely.

They'd all be in the drawingroom by now, taking a glass of sherry. They'd be in and out of the loo, as they like to call it. Lots of giggling from the ladies. Ah, here they came, shepherded in by Master George. Mrs Hester had Father Keith in tow now.

'This all looks superb, Mrs Sheridan,' she heard him say, and Mrs Hester told him it tasted as good as it looked and they had Mrs Sharkey to thank for it all. Pleased, rewarded, Mrs Sharkey took up her place to attend to the varied needs of the guests.

'This wasn't expected, Mrs Sheridan,' Father Keith told Hester as he savoured a vol-au-vent. 'It was more than enough to have the use of your garden, and now you include all these good things. May I have another?'

Hester saw he had plenty. George, having given the matter serious consideration, had fetched up two bottles of his father's best claret and was handing it round. The day which he had rather dreaded was a huge success after all. Even the Lamberts had the merit of affording him some amusement. Ernest looked disgustingly well-fed due to the business lunches he gorged every day. Ella, a puzzling sort of woman, had been positively smarming up to him though he didn't remember more than a casual greeting from her when they were neighbours in The Clearing. Now she kept gushing on about *Corsair* and his brave exploits as she called them. She meant well, he supposed, thinking how much better she would look if she had spared a little paint for her neck instead of finishing off at the contours of her face. He couldn't help thinking of Lady Wishfort in the restoration play who looked in the glass and compared her reflection to an old peeled wall. The idea made him smile. Presently he couldn't help laughing and wishing he could share the joke with Sally, but Ella thought he laughed at something she had said and preened and perked in front of him like a parrot. This made him laugh still more. She ought to be on a perch. Give her a drop more claret and she'd be calling him 'pretty boy'.

Hester, observing this unaccustomed mirth, prised the bottle from him and went to refill Guy's glass but he prevented her by putting his hand over the top.

'It's delicious, but no more,' he said. 'Fact is I want to ask a favour of you, Mrs Sheridan.'

There was nothing arrogant in his expression or manner now. 'I hope it's one I can grant,' she said.

'May I borrow Kate for this evening?'

The request was so unexpected she blinked but before she could say anything he went on: 'We were talking — Kate and I — and she happened to say how much she wanted to explore London, especially Soho. Well, we all know Soho simply isn't for young girls, don't we?'

'Do we? I should think they'd be quite safe so long as they went in the daytime, and not alone, of course.'

'That's just it, don't you see? That's just what I'm saying. So as Kate seemed so keen I offered to take her to dinner there — to a highly respectable restaurant, one we often go to when we're on leave. She liked the idea but if you have any objections ...'

Hester had plenty of objections. They shot through her mind like arrows with labels on them: She is too young. You are too charming. She will fall for you. You will lead her up the garden. I will not have her hurt. I do not like you.

'Don't you think it would be better if you made up a party?' she asked.

'That would take time to organise. It's a super idea, but this evening?'

111

'It would be very nice, Guy. Only how do you propose to get her home? Not on the back of a motorbike, I hope.'

'I have a nice little M.G. now and I'll bring her home in that. I'll take great care of her, I promise you.'

Ella, glass in hand, interrupted them before Hester could reply. 'What are you two so deep in consultation about?' she asked. 'I'm dying of curiosity.'

'Guy was asking if he can take Kate out to dinner tonight and I was just about to consent,' Hester said.

'Why, what a splendid idea!' cried Ella. 'It's been such a successful day and it will be so nice for the young people to round it off with a pleasant little dinner.'

Hester had to agree. The party was over. The clearing up was about to begin. Guy was talking to Kate, obviously telling her his plan for the evening had been approved, for she was clasping her hands together, going up on tiptoe, laughing, excited. Oh, Kate, dear, do be careful, she prayed. Don't fall for him. Don't let him break your heart.

Kate had a very limited wardrobe. Dresses, coats and shoes that might still have done quite well were all lost when the rocket destroyed The Clearing. She had been allowed extra coupons for replacements but not nearly enough. She remembered a most becoming pale yellow silk dress with a scoop neck and a pattern of autumn leaves embroidered round it that would just have done, but it was no use thinking of that. Only the utility clothes, which were all she had, were so uninspiring.

'Oh, Sal, what can I wear?' she asked, for Sally had followed her upstairs to help her get ready. 'Suppose everyone's in lovely things at the restaurant?'

'They're all rationed, the same as we are,' Sally said.

'Yes, but people have beautiful clothes from before the war. I've only got skirts and jumpers.'

'Skirts!' exclaimed Sally. 'You've got that super black ballerina Mum made out of the corded silk she had. It's perfect. Haven't you got a blouse?'

'I've got my chiffon! Oh, what a brick you are. I'd forgotten.'

The blouse was one of Kate's most treasured possessions.

Perhaps the most treasured of all. She had the scrapbook, the amethyst necklace her father had given her, and the blouse. Although her mother had not been the most successful of dressmakers she was an expert at blouses, having been taught by her own mother, and in turn she had begun to teach Kate. They made the blouse between them. It was of cream chiffon with sets of the finest pin tucks alternating with insertions of real lace. The long full sleeves ended in cuffs of the same lace fastened with minute pearl buttons. Kate remembered measuring for the tucks and admiring the ease with which her mother made them. Her mother's needlework was of the finest and in the end most of the sewing had been hers. Kate had always been glad of this. And now, this evening, she was going to wear the blouse for the first time.

'Oh, Sal, I'm so excited! Just fancy going out with him! I can't really believe it.'

She was out of the cotton dress she had worn all day and was looking for the blouse. It was in a drawer wrapped in tissue paper. She shook it out and laid it on the bed.

They stood looking at it, and Kate drew in a deep breath, almost a gasp, for it filled her with such an overwhelming emotion — the needle patiently, carefully sewing the tucks, the hand holding it. A rather plump, pretty hand with just the plain gold wedding ring. Oh, where were they?

Sally sensed the way Kate felt and put her arm round her. She was afraid for her. If her own parents had been killed she would have been completely devastated. She knew that and had often thought she had everything and Kate nothing, and to be alone, utterly alone, must be the most terrible thing in the world. It made Kate vulnerable. She was bound to want someone of her own. It was only natural. And now Guy Lambert was on the scene and he was not the right one. She longed to tell Kate not to get carried away but she could not say anything like that now.

Instead she lifted the blouse carefully from the bed and held it for Kate to put on. 'It's beautiful,' she said, 'truly beautiful. Come on, let me fasten the skirt. Now turn round and look in the glass.'

Kate turned. She saw a tall, slim, elegant girl quite unlike the everyday Kate. This was a glamourous girl, a girl whose

113

eyes were rather too bright, and with a little too much colour in her cheeks. A girl on the verge of tears, on the edge of laughter, a girl surprised.

She turned back to Sally.

'Yes, you'll do,' said Sally. 'You'd better have your necklace.'

The treasured necklace was clasped round Kate's neck and set in the right position.

'Will I look as good as the others?' she asked.

'You'll knock 'em in the Old Kent Road,' said Sally, and they went downstairs together, Sally laughing with a heart like lead and Kate laughing too, but she was on top of the the world.

'Why do we distrust him?' Hester asked. She and Sally had retired to drink coffee with George in his study. He put down his book.

'He's not such a bad young fellow,' he said. 'I had quite a long talk with him and he's very modest about his achievements. Kept talking about the marvels of the Typhoon. In fact, that's all he did talk about.'

'Well, I just hope Kate won't lose her head over him,' Hester said.

'He might lose his over her,' said George. 'And I really don't see what we have to worry about just because she's having an evening out.'

'Call it intuition,' Hester said.

Sally had not spoken and George felt rather sorry for her. After an exciting day, and with Kate off enjoying herself, the evening would be very flat for his daughter. He racked his brains, picked up the paper and turned to the amusements page. If they hurried they could get up to town by eight o'clock and most shows started at eight-thirty. Gilbert and Sullivan at the Savoy. Why not?

He went out to the hall, rang the theatre and was lucky enough to get three returns. Dress Circle. What a bit of luck. He went back to the study. Sally had picked up his book; Hester stared into space.

'Come on, girls. Get your skates on. We're going to the theatre,' he announced. The surprise and pleasure on their faces proved he had done a very sensible thing.

114

Dinner jacket, black tie. George could look almost handsome at times. Sally wore a pretty shot-silk dress and Hester was superb in black. A taxi took them to the station.

Mrs Sharkey saw them off and then went back to the kitchen where Sam was reading the evening paper.

'Bit quiet now, Mum,' he said. 'Anything on the wireless?'

'Saturday Night Theatre,' she told him.

'Said it was quiet, didn't I?'

'We'll have a plate of ham.'

'Anything to drink?'

'You might open a bottle of stout. I can just do with a swig.'

Kate sat in the back of the Lamberts' Rover and wondered when she would wake up. Occasionally she stole a glance at Guy beside her and once he caught her looking and gave her a broad grin. He told her he had a sports car now and could almost touch eighty.

'No!' she exclaimed.

'I'll show you on the way home. You're not afraid of speed, are you?'

'I love it!' She had no experience of fast cars but knew she wouldn't be afraid if he were driving.

As he was on leave he was staying with his parents in the house they had just bought. It was in one of the many outer London districts that were becoming known as London villages, the 'village' being a few shabby little streets clustering round a post office, corner shop and pub. There the resemblance to a village ended for the houses that were built in the twenties soon covered ground that had once been open country and had nothing of the village about them. Some were the work of speculative builders, many were architect-designed, but there was no attempt at uniformity so a four-roomed bungalow might squat between two five-bedroomed houses. Some were pebble-dashed, some plain red brick, many had diamond-shaped window panes. Yet, in spite of the mix of design, there was an air of prosperity about this up and coming district.

Ella was almost, though not quite, pleased with her house. 'Of course, dear, it's nothing like The Clearing,' she told Kate, speaking over her shoulder as they drove along. 'But after living in hotels for so long we were thankful to find The Laurels, though there's not a laurel to be seen. They're all rhododendrons.'

'Oh, I love those,' said Kate. 'Laurels are usually so dusty.'

'You're quite right, dear,' Ella agreed. 'I'm looking forward to seeing the rhodies in the spring. You must come over.'

'Thank you,' breathed Kate. Guy squeezed her hand.

'Of course, dear, furnishing is no joke,' Ella went on. 'We had to start from scratch and this utility stuff is trash. Daddy' — she often referred to Ernest as Daddy — 'is going to look about for antiques, but he has so little time. He works late most evenings, you know.'

'It must be very difficult,' Kate agreed, not knowing what else to say.

'Ah, well, here we are. Home at last.'

Ernest drove into the circular driveway and drew up at the door of a double-fronted bay-windowed house. It was already dark and impossible to get more than an indistinct impression of the place.

Ernest got out and went round to help Ella alight while Guy did the same for Kate. They all stood straightening their clothes and then went in, Ernest first to switch on the lights, then Ella, and then Kate with Guy holding her arm. The hall lights were brilliant and they blinked after the dark outside.

'Come into the lounge and make yourself at home, Kate dear,' Ella said. 'Daddy, put the percolator on. I'm sure we'd all like some coffee.'

Ernest, without a word, disappeared in the direction of the kitchen. Ella sank down on one of the sofas and Guy closed the curtains.

'You've time for coffee, haven't you?' Ella queried, easing her heels out of her shoes.

'Just about,' Guy said.

'Tell Daddy no coffee for me,' said Ella. 'Just a pinch of bi-carb in a glass of hot water.'

116

Guy nodded and went.

'Have you got indigestion?' asked Kate anxiously.

'It's always the same with me,' said Ella. 'Just a smigdeon of anything off my diet and I'm thrown out for a week. It may have been the vols-au-vents. So delicious, too. You see, dear, I must have my three meals a day at strictly regular intervals. Otherwise — constipation. Do you suffer from constipation, Kate?'

'No,' she said, rather taken aback.

'Keep to a strict regime and you never will, dear. Now Guy is as regular as clockwork. I often say I can set the clock by him. Up he gets and in he goes, just like that.'

Kate hoped Guy wouldn't come back yet.

'With me it's strain, strain, strain. My doctor tells me I'm lucky still to have my sight. You can lose your retinas through straining. Did you know that?'

'No I didn't.'

'Ah, here's the coffee.'

Ernest brought in three cups of instant coffee on a tray. 'There's no bi-carb,' he said.

'Oh, dear. And tomorrow's Sunday. I think I'd better have the tiniest tot of brandy. And a splash of soda.'

She sipped the drink Ernest gave her delicately and hicupped quietly, her hand to her mouth. 'Pardon,' she said with each successive burp. 'Oh, dear. Pardon.'

Ernest began to talk about the fête in a heavy kind of way. It had been very well organised and the man in the dog collar must be shaking hands with himself as he collected his ten per cent.

'Father Keith wouldn't take anything for himself!' exclaimed Kate. 'It's all for the church floor.'

Ernest chuckled. 'I wish I could believe you,' he said.

'I'm sure you can,' said Ella with another genteel burp. 'Oh, dear. Pardon. Mrs Sheridan was telling me about all the work he and his people have done and I'm sure none of them made a penny for themselves.'

'It was a jolly good show and it's time we were going,' said Guy. 'Ready, Kate?'

She put down her cup and stood up. 'Ready,' she said.

Ella struggled to her feet; Guy kissed her and gave her

a hug. 'I'll start the car,' he said. His father followed him out but Ella detained Kate for a moment to make sure she was quite comfortable.

'It's lovely to have you here,' she said when Kate reassured her on this point. 'I've been the one woman in a house full of men and I often long for another woman to talk to. I'm sure you can guess how hard it is at times. One gets lonely.'

Kate wondered what to say and for fear of making the wrong remark just nodded and smiled – sympathetically, she hoped.

'I knew you'd understand,' said Ella, and she stood beside Ernest on the front step and watched Guy tuck Kate into the passenger seat of his smart little M.G. and get in beside her. She fluttered a handkerchief as they drove away.

'Mother's taken a fancy to you,' Guy said. 'And now for a super evening on our own.' And he revved up the car with a tremendous noise and there was Kate, entranced, bewildered, and hoping she wouldn't wake up yet because it must still be a dream.

He took her to the little restaurant in Soho favoured by R.A.F. officers and she felt like Cinderella arriving at the ball. The proprietor really did kiss her hand and give her a red rose, just as Guy had said. He was in full evening dress, his black moustache twisted up at the ends, his hair dyed to match. He greeted Guy exuberantly, saying he had a special table reserved and escorting them to it. There was a bowl of red roses on the table, there were candles in little sconces with pink shades on the walls. To Kate it was all full of glamour; she tried to take in as much as she could without looking too hard.

Several officers were already dining and some were known to Guy and came over to be introduced. Two of them slapped him on the back and called him a lucky old devil. 'Lambert has all the luck,' one of them said, his eyes on Kate.

'Why did he say that?' she asked. 'Have you won something?'

'I hope so,' he said.

'Is it a secret? Tell me.'

He only laughed and said, 'One of these days.' He couldn't tell her that all the boys wanted a beautiful blonde for the evening and envied him because he had got one. And not just for the evening, he decided. As he took his seat opposite her he knew this was the first of many times they would be together. Everything about her fascinated him; the turn of her head, the lovely oval of her face, her puzzled look as she tried to understand the menu and then gave it up and asked him to choose for her. He loved her unspoiled naturalness, her extraordinary innocence.

She was fascinated by the wine waiter when he poured a little into Guy's glass for his approval and then filled hers, topped up Guy's and returned the bottle to the ice bucket. The wine was pale gold with a sparkle. Guy raised his long-stemmed glass, she did the same, and they clinked. 'To us,' he said.

'Is it champagne?'

'Only hock, I'm afraid.'

'It's lovely.' She took another lingering sip. There were bubbles. She put the glass down and watched them rise to the top. 'They never stop,' she said. 'I like fizz, don't you?'

A man with a camera appeared and asked if he might snap them.

'Do you mind?' Guy asked her.

'Not if you don't,' she said.

Flash.

The man moved to other tables. 'We collect them as we go out,' Guy told her.

There were three courses to the meal and she was afraid it would be over too soon. The food was excellent in spite of the difficulties rationing imposed. The proprietor had ways and means of pleasing his customers so the regulars crowded in and the place buzzed with talk and bursts of laughter as friends spotted one another and shouted greetings. It was like being at party. Someone blew up a balloon and burst it. Someone whirled a rattle.

Another officer came over. He had a limp. Guy told her of his war record and of how he had escaped from a prisoner of war camp and been more severely crippled by frost bite than by war wounds. She loved hearing him talk, felt she could listen for ever.

A young man in uniform was led in by a middle-aged man

and settled at a table near theirs. His face was disfigured by burns. He was blind. Guy went over to speak to him, and she felt tears prick her eyes. The young man was talking eagerly to Guy and the older one, clearly his father, kept hold of his son's hand and joined in the talk. Her tears were going to spill over and she couldn't find her handkerchief. Anyway, she mustn't let anyone see.

Guy was back. 'We were in the same unit for a time,' he said. Then he saw her tears. He reached across the table and took her hand. 'Dear, dear, little Kate,' he said. 'Here, have my hankie.' She wiped her eyes and smiled.

Coffee was brought and the wine waiter was there again, asking if they would like liqueurs. 'Would you?' Guy asked.

'Are they nice? I've never had one.'

'Try one. If you don't like it I'll drink it for you.'

She had never seen such ridiculously small glasses. They looked as though they had come out of a doll's house.

'Liquid sunshine,' he said, and she thought it a most accurate description. 'Take a sip.'

'Ooh. It's lovely.'

'Like it?

'Delish. I've never had anything like it.'

'You didn't have it at home then?'

'We always had claret. Daddy always gave me a very small glass and I hated it. So sour. But he said it was only civilised to take wine. I like port much better. This is wonderful. What's it called?'

'Benedictine.'

'What a nice name.'

'Dom for short.'

'Dom? Shouldn't it be Don?'

'No. It's made by the Benedictine monks and their title is Dom.'

Although the glasses were so small the liqueur lasted a long time and she savoured every sip because she did not want to finish it. She did not want to leave the restaurant with its unique, exciting atmosphere but soon there was no excuse to stay longer. The bill was presented folded on a plate and she watched Guy look at it carelessly. He smiled at her and took out his wallet. She hoped it would not cost too much and wondered why the proprietor was approaching their table, but it was merely to enquire if Wing Commander Lambert was satisfied with everything. She tried to look unconcerned but felt like a country bumpkin out with a suave man of the world for Guy was dispensing tips to the wine waiter, their table waiter, the head waiter, as though he only had to put his hand in his pocket to find a gold mine there.

The photographs were on a side table by the door. Guy found theirs and paid, one each. 'Aren't they awful?' he said. She thought they were wonderful. Another treasure to be cherished.

Out in the street he drew her arm through his and said it was much too early to go home. He knew a nice little dive where they could go and dance. Darkness hid the scars of bomb damage, a great deal of noise came from the pubs they passed; a drunk, weaving from side to side, almost collided with them. She heard dance music.

'Here we are,' he said.

Could it be a night club? If so it was extremely small. There were tables all round the walls and a minute dance floor packed solid with couples too close together to do anything but lift up their feet and put them down again. Before she knew what was happening she and Guy were on the floor too, gyrating in time to the music. 'I'm an awful dancer,' she said. 'I've never learned.'

He squeezed her hard. 'That doesn't matter,' he said, 'you can't go far wrong in this crowd.'

He held her so close, the heady atmosphere was almost more intoxicating than the hock or the Benedictine. When the music stopped they sat at a little table with a large jug of orangeade between them. All round there was talking, noise, laughter, and then the three-piece band again and a saxophone played as she had never heard it before: 'I'll See You Again'. She listened, enraptured, knowing the words, hoping they were prophetic. Guy was gazing at her, he was holding her hand. 'Our tune,' he said, but there was so much noise she could not be sure if that was what he had really said or if it was what she wanted him to say.

Time to go home but she had no idea of the hour. Then

driving through the almost deserted streets and out of town on
to the open road, and sometimes Guy was speeding to show
her what the car could do, sometimes taking it steady, and
when they were nearly there she was afraid this might be the
one and only treat of her life for he might not ask her again.
Perhaps, years ahead, she would tell her grandchildren she
had once been taken to dinner by the most famous flying
ace of all. Only there might not be any grandchildren for
she could not marry anyone but Guy.

Half a mile from the house he drew into a siding and
stopped. She held her breath. What was going to happen
now? The headlights illuminated the grassy bank. She could
see clover with its mauvy pink flowers, the beech wood
stretching away from the road and the greyish trunks of the
nearest trees. He switched the headlights off. This strange
new sensation held a tiny prickle of fear. She was afraid
she might make a wrong move, do something to offend
him. She sat very still. He put his arms round her and
gently stroked her face. Then he took her in his arms and
held her close. Her head was on his shoulder, his
face against hers. He kissed her, smoothed her hair. It
was sheer ecstasy to feel his lips on hers again and again.
There could be nothing more blissful than these protracted
kisses, his arms enfolding her, her arms about him. Time
went by unnoticed. It did not exist.

A passing car sounded its horn and broke the spell.

'I must take you home,' he said.

Was this to be the one and only time? She clutched
her hands together. 'It's been such a wonderful evening,'
she said.

'Enjoyed it?'

Her 'Oh, yes!' was fervent.

'Then you'll let me take you to dinner again, won't you?
I've got a few more days leave and I want to see you on
every single one of them.'

'I want to see you.'

'Thank my lucky stars!'

His response freed her of all her inhibitions. 'Why are
you so thankful?' she asked, laughing.

'I was afraid you mightn't like me.'

122

'I was afraid, too.'

They were both laughing, holding hands, at ease with each other. Then he saw the car clock and gasped. 'My God!' He started the engine and this time really touched eighty and soon they were crunching over the gravel up to the door of Heron House.

There was no chance of another kiss for Mrs Sharkey was waiting on the step.

'See you soon,' he said.

She watched as he turned out of the gate and heard the car streak away. Then she went in.

'A nice time to come home,' said Mrs Sharkey, arms akimbo.

The grandfather clock in the hall chimed two o'clock.

Mrs Sharkey brought the morning tea round at eight o'clock. She only did this on Sundays, not on weekdays. She yanked the curtains back in Kate's room so the sun shone full on the bed and stood looking at the girl with an impenetrable expression. Kate was just waking up.

'It's all right. I won't tell no one,' Mrs Sharkey said enigmatically.

'Tell them what, Shark darling?' Kate sat up on this wonderful morning, the first of her new and blissful life.

'The time you got home, Miss,' said Mrs Sharkey.

'I don't mind if you do,' said Kate. 'I shall tell them myself anyway. Oh, we had such a heavenly time and I'm so happy I don't know what to do with myself.'

'Better drink your tea for a start.'

'I'll take it in to Sally,' said Kate, getting out of bed and putting on her dressing gown.

'Don't let it get cold,' Mrs Sharkey said. She was worried because she feared Kate was the kind of girl men seduce. Especially handsome men in uniform who think they can get away with anything. Kate, an orphan, green as grass, wouldn't think ill of nobody, judged them all by herself, would never suspect or guess at danger. Didn't ought to have been allowed out with that young man. Hero he might be but male he was. Mrs Sharkey went muttering away to herself as she descended the stairs to the kitchen.

If she had known Guy Lambert better she would not have fretted. He had never seduced a girl in his life and would have thought it wrong to go to bed with one unless she was his wife. He had a strict moral code. Black was black and white was white and the two never merged into a comfortable shade of grey for him.

In this he was at one with his mother. Ella Lambert would not have consented to meet a divorced woman. She believed in absolute fidelity and expected unmarried people to lead celibate lives. If they did not, as she was at pains to drill into her boys, they would get syphilis and their noses would fall off and they would go blind. She dinned this into them with such force that one of them believed her. Guy. Her success with him was absolute.

Although he rather liked girls and enjoyed a harmless flirtation now and then, his real passion in life was the aeroplane. He never forgot the wonder of seeing a plane in flight for the very first time. Toy trains, cars and boats were pushed aside. He lived and dreamed aeroplanes and told everyone he was going to be a pilot when he grew up. He saved every penny he could scrape together to buy a model plane. On Saturdays he would cycle miles to the airfield nearest home to watch the planes take off and streak up into the sky. In imagination he was there too, rising, rolling from side to side, looping the loop, diving steeply, pulling out of the dive when it seemed it had gone that much too far. He never thought there was danger in it and knew instinctively that flying would come to him easily, just as swimming had.

He read every book he could find on the subject of aircraft and aero engines and gloried in accounts of the early days of flight. He begged his parents to let him take flying lessons and when they refused set his mind on finding a way of his own. Perhaps he could get a job with an aircraft company or one that built engines. An apprenticeship? That would be the most practical way, better and quicker than gaining an engineering degree and taking a job without any experience to back it up. As an apprentice he would be in actual contact with engines, he would learn how to assemble them and the thought of being given a blue print and working with it made his hands tingle to get going. But when he broached the subject at home his parents threw cold water on it. You want to be a fitter? Whatever next? That isn't the way we Lamberts go on. Get your BSc, my boy, and then you'll go in at a higher level.

He was up against a brick wall, frustrated, longing to kick out. He had no interest in politics, in the comings and goings of statesmen; tales of Jews making their escape from Germany and seeking refuge in friendly countries went over his head and it was not until Hitler marched into Austria that he began to take notice. War threatened. Events, appalling though they were, might open the gates he longed to see swing back. He could enlist and the best way to do that was to take up the place he had won at Cambridge and join the University Air Squadron.

He did not exactly want war but when there was no declaration in that uneasy August of 1938 he felt an acute sense of disappointment. Still, as a member of the U.A.S. he could learn to fly and that was what he wanted more than anything. When war came the following year he was a qualified pilot and one of the first to be called up.

He would have been surprised to know that little Kate Hope, the schoolgirl who lived at The Limes, treasured a cigarette card he had accidentally dropped. It would have surprised him still more had he known that the first entry in the scrapbook she started at the outbreak of war was his photograph. She had cut it out of the local paper and the caption said he was one of the first pilots to be called up and gave details of his parentage, education and love of flying. They gave him a half-page spread.

Kate had decided she could only devote her book to one of the forces and chose the R.A.F. because Guy was in it. She had to include cuttings about the retreat from Dunkirk, though, because Mr Sheridan had taken part in that.

She was always glad she had taken the book to Heron House when she went there to stay for those few days before her mother and father were killed. Those days had turned into years and now, on this momentous morning after the garden fête, she took it into Sally's room along with her cup of tea and planted

125

it on the bed with the photograph from the restaurant on top.

'Look. We were snapped!' she said.

'Another for the book?' Sally looked at it critically. It was the usual floodlit snap, the colours crude, features ironed out, eyes staring. 'It's not nearly good enough,' she said.

'I know, but it's just for the record. Who would have thought yesterday morning that I'd be dining out with *him*?' She spoke 'him' in an almost reverent tone.

'Tell me all about it.' Sally patted the side of her bed and Kate sat down ready for a long heart-to-heart.

'To begin with, it's changed my life,' she said. 'I know how the sleeping beauty felt when she opened her eyes on a brave new world.'

'That was Miranda. But go on.' Sally was sitting up with her knees under her chin and her arms clasped round them. 'I'm listening,' she said.

Kate did not need further encouragement to launch into an account of the preceding night but Sally kept interrupting. She expected Kate to give a detailed description of the Lamberts' new house, the size of the room they had sat in, how it was furnished, and whether she had been shown the kitchen, the bathroom, the lavatory, and had they got more than one of those? And Mrs Lambert's health. Everyone knew she was delicate or pretended to be but no one suspected the trouble was plain old constipation. Hasn't she ever heard of Epsom salts or senna pods, Sally wanted to know. And a good old raw cooking apple, eaten unpeeled, could do wonders.

'But she was ever so nice to me,' Kate protested. 'Really friendly. She has got her good points, Sal.'

'Hard to find,' Sally said. 'But what about him? Guy, I mean. Is he constipated too?'

'You are a pig. You're spoiling it.'

'Sorry. What was the restaurant like?'

'All candlelit.'

'That's so you won't see how dirty the cutlery is.'

'It wasn't. It was all super. But I felt so green. They planted an enormous menu in front of me and I just went dizzy. I was all at sea and so afraid I'd do something preposterous and shame myself, I

126

asked Guy to choose for me. He seemed to expect that.'

'So what did you eat?'

'Nectar and ambrosia.'

Sally collapsed groaning. 'Fetch a pot. I'm going to be sick.'

'You're really mean. Shan't tell you any more.'

'You know you're dying to. Was it chicken?'

'Fish first, in scrummy sauce. I think it was chicken next, but that had sauce over it, too. But I think it was chicken.'

'Could have been rat. They do them up very tasty these days and Soho abounds in rats of one kind or another, you know.'

'That's the end. Not another word.'

'Ice cream?'

'Yes, if you must know. And we ended up with liqueurs. Ooh, I can't tell you how super! It was called Dom, and you must have some first chance you get. Guy called it liquid sunshine and that's just what it was. It made you smell fields full of clover and honey and wild flowers and herbs.'

'You're off again.'

'After all that we went to a poky little place and danced. And then we came home.'

'He didn't happen to stop the car and start eating you, did he?'

'How did you know?'

'Because that's what they all do.'

'Really? We are well up in the ways of the world.'

'We need to be.'

'You're trying to spoil it for me, talking so clever.'

Sally became very serious. She had been twigging Kate because she was afraid she would get the wrong idea about Guy.

'Let's be sensible for a minute,' she said. 'The last thing I want is to spoil things for you, but you've always had a crush on Guy and it's dangerous. I'd hate it if you got hurt and it can happen so easily. He's sure to have strings of girls after him and even

127

if he takes you out to dinner you're still only one of a crowd.'

'You're a real expert at mucking things up.'

'I'm only warning you.'

'There's no need. You weren't there. You don't know what he's like.'

'That's true. I'm glad you enjoyed yourself, honestly I am, and I wouldn't have breathed a word, only you are such a simp.'

'Am I? Well, I'll tell you something, clever Dick. Guy's just as much a simp as I am. He was afraid I might not like him – after giving me that super evening. That's what he said. And I was just the same. I'd been afraid he might not like me and would never want to see me again, but he does. And if you say any more horrible things I shall think you're plain jealous. And anyway, you're rotten to muck up my wonderful evening, even if it's to be the only one of my life.'

Hot tears stung Kate's eyes. She snatched up her scrap book, pushed the snapshot inside haphazard and made for the door. Sally jumped out of bed and ran after her into her room. She put her arms round her. 'Don't be cross. I'm such a fool, opening my big mouth and talking like an ancient aunt. Don't let's be bad friends. Please.'

Kate freed herself and went over to the window. She could see the place where the rostrum had been set up and the lemonade stall where it all began. Through the trees the river sparkled; there was the cedar tree where they had walked and just past it the spot he had stopped at and asked her to dinner.

The rostrum, the stalls, all the solid paraphernalia of the garden fête had gone but the insubstantial things remained, words spoken, looks exchanged, these could never be removed. They were hers to possess, to cherish, to recall; they belonged to her absolutely and to no one else and they would sustain her. She would be a fool to let Sally's ill-informed warnings hurt her.

All this went through her mind in a flash and with such a wealth of riches to draw on she could not be ungenerous.

'We *are* friends, Sal. Of course we are.'

128

Sally gave a sigh of relief but before either of them could say more they were almost deafened by Mrs Sharkey bashing the gong in the hall and shouting up the stairs to know where everybody was, and what was the use of her frying all them mushrooms if some bomb'eads hadn't the sense to come down and eat them?

'Golly! I haven't even had a lick,' Kate said.

'Hurry up and have one and I'll go down as I am,' said Sally. 'We mustn't upset the old girl after all she did yesterday.'

The house was stirring. Hester, properly dressed, came along the corridor fastening her watch on her wrist. The bathroom door opened and George emerged with a blob of white lather on one ear. Kate, on her way in, wiped it off with a kiss. 'Darling old Uncle,' she said.

He gave her a quick hug. 'At the gallop,' he said. 'Shark's after us.'

'Do hurry, all of you.' Hester paused, kissed Kate good morning and said: 'We want to know all about your night out, darling. Don't be long.'

Kate closed the bathroom door and looked in the glass. What a contrast from yesterday! Her reflection was far from pleasing. There was a stain at the side of her lower lip. She peered close, rubbed it, went at it with soap and water. It was tender to touch. She sat on the side of the bath and looked in a hand mirror. It seemed like a bruise. But how? Was it the way he had kissed her? Pressing his lips on hers – was that it? It must have been.

Sally was shouting from downstairs. She dragged a comb through her hair, dashed cold water on her face, held a flannel of cold water to her eyes. That was better. Her cheeks were glowing, tingling with the cold. She rushed down.

'Sorry I'm late,'

'Never mind, darling. We're all behindhand today. How well you look.' Hester put her arm round Kate's waist and gave her a squeeze. 'Did you have a lovely time?' she asked.

'Super.'

'So did we. We went to see The Gondoliers at the Savoy.'

129

'Then we were all in town together. Was it good?'

'Smashing.'

Mrs Sharkey marched in with a tray bearing a huge dishful of mushrooms, all black and buttery, and a plate piled high with toast. 'Young Sam was up at five this morning gathering these here,' she said. 'Sorry there ain't no lemon. All the lemons went yesterday.'

'Never mind, Shark dear,' Hester said. 'They'll be lovely just as they are.'

Mrs Sharkey withdrew. Hester served the toast and mushrooms round. Just as they began the telephone rang and Sally, nearest the door, went out to answer it and was back at once.

'It's for you. It's him,' she said to Kate.

She ran out, her heart beating fast. His voice on the telephone was wonderful.

'Is everything all right? I'm sorry we were so late. Were there ructions?'

'No. Everything's fine.'

'When can I see you? Can I come down this afternoon?'

'I should think so. Perhaps I'd better ask. Hold on a minute.'

Life was going twice the speed of eighty miles an hour. She had to take a deep breath before she went back to the dining room. She stood outside the door. Then she opened it and put her head round. 'Will it be all right if Guy calls this afternoon?' she asked.

'I suppose so, dear.' Hester was pouring more coffee. 'Ask him to tea. And do have your breakfast or it won't be worth eating.'

Kate closed the door.

Hester exchanged a look with Sally. 'Coo!' Sally said.

George looked up from his plate and told Hester not to frown.

'I'm sorry, but I don't like this and I don't like him,' she said. 'Never did.'

'Just because he was an insolent young pup when we lived in The Clearing?'

'I don't like the Lamberts and they don't like me.'

130

'They could hardly have been more friendly yesterday.'

'That was different. It was an occasion. I don't want Kate to get ideas about Guy.'

'I think she's got them already,' said Sally gloomily.

George looked from one to the other. 'I never heard such bosh,' he said. 'Just because he takes her out and rings her up we're in the high drama league.'

'George,' said Hester, 'Kate is rather special. She has to be protected.'

'I know it. But calm down, you two. Take it easy.'

No more was said for Kate came back and the talk was all of yesterday, of The Gondoliers, the great luck of getting seats, the restaurant in Soho, the night club, the young airman with the burnt face. Kate almost wept as she told them about him. Then they were back to the Lamberts' house and the awfulness of utility furniture. But through it all Hester thought she could sense Kate's feverish excitement and it worried her.

Any girl would be pleased and flattered to have Guy Lambert notice her but to be singled out, as Kate had been, might well create hopes and send them winging high. That scrapbook she kept so religiously told its own story. It was devoted almost entirely to Guy just as though she had a fixation. It was understandable in a way as they had been near neighbours but as far as she could make out he had never condescended to speak to Kate then. He had spoken to Sally because she spoke to him, but he only told her little girls should be seen and not heard to which she retorted that big boys might be heard but they should certainly never be seen and the sooner he disappeared the better. Not a very amiable exchange.

After breakfast George rolled up his sleeves and went to help Sam measure and saw planks for *Corsair*'s decks. They worked so amicably together that very few words were needed. When it was time for coffee Sam made it and they sat side by side with their backs against the windscreen and drank it. Passing yachtsmen hailed them and they both raised an arm in salute. Many of the craft were going to boatyards to be laid up for the winter. Sam spoke their names as they passed. '*Wild Witch*, her as didn't get to Dunkirk — engine failed at Gravesend. *Troubadour* — too small. They tried to turn her back at Queensborough.'

'That's the one that made it to Ramsgate and crossed by himself,' said George.

''S'right. Brought back fifteen men.'

George nodded. He felt comfortable, at ease with himself and everyone else, and the only slight shadow was Hester's concern over Kate and this young airman which he felt was exaggerated. Hester was not usually one to worry and her dislike of the Lamberts was out of all proportion. He did not understand these intuitions of hers and felt bound to stick up for them. Ernest, the deadliest bore he had ever met, was a good provider. Ella was just another stupid, blinkered, self-deceiving woman. Guy was a brave intrepid pilot, not at all a bad young fellow, and Tom, his elder brother, was an unknown quantity.

George had rarely seen Tom as he seldom came home and was said to be in very poor health. Lungs. Asthma. Something of that sort. As a consequence he had not been called up for military service.

And this afternoon Guy was coming to tea. He caught a glimpse of Hester at that moment. She was picking up odd scraps of paper with a spiked stick and Kate was helping her. Now why, he wondered, had Hester been instrumental in getting Guy to open the garden fête? He must ask her. She had brought the Lamberts back into their orbit and thrown Kate and Guy together. Although it could have been Guy and Sally. Why not? But Sally, his Sally? No, he could not see her losing her tough little heart to Guy. Whoever screwed her head on had given it an extra turn. Thinking of her plain, perky face brought a smile to his lips. She warmed his heart.

They had midday dinner on Sundays which did not leave much appetite for tea. Sunday afternoons were inclined to be dull. Having eaten a larger meal than usual George would sit with an open book in his hand, fall off to sleep and drop it. Then he pretended he had not been asleep at all and the performance would begin all over again. The third time the book fell Hester always picked it up, slammed it shut and put it down well out of his reach. 'Now have a proper nap, George,' she would say.

After that she and the girls often went for a walk along the towpath or into the village. All three felt something ought to happen; they would have liked a concert or a play, an amateur production would do, but being Sunday there was never anything of the kind.

They noticed other people out for walks, just as they were. Couples, groups, family parties of six, eight or more, talking noisily. Then there were the singles, middle-aged to elderly as a rule, sometimes with a dog. Kate felt sorry for the single women and imagined they were childless widows. Sundays must be wretched for them; she was sure the chatter of family parties must hurt. She saw them going back to neat little flats and having a solitary cup of tea and a biscuit, listening to the wireless or hoping someone would telephone them. Perhaps they would write a letter or, in desperation, start to polish the furniture.

This particular Sunday was different. They stayed at home as Guy was expected. The time dragged by till four o'clock and still he had not arrived. Kate listened for his car. Half an hour later the door bell rang and Sally answered. Guy. Kate heard their voices and sat very still. It would not do to dash into the hall as though he had come especially to see her although she knew he had. Hester put down the paper she was reading; George straightened his tie.

How her heart fluttered when he came in. He shook hands with Hester: 'Mrs Sheridan', with George, and then turned to her. 'Hello, Kate,' he said. He seemed completely at ease and said he would have arrived earlier but he missed the train. So he hadn't driven down? Not enough petrol. He saved what he could get for essential journeys like bringing Kate home last night. He told them he was at Tangmere now, near Chichester. They should all see Chichester Cathedral sometime. Did he do much flying now? Not as much as he would like but he'd had such luck flying – Spitfires when the Battle of Britain was on and after that Typhoons.

'And which do you prefer?' George put the question sitting forward in his chair.

'Typhoons every time. No doubt of it.'

133

'I've heard they're difficult,' George said.

'First time up they are. You have to get used to them. It's a very heavy engine. I'll never forget the first time I took one up. It spat and snarled and practically swore. It has a Sabre engine, you see. Fantastic. Down the runway like the hammers and up like a rocket. I think I passed out for a split second, but after that first flight I was in love with the Typhoon for ever more.'

Anyone could see he was enthralled by aeroplanes. He went on talking and talking about them, and George listened. The others heard without understanding the technical jargon but his enthusiasm carried them with him.

At five o'clock Hester said they were going to have schoolroom tea in the diningroom. Mrs Sharkey had set out three different kinds of jam to smother the taste of the margarine; there were sticks of celery in a crystal jug, cucumber and tomato sandwiches, rock cakes, and a triumphant sponge sandwich thickly layered with lemon curd.

'We spend our lives disguising the taste of margarine,' George said.

'Don't you get butter?'

'Only a measly bit.'

'Good Lord! We get pounds in the mess.'

'We have two ounces a week and Dad eats all his in one go,' said Sally.

'I don't like bread and scrape,' said George.

'What about you, Kate?' Guy asked.

'I scrape mine and lay on golden syrup.'

George remarked on the fact that food shortages had given people an extra cause for complaint; it had ousted the weather and surgical operations.

'What will it be when we get back to normal — if we ever do?' Hester wondered.

'Scandal, my dear. Gossip. Backbiting,' he said.

'Much more fun,' Sally said.

The rest of the afternoon passed pleasantly. They sat on the verandah after tea but Kate fretted inwardly because she wanted Guy to herself if only for a few minutes. The opportunity came when he said it was time to go and George suggested seeing him to the station as a walk would do them all good. Sally did not wish to be done good to: she wanted to catch up with her reading. Consequently Kate found herself walking with Guy while George and Hester followed a short distance behind.

'We're so near and yet so far,' Guy said. 'I know what that saying means now.'

'So do I,' Kate agreed fervently.

'It's tantalising. Why don't they fall in the river and leave us alone for a minute?'

'Only a minute?'

'We'd have to dive in and save them. Still, it was nice of them to let me come. Will you write to me?'

'If you promise to write back.'

'I will. Every day. And I'll think of you all night.'

She felt the most delicious sensation running through her.

'I have to go back to camp tomorrow but I'll get a late pass and come up to town one evening. We can have dinner and then go to a dance or a film. Which would you rather?'

'A film.' She was thinking of the back row of the cinema, the thrilling darkness and his arm round her.

'I'll ring you. How would it be if you stay with my mother overnight and come back next day?'

'Sounds wonderful.'

It was all happening so fast she felt half bemused. Those quiet, sad years when she had learned to live with grief and hide it were past and gone. Here was Guy who had always seemed so far above and beyond her walking by her side, making plans for future meetings, saying how wonderful it was to have met her again, wishing they could kiss when they reached the station.

And here they were on the platform and here was his train steaming in. Handshakes all round. Then he was leaning from the carriage window waving and they were waving back until the train was out of sight.

George's good opinion of Guy was strengthened after his visit but Hester persisted in her reservations.

'I agree it seems to be coming on a bit fast but it's not to be wondered at,' George argued. 'If they're serious it would be a good match for both of them.'

135

Hester shook her head. 'She's much too young and too sheltered,' she said.

'Hark who's talking,' replied George, and he kissed her on the lips and patted her shoulder before going back to his books.

There was a letter for Kate every morning and she spent hours writing back. Guy sent flowers, chocolates, he even sent a pound of butter he had scrounged from the cookhouse. 'That's the boy!' said Mrs Sharkey when Kate handed it over. He rang up several times a week. She stayed with the Lamberts twice and went shopping with Ella. It had all been lovely, she said when she came home. Mrs Lambert had been so kind.

Hester had never been a wet blanket and she took pains to hide her unease now. Nothing would have pleased her more than to see Kate happily married but not to Guy Lambert. He was not the man for her. Although she could not fault his behaviour in any way, she was sure his arrogance and ruthlessness were only in abeyance. They would surface again and he would break Kate's heart.

Meantime there was nothing she could do. If it had been within her power to check the progress of the affair Kate would hate her for it; if Guy were to cool off, slow down and finally walk out the result would be near fatal. The only thing to be done was to wait and hope her worst fears would not be realised.

Sally shared her concern but went so far as to concede that Guy was not nearly as stuffy as he used to be.

'That's because he hasn't been under his mother's thumb for five years,' said Hester.

George was beginning to think he should say something to Guy – ask him his intentions like the proverbial Victorian father. The only thing against it was that Kate was not his daughter, not even his ward. Before he could decide what to do Guy saved him the trouble. He arrived one day and told George he loved Kate with all his heart and wanted to marry her. He spoke of his hopes and aspirations for the future. He would be demobilised within the next few months and had been offered a job by a leading aircraft firm. The prospects were good. There was a house

136

for sale on the outskirts of London where his parents were living and if Kate liked it his father would secure it for them. It was conveniently close to the firm he would be working for. Until he was free to take up his post they could live in a furnished flat in Chichester. He seemed to have it all worked out.

'And what do your parents say to this?' George asked.

'Oh, they're all for it,' said Guy.

George did not see how he could pour cold water over a young man who had served with distinction all through the war. He advised the wisdom of not being in too much of a hurry but Guy had an answer for everything. George hoped Hester would not accuse him of being too easily won over.

'It's simply that I'm not happy about it,' she said when he told her. 'People laugh at intuition and that's all I can call it. I wish I could share your optimism.'

Kate, of course, was on cloud nine. She flung her arms round his neck, called him her darling Uncle George, and declared it was absolute heaven. 'You do approve, don't you? Say you're pleased. Do say.'

'I certainly approve of your happiness,' he said, 'but there's no great rush, is there?'

'Of course there is. I want to wash his socks and iron his shirts and cook his dinner. There's no sense in waiting.'

'Well, we must think about it, my dear. I'd advise a year's engagement.'

'Uncle George! You didn't wait five minutes for Hester. She's often said so. Look, you're blushing!'

He had to admit Kate had caught him out; he had rushed into marriage and never regretted it.

'We won't regret it either,' said Kate.

Hester now saw the marriage as inevitable but she felt bound to raise one more consideration. 'Kate, darling, don't be angry at what I'm going to say. Are you absolutely sure this isn't infatuation?'

Kate declared it was not. 'It might have been when I was twelve and didn't even know him,' she said. 'Not now.'

'Or hero worship?'

'Everyone hero worships him. Who could help it? But

137

now I really know him I like him more and more every day. I do honestly love him, Hester. You must know how it feels to be passionately in love. And not only that but to like someone. You must know.'

Hester had not expected this. She understood exactly what Kate meant and such emotions stirred in her that she felt the colour run out of her face. Her throat was dry, Gianni was in her heart, her mind. He was her life and she longed desperately to see, hear, touch him. Sweat broke out on her forehead. The palms of her hands were wet.

'Are you all right?' Kate's anxious voice cut through the swathes of memory and brought her back to the interlude she was existing in now. For that's what it was. Gianni was her life.

'Will you get me a glass of water, dear? I've come over a bit faint. It's the heat.'

Kate hurried away wondering. It was not a hot day but middle-aged women had hot flushes in the coldest weather, she had heard. Poor Hester. But she wasn't middle-aged yet . . .

Mrs Sharkey shook her head. 'She's not herself these days,' she said. 'Change of life. Swimsuit one minute, fur coat the next. Give her the water and I'll make a nice strong pot of tea to follow.' Kate went away smiling. She had never yet discovered Mrs Sharkey making a nasty pot of tea.

The proposed quiet wedding developed into a large affair as so many people wanted to come. The reception inside Heron House became a huge marquee in the garden. The bride was in white — Ella Lambert had kept her own wedding dress and it was altered to fit Kate. George would give her away. Top hat and morning dress. Was it a grey or black topper? Better consult an etiquette book.

Kate was the centre of attention, and amidst all the fuss and excitement wondered what Sally was feeling.

'Would *you* like to get married, Sal?' she asked.

Sally thought for a moment and then said: 'I'm too happy at home with Mum and Dad. I doubt if I'll ever meet anyone who could tempt me to leave them. Not for ever.'

The two girls were in the drawingroom. It was one of

those quiet evenings, the sky a soft grey with not a breath of wind. Kate, looking out, felt the peace, the tranquillity, and for a moment so brief it had gone before she could capture it, she did not want to leave either. There was so much gratitude in her heart, so much love for them all, that tears came to her eyes.

'Oh, Sal, where would I have been without you – darling Hester and Uncle George and you? We won't drift apart when I'm married, will we?'

'Not if I know it!' Sally said.

The wedding was every girl's dream come true. A Battle of Britain hero marrying the girl next-door. Only eighteen years old and her parents killed by enemy action. How sad, how lucky, how romantic! No one mentioned that besides being untrammelled with relations the bride was rather well off in her own right so Wing Commander Lambert was doing pretty well for himself too.

Each day was better than the last. Kate enjoyed every moment with Guy. They were living in a small flat in Chichester while he waited for his demob papers to come through, and life was pleasant there. When he was on duty she explored the town, spent dreamy hours in the Cathedral, and wrote ecstatic letters to Sally. How she poured out her heart!

When Guy was free they drove about the countryside, ate bread, cheese and pickled onions at wayside pubs, and washed it down with cider. They often spent evenings in the mess drinking gin and lime; the talk there was easy and she got on well with the officers and their wives, and was thrilled by tales of wartime exploits. They were all young, they were survivors, the future was theirs and they were full of plans so there was no end to the talk.

She was sorry to leave the good comradeship that prevailed at the camp when Guy returned to civvy street, but on·the other hand there was so much in store for them. They were lucky to be moving into a house of their own and everyone assured Kate she would soon make new friends.

There was the excitement of Guy's job, his first as a civilian. He did not know if he would like it but often told her, like it or not, he meant to succeed and if dogged perseverance had anything to do with it he would soon make his mark. She resolved to do everything in her power to help him.

The house they had decided to buy was in a long straight road with cherry trees on either side. It was called The Avenue and was the most prestigious road in the district and only half an hour's walk from Spencer Road where Ella and Ernest lived.

Ella was delighted to have them so close but when Sally heard of their choice she turned both thumbs down.

'What a daft idea. The further away from them the better,' she said.

'They won't interfere,' said Kate.

'*He* won't but look out for *her*,' Sally warned.

'She's being absolutely sweet,' declared Kate.

'Worse and worse. I can't abide sweet people.'

'You're being piggy. She's asked me to call her Ella as she couldn't expect me to call her Mother. She says she thinks of me as the daughter she always wanted. I believe she means it.'

Sally gave Kate a long look. 'Don't make me cat,' she said. 'Honestly, Kate, I'd never have expected you to swallow all that guff.'

'It isn't guff.'

'Sickly sentiment then.'

'I don't see anything wrong with sentiment. She *would* have liked a daughter.'

Sally was spending the day looking over Kate's house with her. It was only partly furnished and she found herself thinking of the Hopes' house in The Clearing. She remembered the unique objects, the clocks, the Meissen figures, all lost and gone forever just as they themselves were gone. And here was Kate in this ordinary house married to a man she, Sally, thought most unsuitable for her. Her anxiety for Kate made her wish she had not decried Ella. She had no right to criticise and perhaps set Kate against the Lamberts.

'Oh, dear, darling Kate, don't take any notice of me. I really am a pig and I'm glad you get on so well with Mrs Lambert. It's nice to like your mother-in-law.'

'I hope you'll like yours when you get one,' said Kate, thinking how lucky she was compared with Sally who was stuck with books and exams while she had Guy and instead of certificates would have children.

Sally had no desire to live in suburbia but thought she would enjoy observing the residents just as she always enjoyed people watching, as she called it.

'What are the neighbours like?' she asked.

Kate told her there had scarcely been time to get to know any of them but on the whole she fancied they were rather stuffy. 'Except for the Fortunes opposite. I think he's a bit shy but she isn't. Look, there she is, just going in her gate.'

'There's not much of her,' said Sally.

'Her voice makes up for it. She's from Lancashire.'

Ada and Jack Fortune were middle-aged. Jack taught maths at a minor public school a bus ride away. Ada kept house and did jigsaw puzzles. They had been the first residents in The Avenue and had moved in when the houses were being built. That was in the twenties when the cherry trees were not much bigger than standard roses.

The houses had won their architect an award. As time went on they lost their Ideal Homes image and by the time Kate arrived looked what they were: well-maintained houses transformed into homes by their owners. The flowering cherries had matured and their branches arched across the road and almost met in the middle. In spring the extravagant display of frothing pink attracted crowds at weekends. Midweek, when the trees were at their best, august personnages drove along the road at a snail's pace in their Daimlers, graciously waving to nannies and their charges.

The flowering season was short: high winds and blustery showers soon demolished the blossoms which covered the pavements and front gardens in a sodden brown carpet. The non-appearance of road sweepers often drove the residents to do the clearing up themselves and although this did not please them it offered the excuse to ask one another what they paid rates for, but on the whole the road could not be called a friendly one. There was no popping in and out of one another's houses in The Avenue; the neighbourly atmosphere of older terraces had never existed there and the few who had lived in less buttoned-up places sometimes felt out of their element.

Among these were the Fortunes, or rather Ada, for Jack, with his work, his garden and his model trains, had very little time for neighbours, especially if they were the kind who fancied themselves.

Ada was not so fortunate. She missed the friendly atmosphere of her northern home and when new people moved into The Avenue she invariably called on them with a small gift, a packet of biscuits or a quarter of tea, as a welcome. It was sometime before she realised these overtures of friendship were not appreciated although, as she told Jack, she would have been glad of tea and biscuits when they moved in themselves as she had forgotten to bring any with her. To avoid the blank looks that greeted her gifts she substituted flowers, just small bunches, and it was just such a bunch she took over to the Lamberts when they arrived.

She was particularly interested in them as she had read all about their wedding and was thrilled when the milkman told her they had bought the house opposite. She relied on the milkman for news and always gave him a cup of coffee when she paid her weekly bill. She would ask him into the kitchen and they sat at the table and had a really good, old-fashioned chat. Sometimes, when her current jigsaw puzzle threatened to defeat her, she took him into the diningroom to see if he could help. Jigsaws took up a lot of time and one day Mrs Hooper, who lived next-door but one, came and rang the front door bell.

'I'm waiting to pay my milk bill,' she announced when Ada opened the door. 'What has become of the milkman? His float has been outside your house for three-quarters of an hour by my watch.' She tapped her watch with a stout forefinger as she spoke. Ada peered at it.

'Eeh,' she said, 'how time flies.'

'Kindly tell the milkman I am waiting,' said Mrs Hooper, 'and if you want to entertain him every Friday, pray do so after I have paid my bill.'

Mrs Hooper was a short, fat woman and wore a square

double-breasted coat and square shoes. She had a mauve complexion liberally plastered with very pale powder. Ada took all this in and decided that the belligerent manner and unbecoming appearance combined to make Mrs Hooper a person she did not want to know. She folded her arms. 'Lad's entitled to his tea break,' she said.

'Then let him take it sitting in his cab so customers can pay him there,' said Mrs Hooper. 'Tell him so from me.'

Ada counted the buttons on Mrs Hooper's coat. 'Tell him yourself,' she said, shutting the door so smartly that Mrs Hooper was lucky not to get her nose boxed.

This exchange did nothing for Ada's popularity in The Avenue but by then she had decided she wanted no more of her neighbours than they did of her. All the same she could not prevent hope rising when the Lamberts came. She was not disappointed. Guy was not at home when she called. Kate opened the door and smiled when she saw Ada clutching some flowers and looking apprehensive.

'Oh, you're from opposite, aren't you? Are these for me? Lovely! Do come in. I'm afraid we're in a frightful muddle.'

'Eeh – don't let that fash you. It's nothing to the state we were in the day we came. The road wasn't made up then and it was pouring. The mud! It came over our shoes. We had to buy Wellies. But don't let me rattle on. I'm a proper rattle.'

Kate was feeling rather lost at that moment and not at all sure she liked the furniture they had bought. When she compared it with the things at Heron House which were old and beautiful she was almost disconsolate and wondered how she could ever make the house look like home.

She took Ada into what was to be the drawingroom and they sat at either end of a large chintz-covered sofa. Kate was not at all sure she liked the chintz. She had become accustomed to the ash rose velvet of Hester's settee but that was an antique and although the velvet was rather worn there was an air of grandeur about it. Now she found herself talking about this kind of problem to Ada and feeling reassured by the sympathetic response. She realised, almost for the first time, that she was a married woman in her own home,

143

having a rewarding talk with another married woman who was giving her encouragement.

Ada Fortune had considerable experience in everything connected with running a house and she was extraordinarily good at assessing people. She saw at once how vulnerable Kate was and how unsure of herself and she hoped she could help in an unobtrusive way.

Kate, for her part, felt sure she was going to like this plain-spoken, homely little woman with her sharp features and Lancashire accent. Soft brown eyes and a ready smile mitigated the sharpness of Ada's face and Kate soon got used to the 'Eehs' with which her conversation was peppered.

'You must come over and see our garden,' Ada said. 'Jack's been working on it for years now. He'll be able to spare you plenty of herbaceous plants when he splits them up in the autumn.' She glanced out of the window. 'The Ellises let it go,' she remarked.

'I shall have to tackle the curtains before I do anything else.'

The Ellises had left their ancient buff-coloured curtains up at the windows. They served as a screen but Kate had decided they must be replaced with the least possible delay. Ada possessed a sewing machine. 'I love doing seams. You must let me do the seams!' she exclaimed, full of enthusiasm. She was still in full spate when Guy walked in and took them both by surprise. Kate jumped up.

'Come and meet Mrs Fortune,' she said.

Ada was on her feet. 'Eeh, what a lovely surprise!' she said.

Guy bowed stiffly. 'How do you do?' he said.

'Nicely, thank you,' replied Ada who had never got used to this form of greeting which she thought very strange and meaningless. 'And you, Wing Commander Lambert, how are you?' she asked.

'I'm out of the R.A.F. so the title doesn't apply now,' he said.

Kate noticed his cool tone and supposed he did not realise that Ada was a near neighbour so hurried to explain and went on to tell him of the kind offer of plants.

Ada watched Guy's face as Kate spoke. He was very

144

good-looking, she decided. He had fine features and a well-shaped head. His eyes were a most unusual colour. Rather like chips of stone. And cold. She did not like his eyes.

'I must be going,' she said. 'Your husband will be wanting his tea, my dear.' To Guy she said: 'We're just opposite. We've been here over twenty years so we're the oldest inhabitants ...' She went on talking and wished she could stop. He was edging her out.

'Goodbye for now, love,' she said to Kate. Going down the path she was sorry she had called her 'love' but she had dropped back into the parlance of her old home which was not acceptable here. Young Mr Lambert would not approve, she felt sure. He had flustered her, made her feel insignificant.

'What are they like?' Jack asked when she went in to her own house.

'She's a dear, but I don't take to him,' Ada replied. 'Stuck up, that's what he is.'

The moment the door closed on Ada, Guy swept Kate up in his arms, hugged her, kissed her, held her tight.

'Who was that old bag?' he asked.

'I told you. Mrs Fortune from over the road.'

'Eeh, bah goom,' he said. 'I was afraid she's start singing "The Biggest Aspidistra in the World"'

They collapsed on the sofa, she so happy he was home, he glad to be there. It was bliss, sheer bliss. The chintz covers were quite tasteful after all, the colours softened, everything was wonderful when he was there. He gave her a safe feeling, the sense that nothing could go wrong.

'What about your day? Did you feel strange?' she asked.

'It was a bit like the first day at school — you don't think you'll ever match names to faces. Very funny faces, some of them. I was just shown round, given the lowdown on the place, introduced to people — you know how it is.'

'I don't really. I've never had a job.'

'You've got one now. Looking after me.'

'Good. I shall start you off with a White Lady.'

'Are you telling me you know how to mix one?'

'Uncle George taught me. He's an ace. I've got it all measured out and I'm longing to try the cocktail shaker Tom gave us.'

Tom had not only given them the shaker, his present consisted of a fine silver tray, an ice bucket, a set of crystal glasses and all the other paraphernalia necessary for mixing and serving drinks.

'Good old Tom,' said Guy. He watched her crack up the ice by wrapping the small blocks in a tea towel and attacking them with a rolling pin.

It was not easy. She went up on tiptoe and pressed down with all her might and he wanted to take over but knew that would disappoint her. She did well. At last the ice was crushed; she shook the mixture like a bar tender born and the glasses frosted over when she poured it.

'Success!' he shouted.

Was it the best drink they had ever had together? What about the hock that night in Soho? Or was it the champagne at their wedding when they turned to each other? And what about the first gin and lime in the mess with all his friends clustering round? Was it then?

'It's now!' they said in unison.

Next day she had a letter from Mr Proctor, her father's partner at Orlando Hope's. He said there were genuine pieces of period furniture to be found out of town and suggested the wisdom of searching for some in their spare time. There was no need to go very far, he said. Antiques shops were opening up in all the country towns and she would be sure to find things she really liked. He mentioned the best places to try so they went on a treasure hunt the following Sunday and it was not long before Kate discovered a pair of oval-backed Adam chairs. They were of satin wood with embroidered upholstery, just the kind of chairs her father would have chosen, and she had no hesitation in buying them. When they were delivered and installed in the drawingroom the whole tone of the room changed. It was as good as a burst of sunlight.

She immediately warmed to the whole house and saw

how easily she could chase out the rather sterile atmosphere created by the Ellises' dingy brown oilcloth.

'The Ellises' were brown all through,' Ada Fortune told her. 'They were like a couple of dried-up cigars. You'll find wood blocks under that oilcloth and the hall is tiled. Done by Italian craftsmen. Wicked to cover it up.'

Kate found all this was true and set about restoring the good features of the house. She saw it furnished to her own taste with period pieces like the Adam chairs, and if she learned upholstery she could cover the sofa in more suitable material than the chintz. Ada went with her to buy curtain material and they spent the best part of a day in an exclusive shop and came home delighted with the fabrics they had discovered.

Ella was rather put out when she saw the purchases later in the week. 'You should have asked *me* to go with you, dear,' she said.

'Ada offered and I didn't think anything of it,' Kate said.

'Well, dear, I'll always come. I enjoy a little jaunt.'

'It was a very tiring day,' said Kate. 'You would have been exhausted.'

'I daresay, but it would have been worth it to help you.'

Kate felt irritated and hoped her mother-in-law would not expect to be consulted about everything.

'Who is this Ada person?' Ella asked. 'I get the impression she's a rather common sort of woman.'

If she is it's a pity there aren't more like her, Kate thought, and with the excuse that the kettle was boiling, she went into the kitchen and kicked the leg of the table. Ella hadn't even met Ada so how could she get any kind of impression unless Guy had given it to her? She remembered Sally's warning and thought about it while she set the tea tray, then she went back to the drawingroom to set Ella to rights.

'You've got the wrong impression of Mrs Fortune,' she said. 'She has a strong Lancashire accent but that doesn't make her common.'

'Really, dear?'

147

'Not at all. She is really kind. The sort of person you can trust.'

Ella stirred her tea. 'I'm so glad, dear. But, you know, one does have to be careful not to rush into friendships and then regret them.'

'Yes, that can be very awkward, but I always remember the way Mummy ran over to the Sheridans when they arrived and asked them in to tea. You might have thought that was a risk.'

'It could well have been,' said Ella.

'As it happens they turned out to be the best friends we ever had. I feel just the same about the Fortunes.'

Ella cleared her throat, nibbled a biscuit and asked if they were going to lay turf or sow grass seed. Kate felt she had held her own that time and said they had not decided. 'Another cup of tea?' she asked.

'Please, dear. And have you an aspirin? I feel my headache coming on.'

Kate had already noticed that Ella had persuaded herself she was delicate. She magnified the slightest ache into a cause for anxiety and expected everyone to coddle her as much as she coddled herself. It amused Kate to see her reclining on her large sofa surrounded by cushions, a bottle of pain killers and a glass of water to hand, and also a box of chocolates. She was given to puffing and blowing in a very genteel manner if one did not enquire frequently after her health and yet she always found the energy to do anything she liked. Let anyone suggest an outing, a film or a play, and she was up and ready to go, as sprightly as a sparrow.

On Sunday they were invited to tea with her. Kate wanted to go on a treasure hunt again but when she told Guy he said his mother would be disappointed not to see them. 'Though we could take her with us,' he said. 'She doesn't get about much.'

'What about your father?'

'He always plays golf.'

'Doesn't she go the clubhouse with him?'

'It's not her scene,' he said.

Kate had been longing to spend the whole day with him

but she fell in with his wish. She had such an overflowing measure of happiness she decided it would be mean not to indulge Ella a little.

At first the day went well. Ella sat in the back of the car saying she was so comfortable she didn't think she would get out. This pleased Kate; it meant they could wander round at their own pace. But the first place they stopped at Ella got out and went marching in to shops, examining chairs and tables and chests and calling out to them to come and look at this or that. It was all most distracting. 'Kate, you must come and see these plates,' she called from the other side of the road. 'They're the very thing for your sideboard.'

Kate did not want plates on her sideboard. She was not looking for ornaments. She wanted a pier table for the hall. Sometimes Guy deserted her and accompanied his mother. Kate lingered in front of a shop with an unpromisingly dirty window. It was packed out with old wardrobes, shoddy-looking chests, fenders, fireguards, dusty rugs. Nothing of much worth. But wait. Two men inside were moving things about and she guessed they had just cleared a house. They began carrying things outside: two quite good Windsor chairs, a desk, and then, as though it had been waiting for her, a pier table such as she had not seen since the one in Orlando Hope's. It was almost as though Ollie himself had put it there for her. 'How much?' she asked one of the men. He told her. She felt a surge of real triumph. Marquetry and satinwood.

Ella and Guy were straggling along on the other side of the road and she called over to them. They crossed. 'There's nothing worth having over there,' Ella said, 'or here by the look of things.' Then she saw the table. 'Oh!' she exclaimed. 'Oh, that's mine.'

'Oh, no. I was just going to buy it,' said Kate.

Guy had wandered off to the shop next-door. One of the men came out with another chair and Ella accosted him. 'I'm having that table,' she said. 'Will you take a cheque?'

'Certainly, Madam. Come inside.'

Kate was dumb. Guy was quite a long way down the street by now. She was so angry she could have choked.

Ella came out of the shop and said pleasantly: 'All settled. Such a bargain, too.'

'Ella, *I* was going to buy that table. It's just like the one in Daddy's shop and I wanted it for our hall.'

'Well, dear, you weren't sharp enough, were you? Never mind. I expect there'll be plenty more.'

'That's most unlikely,' said Kate. 'I called you over to look at it because I was going to buy it.' She was so full of resentment she did not know how she would get through the rest of the day and when Guy rejoined them she told him she wanted to go home.

'Don't you want to look at anything else?' he asked.

'I've had enough.'

They got back in the car and Ella began telling him about her wonderful bargain. Kate sat with her hands clenched feeling ill with disappointment and rage. She had been betrayed. this beastly woman with her endearments! Oh, for Hester, for Sally, for Mrs Sharkey! Anyone but this horrible scheming creature.

Guy never liked talking much when he was driving so he scarcely noticed what Ella was rambling on about and appreciated Kate's silence. It was not until much later that evening, after they had survived Sunday tea at Ella's, that he began to wake up to Kate's mood.

'Anything wrong?' he asked.

'The table. Your mother snapped it up under my nose when I was on the point of buying it.'

'Why on earth didn't you say?'

'I did. I'll never see another like it, and I wanted it.'

'I wish you'd put your foot down a bit harder.'

'You were at the other end of the street and it all happened so quickly.'

'Poor old Kate,' he said, and put his arm round her. 'We'll have to make sure we get there first next time.'

What was the use of reminding him the whole object of the excursion was to find things for their house, not for Ella's? They could have furnished it from top to bottom with modern furniture of the kind to be seen in every high street store but that was not Kate's style. Her idea from the first had been to wait until some irrestible piece caught her eye as it had done today. She had to do some very serious thinking and once she regained her calm made up her mind never to go on such another outing. Next time she would go with the Fortunes. They had an Austin 7 and had already told her they enjoyed taking little trips and would be pleased for her to go with them any time.

Having settled that in her own mind she told herself she was a fool to get upset over things: only people mattered and she had Guy and so much else besides. It was not his fault he had such an unspeakable mother. She flung herself into his arms and made such a fuss of him he said, 'Here! What's all this?' and carried her upstairs to bed.

One afternoon a few days later she opened the door to a thunderous knock and saw two men on the step with the table.

'Mrs Lambert?'

'Yes.'

She looked at the docket he thrust under her nose. It was addressed to Mrs Guy Lambert, 24 The Avenue.

'Where would you like it, love?'

'In the hall. Over there. That's fine.'

When they had gone she stood looking at it and felt very strange. She had distinctly heard Ella tell them to send it to The Laurels, Spencer Road, but there was no doubt it belonged where it was. 'I'm keeping you,' she said aloud, and she touched it lovingly, her fingers making marks in the dusty surface. She found a soft cloth and began to dust it. She was intent on this when Guy came home.

'Oh, good. It's come,' he said.

'Your mother told them to send it to The Laurels,' she said.

'I persuaded her to change her mind.'

'Guy! But how on earth?'

'We had a little chat. That's all. Mother quite understood when I put it to her.'

Kate was overwhelmed with gratitude and only too ready to reinstate Ella in her good books. To think Guy had done this for her, had realised how much it meant to her!

Guy supposed the table was all right in its way but he could not see why either of them should be so worked up

151

about it. His mother had been most reluctant to give up her right to it and came to the point of quarrelling with him.

'How can you be so hard on your poor old mother?' she had said. 'Kate has years before her and I have so few. I'll leave it to her in my will.'

'Mother, you are giving it to her now. Here's my cheque to repay you. I mean it.'

In the end she gave in with a marked ill grace and only because she was afraid of falling out with her favourite son. The episode made her so ill she had to go to her special hotel at Bournemouth to recuperate as she feared her blood pressure had risen far beyond its safety limit.

Hester came to spend the day with Kate and heard all about the table. 'I can't tell anyone else, not even Sally,' Kate said. 'She'd never stop laughing. She warned me against Ella, you know.'

'You'll have to be very firm with your mother-in-law,' Hester said. 'She's an old fraud.'

'Perhaps I was silly to get so upset but Guy was absolutely super. Don't you agree? He didn't tell me he was going to put his oar in, and to think he persuaded her to hand it over. And he paid her for it, too. So it's really a present from him. Don't you think that's wonderful?'

'Yes, darling, I do. Things are turning out very well for you.'

'So I was right to marry him, wasn't I? You were afraid I was making a mistake.'

'I'm only too glad you're proving me wrong. I don't think I've ever seen you looking so well, Kate. You're positively blooming.'

'Am I? Well, I'll let you in to a secret. I'm pretty sure I'm preg.'

'So that's it! Oh, I'm so glad. When?'

Kate was laughing. 'It's only six weeks. Much too early to start looking important,' she said.

'What does Guy say? Isn't he delighted?'

'Knocked off his feet! You should have seen his face when I told him.' She had only told him the night before and his first reaction was incredulity. After that the expressions that passed over his face as her news sank in made her sorry she couldn't catch them on film.

'I wish you could see yourself!' she exclaimed. 'You're going to be a daddy. Say you're pleased.'

There was the slightest hesitation before he answered. Then he said: 'Of course I am. A bit staggered. It isn't a thing to be taken lightly, is it?'

'It's stupendous. We'll still be young when the children are grown up. Think of that,' she said.

'Children?'

'We're going to have four.'

He was overwhelmed with love and pity and apprehension and annoyance all at once. He kissed her, praised her, and managed to keep the dismay out of his voice. He did not want children so early in their marriage. He wanted Kate to himself; a child would be an intruder and would put a brake on their activities. Besides that he had his way to make and this was not the time to start a family. Well, there was nothing to be done now but make the best of it. He had only himself to blame for this slip-up but he would make sure it didn't happen again.

Kate did not suffer from the inconveniences that so often attend pregnancies. She had never felt so well or enjoyed life so much. After the horror stories his mother had told him Guy would not have been surprised if she had kept her feet up for nine months and survived on a diet of oysters and champagne.

Hester and Mrs Sharkey were both busy making tiny garments and Kate had the joy of opening their parcels and exclaiming at the contents. Ella, restored and amiable, was excited at the prospect of becoming a grandmother and took it upon herself to sew little frocks. She did it very well and was pleased to accompany Kate on shopping expeditions for nursery furnishings. The rumpus over the table had sunk into the background and was all but forgotten.

Ada Fortune was quietly making things, too. Her knitting far surpassed anybody else's and she liked doing it. Kate often went over and sat with her in the garden, especially on Tuesdays when Jack took himself off for the day. Ada never asked where he

153

went or what he did. 'It's his day, you see, love. He needs the change.'

Jack looked out of the garden door as she spoke.

'Just off, girl,' he said.

'Done your flies up?'

He had.

'Got your teeth in?'

He gnashed them at her.

'My, but I have to keep my eye on him,' Ada told Kate. 'The times I've had to run after him with his teeth, you wouldn't believe. He doesn't seem to notice. Same with his flies. You'll get arrested, I tell him. Not with you looking after me, he says.'

Kate wondered if she would have the same problems with Guy as the years rolled on but she couldn't imagine it and Ada was certain she would not. They both chuckled over the strange ways of husbands — 'You'll soon learn husbands are not at all the same creatures as men,' Ada informed her — but she had the feeling that Kate's marriage would not develop into the warm companionship she enjoyed with Jack. She saw very little of Guy. He was standoffish when they met and she knew Kate worked extra hard to compensate. They were in love, no doubt of that, but she had the feeling Kate was watching her step. 'You never know when he'll turn and snarl at you,' she told Jack.

Kate had already discovered Guy must have his own way in everything and it was not worth opposing him. She admired and loved him beyond words so life ran smoothly, and rather to his surprise he liked being a civilian and working in the world of commerce. Boosted by his war record, and with his quick grasp of affairs and handsome looks, he could not fail to make his mark.

He often told Kate his job was a piece of cake with jam on it.

'You deserve it.'

'Think so? Well, perhaps I do.'

She looked forward to their evenings. They were the best part of the day and as seven o'clock approached she would feel the same exciting exhilaration she had known in those enchanted days when they first fell in love. She would open the garage doors ready for him to drive in and be in the hall dashing to get the door open before he could get his key in the lock. And then that wonderful, joyful embrace — the marvel of having him home, of being together in their own house. They both exulted in their good fortune.

He liked to tell her about his day and she wanted to hear. He was on the sales side and that meant meeting prospective customers. Later on he would have to travel a good deal both at home and abroad with the Sales Manager. She did not relish the idea of being separated but never let him know it. He was absorbed in his work, throwing all his energy into it, and she was ready to give him the support he needed. She knew he was marked out for success and was not surprised when he told her the Managing Director had singled him out for a talk after a meeting. This, he told her, was a signal honour and had caused a good deal of interest and speculation when the news got round.

'You'll get a promotion before you're much older,' she said.

'Shouldn't be surprised.' His tone was casual but he talked of nothing else the whole evening.

There was not much for her to tell him about her own days. He had made it clear he wanted no truck with the Fortunes so she didn't mention them or tell him what a fantastic garden they had or about Jack's model train set. There was nothing new from Heron House either. But although he was indifferent to these things he was not indifferent to Kate herself. He was delighted with her, proud of her, happy to be with her, and he showed it in many ways, surprising her with his consideration and thoughtfulness. She had only to admire something in a shop window and it was hers or express interest in a film or a play for seats to be booked.

Their daughter Fiona was born into this congenial atmosphere and proceeded to disrupt it by crying incessantly every night. Nobody knew why and no one could find a cure. Some babies cried and others slept like angels the whole night through, apparently. Kate spent long weary hours walking up and down with her. She did not expect Guy to take a turn, neither did he offer. It went without saying that in order to do his job efficiently he must have his full night's sleep. Kate made sure he got it.

Hester was wondering what to do with the rest of her life. She could look back on a past with some purpose in it. From the time she married George and had Sally there had been things to do; having a family to care for was good, running the home was fine, looking after the evacuees was worthwhile, and she had helped Kate through the trauma of losing her parents. Now she was no longer needed. With Sally in her element at Oxford, Kate married with a child and George absorbed in his work and only home at weekends, what was there for her?

Gianni had told her to learn Italian but what was the use now she would never see him again? Just because it was something worth doing, of course. She bought 'teach yourself' books but they brought him back vividly and yet made him seem further away. She could hardly bear to hear others speak of him as the Wards so often did because she could not respond for fear of giving herself away.

Those Wednesday afternoons when she went to mind the children had been oases in her life. While they were having their afternoon rest and Alfred and Lorna were out, she and Gianni had the house to themselves. It was bliss seasoned with the spice of danger. Those protracted kisses, the strength of his arms, the feel of his smooth skin, were potent even in retrospect. And then the evenings when she stole into the Wards' garden to find him waiting for her. The darkness, black sky thick with stars — never a moon. Never on moonlit nights.

She had never imagined she would find herself in such a situation — blameless husband, passionate lover, and no question of choosing between them. Her fate, and she might as well accept it, was to be a sensible, affectionate wife to George; to read good books, listen to the third programme, take health-giving walks and be grateful for her many blessings. These good resolutions were tried to the utmost when George told her he had been invited to go to America to take up a University Fellowship.

'It's a splendid offer,' he said. 'I've always wanted a

chance like this and you'll love it. It will be a complete change, my dear.'

'How long is it for?' she asked.

'Two years, perhaps longer. It all depends. We go in the autumn though I suppose we'll have to learn to call it the fall.'

'Yes,' she said, and sat very still, feeling as though her whole inside was rolling over. George didn't notice. He went on talking about this unexpected happening in their lives which had come at such an opportune time with their two girls doing so well and nothing to worry about that he could think of. He saw it as his last opportunity. For her it was the final curtain.

Another continent, the new world. Gianni — the ocean between them. It was bad enough as it was but this put paid to any hope of meeting him again. I can't go on, she thought, but of course she did. She had no option.

She told Lorna Ward about it the next time she went to the farm.

'How exciting,' Lorna said. 'Aren't you thrilled?'

'More stunned. I shall be a fish out of water there.'

'Of course you won't. Anyway it's something for me to tell Gianni next time I write.'

The awful heart thumping started as it always did when he was mentioned. She tried to sound casual. 'You hear from him then?' she asked.

'Quite often. He always asks after you.'

'Really? You never told me.'

'You never seemed interested.'

'Well, he was only a ship in the night.' She hated herself for saying that.

'I don't agree,' Lorna said. 'We got very fond of him. And he had a terrific crush on you.'

'Oh, tripe,' said Hester, furious because her face flamed.

Lorna laughed. 'Oh, come on, Hester! We all like a bit of admiration, especially from a smasher like Gianni. I often thought what a wonderful couple you'd make.'

'You'll be late for the pictures,' Hester said.

She didn't find it easy to amuse the twins that afternoon

and when they were asleep gave way to depression. She had plenty of acquaintances; no one to whom she could speak of her innermost feelings as she would have done with Mary Hope. Sometimes she went to St Michael's when there was no service just for the atmosphere of peace that pervaded it, but it didn't enter into her. She came away even more distressed than when she went in.

The spring was passing, soon it would be summer and she would think of Santa Carlotta, try and fail to find it on the map. She recalled the magical names and enchanted places Gianni loved to talk of and longed to see them with him. He liked dancing, music, fun, parties. He liked girls but he loved her. When they were together their companionship was so warm and affectionate. They teased each other, laughed, were happy. Now, as she walked by the river, all she felt was emptiness.

It was a mild afternoon, the sky a soft, feathery grey with the hint of blue here and there. She went further than she intended and when she turned homeward rain began to fall, soft and fine, like a mist. It made the river, the trees, the occasional rowing eight seem unreal, as though a transparent curtain had come down and put them slightly out of focus. The voice of the cox came echoing as though from far away. She saw the outline of *Corsair* now and the wet decks shimmered in the light. Raindrops sparkled and fell from the leaves.

She was alone on the footpath but ahead people were coming from the town, straggling for the most part except for a man in a white suit who walked briskly and would soon outstrip them.

Now he was ahead of them all, moving faster, breaking into a run. She stopped, drew aside, her heart racing for there was something of Gianni about him and she must wait, calm down, keep still until he passed.

She scarcely dared look up when he spoke for fear he would vanish but the only things to vanish were her doubts, fears, uncertainties. At last she and Gianni were together.

Ernest Lambert occasionally felt it behoved him to invite the Sheridans to dinner. Entertaining at home was not a good idea as it put too much of a strain on Ella so he always took them to a restaurant.

On one of these occasions and one only he decided to dine out of town. He had heard that Monkey Island, on the river, was a good place to go, and as he had just taken delivery of a new Rover and wanted to run it in he got in touch with George and arranged to drive him down to Heron House with Ella and pick up Hester. They would go for a run first to see something of the countryside, so what about an early start?

'We won't tell the girlies,' he told George when he picked him up in the afternoon. 'They'll enjoy it all the more coming out of the blue.' Ernest always referred to the women in his circle as girlies. 'Another little drink for the girlies?' he would rumble in his deep voice. It was the kind of voice that came from such a depth it was hard to realise what he was saying until after he had said it.

George felt himself cringing away as Ernest spoke and grew tired of having to ask him to repeat everything. He amused himself by trying to devise different ways of asking.

'I suppose your old woman will be at home?' enquired Ernest.

'What? Oh, yes. Hester's always at home. Ought to get out more.'

'Same with mine. Grouses about it, too.'

'Eh? Oh, grouses, does she? Hard luck. Mine doesn't.'

'Ah, well, you've got a peach there. Still, I must say little Fiona's made a big difference to Ella's life. Thinks the world of her. Can manage her, too, and that's more than poor Kate can.'

They had arrived at The Laurels where Ella, not expecting her husband till evening, was peering through the window to see who had driven up. Half an hour later they were on the road to Henley. The misty rain had cleared and the sun was shining.

It was a smooth run, the car performed well so Ernest was happy driving at the prescribed speed. They arrived at Heron House in the middle of the afternoon and George recollected it was Mrs Sharkey's half day and she always went to the cinema accompanied by Sam.

'Hester will be on *Corsair*. She likes to sit on deck when it's fine,' George said, so they strolled down to the river. But she was not on deck or in the saloon.

'She'll have gone for a walk along the towpath. We might as well sit here and wait,' he said.

He put the chairs out and made some tea and they sat drinking it and watching people strolling by the river and one or two anglers on the banks just ahead of them. Ella said it was just too wonderful, the water had such a calming effect, it was as good as a rest cure.

After an hour Ernest began to get fidgetty. The people they had seen walking upstream had all come back and at this rate they would not be able to fit in the tour he had planned. George, too, thought it high time Hester was home and suggested returning to the house. He had no guarantee she had gone along the towpath, she might just as well have gone to the village in which case they would not have seen her come back. Ella insisted on washing up the tea cups and Ernest regretted not having told Hester they were coming. How did her silly old fool of a husband know if she was in or out? No woman in her senses stuck in all the time. It seemed George took a good deal for granted.

They trailed back over the lawn, past the cedar tree and into the rose garden. 'She sits here and reads quite often,' George said. She was not there this afternoon but Ella wasted a lot of time admiring the roses and George offered to cut her some to take back. She went round choosing them and Ernest waited, champing.

Next came the walled vegetable garden. He prayed they were not going to gather beans or any other produce. There was plenty of it but to his relief they passed on and came to the barn.

'Oh, the barn!' exclaimed Ella. 'I've never been inside a barn.'

'There's nothing to see. Have a look,' George said.

The door was partly open so they all went in. It was just a large empty building with very little light and after the brilliance outside it took time for the eye to get accustomed to it.

There was certainly nothing to see but they heard a slight

160

rustling, a disturbance of the stillness, and Ella said, 'Oh, I do hope there aren't any rats in here. Isn't that something over there in the straw?' She was pointing to a pile of straw in a far corner and drew in a sharp breath as a man and woman started up, disturbed by the intrusion. They had been stirring, stretching themselves, emerging from one of those luxurious drowsy sleeps that often follow love in the afternoon.

Not one of the three could move. It was just as though they had been frozen on the spot, like children playing statues who freeze into an attitude when the music stops. Dumb, stricken, they stood gazing at Hester and the man beside her. She gasped and grabbed his jacket to cover herself. It all seemed to be happening in slow motion, like the playback of a race. Later Ernest recalled noticing the snazzy pants the man was wearing. Pale blue, as far as he could tell in the dim light.

George did not move and the man addressed him. 'If you will give Mrs Sheridan time to collect a few things we will leave immediately,' he said, and from his accent it was clear he was foreign.

That evening, when Ernest told Guy all about it, he said he just couldn't believe it was happening. 'Old George didn't even knock the fellow down,' he said. 'He just stood there, ash grey, and then he turned and bolted, went stumbling down to the river.'

Ernest dragged Ella out. She was gibbering, of course.

'Trust your mother,' Ernest said. He told her to wait for him in the car and started to run after George who was already a long way ahead on the towpath. He knew he would never catch him and perhaps it was as well to leave him alone in the state he was. He went back to the car and drove it a little way from the house so he could waylay the Sharkeys when they returned from the cinema. Ella felt a migraine coming on. She was in one of her states and no wonder. Sick as a dog. He managed to get her out of the car before she damaged the upholstery. Never any good in a crisis.

It was nearly an hour before the Sharkeys returned and Ernest had the unenviable task of telling them what had

161

happened. It was no surprise to find they didn't believe him but when at last they took it in Sam set off to find George while Mrs Sharkey went weeping and wailing indoors to see if Hester had really gone.

Ernest said he hoped he would never have to go through such an experience again. Hester was not there but the house was full of her — her open book on a table in the drawing room, her sewing rolled up in a chair, her sun hat in the hall. It was a shock to him so how must George feel, and Mrs Sharkey and Sam? Mrs Sharkey refused to believe the evidence of her own eyes though it was clear Hester had packed up a few things to take with her — her small attache case had gone.

'I'll ring Miss Sheridan. She'll know what to do,' Mrs Sharkey said. 'Like as not she'll be after them. If you ask me, Mr Lambert, Mrs Hester's been barnacled.'

Ernest had no idea what Mrs Sharkey meant but thought it best to agree. 'I've no doubt you're right,' he said.

She made her telephone call and came back wondering what was to become of Mr George and poor little Sally. He could only shake his head. 'And Kate, poor dear?'

He quailed at the thought of the distress in store for the girls. There they were, innocently going about their own affairs, completely unaware of the catastrophe at Heron House. They would have to be told and that reminded him to ring Guy, tell him there was a bit of trouble at the Sheridans and ask him to call at The Laurels before going home so he could be told about it.

Ernest felt bound to stay at Heron House till he knew George was safe for he was afraid he might do some damn fool thing like jumping in the river. In the meantime he could only wait and listen to Mrs Sharkey's meanderings.

'Mrs Hester didn't know any men. Never had any gentlemen visitors apart from Father Keith now and then and it wouldn't be him, him being cellybrit,' she said.

'From the few words this fellow said I'd guess he was a foreigner,' remarked Ernest.

Mrs Sharkey had been sitting in a slumped attitude but she jerked upright as though set off by a spring. 'Foreigner?' she repeated. 'Not Eyetalian, Mr Lambert?'

'Could have been,' said Ernest.

She slapped the table with the flat of her hand, 'I knew no good would come of it,' she declared. 'Off to that heathen Catholic church every Sunday to hear them Eyeties sing. I told her she should stick to Chapel, not that she ever went there neither. Ten to one it's an Eyetie.'

'You may be right,' he said.

'I warned Mr George when the girls started fraterising but I never thought as Mrs Hester — oh, dear, Mr Lambert, what is to come of it all?'

Again he shook his head. He knew there had been an Italian P.O.W. camp close to the Sheridans and the prisoners worked on the land. Towards the end of the war, he had been told, they were given a lot of rope. They were liked by the indigent population as they were well-behaved and amenable. Many of them were good-looking and the girls preferred them to the Tommies and hung about like alley cats waiting to see them.

As this idea sunk in Ernest's indignation rose. His son Guy had risked his life countless times in the defence of his country while Hester was wallowing in the straw with one of the enemy. She was a traitor. She had deceived her husband but, worse still, she had deceived his son and that was far worse in his eyes.

His train of thought was interrupted by the arrival of Miss Sheridan and it took some time to tell her what had happened. She did not waste time over Hester. 'We'll deal with her later on,' she said. 'George is our concern now and he had better be left to me.'

Ernest felt the whole situation could be safely left in her hands. He imagined her going after Hester, bringing her back by the scruff of the neck and knocking hers and George's heads together hard. To his great relief Sam returned while they were talking. He had found George sitting on a bench two miles upstream and had brought him back and left him on *Corsair*. He refused to enter the house.

'Make a big pot of tea, Sharkey, and let Sam bring it down. And some food,' said Miss Sheridan. She turned to Ernest. 'Thank you for all your help, Mr Lambert,' she

163

said. 'You've had a very tiring day and will be wanting to take your wife home.'

Ernest had forgotten all about Ella. He should have brought her indoors, not left her half a mile down the road. He would never hear the last of it.

'When we have more news I shall let you know,' Miss Sheridan was saying. 'I'm afraid your daughter-in-law will be most upset. She's so fond of Hester.'

'By golly, so she is,' Ernest said. This defection of Hester's was going to be a blasted nuisance all round. He was thankful to leave.

Ella was on the back seat of the car, moaning. Ernest himself was very tired and considerably upset by Hester's deceit. It was abominable. He would not have been shocked at her having a lover, it was only to be expected as George, poor old devil, was old enough to be her father. Older. But she needn't have lain in the straw − not with one of the enemy.

At 24, The Avenue, Kate was hoping Guy would be home in time to have drinks in the garden before dinner. It was a perfect evening and the patio with its comfortable chairs and tubs of flowers was enticing.

Fiona was asleep in her cot upstairs so there should be several hours of peace to enjoy. She was six months old, beautiful, healthy, much admired when she was pushed out in her pram, but she was not the contented, good-tempered baby Kate had expected her to be. She was an undeniably fractious child and Kate could not make out why. She had asked Guy if he was disappointed because their first child was not a boy but he declared he was delighted with his little daughter.

'She's a beaut,' he said.

'It'll be a boy next time,' said Kate, and was surprised when he did not respond. 'Don't you want a son?' she asked.

'Oh, there's plenty of time,' he said carelessly. 'Let's get this one over first.'

'If that's how you feel, I'm sorry we didn't have quads,' she said. 'You know I want four.'

The silence with which he received this remark set her

wondering. It was the first time she had spoken to him in a slightly argumentative way and she was sorry. Was there the hint of an atmosphere? And had she caused it? Or had he? Best not to dwell on it and it would pass — that is if it was actually there. Later she decided she had imagined it for everything was as before and the best part of each day was the evening when he came home to tell her how things had gone at work.

That half hour before dinner was especially precious to her. It was an oasis, thirty minutes of bliss before she dished up the dinner, and that too was an occasion. She always took great pains with it; this evening there was a piece of turbot gently poaching in the oven and a rather tricky sauce on top in a double pan. It would only need seasoning.

Guy was late. She kept going down to the gate although she knew that would not bring him any faster. Half an hour. Three-quarters. It was too late for the garden now. Disappointed, she brought the tray back in and closed the doors. Dusk. Then dark. He did not like her to ring the office. Still, the security man might be able to tell her when he left. As she lifted the receiver his car swept in so she put it back and hurried to open the door.

'Hallo, Katey.' He had never sounded so subdued or looked so limp. He put his arm round her, patted her shoulder.

'You look worn out. What's the matter?' she asked.

'I've been at Mother's. Dad asked me to call in on my way home. They'd just got back from Heron House.' The tone of his voice with all the lightness gone from it, his hesitation, the anxious way he was looking at her, meant something was seriously wrong.

'Let's sit down,' he said wearily.

If only he would get it out, whatever it was!

He took her hands and held them. 'Hester has gone away,' he said. 'It all happened this afternoon. She has left George.'

'Left him? Why? What do you mean?'

'She has left him for someone else.'

Kate pulled back. 'I don't believe it,' she said.

'I'm afraid it's true, Kate.'

'No,' she said. 'No!' How could he expect her to believe anything so monstrous? 'No!' she almost screamed.

'You've got to believe me. She's eloped.'

Eloped? The drama of it! He'd be saying she was on her way to Gretna Green next.

'You're having me on,' she said.

'Mother was there. So was Dad.'

She could see them both with their jaws dropped. She began to laugh.

He gripped her shoulders hard. 'For God's sake, stop giggling and listen to me,' he said.

Her silly, nervous laughter stopped.

'Dad drove Mother and George down to Heron House this afternoon. The idea was to collect Hester, go for a drive and then out to dinner. Hester was not expecting them. She was entertaining someone else. You can imagine the rest.'

Kate heard what Guy said but couldn't take it in. Things like that simply did not happen. Not to dependable people like Hester. There was a misunderstanding somewhere.

'Hester would never leave Uncle George,' she said slowly. 'She's too fond of him. They are a real family. It's out of character.'

'You obviously don't know her character. She's chosen to leave her family and that's the end of her.'

She began to shiver and he held her close, trying to calm her. 'Miss Sheridan's there now taking care of things,' he said. 'Relax. We won't talk any more.' He knew Kate looked on Hester as her second mother so she was bound to take this hard. He accepted that but he disliked Hester although he could not have explained why. She had always been pleasant enough and he would not deny she was stunning to look at, but there was a latent quality in her that repelled him and he could not identify it. His mother felt the same. It was a kind of gut reaction.

He had spent an exhausting two hours at The Laurels with his parents, trying to make sense of his father's jumbled account of what had happened and to soothe his mother. Ella was genuinely ill this time. Her migraine was much worse than usual and as she could not stop shaking they sent for the doctor who gave her tranquillisers and advised complete rest and quiet.

'A nice how-de-do,' Ernest complained, and Guy agreed with him. He considered he had told Kate as much as she needed to know, for the present anyway, and was just going to suggest having something to eat when she sat up straight.

'There's more to all this, Guy,' she said. 'If she's really gone, who did she go with?'

'Nobody knows for certain.'

'But you said they were seen together. Did Uncle George know him?'

'George just bolted.'

'Mrs Sharkey would know who all the visitors were.'

'Mrs Sharkey thinks he was one of the Italian prisoners. He certainly spoke broken English. Dad heard him. I expect we shall be told in time. Now I don't want to say any more.'

'You must. I'm not a child. Where were they? In the house? On *Corsair*?'

'They were in the barn, the pair of them. Mother, Dad and George went in there in all innocence and that's what they saw. It was horrible for Mother. It's made her ill.'

So Ella was ill, and Guy was more concerned for her wounded feelings than anything else.

Kate took a grip on herself and dug her fingernails into her arms so it hurt. Pictures began to flash through her mind. Those Italian prisoners they could never regard as enemies. The way she and Sally used to talk to them, give them sweets – but she mustn't think of that now.

'I'm not going to listen to one bad word about Hester,' she said. 'Where would I have been without her? I don't have to tell you what she meant to me.'

'That doesn't excuse her.' There was a cold note in her voice, a hard, unrelenting tone she had never heard before.

'This is all very hot and steamed up,' she said. 'I expect she'll come back and we'll wonder what all the fuss was about.'

'George wouldn't have her.'

'Of course he would.'

'Well, I wouldn't if I were in his shoes.'

'Suppose she gave in to her feelings just once. It doesn't have to be the end of her marriage,' she protested.

'So that's what you think! This is a side of you I don't know, Kate. An act of that kind is the end of any marriage.'

'What about forgiveness?'

He brushed this aside with an impatient gesture. His father's graphic description of Hester grabbing the fellow's jacket to hide herself was fresh in his mind. '*You* may be soft about Hester,' he said, 'but what about George? What about Sally? It's pretty devastating for them, isn't it?'

She began to cry. Another world had come to an end. The peace, security and kindness of Heron House had gone forever. 'It's awful. Just awful,' she sobbed.

He soothed her, said they would have to get used to the situation and see what they could do to ease the pain Sally and George would suffer. 'We're so lucky. We've got each other,' he said.

This was more like the Guy she loved so dearly. It was good to feel his arms round her.

'I'll tell you one thing, Kate,' he said later on, and there was a note of satisfaction in his voice, 'I never liked Mrs Sheridan. Neither did Mother. She's a cheap, treacherous, common trollop!'

'Oh!' she cried, pulling away from him. 'How can you? How *can* you?'

'I can because it's true and I'm jolly glad you won't be having any more to do with her,' he said.

'But I shall. I'm not going to drop her.'

'Get this clear, Kate. I will not allow you to associate with that woman. Understand?'

'No, I don't,' she said.

It was just as though a gulf had opened between them. In the kitchen the sauce was burned and so was the saucepan. Upstairs the baby began to cry.

Sleep, what there was of it, was fitful and when morning came Kate felt more than the weight of Hester's departure hanging over her. She had come hard up against Guy and would have to hold her ground at all costs for she could

168

not allow him to dictate to her where her principles were concerned. She did not feel called upon to condemn Hester or to choose between her and George. She loved them both and was loyal to both. In all probability Hester would be looked on as an outcast now but that did not cancel her good qualities or the way she had helped Kate survive so she would not disassociate herself from her no matter what Guy might say.

But being at loggerheads with him made her wretched. She wanted him to understand how she felt, but the tone of his voice, the set of his mouth, the words he had used, told her it would be useless to try.

There was a strained atmosphere at breakfast. She longed to say something but words refused to come. At length she stammered out: 'Don't you think we should talk a little, Guy?'

'Not now. I have a hard day ahead.'

'It will be all the harder with this misunderstanding between us.'

'There's no misunderstanding. You know my sentiments. I know yours. There is nothing more to say.'

'But there is. I had no idea you judged people as you judged Hester. What right have you to call her a cheap, treacherous trollop?'

'The right of a man who was serving his country while she was wallowing in the straw with the enemy.' He was leaning across the table glaring at her and she was frightened, but she had to overcome her fear although her heart was beating very fast.

'You must not ask me to condemn her,' she said. It took all her courage to say it.

'Then don't expect me to change my attitude.' With that he left the room and a moment later she heard the front door close. She went on sitting at the table hoping he would come back and repair the damage with a kiss, but outside the car revved up, turned into the road and drove away.

She thought of Heron House and looking back saw the years there as idyllic in spite of her sorrow. George. Hester. Sally. Dear old downright Mrs Sharkey. The kindness, the good humour that prevailed there. Now it had all gone and

169

there was no one she could turn to for a word of comfort. Aunt Josephine was there and Kate would have rung her but she feared George might answer the telephone. She could not get in touch with Sally, there was no way of getting news. She would just have to be patient and carry on with her everyday tasks as though nothing had happened. She cherished the hope that Hester would come back and puzzled her head over which of the Italians she had run away with.

Waiting, getting through time, was hard. She took Fiona for walks, stopped to talk to acquaintances and asked Ada over for tea while Fiona was having her afternoon nap.

'You look a bit peaky, love,' said Ada.

'I didn't sleep very well.'

'You should get Guy to take you away for the weekend. Your mother-in-law would look after the baby, wouldn't she?'

'Yes. She loves having her. Manages her much better than I do.'

'Well then, that's settled.' Ada went on chattering away. Her sisters were coming to stay with her; Jack was getting a new aerial for the wireless, a really high one, and they were going to place it at the end of the garden and expected wonderful reception. Kate managed to respond, satisfactorily she supposed as Ada didn't appear to notice anything amiss. She was not to know that Ada had seen Guy drive off with a face like thunder that morning and had remarked to Jack that she would not care to get on the wrong side of that young man.

It was another lovely evening, just right for drinks on the patio. Kate hesitated about taking the tray outside and then decided it would be stupid not to. The best way was to behave as though there was no friction. She made fish cakes out of the turbot that had gone uneaten the night before, prepared vegetables, made a fruit salad. Then she bathed Fiona and put her in her cot praying she was not going to howl. As she went downstairs Guy came in much earlier than usual.

'Hallo, Katey,' he said, quite cheerfully.

'Oh, I'm so glad you're early.' there was a momentary pause, then he kissed her and she clung to him, thinking

170

he had changed his mind. 'Did you have a good day?' she asked.

'Tell you later. What about you?'

'Pretty good.' She could believe it had been now he was in a better mood. 'Drinks outside?'

'Lovely. I'll just get out of this rig. Hope there's some ice.'

'There is.'

'Down in a minute.'

She was almost ashamed of the relief she felt as she knocked ice cubes into a bowl and cut slices of lemon. Guy came down in a short-sleeved silk shirt with a cravat.

'To us,' he said, as he handed her her drink.

This was her precious half hour, sitting here with Guy, hearing the evening sounds. A blackbird was shouting its head off in the apple tree up the garden.

'I saw Major Harvey today,' Guy said. 'He sent for me. I'm to go up to Newcastle for a day or two to the new factory.'

'That's good, isn't it?'

'I'll say. It's two steps up the ladder. I'm afraid it's put one or two noses out of joint.'

'Oh dear. You don't want enemies. Still, it's exciting, isn't it?'

'It's my chance. Katey.'

He went on talking about the new project his firm was embarking on and his part in it for the rest of the half hour and then all through dinner and long afterwards. He was so wrapped up in his work and the opportunities it offered him that he seemed to have forgotten the furore of yesterday. It was just as well, she thought, and seeing how eager he was to succeed she determined to help him in every possible way.

She could begin by not letting him guess how much she would hate being alone while he was away.

Kate did not relish the prospect of meeting Ella and deferred visiting her for the next day or two. The door of The Laurels was opened by Mrs Blunt, the daily help, who jerked her head in the direction of the drawingroom and remarked with

171

a wink that Mrs Lambert was very poorly and making the most of it.

Mrs Lambert was reclining on the sofa clad in a rose pink negligee with black pads over her eyes.

'Who is that?' she asked in a trembling voice when Kate and Fiona went in.

'It's only me, Ella. I haven't been before as you needed to rest. Here's Fiona to see you.'

Fiona approached the sofa at an alarming speed on all fours, emitting a series of sharp short shrieks as she went.

'Oh!' cried Ella, clapping her hands over her ears. 'Oh, for heaven's sake. My head! Have you no control over that child?' She removed the eyepads and Fiona sat up, gurgled and laughed and held out her arms to her grandmother. 'Oo's a good girl then?' said Ella in a silly affected voice. 'Oo shall come up with Granny, then? Oo shall have biccy in a minny winny?' Then in her normal tones: 'Lift her up beside me, Kate dear. And will you ask Mrs Blunt to bring in the tea now?'

Kate wished Ella would not talk to Fiona in ridiculous baby language but she lacked the courage to object openly. When they were settled with their tea and Fiona was crumbling up biscuits all over herself and the sofa Ella began on the subject they both had in mind.

'Have you heard from a certain quarter?' she asked. Apparently names and locations caused her too much pain to utter.

'Not yet, but no doubt I shall,' said Kate.

'Nothing can be said in defence of that woman,' said Ella. 'I feel sick at the thought of her. You can have no idea how that dreadful scene I witnessed has affected me. Of course I'm not just sensitive, as you know, hear. I'm hypersensitive.'

'Then you must try not to dwell on it. The whole affair is distressing to us all. It breaks my heart to think of Heron House and the Sheridans who have always been so good to me. And to know that darling Hester isn't there any more — oh, I do so hope things can be patched up and she'll come back. Surely she will?'

'Whatever are you saying?' demanded Ella. 'If she did

have the effrontery to come back, I hope everyone would cut her. Including you, Kate.'

'That I would not,' she declared hotly. 'I'm very, very sorry for what's happened. It's dreadful for Uncle George and Sally and please don't think I condone Hester's behaviour but I will never join her detractors.'

'You were not there on that dreadful day, Kate. You can have no idea what it's like to see a couple lying naked in front of you. If I could blot that picture out of my mind, believe me I would.'

'Perhaps it would help you to forget if we don't speak of it,' Kate said.

But nothing would stop Ella now she was in full spate and Kate had to listen to her account of her sufferings, her long wait in the car when nobody seemed to think of her or consider her feelings, several times over.

At the first opportunity she said quietly: 'Yes, it must have been very hard for you, Ella, but I can't join you in condemning Hester. I know she's fond of Uncle George, there's no doubt of that, but he is so much older and how can any of us tell what drove her to this?'

'What does that matter? She could resist, I suppose. Don't we all have to resist temptation?'

Kate was having to resist the temptation to scream at her mother-in-law. To see her sitting there steeped in virtue was almost more than she could bear. She sipped her tea. Ella sipped hers and asked Kate to pour another cup. Fiona began to tug at the pendant Ella wore on a chain round her neck. It was a locket containing miniatures of Guy and Tom as children and Fiona knew it could be opened. Ella snapped it open for her. Fiona snapped it shut and demanded it be opened again. This went on several times till Kate said: 'Don't let her worry you, Ella.'

But Ella always had time and patience for her grandchild although after a while she returned to the subject of the Sheridans.

'I see that you and I must agree to differ, dear,' she said. 'But we won't quarrel. I'm glad Guy shares my opinion and you must give him credit for seeing through that woman from the first. And poor Mr Sheridan − well − she never bothered much about him. If she had she would have smartened him up, poor man. I shall let him know he will always find a welcome here. He needs friends now, if ever he did.'

'I'm sure he has them,' said Kate.

'And Sally. Have you heard from her?' asked Ella.

Kate shook her head. She was worried about Sally for she had not heard a word so far and had no idea how much she knew of events at home.

'It's a mercy she was away,' Ella said. 'She has her career in front of her so that's something. But poor Mr Sheridan has nothing. His life is over.'

'I very much doubt that,' said Kate.

'We shall see.' Ella turned her attention to Fiona again. The child was behaving exceptionally well as she always did at The Laurels. She was different with Kate. The child's piercing shrieks when they were in shops caused her acute embarrassment because she could not stop her and other mothers paused to ask what was wrong while grandmothers shook their heads and offered advice, none of which had the desired effect. But Ella seemed to have a beneficent influence.

'It's time for us to go,' Kate said. 'We don't want to wear you out, Ella. Say goodbye to Granny, Fiona.'

She went red in the face and clung to Ella who only had to say one word to prevent the imminent screams. 'Now, Fiona,' she said, 'you are going home with Mummy and you shall come to see your Gran Gran on Sunday.' There was no screaming or crying. Ella turned to Kate. 'You must be firm with her, dear. You simply must not allow her to get the upper hand. Children need discipline.'

Kate went home feeling unutterably depressed. The child she had longed for so ardently did not seem to belong to her. She thought of old stories about changelings and could almost have believed Fiona was one of them. She often told Guy she would be different if she had a brother or sister but he did not agree.

'One's enough to be going on with,' he said whenever she mentioned it.

'We should have another though.'

'You don't seem able to manage this one.'

174

'That's not fair.'

'Well, do you?'

The usual argument followed. It always did and she could never persuade him.

All was turmoil at Heron House and Aunt Josephine was faced with the formidable task of restoring order. It was not easy but she went about things in a practical way by going down to *Corsair* and asking George if he wanted dinner served in the saloon or in the diningroom.

He looked at her in a dazed kind of way and said he couldn't eat a thing. She persuaded him by saying Mrs Sharkey had taken the trouble to prepare a meal so wouldn't he just peck at it? 'You'd better come up to the house. It's no good sulking in your tent,' she said.

'I'm bewildered.' He sank his head in his hands again.

'Small wonder. Now come along.'

He followed her. He was in a state of shock, mystification, anger, grief. There was no place for him in a world without Hester and that overrode the necessity to sort things out, to discover what had really happened and why. He felt as though his heart had been torn out leaving a raw gaping hole; then he was lulled into thinking the whole thing was a bad dream and Hester would soon be home.

But her passport had gone. They had been to France in 1938 and she had a new one for that holiday so it was not yet due for renewal. He caught a glimpse of himself in the dressing table glass. God! What an old, ugly damned face he had. That fellow in the barn was young and good-looking. Was he the one who sang solo in church? *Panis Angelicus*. The girls called him Gianni. They had asked him his name and persuaded themselves he gave them the glad eye. It had amused him and horrified Mrs Sharkey. He remembered telling Hester his admiring glances were for her and noticing the way she brushed the remark aside. He often forgot she was young. He forgot she had never been to dances like other girls or had the fun young people have. He remembered how she looked at photographs of young women in glamorous dresses in the glossy magazines; they were taken at charity balls, at the races, at first nights. Now he wondered if she envied them. She read romantic novels, wept at romantic films, she doted on Garbo in Camille — or was it Robert Taylor? Gianni was rather like Robert Taylor. Dark. Handsome.

'George, we must think about Sally.' Aunt Josephine's voice stirred him out of his rambling, disconnected thoughts. 'She mustn't hear about this from anyone but you, my dear. I'll drive you to Oxford tomorrow.'

Next day brought Kate a long letter from Aunt Josephine and she was glad it arrived after Guy had left so she could read it alone. Their suspicions about the Italian prisoner were correct. Hester had gone away with Gianni Morelli and by now she was most likely at The Hotel Villa Laura in Santa Carlotta. Aunt Josephine did not apportion blame but naturally enough George was devastated.

'I spoke very plainly to him,' Aunt Josephine wrote, and Kate could almost hear her voice and picture the scene as she sought to help her nephew accept the situation he found himself in.

'Think for a moment, George. You have had twenty happy years with Hester. That's more than many people have in a lifetime. Remember those happy years and be grateful for them. Don't harp on her wickedness for deserting you. Think of her good qualities. Think of her patience with you and Sally eternally spouting Shakespeare at her. Think of her typing out your notes, your lectures, your addresses. Upon my soul, George, you've had a good twenty years, very good. So pull up your socks and get weaving.'

'What at?' he asked.

'Go and see Sally. I said I'd take you.'

But Sally had heard from Hester who wrote from Dover and she went straight to Heron House to be with her father. She stayed there for a week, walking with him, talking, taking *Corsair* off the moorings and cruising upstream or down according to their inclination, and all the time smothering her own distress in order to salve his.

'You see, my dear, I quite forgot your mother was so young,' he often said.

In the background Aunt Josephine was making plans,

considering one scheme then rejecting it for another. She was wary of hasty decisions made at critical moments and regretted afterwards. It would be a great pity, she thought, to get rid of Heron House. George had mentioned doing so several times and said if he hadn't been such a bloody fool as to send Hester there to escape the bombing, this would never have happened.

'Staying at The Clearing wouldn't have been such a good idea either,' Aunt Josephine reminded him. The germ of an idea she had in her mind was beginning to take root. She tried not to think about it too much for fear it might give up on her so she pretended it wasn't there. To gain time she suggested George and Sally should go off on a little tour. It would do them both good to get away, there was nothing like a change of air to benefit the liver, she declared. 'Do something you've never done before — like staying at Southend for a week. Lots of shell fish and mud. Or better still hire bicycles and tour the Essex coast. Splendid exercise. Good for the lungs and wonderful for the leg muscles.'

It did not take a great deal of persuasion to induce George to agree. His state of mind was such that he needed to be led.

Before they set off Sally went down to spend a day with Kate. A week had gone by since Hester's departure but already it felt like years and Kate had been worrying and fretting and bottling up her feelings because of Guy's disapproving attitude.

The two girls fell into each other's arms and kissed and cried together, too full of emotion for words at first but eventually able to talk. Knowing the circumstances, and greatly to her credit, Ella took Fiona off Kate's hands for the day so that she and Sally could talk to their hearts' content.

'I couldn't come before,' Sally said. 'As soon as I got Mum's letter — she wrote to me — I dropped everything and streaked off home and I couldn't ring you because Dad was there. He's shattered, Kate. Aunt Josephine's there. I don't know what would have happened without her.'

'Isn't there any hope of Hester coming back? A reconciliation?' Kate asked.

Sally shook her head. 'It wouldn't work.'

'Isn't there any more news of her?'

'I'll show you her letter.' Sally was crying as she spoke. 'She wrote to Dad, too. I couldn't help seeing how his letter began because it fell out of his hand on to the floor and he just went out of the room. I picked it up. It began 'My dear George,' and it went on − 'for you *are* dear to me, George, and always will be.' I didn't read any more. I just put it back in the envelope and left it on the table and later it had gone.'

'I'm sure she's fond of him,' said Kate.

'We've been so happy as a family,' Sally said. 'The four of us.'

'I know.' Kate was so grateful to be included but all the more sorrowful because the family was no more. 'Oh, Sal, won't things ever be right?' she said.

'They'll never be the same,' Sally said, 'and you know, Mum has been different lately − well, for quite a time now. She's seemed sort of far away.'

'I suppose she was with Gianni in her mind.'

'She was quite desperately in love. In her letter she says Kate will understand and so will you one day, Sally. But I don't mean to fall in love. It's too devastating.'

'You won't be able to help yourself, Sal.'

'Want to bet?'

'On a certainty? I wouldn't dream of it. But what about Uncle George?'

'He had an offer to lecture in America some time ago. Now he's lost heart but I'm quite sure Aunt Josephine will persuade him to take it up. I know she's working on it. She sits there thinking so hard you can almost tune in to her brain. Don't you think it would be the best thing for him, Kate?'

'I certainly do.'

Sally was quiet for a long time. At last she said, 'Oh, dear. To think of them both being out of the country. I'll feel like the orphan of the storm. I feel bruised. I know exactly where my heart is because it hurts.'

'You gave me so much comfort when I needed it,' Kate said. 'What can I do for *you*, Sally?'

178

'Give me a kick in the pants and tell me to snap out of it,' she said, snuffling and crying and laughing all at once. 'I love them both so much, never so much as now. Why do we have feelings? Wouldn't it be better not to feel?'

'No, it would not,' declared Kate. 'You'd miss all the wonderful things as well.'

They talked on and on, going over the time when the prisoners were there. 'It was the one who sang *Panis Angelicus*,' Sally said. 'Do you remember him?'

'He was the one I liked best,' Kate said.

'So did I. Remember how we thought he was always looking at us? Of course he was looking at Mum. Poor old Mum.'

'She isn't old and she *is* lovely,' said Kate.

Sally was not surprised to hear how the Lamberts had reacted. 'What else would you expect of them?' she said. 'Sorry, I didn't mean to include Guy.'

'Don't apologise. He's of the same mind,' Kate said.

'That must make it difficult for you.'

'It does. I can hardly expect him to approve but he's so vehement – so shocked and narrow-minded. Almost more so than his mother.'

'Don't let it come between you,' Sally said. 'Hold on to your own opinion but keep it to yourself whatever you do.'

Kate had already decided on that but it was hard to smother her feelings when she so often longed to bring them out into the open. That was when she began to find loneliness can exist within a marriage and she was not prepared for it. It was a bitter thing. She had not known it was possible. How could you be lonely when you had a husband who was all you ever dreamed of? Something had happened that was beyond her control. She saw him in a different light now.

But perhaps that's how he sees me, she thought. He may be feeling alone too. He's disappointed because I can't bring myself to take his high moral stand and see things in stark black and white, as he does.

Oh, we must get together again. We must be as we were. How can either of us be lonely when we eat, sleep, live together?

*

179

It took Aunt Josephine some time to formulate her plans and put them into action. She took the long view. George had over seven years to use up before he retired. Sally would come down from St Hilda's next year and no doubt get a job in London. Well then, let George exchange his small West End flat for a larger one so Sally could live there and so could he when he came back from America. She was determined he should go there. Change of scene, change of contacts, buck his ideas up, give him a different lease of life. And Heron House, that must not go out of the family on any account. The answer was to lease it for fixed periods to visiting American academics with Mrs Sharkey remaining there as custodian, housekeeper, whatever title she chose to select. Then when George did eventually retire he could come back there to live and enjoy visits from Kate and her family – she was bound to have more children – it would be a serious mistake to stop at one, especially one like Fiona who, from all accounts, was a little fiend.

Sally, of course, would be married with a family by then and although the name of Sheridan would be lost the line would go on and Sally could always persuade her husband to change his name by deed poll. That would be quite acceptable.

So, having put each scheme neatly in place, Aunt Josephine presented the package to George and as he was in no condition to decide anything for himself he agreed meekly.

It all took time but with Aunt Josephine in charge he did not have to worry at all except for feeling lost. Utterly lost without Hester. He sometimes wondered if he looked like a stray dog running round searching for its owner.

It was surprising how quickly the morbid excitement over Hester's elopement fizzled out. A whole year had gone by and Kate still felt bereaved. Hester was the one person in the world she could discuss her problems with but loyalty to Guy would have prevented her from asking even Hester's advice about the invisible wall that stood between them now. And it would not have been there but for Hester's defection.

I will not be defeated, she told herself, and she stuck out her chin much as Sally was wont to do years ago when she felt her lack of one severely. Kate had a lovely chin but she caught a glimpse of herself sticking it out in the glass and the sight made her laugh.

That's our trouble. We don't get enough laughs, she said aloud and she ran across the road to the Fortunes where she was sure to get at least one.

The pole for their aerial had at last arrived after a very long delay and Kate was amazed at its length.

'However are you going to get it up?' she asked.

'Jack has it all worked out,' Ada said. 'Jane and Jessie are coming down for the weekend and the four of us will start at the top end near the house and just raise it as we walk towards the base. Then it will simply slip into its socket. Easy.'

Kate thought it sounded far from easy. 'I'll come over and help,' she said.

Jane and Jessie, Ada's twin sisters, were very small women with matchstick legs that looked ready to snap. They wore identical clothes but in strongly contrasting colours. Jane favoured egg yolk yellow, Jessie wore bright red, and all three sisters wore mob caps in the mornings and kept them on till just before lunch. It amused Kate to see the three caps bobbing about as they put out milk bottles, shook dusters from windows and diligently swept the front paths.

On Saturday afternoon Kate went over to help with the pole while Fiona was having her sleep and Guy was mulling over the week's reports.

'Shan't be long,' she said, but it was soon obvious that hoisting the pole was going to take longer than any of them expected. The idea was that they should stand in line beside the pole and lift it in stages. When Jack gave the word 'Up' it was to be knee high; 'Up, up' to waist level; 'Up, up, up,' and it would be shoulder high. Four 'Ups' and it would be over their heads and they would advance hand under hand till it was erect and ready to be pushed into its slot.

'Simple,' said Jack as they began.

It might well have been simple if the sisters had obeyed his instructions implicitly but no sooner had the first action been performed and the next in progress than one of them would let go. This put the whole exercise out of joint. They once had it shoulder high when Ada shouted that her foot had gone to sleep.

'We want someone taller and stronger,' said Kate. 'What about Mr Hooper?'

The Fortunes were barely on speaking terms with the Hoopers. They tried again by themselves. Of course they all knew Guy was at home and Kate knew they knew and felt embarrassed. He would not be pleased to be called upon but eventually, when it was clear that success was almost further away than when they started, and they were all mopping their brows and flexing their muscles, she went over the road to fetch him.

He took some persuading but at length he followed her and this time he was the one to shout commands taking up his position nearest to the socket. Things went better. They got the pole shoulder high and inched it gradually over their heads, but at this stage their arms weakened.

'Eeh, I've a mind to take my teeth out,' quavered Jack.

'No you don't,' yelled Ada. 'Not while this pole's resting on my head.'

Guy, furious at having been roped in, was taking the bulk of the weight. 'Come on, all of you,' he shouted in the tones of a company sergeant major. 'One, two, three, heave.'

They were too frightened of him to disobey and this final effort paid off. The pole was upright and in its socket, the tallest wireless aeriel in the district.

They stood back to admire it and Jack, who now had his teeth safely in his pocket, began to thank Guy in accents that were incomprehensible, although he distinguished the word 'lad' several times. He objected to being called 'lad'. He was not pleased either when Jane grabbed one hand and Jessie the other with the suggestion they should all dance round the maypole but there was no stopping them and he was deafened by the sound of shrill Lancastrian voices singing 'Here we go round the mulberry bush'.

Kate was so pleased the pole was in place and certain it would not have been without his help that she was unaware of his displeasure.

'You'll take a cup of tea, Mr Lambert?' Ada asked.

'Thank you, but I must go back,' he said. 'I have a great deal of work to get through.'

'Oh dear, did you put it down to come over and help? Now that's neighbourly. Jack, do you hear that? We interrupted Mr Lambert's work.'

'I'm sure he doesn't mind,' Kate put in. She was enjoying herself. Ada and her sisters were dears, it was nice to be with them, and she would have liked to stay to tea.

'Come along, Kate. Fiona will be waking up,' Guy said.

Kate realised this was likely and said they had better go. They were accompanied to the gate by the whole family, still loudly thanking them and waving goodbyes as though seeing them off for a voyage round the world.

'They'd never have done it without you,' Kate said with a last wave to the Fortunes as she closed their own front door.

Guy turned round on her. 'You had a nerve dragging me over there,' he said. 'I don't want anything to do with that ee bah goom crowd and you know it.'

Kate did not intend to be put down or to apologise.

'You've done them a good turn and I'm not the one to tell them you did it against your will,' she said. She put the kettle on, made tea and talked about the play group Fiona had joined.

Volcanoes, earthquakes, eruptions – Sally felt Heron House and everyone in it had been subjected to even worse disasters, and though they might pick themselves up it would take a long time to dust themselves down and start all over again. All the same, when she compared her lot with Kate's she much preferred her own.

She often went to stay at 24, The Avenue when Guy was away on a trip and once when he was there. Once was enough. It tried her patience to see Kate running round trying to please him all the time. He dominated her, yet she pretended she was happy and never deviated from her devotion to him. If only she would let go and have a good swear sometimes, Sally thought. She had lost the radiance that lent a special sort of glamour to her looks and everything else about her.

She still played the piano, decorating popular songs with brilliant trills and arpeggios, improvising on themes, really enjoying herself, but not when Guy was there. He nearly always brought work home and spent the evenings poring over plans and estimates and making notes in his small, neat handwriting. The piano disturbed him. He never said so in words; he just put down his pen, sighed audibly and leaned back with eyes closed, thus conveying his objection. Kate would immediately stop and start apologising. Quite the wrong tactic, Sally thought.

He put the brakes on conversation, too. She couldn't mention Hester in his presence. If she did he went out of the room and Kate would say: 'I've learned not to mention Hester, Sal. It's better that way. We can talk when we're on our own.'

'Of course we can, but it isn't natural. It's like disowning a large part of your life.'

'Oh, well, that's how it is.'

It was not pleasant to be restricted in this way and there was no denying the strain it imposed on Kate. This marriage that had begun so well was threatened from within and without, and Sally felt great pity and concern for Kate. A snooty husband and abominable child – who would want to swop with her? The risks of matrimony are not for me, Sally told herself, and she was all the more pleased with her job at the Treasury and the flat George took for her before he went to America. It was in a quiet street off Park Lane, beautifully central and only twelve stations from Kate on the District.

Of course she missed the family life and it hurt to have her mother and father so far away but Heron House was still there and so was Mrs Sharkey who now chose to call herself the chatterlaine, scorning the more plebeian title of housekeeper. The house was let to American professors and their families and she kept a vigilant eye on them. Let but the ghost of a scratch appear on a table and she was after them with bitter reproaches and promises to inform the even more formidable Miss Sheridan if such a thing ever happened again.

'Anyway, they're only tempry,' she would say when

discussing their shortcomings with Sally who went to see her once a month.

She provided meals except on Sundays but when requested, or rather begged, she deigned to give them tea and her Sunday teas became a legend — cucumber sandwiches, thin bread and butter and jam, and madeira cake. The great silver teapot, the eggshell thin china set out on an enormous silver tray, were wheeled into the drawingroom with the cry: 'Here you are then, bomb'eads. And no crumbs, *if* you please.'

She never doubted Mr George would come back one day and secretly dreamed Mrs Hester would, too. It broke her heart to think of Mrs Hester living in heathen Italy with a wog and it was no use telling her he was no such thing. 'There'll be an end to all this. Mark my words,' she would say.

At least Sally could reassure her about Mr George. Judging from his weekly letter he was thoroughly enjoying himself in the States. He had been apprehensive at first, thinking he was too old and passé to rate as anything but a nonentity. To his surprise and near incredulity he found himself whirled into a social life that was overcrowded with invitations. 'Much of this and your old dad will get bigheaded,' he wrote. Sally's heart swelled with pride and love for him. It was such a relief to know he was rising above his despondency and she felt she could enjoy her own pleasures all the better unhampered by his sadness.

The Hotel Villa Laura! It was as romantic as its name when Sally saw it for the first time. She had been full of trepidation on the long train journey, for three years had gone by since Hester ran away with Gianni and their meeting might not be easy.

The little railway station at Santa Carlotta was as rustic as any wayside halt at home. Only a handful of people alighted and by the time she got outside the single taxi was trundling away and only a small horse-drawn carriage remained. It was a very smart turn-out and the driver was in an equally smart uniform. Sally consulted her phrase book and wished she had kept up her Italian classes. She approached the carriage. '*Vorrei andare a* —' she began nervously, but the driver was already down from his seat.

'Signorina Sheridan!' he exclaimed, and it was not so much a query as a greeting. He followed it by gabbling away so fast she could not distinguish one word from another and although she said '*Non comprendo*' several times he just rattled on, his talk punctuated with the words 'Signora Morelli,' and 'Villa Laura' from which she gathered he had been sent to fetch her and was not about to whisk her into the hills and hold her for ransom.

He stowed her luggage, helped her in and they were off, the horse trotting smartly. She felt she was on a film set for the road was lined with oleanders and the scent was swoon-making. Besides that the driver was singing '*Funiculi Funicula*' at the top of his voice and seemed to expect her to join in for he kept looking back and making encouraging signs. He appeared to be conducting an invisible orchestra and she wished he would keep his eye on the road.

They arrived and drove through the wide-flung gates and there was the villa. It stood well back from the road in large, well-kept grounds and Sally caught her breath at the sight of it.

Six wide marble steps swept down from the entrance and an enormous bougainvillaea came trailing over the ballustrade. The house seemed to shimmer, translucent like a shell, and there were green shutters at its windows. It was almost impossibly lovely. And to think her mother was somewhere inside, that she lived in this fairytale palace.

Now the driver was helping her out but her feet had hardly touched the ground when Hester came running down the steps. 'Oh Mum, darling Mum,' cried Sally as her mother clasped her in her arms and Sally felt all the pent-up emotions of the past few years spilling out in tears. What could they say? Where to begin? Hester soothed her just as though she was a child picking herself up after a fall and running to her for comfort.

They went in, arms entwined. The entrance hall was dim after the brightness outside and Hester was taking Sally up a wide staircase and into the room that was to be hers. She was saying how tired she must be after her journey – 'So why not just have a lick and promise now and then we'll have tea? Oh, you dear, darling little Sal! It's so wonderful to see you. Why am I crying when I'm so happy?'

Sally knew she need not have felt anxious on her way. Hester was just as she had always been, the dear, kind-hearted Mum of her childhood, the mother she had never ceased to love when others derided her, the mother she missed and longed for when things went right, still more when they went wrong.

Hester, too, had wondered about their reunion. They had corresponded at regular intervals but writing was so different from talking and she would not have been surprised by some restraint so it was a great relief to find she could come straight to the point and ask how George was doing.

'Bearing up very well now,' Sally said. 'I don't mind telling you he was shot to pieces at first.'

'Tell me,' Hester said.

So Sally did, and Hester told Sally about her long, painful struggle to overcome her love for Gianni.

'If he hadn't come back I'd still be at Heron House,' she said, 'but he couldn't conquer his feelings for me anymore than I could for him. And he did try, Sal. Well, you can imagine. The Morellis are splendid people but the idea of Gianni marrying a divorced woman who couldn't give him any children – well, just think.'

'Problems all round,' said Sally. 'What made them give in?'

'He was in such misery. They quite thought he'd die.'

'It must have been hard for you when you got here.'

'No. They were superb. They welcomed me, took me to their hearts, as people say. They've made me feel I really belong.'

'Mum, I'm so glad, truly I am.'

'I expect you heard all kinds of bad things about me and there's no way I can justify what I did,' said Hester. 'I shall never pretend that what I did was right. Or justifiable.'

'You were never a hypocrite, Mum.'

'There's just one thing I'd like you to know. Gianni and I never made love till that one fatal time. I wish you'd tell Dad so when you get the chance.'

Sally nodded and there was a pause. Then Hester said

cheerfully: 'And now, my dearie, you can see how I'm placed here so let's go out on the balcony and have tea and you can tell me all about yourself and Kate and my dear old Sharkey.'

The balcony overlooked the garden at the front of the hotel and presently they were sitting there together with a large pot of tea and some delectable cakes. In the middle of the lawn a fountain played, the water spouting out of a pipe played by a shepherd boy. It fell into a large scallop shell where waxen water lilies floated. People strolled about on the lawns, came and went through the open gates, stopped to talk to one another. There were several tables on the lawn and tea was being carried out, or cool drinks in tall glasses on silver trays. It was a scene of leisure, of prosperity, of well-being.

Sally bit into an eclair and the cream ran down her chin. Hester laughed and said, 'Well, go on. You've told me all about Aunt Josephine and her machinations. Now what about Kate?'

'She's making the best of it,' Sally said.

'That sounds ominous. Aren't they in love any more?'

'In a way,' said Sally. 'Of course Kate's no diplomat and I bet Guy's difficult. Fiona's a little swine. Born bad, so that doesn't help. He's getting on like a forest fire, incidentally.'

'That's good, surely?'

'Good for prestige and the pocket. Not that money's needed. Kate has enough of her own.'

Hester felt a slight chill as Sally talked of Kate. It was impossible to make out the cause of the rift between Kate and Guy, if indeed there was one, and Sally could not tell her mother that their differences had never shown up till she ran away with Gianni Morelli and rocked the family circle.

'What about the senior Lamberts?' said Hester, when they had exhausted the subject of the younger ones.

'As they always were. He's all paunch and pockets. She still enjoys ill health. But, to be fair, she's really fond of Kate. There's no doubt about that. And she's very good with baby sitting.'

'Things could be worse, I suppose.'

'Yes. But there's no gaiety about any of the Lamberts,' Sally said. 'They're so prim and proper. They're what Dad calls suburban.'

'That's it!' exclaimed Hester. 'Dad always hits on the right word.'

Sally noticed that Hester always referred to her ex-husband as 'Dad' and wondered if that's how she thought of him. There was no doubt that George looked as though he was her father and Gianni was indisputably her husband.

Guy had done remarkably well in the five years since he left the R.A.F. It was as though he had been marked out from the first by Major Harvey, head of his department, and yet, as he so often said, he had no one to push him so why was he scaling the ladder at this rate?

'With your record? Where's the mystery?' asked Kate. This pleased him. He liked to hear her praise him.

He worked long hours, the demands of his job came before everything, and she did her best to help him in every way she could but she was not cut out to be the wife of a hard, ambitious man which was what Guy had become. Qualities in her that bewitched him when she was eighteen were drawbacks now she was twenty-five. Her shyness, her inability to mingle easily with his colleagues and their wives at social gatherings, and a positive genius for saying the wrong thing were not exactly assets.

His work took him away a good deal and although she did not like his absences they made the times he was at home all the more precious. She felt as though she was on honeymoon again, recapturing the joy of waking up in the morning to find him by her side. This made up for the strain of party-going with his new friends. She had been at ease with his R.A.F. comrades and loved the evenings in the mess, the informal dances, the sheer bonhomie, but these commercial people were different. She could never think of anything to say at the parties they went to. Guy would drift off leaving her marooned with a glass in her hand, trying to smile.

'It's no use. I'm not a cocktail person,' she would tell him.

'You needn't be a wet blanket,' was his answer.

This hurt, and yet he had so many good points. He insisted on her having a car so she would not be tied to the house; they went to a play or a film at least one evening a week and Ella looked after Fiona. She was happy then but could not understand why he got so irritable if she asked him when he would be back from a trip. Not to the hour, just simply the day. He objected. He could not be tied and what was more refused to be, not even for special occasions like birthdays, anniversaries.

'You and your old-fashioned ideas,' he scoffed. 'All this cut and dried stuff with meal times and occasions. You're a Victorian aunt.'

'I think it's just good manners,' she said.

'Can you imagine a conference with me asking to be excused while I ring the little woman who's just about to dish up a chop for my dinner?' He never failed to make her feel silly and small.

'It's my dinner, too,' she countered.

'Now, look. You just have your dinner and don't worry about mine. If I'm late I'll eat out or make do with a sandwich. All right?'

It was useless to say more. She made matters worse every time she opened her mouth and there was no one to turn to for advice now Hester had gone. She would not have discussed her problems with anyone else in the world – not even Sally.

But it was not just meals and times, it was everything. They should have been able to sit together and talk, exchange thoughts and ideas, see things together, hear things – the rain on the roof, the wind in the trees – live together in the kind of companionship she thought of as marriage. Her own mother and father had been ideally suited so she had no experience of clashing temperaments. She had expected her life and Guy's to merge together in the same kind of partnership.

There was no denying her disappointment but she never stopped hoping things would improve. They would have another child eventually and in the meantime she would remember to choose times when he was not overworked to tell him of any domestic problem; she would never mention

Hester in an unguarded moment or talk of the happy times she had enjoyed with her.

Her reward was the glow she felt when he was his old self, when she could turn to him in bed and feel his protective arms round her and say, 'We're all right, aren't we?'

'Of course we're all right. What a silly little shrimp you are.'

He only had to say something as simple as that and all was right with the world. Or almost.

Things improved still more when Tom Lambert's firm moved south and he came back to live with his parents. Kate had only a slight acquaintance with Guy's brother but she found he was easy to know and easier still to like.

The first time she was alone with him was when he called one evening just as she was about to put Fiona to bed. Fiona, as usual, did not want to go.

'Shan't, shan't, shan't!' she said.

'What's this? Mutiny?' asked Tom.

'Come along, Fiona. Let's have no nonsense,' said Kate, embarrassed to have her brother-in-law see what a refractory child she had.

'I won't go to bed till Daddy comes home,' shouted Fiona.

'Oh yes you will.'

Fiona opened her mouth and emitted a high-pitched scream followed by another and another. Kate could have sunk through the floor. Tom looked on in amazement. Then, without any notice, he raised his forefinger and stabbed it at the child, at the same time making a most ferocious grimace. Fiona's screams stopped. 'Up those stairs,' he ordered. She began to clamber up one at the time, stopping to peep at him through the banisters every so often. Kate had no more trouble getting her to bed.

'How on earth did you manage that?' she asked when she came down.

'Just the element of surprise,' he said. 'Are you going to offer me a drink, Kate?'

'Of course. We'll both have one.' She poured gin and tonic. It fizzed deliciously. 'What must you think of me,

not being able to control a creature as small as that?'
she asked.

'A little perisher, isn't she?'

'Guy can manage her. She eats out of his hand. Gosh,
isn't this gin lovely?'

'I'll say. It's all the better when you're not supposed to
have it.'

'Are you on the wagon?'

'Supposed to be. Still, once in a while, you know.' He
smiled at her, raising his glass. Then he said, 'We've never
had much of a chat, have we? I've always wanted to tell
you how sorry I was about the Sheridans. You must feel
it very much as they were such good friends of yours. And
of your mother's and father's, too, I believe.'

'They were. And they're still my friends, both of them,'
she said.

'And their funny little girl — Sally, wasn't it?'

'That's right. She's not such a funny little girl nowadays.
In fact, she's quite attractive in an odd sort of way. What
do the French call her kind of looks? *Belle malade*, is it?
It means ugly-beautiful.'

'I think you mean *belle laide*,' he said.

'Yes, of course I do. She came down from Oxford with an
honours degree and she's working at the Treasury now.'

'Twopence to speak to her, I suppose?'

'Sixpence.'

'I must save up. And Mr Sheridan?'

'He's in America and doing well. The Americans simply
swoon over his English accent and his voice. Especially the
girls. Sally says he's quite a pin-up boy.'

'I never really knew him, more's the pity. I feel as though
I've missed out.'

Kate found Tom so sympathetic and responsive that she
was soon talking about the Sheridans without restraint and
it did her good to recall the happy times she never thought
would end until Mrs Sharkey and Sam went to the cinema
together. It was Mrs Sharkey's day off, Kate explained, so
she was perfectly entitled to go and as she said herself,
how could she have foreseen that Gianni Morelli would
choose that very day to turn up when poor Mrs Hester

was alone? 'Tisn't as if it was a good picture I saw,' she told everyone concerned. 'It was a stoopid picture, worst I ever saw. Should a come out. Might a got home in time to stop 'em committing adulchery.'

Mrs Sharkey could not bear to look at the barn. She seemed to think the Eyetie had dragged Mrs Hester there against her will and nothing would convince her otherwise.

'So you see, Tom, that's how it happened,' Kate said. 'A whole world came to an end. Only a very little world, but it was George and Hester's and Sally's and poor old Mrs Sharkey's. And mine, too, though not in the drastic way it was for them.'

'I'm glad you told me,' he said. 'I've heard my mother's version and a very spicey one it is. But then Mum's account of anything needs to be treated with caution, especially if it reeks of scandal. But do tell me, between ourselves, is Hester really a wicked woman?'

'She most certainly is not!'

'I'd like to meet her again.'

'Then you'll have to go to Santa Carlotta – the Hotel Villa Laura. Why not? You could spend your summer holidays there. Sally says it's beautiful.'

'She's been there then?'

Their conversation was brought to a halt by Guy coming in. He had obviously had a good day for he was in the best of humours and very pleased to see his brother. He had always been devoted to Tom and would listen to him and take his advice. Tom, for his part, admired his young brother's courage and daring and was proud of him. He never felt the slightest tinge of jealousy because Guy was the apple of their mother's eye, it seemed natural that this should be so, and although Tom was older he was content to take a back seat.

He accepted Kate's invitation to take pot luck with them and stayed the whole evening. It was the best evening she had spent for a very long time for he created an easy atmosphere and drew her into the talk which made a change for her. So often, with Guy's friends, she would sit dumbly by, unable to offer a remark or contribute an opinion. She saw Guy was looking at her with some surprise for she was laughing, cracking back at Tom, teasing, holding her own. He had a tonic effect on her.

'Isn't it splendid having Tom home,' said Guy when his brother left. 'He really is the tops. It's a pity his health is so bad.'

'What's wrong exactly?'

'I suppose it boils down to no stamina. He was always ill as a boy — pleurisy, pneumonia, bronchitis. One thing after another and it's weakened him.'

'Perhaps he'll be better down here. It isn't so cold,' she said.

After his initial visit Tom came frequently and Kate's liking for him increased the more she knew him. It seemed as though the whole tone of their lives improved through his influence. She could almost forget she was at odds with Guy over Hester so time went by smoothly and could have been almost perfect but for Fiona who became increasingly difficult. She showed great affection for her father, none for Kate who could not help worrying about it although Guy said there was no cause for concern.

'I'm a bit of a novelty, that's all,' he said. 'She doesn't see very much of me but you're with her all the time and you're the one who has to tick her off when she's naughty. It's tough on you now, but she'll get over it.'

'I hope so,' Kate said, but she still wondered and could never forget the time Fiona turned on her with real hatred in her face. She had been invited to a school friend's birthday party and was all ready to go when Guy came home unexpectedly.

'I've taken the afternoon off so let's drive down to Maidenhead and have tea there,' he said.

'Yes, yes yes!' cried Fiona.

'But you're going to Mandy's party,' Kate reminded her.

'Not now. I'm going with Daddy.'

'No, Fiona. You're invited and expected. Come along now. Put your coat on.'

'Couldn't she skip it?' asked Guy in an undertone which Fiona picked up.

'Certainly not,' said Kate.

'I'm going with Daddy!' Fiona stamped her foot. Her face blazed.

'Fiona, put your coat on at once. It's time we left.'

'Daddy, don't let her make me go. I don't want to go to the party. I want to come with you.'

'I'm afraid you can't, pet,' Guy said. 'Mummy's right. You have said you'll go, so go you must. No more nonsense now.'

Fiona had worked herself up into a rage. She started to scream and kept on with piercing shrieks in the worst tantrum they had ever seen till Kate caught hold of her and shook her so hard she stopped from sheer surprise.

'Look, suppose I take you to the party,' Guy said. 'We'll go to Maidenhead another afternoon.'

Fiona was slightly mollified. 'Will you take me in the car?' she snuffled.

'If you're good.'

'Will you stay at the party and bring me home?'

'If I'm asked.'

At the front door Fiona turned round and said: 'We shan't want *you*, Mummy.'

Kate ignored this and addressed Guy. 'Here's Mandy's present,' she said, handing him a packet wrapped in gift paper and tied with pink ribbon. 'Wish Mandy a happy birthday from me, Fiona.'

Fiona ignored her.

Kate went in and got on with some sewing she had on hand.

Guy stayed at the party and apparently enjoyed it, or at least the children enjoyed having him there. When they came home Fiona compared notes with him on all that had happened without including her mother. That evening when Kate put her to bed she could feel a kind of resistance. She bent for the goodnight kiss but Fiona turned away. 'Aren't you going to give me a kiss?' she asked.

'No.'

'Why not?'

'Because I don't like you.'

'You know you don't mean that.'

'I do. I love Daddy but I don't like you. So there!'

Kate turned out the light. She tried to brush off this exchange but in her heart she had the chill feeling that Fiona really meant it.

The worst of it was that the child's attitude did not change over the years. Fiona soon began to notice the small differences between her parents and seized on the slightest criticism her father might make of her mother. 'Darling, I wish you'd shown a bit more enthusiasm when I asked the Pattersons here,' he might say, or 'I think your pink suit's better for the cricket match this afternoon.'

It was as though Kate never did anything quite right and Fiona's face would assume a superior expression which implied she agreed with her father and deplored her mother's stupidity. 'Fancy putting on that rotten old blue dress when you're going to meet Daddy's friends,' she seemed to say without uttering a word.

Kate looked forward to the time when Fiona would go to boarding school which she did when she was eleven years old. She enjoyed term time with the rather guilty feeling that she ought to be missing her daughter and wondered where she was at fault.

'Is it me?' she asked Sally one day.

'No, it is not,' declared Sally emphatically. 'You've been landed with the reincarnation of a disagreeable ancestor.'

'I don't know anything about my ancestors,' said Kate.

'What about Guy's? Fiona could be the reincarnation of Ella Lambert.'

'Don't be an ass. Ella's not dead yet. And she's not all that bad,' said Kate.

Tom called at that moment and contributed a few of his own ideas about ancestors, reincarnation and allied subjects. Kate drifted off to the kitchen to make tea and it amused her to hear Sally and Tom talking although she could not hear what they said. The tones of their voices blended harmoniously together, Sally's chuckling laugh, Tom's unexpectedly deep voice. It occurred to her that Tom almost invariably called when Sally was there. They obviously liked each other and she wondered if a little gentle matchmaking would be in order. Perhaps a foursome to the theatre sometime?

The idea caught on. Guy was always at his best in Tom's company and although he was wary of Sally he did not dislike her. Their outings and excursions became a weekly event and Kate revelled in them. Tom would always see Sally home to her flat afterwards.

When they were alone Kate liked to sit on the floor with her head on Guy's lap and her arms round his knees. 'I'm so happy,' she would say.

He stroked her hair, petted her, pulled her up on the sofa beside him. 'You dear, silly little Kate, it doesn't take much to please you.'

'Much!' she exclaimed. 'I've got everything. I'm the luckiest woman alive.'

This was not strictly true. She wanted another child but she had never been able to coax Guy into agreeing. Time was going on and her dream of a large family had almost slipped away.

Sally heard from her father at regular intervals and usually showed Kate his letters. He had gone to the States thinking he was finished only to find he was beginning again in a way he would never have thought possible. It was generally agreed that his knowledge of the eighteenth century, both historical and social, was without parallel and his published essays always attracted a good deal of attention. At home his lectures were well attended but here they were packed out. His turns of phrase, his humour, the way he threw in odd anecdotes, soon got him the reputation of being quite a star. All this pleased Sally considerably and relieved her of some of her anxiety on his account. She had always appreciated his work, loved to hear him talk on his favourite subject or tell her of his finds in research, but even she was flabberghasted when she heard he had been asked to appear on television. Such a thing had never happened at home.

'Isn't it smashing!' she exclaimed, as she and Kate pored over the letter that brought the news. 'Good old Dad! I must write and tell Mum.'

After this everything snowballed. Apparently George attracted such a large audience and was the recipient of so many letters and invitations he had to engage a secretary to deal with it.

Monny Brown was one of the many he interviewed and he chose her because she was not too young or too beautiful or too overqualified. She also had a soft voice. She had other attributes which he discovered as time went on. She could make a good cup of tea and he liked tea much better than coffee. She did not talk too much. She looked pretty when the weather was warm. With all her quietness she still got things done with an efficiency that baffled him. She dealt with the mail before he had even read it; she arranged his tours, booked hotels, saw he was not pestered by the innumerable luncheon club ladies who wanted to engage him and, all in all, she made his life so smooth that he could get on with his work in peace.

He was to discover how valuable she was when she had to stay away with a devastating cold. He simply did not know what to do without her. He went round to her apartment with a huge bunch of flowers and a bottle of whisky and found her with lank hair, a red nose and eyes bulging with cold.

'Don't come near,' she croaked.

For answer he hugged her hard, kissed the top of her head and said: 'I can't get on without you, Monny. You'll have to marry me. Will you?'

'When I get rid of my cold,' she said, and put the kettle on.

And so George, who thought happiness had gone for ever, found it had come back in a different guise. He often told Monny he loved her more with every day that passed and there was no doubt she loved him.

Sally felt like throwing several hats in the air when her father telephoned her. It was one of many calls he had made but hearing his good news and his pleasure when she told him how glad she was for him and for Monny and for herself made them feel as close as though they were in the same room.

There was one small disappointment for her. Kate, the one person she was burning to tell, had gone away for a motoring weekend with Guy and she would have to wait till Sunday night before she could share the news. Aunt Josephine already knew and approved. She rang Sally to say so. That left Mrs Sharkey. It was Saturday so off she went to Heron House.

On this fine afternoon the house looked exactly the same as when they all lived there and she could hear the noise of the motor mower so Sam must be cutting the grass. Strangers were sitting in the garden – the Americans, she supposed. They looked very much at home.

She went round to the kitchen door and caught a glimpse of Mrs Sharkey sitting at the table with the newspaper spread out in front of her. Sally wondered what she was making of it today for Mrs Sharkey's method of reading the paper always left her in a state of indignant confusion. 'Lot o' nonsense,' she would proclaim. 'Don't make sense.' As she read down the first column and then the next without ever following the instruction to turn to a page further on this was not surprising but no amount of explaining could ever convince her there was more than one story on each page and if there was it was because the printers didn't know their business. 'Drunk, the lot of 'em,' she would say.

Sally tapped gently on the window and at the sight of her Mrs Sharkey's face broke into a broad smile and she hurried to open the door.

'What brings you so unexpected, my lamb?' she asked as Sally hugged and kissed her.

'Wonderful news from Dad, Shark darling!'

'Is he coming home?'

'Not yet. He's married.'

Mrs Sharkey stepped back. 'Course he's married. Always has been. That's not news,' she said.

'*Re-married*, Shark.'

'What's this you're telling me?' A look of disbelief had wiped the smile from Mrs Sharkey's face. She sat down again and Sally sat too and put her hand over Mrs Sharkey's.

'He's married a marvellous American girl and he's very happy. I am, too. And so must you be.'

'That I'm not,' declared Mrs Sharkey. 'Mr George is married to Mrs Hester and nothing can change it.'

'But Mum and Dad are divorced, Shark. They're both free to marry again.'

'Stuff and nonsense. Mrs Hester was kidnapped by that

199

wicked Eyetie and why Mr George didn't go and rescue her I shall never know.'

She looked so grim and forbidding as she spoke that Sally was at a loss to know how to win her over. The old girl had always been devoted to Hester and would never understand why she deserted George. It was clear she had been hoping for a reconciliation and now she knew it would never be.

'Wouldn't you like me to tell you all about it?' Sally asked.

'You've told me.'

'I wish I could help you to see the good side of it. After all, it was rotten for me when they split up. I felt as though the world had come to an end, but I wasn't a child and I just had to put up with it. Mum's happy with Gianni and now Dad's happy, too.'

'Well, he don't deserve to be. Neither of 'em do. Happy indeed! What about their dooty? Took vows, didn't they? Neither of 'em's dead yet so vows still hold.'

'They got married in a register office, Shark. So there weren't any vows. Not like in church.'

'You telling me they lived in sin all those years?'

'Of course not. Oh, Shark, you're impossible.' Sally got up. Her journey had been wasted and there was no point in staying if she was not going to get any further. She went to the door.

'Where you going?' demanded Mrs Sharkey, looking up.

'Back to London.'

'Oh no you're not. Not without your tea. Never heard of such a thing. Sit down at once.'

Sally smiled inwardly and sat down meekly while Mrs Sharkey filled the kettle and slammed the crockery about as though she was punishing it. 'Going off without your tea,' she kept muttering. Sally stayed quiet. The less said the better, she thought, although there was a lot more she wanted to say.

Mrs Sharkey was spreading bread and butter, getting out the jam. She took Sally's bag off the table and threw a cloth across. She banged down two plates, got half a cake out of a tin. When it was all ready she sat down herself, poured

200

the tea, and handed the bread and butter. There was a lace doyley on the plate and Sally realised Mrs Sharkey was not relaxing her standards even in the kitchen. Perhaps it was no wonder she could not approve of people divorcing and remarrying, especially people who were so close to her. There was a long silence till at last she spoke.

'What's her name then?' she asked in a sulky tone.

This took Sally by surprise but it meant Mrs Sharkey was coming round.

'Monny,' she said.

'Monny? Huh! What sort of a name is that?'

'Short for Monica.'

'Huh.'

Another long pause. Then: 'Young?'

'She's not a chicken.'

'Just as well.'

Long silence. Then: 'Slice o' cake?'

'Please.'

'It's on the dry side. You can jam it if you like.'

'Oh thanks, Shark. That will be a treat.'

It was madeira cake − Sally's favourite. 'You know,' she said, 'I wouldn't be a bit surprised if Dad comes back here to live later on.'

'Time I retired if he does.'

'Oh, Shark, why?'

'Think for yourself. Can you see me taking orders from a person called Monny? And her his second?'

'You're spoiling it all for me,' Sally said.

'I don't want to do that, as well you know, but I've got my feelings.'

Sally half expected a loud sniff to follow this remark but it didn't although the ghost of it hovered in the air.

'We both have our feelings,' she said. 'I'm only sorry you can't take pleasure in Dad's new happiness the same as I can.'

This time Mrs Sharkey did sniff and at the same time took an enormous snow white handkerchief from her apron pocket and wiped first one eye and then the other. She was crying for something that could never be, the restoration of what she always thought of as her family, intact and as it

201

had been long ago. But that was all before the war and the war had changed everything. The girls had grown up, Mrs Hester was seduced by an Eyetie and poor Mr George had gone to America. Been there years now. Six, was it? Or eight? Eight. Eight long years. Oh dear, oh dear. Still, it was not for her to damp Sally's joy. If *she* didn't mind her father remarrying why should anyone else complain, especially as Sally had pulled her chair up close and had her arms round her and was saying sweet, endearing things.

'Take no notice of me, Sally,' she said at last. 'I'm just a silly old woman who takes good news for bad.'

This revived Sally's spirits but she still felt rather dashed and longed to impart her news to someone who would greet it with real enthusiasm. As it was she looked forward to a solitary weekend and wondered how to fill it. Of course she could write to Dad and she must certainly let Hester know but, oh, for the sound of a familiar voice, the touch of a hand.

The telephone was ringing as she entered her flat.

'Hallo,' she said, her voice rather flat.

'Look, I don't see why you and I have to give up our weekend treat just because the other two are off on a jolly. How about dinner, Sal?' It was Tom. That wonderful deep voice.

'Tom! Oh, I'm so glad you rang. I've had some good news and I'm bursting to tell someone. Not over the 'phone. It's too special for that.'

'Be with you in half an hour,' he said, and rang off.

He had never been inside her flat and she wanted his first impression to be good. Just time to rush out and buy some flowers from the stall at the corner. Pink roses, carnations, lots of feathery green stuff. She arranged it all in a copper bowl, straightened curtains, plumped up cushions, rubbed up the silver drinks tray. When the bell rang she was almost out of breath.

'Well,' he said, looking at her and not noticing anything else, 'what's up? Have you had a promotion?'

'No. It's Dad. Let's sit down and I'll tell you.'

They sat on the sofa and as she poured out her story he took her hands in his, watching how her eyes sparkled behind the rather thick lenses of the glasses she wore and thinking how unselfish she was. He marvelled at the way she could devote herself to both parents, never blaming either of them for their break-up and looking back with nothing but gratitude.

'So you see, Tom, Dad is really happy now and I'm so thankful. Now he's got Monny I don't have to worry any more.'

'Did you before?'

'A bit. Rather a lot, really.'

'Super,' he said, noticing how the sweetness of her expression transformed her far from beautiful face and made her the loveliest girl he had seen in all his life.

The sun was going down and outside the sky was full of little grey clouds which changed to deep pink in its rays and then gradually faded through many more magical shades until they were grey once more.

They were both standing at the window watching this transformation and unknown to each other they were both full of the same longing. If only I had the right to ask her, was the thought in his mind while she was thinking, if only he would.

At last he plucked up enough courage to say: 'Wouldn't you like to get married, Sal?'

'Yes,' she said, without hesitation. 'What about you?'

'Me? In my state of health? It wouldn't be fair to ask anyone. Anyway, who'd have me?'

'I would,' she said.

There was a long pause and her heart sank. She loved him, was in love. She had seen what love did to others and sworn never to let it happen to her yet here she was boldly admitting it and his silence must mean he scorned her.

At last he said: 'It wouldn't be fair to you. I haven't even got a very good job, lucky to have one at all with the amount of sick leave I take. No company wants to insure me. One lung's collapsed; I'm asthmatic, bronchial, my chest sounds like a nest of mice.'

'I know all that,' she said.

'So though I love you with all my heart I can't let you

marry me. I've an idea you quite like me but I won't let you waste your life on me.'

She did not respond straight away. The effort of making his feelings plain had tired him. He sat on the arm of a chair. The light had almost gone. At last she turned from the window and put her hands on his shoulders.

'Tom, if your health is as bad as that we'll get married at once,' she said. 'No arguing. You've lost the motion and you're hooked.'

The long delayed embrace, the rapturous kisses, the things he said! First she was his dear, adorable Sally, then old four-eyes or cuddly little Teddy bear — above all she was his own true love.

Theirs was a quiet wedding. Two witnesses in off the street, then straight to The Avenue to tell Kate.

'You've been very sly about it,' she said when she recovered from her surprise, but she saw at once how right they were to throw caution to the winds and seize their chance of happiness.

'But you were very, very sly. Both of you,' she said again.

'Think so? Imagine the parents of the bride and groom posing for the wedding photo. Dad with Ella, Mum with Ernest. What a record for the album!' said Sally.

Kate couldn't help laughing. It would have made a very odd picture indeed.

Ella Lambert was furious and made no secret of her disapproval. 'I never imagined such a thing could happen in *my* family,' she moaned.

'What's so terrible?' asked Kate. 'They're so right for each other and Sally will take care of Tom as no one else could.'

'Including his mother? Really, Kate.' Ella positively bridled. 'If you imagine Tom has not been taken care of all his life you must be very thoughtless.'

Kate did not think it would be wise to remind Ella that Tom had spent most of his adult life away from home and had not been taken much notice of when he was there.

'However, we'll let that pass,' Ella went on. 'No, it's the fact that a son of mine has allied himself with the daughter of that immoral woman that distresses me. And I hear they've gone to Santa Carlotta for their honeymoon. Surely it can't be true?'

'They've gone to the Hotel Villa Laura, as a matter of fact.'

'It's the same thing, isn't it?'

Kate agreed it was.

'Disgraceful. It seems they give no thought to anybody's feelings but their own.'

'I'm sorry you feel so strongly about it,' Kate said. She longed to say a great deal more but realised every word in Sally's favour would only strengthen Ella's determination to discount each of her good qualities.

Tom had seen a corner house for sale in Magnolia Road and decided to buy it. It was newly built like all the others in the road and not much more than a stone's throw from Guy's much larger and more impressive establishment in The Avenue.

The elder Lamberts lived a good half hour's walk away for which Sally and Kate were thankful although Sally's gratitude far exceeded Kate's. She had never pretended to like her mother-in-law and Ella scarcely troubled to conceal her disapproval of Sally. She remembered her as a very plain, saucy child when they lived in The Clearing, not in the least like pretty well-behaved Kate, but even if she had been a paragon of beauty and virtue she would still have been tainted by her mother's immorality.

Ella still shuddered when she thought of Hester Sheridan and the very mention of her name brought back that scene in the barn. It was all very well for Tom to take a tolerant view but he had not seen what she saw. Guy, dear Guy, understood her aversion and shared her disgust. And to think Tom had married the woman's daughter! But then he wasn't like Guy. Once he actually defended the woman and told her, his own mother, that she didn't know the first thing about being in love.

'You don't know what it's all about, Mum,' he had said. She wished he wouldn't call her Mum. Such an ugly word. Why not Mother, as Guy called her? But that was Tom

205

all over and she feared very much that his character would deteriorate still further under the influence of his horrid little wife.

She did not like their house either. A nasty pokey place in a very common road with very common neighbours. Tom called it a snug little box in a jolly little road and the neighbours only seemed common to Ella, not to them, he said.

Sally loved the house but admitted it had disadvantages. It was at the top of a steep incline so the garden was a problem. There was no way they could have a lawn so they made a huge rockery and she used some of the money from her father's wedding present to buy the right kind of stones. They spent time and trouble deciding which plants and shrubs to choose and where to place them, and as Tom was not strong enough for the work involved Sally managed it with the help of a jobbing gardener and the Allens who lived next-door. The effect was striking: little paths among the rocks, alpine flowers, dwarf conifers.

A path from the patio at the rear of the house led down to the side gate which they used constantly as theirs was a 'No entry' road so reaching the front door meant making a lengthy detour. Consequently it was much easier for cars to stop at the side gate. But that, as Tom often said, was a mere detail. Ella did not agree with him. 'There's no luck in a corner house,' she said.

'Come off it, Mum,' said Tom, for whom life had never been better.

Sally gave up her job at the Treasury when she married. She wanted to be a full-time wife and it seemed no time at all before she was a mother as well. Her son, Paul, was born exactly eight months and three weeks after the wedding.

'I was a virgin bride so you needn't start counting up on your fingers,' she told her mother-in-law when she visited her in the nursing home.

'Really, Sally! What an outrageous thing to say!' exclaimed Ella, dropping the flowers she had brought up to the bedside table.

'It's a whole week short of nine months so people are entitled to wonder,' said Sally.

206

'It is *not* a subject to joke about,' said Ella, po-faced. 'Just an embarrassment.'

Sally managed to stop herself from saying the baby was the dead-spit image of the milkman.

'And now we must think abou the christening,' said Ella after a rather long silence. 'I've kept the robe my boys wore when they were christened. And Fiona, too. She was such a lovely baby. It's Brussels lace and fine tucks with the tiniest pearl buttons . . .' Her mood had softened. She was thinking of Guy as she carried him to the font. He had not cried once. Tom, of course, howled the church down and went blue in the face.

Sally was hardly listening. She was so drowsy and if the old girl enjoyed twaddling on about tucks and buttons why not let her? Soon she would be going home to Tom and a life full of riches. Her miniature daffodils and narcissi would be out in the garden soon. And there was to be a trip to the States in the summer to see Dad and Monny. How fantastic it all was. Monny was pregnant so she would have a little brother or sister by the time they went and Paul would have a baby aunt or uncle. Just as though he appreciated the comical side of this Paul's face creased up in a smile. 'Oh look,' Sally said, 'he's smiling.'

Ella looked and shook her head. 'That, my dear, is wind,' she said.

Tom was overwhelmed by his good fortune. To have a wife and now a son – if he had been so short of breath he would have turned somersaults, and as it was he had much ado not to stop strangers in the street and tell them he was a father.

'What more could any man wish for?' he asked as he and Sally looked out over their domain. They had a house, a garden, they had each other, and their son was a healthy, good-tempered, affectionate child. He was soon holding out his arms to Kate whenever she came near and chuckling when she picked him up. He's not even my nephew and yet I feel he's so close to me, she thought, and her heart ached for her dream children, the large jolly family she wanted so much. But perhaps – who coud tell? – that hope might be realised, and others too. Sally wanted them all to go to Italy and said it would do young Fiona good to be thrown amongst the exuberant Morellis.

Kate agreed. She was able to keep in touch with Hester through Sally although she didn't mention it to Guy and cherished the wish to go to Italy one day. She attended an Italian class one afternoon a week.

'It would be heaven if we could all go to Santa Carlotta,' Sally said when they talked of holidays. 'Try to talk Guy into it.'

'I daren't. He'd explode.'

She knew it wasn't worth risking his indignation by suggesting it. She would have to bide her time and if she concentrated hard enough it would come about, just as Sally had told her the very first day they met.

Sally was always running round to see Kate and it was not long before everyone in The Avenue knew her because she knew them. Not for her the brief nod, the cool, half-embarrassed good morning, for Sally always stopped to speak. She admired front gardens, spoke to children, petted dogs and held long conversations with cats. Kate got to know her neighbours better, too, at least in so far as she could for Guy had no wish to mix with them.

Ada Fortune often declared that it did her a power of good to see Sally because she radiated happiness and Paul became a great favourite with her and with Jack. He was enchanted by their garden with its streams and stepping stones and other such delights. It was magic to a small boy to stand on a stone and look down at the water plants with tiddlers swimming about in swarms, water beetles scudding on the surface, and sometimes the glimpse of a goldfish.

Tom had no ambition at all. His modest salary was just enough for their simple life style and Sally had discovered a new hobby. She enjoyed stretching the money and became expert at it. She could have written a book on ways to spin it out and when she went down to Heron House to see Mrs Sharkey they spent hours in conference exchanging recipes and hints and having competitions to see who could make a pound go furthest.

Kate frequently wished Guy was more like his brother

208

for his success in business was not improving his character. She cherished the belief that the real man she had married and loved so dearly was still there though obscured by his burning desire to be first among his colleagues. They were as determined to reach the top as he. Outwardly friendly, they would have trodden on one another's faces to be first past the winning post. Oh, if he had only stayed in the R.A.F. how happy we would be, she thought, and remembered the impromptu dances in the mess with pleasure while dreading the annual dinner and dance of Guy's firm.

The dinner was the easiest part, the dance the hardest. They always had the first dance together but after that Guy considered it his duty to dance with the wives of all the important men in the firm. She did not understand why these men did not seem to consider themselves bound by the same obligation towards her, and frequently sat out long periods alone.

She had often asked Sally why she was a wallflower and could hardly believe the suggestion that men were afraid of beautiful women and felt safer with the plain ones.

'I hope to goodness I'm not left stranded this year,' she confided to Sally who had come round to help her get ready.

It was winter, cold, dreary and overcast. Kate had a new dress. It was in a striking shade of red, a glowing colour.

'You look stunning!' exclaimed Sally. 'You'll be the belle of the ball.'

'I doubt it. The competition among the wives is fierce.'

'No one's going to better that. Has Guy seen it?'

'He chose it.'

'Good for him.'

Guy came downstairs, handsome in white tie and tails. He was very pleased with Kate's appearance and congratulated himself for choosing the dress. 'I'm proud of you,' he said.

'Just because I look nice?'

'I'm just as proud when you're in your old gardening rig. Come on, we're going to have a whale of a night. Can we drop you off on the way, Sally?'

'Yes, please.'

'What are you and Tom doing this evening?' Kate asked when they were in the car.

'Reading by the fire and thinking of you two wining and dining.'

'We must do that sometime, Guy,' Kate said.

'Do what?'

'Sit by the fire and read.'

'When I retire,' he said.

His remark made her feel cold and shivery but as they drove up to the hotel she made herself a promise. She was going to overcome her natural shyness and enjoy the evening.

Sir Ian Hurst, the managing director, and his wife were receiving the guests. Sir Ian, a tall, grey-haired man – Winchester and Kings, as Guy often reminded her – gave Kate a kindly smile. 'How charming you look, Mrs Lambert,' he said. She returned his smile, encouraged. Guy's hand was under her elbow, steering her on. 'We'll circulate,' he said.

There was soft music from an octet. '"Lilac Time". Tauber,' she said.

'I thought it was Schubert,' said Guy.

Waiters with trays of sherry threaded their way skilfully through the crowd. They both took a glass and toasted each other. Kate's eyes were dancing. She loved the music and she loved Guy. It was wonderful to be with him. When she looked round the room she could not see anyone to equal him for looks or bearing. She glowed with pride and pleasure.

Major Harvey, the head of Guy's department, spotted them and made his way over. He greeted Kate effusively and asked if she had looked at the seating plan. Not yet.

'You're at my table, of course,' he said. 'I don't like the arrangement at all so we'll alter it. Can't have husbands and wives sitting next to each other. You won't mind being parted from your husband, will you, Mrs Lambert?'

'Not at all,' she said, although she minded very much.

When it came to taking their places for dinner she found she was at the end of the table with no one on her left. Guy was on the same side but near the top next to Mrs Harvey so she couldn't see him. She had never met the young man on her right and he was absorbed in the girl beside him and talked to her throughout the meal, scarcely acknowledging Kate until she asked him to pass the salt. Her only hope was to try striking up a conversation with the elderly man opposite. He appeared to be deaf for when she spoke he leaned forward with his hand cupped round his ear and gave the wrong answer to her remark that she hoped it wouldn't snow.

'Yes, indeed. It will be nice if it does,' he said.

Discouraged, she concentrated on the food. Speeches followed the long-drawn out meal. The speakers cracked the usual jokes, they toasted members of the firm, one begged to take wine with all the gentlemen whose hair had receded to the crowns of their heads, another toasted the man with the prettiest wife upon which every man present raised his glass, and so it went on but not, mercifully, for too long as there were only two hours left for dancing and the ballroom and orchestra were ready.

'Sorry we were separated,' Guy said as he and Kate joined the throng leaving the diningroom. 'It wasn't too bad, was it?'

'With no one on my left and the man on my right turning away from me all through dinner?'

'Pity the plan was changed. Still, we'll make up for it now. Let's be first on the floor.'

The orchestra struck up a waltz and Kate adored waltzing with Guy. It was a dream. She was in his arms and he was looking down at her, smiling, pressing her to him. 'Darling Kate,' he whispered. 'Love me?'

She did. It was wonderful, swooningly wonderful. Oh, it was just as it had been; all the enchanted moments crowded in and all the disappointments were crowded out.

The music ended. 'Let's have another dance soon,' she said. He took her arm, led her back to the table Major Harvey had reserved for his party. A quickstep followed. 'Must ask Mrs Harvey,' Guy said. Major Harvey was already on the floor, Guy followed with Mrs Harvey, and soon Kate was alone.

Next time, a foxtrot, Major Harvey asked her for a dance

but after that she was abandoned every time and her heart sank and sank. Guy didn't even return between dances, he was doing the rounds and obviously enjoying it.

After a while, when she seemed to be the only girl sitting out, she was surprised to see Sir Ian Hurst making his way towards her.

'I'm afraid you're not enjoying yourself,' he said, taking the seat beside her. 'That husband of yours should be looking after you.'

So he had noticed. Her colour rose. 'I'm perfectly happy,' she said quickly. 'I enjoy being a spectator − it suits me quite well.'

'You make a very decorative one,' he said.

She laughed. 'At least I'm useful that way,' she said.

'Perhaps you're like me − not in your element on occasions like this? I'd much rather be at home with a book − or even at home without one.'

'So would I,' she agreed fervently.

It surprised her to find how easily she drifted into conversation with the most important man in the room and very soon he was chuckling over some of the things she said. He was drawing her out, encouraging her to tell him what amused her, and without meaning to she spoke of the Fortunes and their wireless aerial, their mob caps, their curious habit of walking single file when they were out. She talked of Henley, of Mrs Sharkey and her malapropisms, and then, because he asked, about her family and her lack of relations.

'But I'm lucky in so many ways,' she said. 'Guy's brother, Tom, married my best and dearest friend and they live near us. We have lovely times, the four of us, running down to the coast at weekends or playing tennis or even weeding our gardens.'

He had sat with her through two dances − quite a long time. When the dancers returned to their tables he said: 'Come and talk to my wife. I believe you only had a brief word when you arrived.'

He offered his arm and they proceeded across the floor with everyone watching. She knew Guy's eyes were boring into her back. He would want to know everything that had passed

212

between them and she hoped she could remember it all.

Lady Hurst greeted her with great kindness. She was an elderly woman of the type that looks like an ideal granny which is exactly what she was — unpretentious, comfortable, and as easy to be with as her husband. She had noticed the contrast between Kate and the other wives with their sharp eyes, their sophisticated repartee. Kate's beautiful, calm face and her simply dressed hair appealed to her but it was plain to see how vulnerable she was, how lost in this smart, brittle crowd.

Sir Ian had left them and was in conversation with another group. Kate did not want to outstay her welcome with Lady Hurst and was able to detach herself gracefully when the Harveys came to speak with their hostess. She did not want to return to her own table and sit alone again so she made for the powder room, titivated a bit and then wondered what to do next. The attendant was sitting in a Lloyd Loom chair knitting. Kate admired the work, the pattern was the same as a pullover she had made for Guy. She managed to use up a whole half hour with the woman and would willingly have gone on if Mrs Harvey had not come in.

'Oh, there you are!' she exclaimed. 'Your husband's looking for you everywhere. It's the last waltz.'

'I'd lost track of the time,' Kate said. She followed Mrs Harvey down the wide staircase and there was Guy at the bottom. He led her on to the floor. The lights were dimmed.

'Where the hell did you get to?' he asked angrily.

'The only place I could think of to retreat,' she said.

'You were missing for a damn' long time.'

'Did it matter? Major Harvey was the only man who asked me to dance. It's very hard sitting out with a fixed smile pinned to your face.'

'You know quite well I have to do the rounds,' he said.

'I know. I know. Next time I'll bring my embroidery.'

How different this waltz was from the first. What a perfectly horrible evening it had been.

'Anyway, what was Sir Ian talking about?'

'I'll tell you later.'

They drove home in uncomfortable silence. Indoors she poked up the fire and the caked dust collapsed into a glowing red mass with sparks flying up and caves and peaks discernible in the midst. She held her hands out to the blaze, thankful to be home. Guy came in and put his hands on her shoulders. 'Look — I'm sorry you didn't enjoy it,' he said.

'I begin to wonder if I stink.'

'Don't take that line for heaven's sake.'

'Why am I always left out? Am I so off-putting?'

'Sir Ian obviously didn't think so. What were you talking about?'

'Nothing really. He began by saying you should be looking after me. I had to pass that off as well as I could.'

He sat down. 'Thanks,' he said. 'It sounds as though I've blotted my copybook.'

'Of course not,' she said. 'But it was lovely talking to him. We got on like a house on fire and were eye to eye in so many things. He laughed when I told him about the neighbours and how you helped the Fortunes raise their wireless pole.'

'Good God! You didn't tell him about them?'

'Yes, I did. And about Mrs Sharkey's funny talk and — oh — everything. All our goings on. He wanted to know.'

'You bet he did. Well, you've cooked my goose good and proper. Don't you know if a man's to get on he must have a wife he can take anywhere? You with your half-witted chat! You've just about put paid to my chance of stepping into old Harvey's shoes when he goes up one next year.'

All the colour had gone from Kate's face. She stood up and said quietly: 'So that's what you think of me? I'm glad I know.'

His scorn had withered her, seared her heart, scarred her incurably. Without another word she went upstairs and to bed. Tears poured from her eyes but she managed not to sob. Later, when Guy came, she lay still and quiet and at last, after he was asleep, she slept too.

Next morning she went silently downstairs in her dressing gown. She wanted time to think before Guy got up and she sat by the fire again. It was out, the hearth was full of grey

214

ash and the colour reflected her mood. What was she to say?
How was she to behave? As though nothing had happened,
she told herself. Go on as usual. Get breakfast. Take him a
cup of tea. Later she would break her rule of never discussing
her differences with Guy and seek comfort and reassurance
from Sally. Having made up her mind about that she felt
a bit better. She made the tea and took a cup up to Guy.
She put it on the bedside table.

'Kate,' he called as she left the room. 'Katey, come
back!'

She closed the door behind her.

He came down dressed for work as she was taking
the breakfast things in. She sat down and helped herself
to toast.

'Kate, I didn't mean what I said last night. Heaven knows
what possessed me to speak to you like that. I'm sorry.
Really I am.'

'I expect you are,' she said. 'You gave yourself away.'

'You know I didn't mean it.'

'Didn't you?'

'Of course not. It was reaction because the evening turned
out so badly.'

'No, Guy. It was anger because you thought I'd let
you down – spoilt your chances. Don't pretend it was
anything else.'

'Katey – '

'It's time you left and you've eaten nothing.'

He looked at the clock, gulped some coffee. She went
into the hall for his coat and held it for him to put on.
She would go on in the customary way. She opened the
front door. He put his arms round her but she turned her
head away so he could only brush her cheek with his lips.

'We'll talk tonight,' he said.

'You'll be late. Let me close the door. It's cold.'

She would have given the world to cry when she was alone
but Mrs Sims was coming and would want to know all about
the dance and she must say it had been better than ever and
her feet were worn out.

Sally was sorry to hear about Kate's wretched evening and

215

its outcome. It was monstrous of Guy to say such horrible things. She had no doubt Sir Ian had really enjoyed his talk with her and admired her naturalness. She might well have enhanced Guy's prospects rather than blighted them. She told her so that afternoon. She knew very well that Kate's loyalty and devotion to Guy was why she had never complained of him before so this time she must be mortally hurt.

'He as good as told me he can't take me anywhere,' Kate said. 'I'm a washout. A hindrance to him. What am I to do, Sal? What would *you* do?'

'Harden my heart,' Sally said.

'It feels like a stone now. And already, this morning, he was apologising, making out he didn't mean it. But he did, Sal. He did.'

'At the time. Not now. He took it out on you because you'd had such a rotten time and he knew jolly well he should have done something about it.'

'It's ruined everything.'

'Think how good it was at first and pretty well ever since. You've had ups and downs with Fiona being so difficult but you've been happy, haven't you? So has Guy. This is a bad patch. You'll recover.'

'Perhaps, but I'll never forget.'

'This may be your chance to start again,' said Sally after a pause.

'How?'

'By getting tough. You give in to him all the way. He wipes the floor with you and you mustn't let him get away with it. You *must* take a stand, Kate.'

Kate felt weak at the knees. She didn't know where she was going to find the courage to behave as Sally advised. She was pretty sure Guy would be full of blandishments this evening; he might bring flowers, chocolates, an expensive present. She must refuse to accept any of it. Not nastily, but firmly. They very last thing she must do was to throw an atmosphere.

'Thank you for being such a brick, Sal,' she said.

'What about some tea and toast?' Sally suggested. 'Paul's playing with the kids next door. I'll pop in and fetch him while you make the toast.'

Kate went into the kitchen and cut slices from the loaf,

then she sat on the floor toasting it with a long handled fork. It was wonderfully relaxing and she began to feel better. Paul came running in, flung his arms round her neck and rubbed his face against hers. He dropped some postcard-sized photographs on the floor.

'Grandpa sent them,' he said.

Grandpa, of course, was George Sheridan and the photographs were of his two infant sons with their mother, Monny.

Kate was looking, at them when Sally came in. 'Aren't they little ducks?' she said. 'My little brothers, and Paul's uncles. He's bewildered by the whole thing. Uncles have to be old men in his book.'

'That's not surprising.'

'I'm looking forward to the day when they all come home and settle down at Heron House,' Sally went on.

'Do you think they will?'

'Certain of it. Dad wants the boys to have an English education and Monny agrees. Won't it be wonderful?'

'It will,' Kate agreed.

'Only another year or two. I don't know how to wait,' Sally said.

She was making the tea, talking from the kitchen, and Kate was buttering toast. Very soon they were sitting in front of the fire, enjoying it and scorching their legs.

'You have to hand it to Monny and Dad,' remarked Sally. 'They've invited us over in the New Year, so that'll be great. There's an advantage in having divorced parents. It extends the family circle.'

'Will you go to Santa Carlotta next year?'

'In the summer.'

They went on talking in a desultory way till Kate noticed the time and said she must be going. It was dark and raining. 'Lucky you brought your Gamp,' Sally said. She looked out anxiously. Tom should be home by now, she thought, as she saw Kate off.

Two miles away Tom was waiting for a bus that never came. The icy wind blew through him and the rain came cascading down. At last there was nothing for it but to walk the two miles home. He kept the picture of Sally and Paul before him as he plodded on. To think Paul was five years old already, and from a baby to a toddler to an infant he had pleased everyone except his grandmother who said he was a very noisy child. Tom had to admit he was. He was a lion, a tiger, an owl or a train, and he made appropriate noises as he raced round his grandparents' garden on Sunday afternoons. Worse still he had taken to calling Ella Granny Boodle and she resented it and hinted he got it from Sally as he was too young to have thought of it for himself.

How thankful they were to get back home on those Sunday afternoons and how thankful he was to be home now. He put the key in the door and went into the warm, comfortable sitting room where the fire glowed red in the grate and there they were, his wife and son. Nothing mattered to him but being home with them.

When Kate went in at her front door she was surprised to find Guy already there. He met her in the hall, greeted her with a kiss and took her wet umbrella. 'I'll bring some coffee,' he said.

There were no flowers, no presents, so she was spared the necessity of refusing them. At least he wasn't going to try bribing his way back in to favour.

They drank the coffee and he said: 'Katey, can we talk?'

'Of course,' she said. 'But not about last night.'

'Are you still cross with me?'

'I'm not going to talk about it.'

'I want to explain.'

'No explanation is necessary. Now please drop it. I'm going to cook dinner.'

He followed her into the kitchen and asked if he could peel the potatoes, a thing he had never done before. The peelings were so thick she nearly asked him if he was going to sell them. He was almost subdued all the evening, had not brought any work home with him and did not talk about it either. She began to wonder if she had handled the situation properly and decided to ask Sally next day.

In the morning when she rang Sally she couldn't ask her

218

opinion because Tom had arrived home soaked through the night before and was staying in bed. Knowing his delicate health she immediately saw her own problem as trivial. As soon as Guy came home she told him the news and they set off for Magnolia Road and were thankful to find Tom much better. He was ensconced on the sofa with a rug over his knees and a shawl round his shoulders. The warmth of the fire had lent colour to his face and Kate said she had never seen him look so well.

Sally had made a large saucepan of soup and insisted they all had some. They sat round the fire balancing the bowls on their knees and spilling crumbs on the floor.

'Lucky Mrs Sharkey can't see us,' Sally said.

They were talking so easily and comfortably, just as they had always done when they were all together. There was nothing wrong – harmony, bliss. Kate began to wonder if she had imagined the unpleasantness after the dance. Now she was to be envied, perhaps as never before. Of all their good times as a foursome, surely this was the best?

They left early so as not to tire Tom even though he declared he felt fine and was going back to work next day.

'I feel wonderful,' he said as they left.

Next morning he died peacefully in his sleep just as the sun was rising.

'Who on earth can be ringing at this hour?'

'Wrong number,' Guy said sleepily and turned over in bed, but Kate ran down to the hall wishing they had an extension in their room.

She didn't recognise the caller's voice at first or take in that it was Sally for she spoke in a hoarse whisper. 'Please come. It's Tom. Please come, Kate.'

No time to waste talking. 'I'll be with you right away,' said Kate.

She hurried back to the bedroom shouting at Guy to buck up because there was trouble at Sally's. She pulled on slacks, a thick pullover. She didn't even drag a comb through her hair before she was off running down The Avenue in the frosty dawn and over to Magnolia Road, latch key in hand.

There were voices from upstairs. She recognised Dr Graham's but before she could go up he appeared on the landing, saw her and shook his head. Then he came slowly down. He patted her shoulder. He was the family doctor and had known her all her life, just as he knew the Sheridans and the Lamberts.

'There's nothing to be done, my dear,' he said, and he told her Tom's life had ended peacefully and without suffering.

'I must go to Sally,' she said when he finished telling her.

'No, my dear. She wants to be alone with him. I've rung the undertakers and they will be here to take him away in two hours' time. Paul is still asleep. Are there any friends who can have him for the day?'

Kate was sure Ada and Jack would be glad to look after him.

'Will you arrange it? And then stay with Sally. Don't leave her alone.'

'I won't,' Kate said.

She was shocked out of her mind and yet she could behave sensibly and talk calmly with Dr Graham. It was as though her feelings were on ice and could be kept there while she made the necessary arrangements. There was so little time — less than two hours now. First she rang Ada and made provision for Paul; then she went next door and asked Mrs Allen to stay in Sally's house while she took Paul to the Fortunes; next she sent a lengthy telegram to Mrs Sharkey. All this was done by the time Guy arrived. He knew what had happened without being told.

He had lost many friends in the war but never anyone close, never anyone like Tom, and the effect was devastating. She was frightened by the way he crumpled up, convulsed with sobs. She was numbed, he was not. The terrible truth struck at him with all its force and she had to restrain him from going up to his brother's room and bursting in on Sally's vigil. She managed to persuade him to go to The Laurels and break the news to his father. The thought of his parents' anguish helped him to control his own.

Her worst fear was that Paul would wake and come

out to see what was going on but this didn't happen. His surprise at seeing her when she opened his door gave way to delight and she found herself almost believing the lies she fed him. Mummy and Daddy wanted to be quiet today so she was taking him to have breakfast with the Fortunes. That would be fun, wouldn't it? Then he could spend the day operating Jack's trains. They might even take him to the Science Museum.

His eyes goggled. 'I've always wanted to go there,' he said.

When he was ready there was just time to walk him to the Fortunes who rose to the occasion with all the kindness she had come to expect of them. She was sickened by her own deception and on the way back her thoughts reverted to Tom and Sally and her frozen heart began to thaw. With the thaw came grief and pain. The idea of either of them without the other was insupportable. Sally had gloried in her marriage, cherished every moment with Tom, been grateful for every chance to help him, never complained about the restrictions his health imposed. Sally had helped her through her own grievous loss. Now what could she do for Sally? All I can, Kate vowed.

But Sally was so stunned she scarcely seemed to know Kate was there. She sat staring in front of her and Kate, beside her, held her cold hands and tried to impart the sympathy she felt. Tried to be to Sally what Sally had been to her.

The telegram bringing the news of Tom's death came as a thunderbolt to Mrs Sharkey. She could not grasp it, read it over and over again and then gave it to Sam, begging him to tell her she'd got it all wrong.

'You haven't, Mum,' he said, scratching his head. 'I wish as you had.'

He sat down opposite her at the table and she cried into her apron, wiping her eyes on the coarse hem and eventually taking a grip of herself and staring at him hard. 'I'm off to London,' she announced in an aggressive tone almost as though he was opposing her. 'I'm off up there and you're not going to stop me. I tell you that for nothing, Sam Sharkey.'

'I'm not stopping you,' he said in an aggrieved tone. 'I think as you ought to go. It's your duty.'

'And who are you to tell me my dooty, I'd like to know? Do you think I don't know my dooty after all these years?'

'Come on, Ma. Go and pack up your traps, have a bite to eat and I'll run you to the station.'

'Very kind, I'm sure,' she said as she stumped out of the kitchen, leaving him to think about Sally's loss and to wish he could do more to help than running his mother to the station. What'll Sally do? he wondered. Tom was moon and stars to her, that he was.

Sam had got the idea of people being moon and stars to each other from one of the novels his mother read. The idea puzzled him and made very little sense but he rather liked the sound of it though he would not have uttered it aloud, not even for a couple of pints.

At Magnolia Road Mrs Sharkey found Sally in a state of shock. Stricken, as she told Sam when she returned to Heron House. Stricken. That's what she was, the poor dear.

Sally had not been able to shed a tear until Mrs Sharkey came but when she saw her she gave her a great hug.

'Oh, you darling old Shark. Thank you for coming,' she said.

With scarcely a word Mrs Sharkey had brought all the kindliness of Heron House with her and it was as though Hester and George were both there to give comfort.

How Sally cried. How she spent herself crying.

Kate's intuition told her evenings and Sundays would be the worst times for Sally. Tom's hand on the latch of the gate, his key in the door. Those were sounds Sally would never hear again but she would think of them. Kate knew this and took care to be with her at those times. After a while she devised ruses to get Sally out of the house.

'Let's join an Italian class,' she suggested. 'There are several at the Institute.'

'I know. I started ages ago and dropped it.'

'Why not take it up again? I'm going to. But it will be beginners for me.'

'Me too. I've forgotten all I knew.'

They both joined. The hours suited Paul's school times.

They could meet him when he came out and have tea on the way home at the one remaining teashop. Several other mothers with their children gathered there so it became a pleasant social event and the proprietor always saved the stale bread for Paul to feed to the ducks on the pond opposite.

At least that was one afternoon a week catered for, Kate thought, and she found things to do on other days.

But Sundays ... Those pre-lunch drinks. Tom had revelled in his brother and Kate coming for sherry and now he was no longer there Kate worried about what they should do. She did not think they could ignore it and Guy agreed with her. They decided to ask Sally and Paul to lunch on Sundays.

'We'd love to come only you must come here for sherry first, just as you always did,' Sally said.

Kate faltered. 'But, Sal, wouldn't you prefer to have it at 24?' she asked.

'No,' replied Sally. 'You and Guy always came to *our* house. I want it to go on like that. It would be a comfort to me. You do understand, don't you?'

Only then did Kate realise what this little Sunday ceremony had meant to Sally. With their limited means the bottle of inexpensive sherry was a luxury to be enjoyed with the two people they loved. Someone had given them a set of good glasses for a wedding present and it was their joy to get them out, and then to sit talking, happy and at ease as they sipped their wine.

She had to blink hard. 'Oh, darling, darling Sal, I *do* understand,' she said.

Often in the seclusion of her own house, Sally felt she would burst with the agony of loss. She would beat on the walls with her fists, knock her head against doors, let her hopelessness tear out of her throat in loud animal noises.

Once, waiting on a railway station, she heard a young calf lowing and found it tethered up in a goods wagon. It had just been taken from its mother and she never forgot the despairing noise it made. Passengers, pausing to look at it, said it would soon forget, soon get over it, but how could they tell how long its misery would last? Perhaps it would keep it inside all its life beating away like a separate heart, and no one would know.

She, too, kept her misery inside. She rallied all her inmost resources and bounced back as Paul's cheerful, loving mother.

How well she's got over it, people said.

Once, at a coffee morning with Kate, they both overheard somebody say just that and walked quickly away.

'Can you understand it?' asked Sally, seething. 'Oh, how I'd like to tell them sometimes. Let's go before I choke.'

'I understand exactly how you feel,' said Kate, and she did. 'But, you know, you *are* resilient,' she went on. 'You're never a misery.'

'No one would want to know me if I were.'

And Paul? Sally was thankful to find he had inherited her resilience. She taught him to be independent, sent him on small errands, and if he mistakenly brought home the wrong brand of tea she sent him back to change it. She talked of Tom a great deal, making sure he would never forget his father, reminding him of the things they had done and the places they had been to as a family.

'We're going to stay with Dad for Christmas,' she told Kate. 'It will be fun for Paul with those little uncles. Another on the way, I'm told.'

'Goodness! They *are* going it,' said Kate.

'It will get Christmas over, that's the main thing, and next summer we'll stay with Mum. Aren't I lucky to have them?'

For answer Kate got up and gave her a hug. 'Darling, Sal, you're a brick,' she said.

Sally often talked of living in Italy when she discussed her changed circumstances with Kate. 'We can stay here within range of Tom's family, or else Italy. The States are out long-term because Dad will come back with his brood.'

'Which do you really favour?'

'I love Italy — but then there's Paul's education. I doubt if Tom would want him to grow up there. And I'd miss you, Kate.'

'And I you.'

Their lives were entwined more than ever now. Without

Tom. Almost without Guy for he seemed lost now his brother had gone. Kate knew he missed him terribly but he didn't say. He wouldn't talk about anything but work, work, work.

Sometimes, in bed, she took his hand and held it to her breast. 'Talk to me, Guy. Talk to me,' she said.

'What do you want to talk about?'

'Everything. Us. Them.'

'Talking won't help,' he said. 'Much better get a good night's sleep.'

She turned away. Bereft, lonely. She could have wept but tears were useless, self-indulgent. I must pull my socks up, she told herself. And I will.

It was almost Easter before Sally came back from America. She had felt so much better there and no one could be dull with George and Monny and their family. Paul was in his element; he insisted on calling the boys Uncle Jamie and Uncle Charles although they were his juniors. He patted Monny's stomach and asked if she had a little aunt for him inside. He called her protuberance his Aunt Eliza.

'Eliza? I don't like that much,' Monny said.

'Why not?'

'It's very stiff and old-fashioned.'

'That's what aunts are like. Ask Grandpa. He's got an aunt called Josephine.'

'I hope to meet Aunt Josephine one day,' said Monny.

'And I hope my little Aunt Eliza won't be like her,' said Paul. 'Not to look at, I mean. She always wears a hat. Has Aunt Eliza got one on now?'

'I don't think so,' said Monny. 'It would be rather uncomfortable for me if she had.'

The time went too quickly and Sally felt the wrench of parting from her father keenly but it was mitigated by the prospect of going to Santa Carlotta in the summer and when she and Paul reached Magnolia Road there was Kate waiting to greet them. She had filled the house with flowers, stocked up the refrigerator and store cupboard, and even started to weed the garden so Sally did not have to contend with the terrible emptiness and quiet she dreaded.

225

'Angel! You really are an angel,' she said when the first greetings were over.

'You'd do the same for me,' said Kate. 'Now sit down and tell me all about everything.'

There was so much to tell and it was all good. Sally had taken to Monny as soon as they met; the little boys were cute; Dad had shed at least ten years and was happy as a piglet in clover, and so generous. He had given Sally a cheque that would more than cover the trip to Italy and all the expense it would incur and was in the process of making her an allowance.

'So you see, Kate, my financial problems have melted away,' she said. 'I can go up to town and buy some shoes and a dress and all that kind of thing without having to scrape. It's such a load off my mind.'

'When will you go?' Kate asked.

'When the mood takes me. I want to wallow in the comfort of home first, catch up with neighbours, go to see awful Ella, and of course dear old Shark. We must spend a day with her. I've got a few presents for people, too. Yours is a coffee maker. I'll bring it along tomorrow.'

She rattled on and Kate marvelled at her fortitude. Somewhere, deep down, she had a strength she could draw on. Somehow, Kate thought, she never lost anyone; separation – even death – did not part her from those she loved. Through all the trauma of Hester's defection and George's misery she had never once blamed either of them although she saw the picture clearly and sometimes described it to Kate. George fell in love with Hester for her youth, beauty, helplessness. Above all he wanted to protect her. Hester felt betrayed for her mother's decision to remarry, causing the little world she had worked so hard to create to be blown asunder. She had liked and admired George from the moment they met and his unexpected proposal opened another door for her. She was flattered. She fancied herself in love but what she really felt was deep affection and trust. Years went by before a prickle of discontent disturbed her and she began to feel something was missing. She had never known romantic love and if it ever came it would be her duty to resist.

226

'But when it did come, she couldn't,' Sally said. 'Poor old Mum.'

Kate was amused at the idea of Hester being a poor old mum. Maternal she was, an old mum she most certainly was not.

Sally went up to town on a fine day in May. She bought a sundress, sandals, a beachbag; things she could easily have bought in Italy but she didn't want to spend her time there shopping. She wanted to laze on the balcony with Hester, go for walks with her, visit the Morellis, stroll up to the piazza to listen to the military band, and most important of all discuss plans for the future.

Things were changing for Hester and Gianni; one or two multi-storeyed hotels had been built close to the sea and others would follow. The day must come when hotels like the Villa Laura would be pushed out of business and Gianni had plans to forestall this.

As far as Sally knew there was no settled plan yet so she didn't mention it to Kate. Better to wait till she knew more. She was thinking about it when she joined a queue for the bus home. She leaned against the bus stop sign and closed her eyes. The sun was warm on her face.

That was the last she knew. She was aware of a monstrous roaring sound, that was all, that and the screaming as a man on a powerful motorbike ploughed into the queue, demolished the concrete post and all but demolished her with it.

The accident brought traffic to a standstill. Police, ambulances, the road sealed off. Kate and Mrs Sims heard the news on the wireless as they were having lunch. One killed, several injured. Later it emerged that the rider made off in the confusion and was never caught. The bike was stolen.

'I'll lay he was drunk,' Mrs Sims said.

'Or doped,' said Kate, peeling an apple.

Neither dwelt on the subject. The diningroom curtains were home from the cleaners and the next job was to hang them. Mrs Sims held the steps while Kate mounted aloft and had just fixed the first hook when a police car stopped outside and two officers came up the path. She dropped the curtain and came down with a horrible fluttering feeling inside. The bell pealed.

'Shall I . . .?' Mrs Sims was still holding the steps.

Kate ran to the door.

'Mrs Lambert?'

'Yes,' she said. 'Please come in.'

They followed her into the dining room. They told her Mrs Sarah Lambert had been hurt in an accident and Kate's name and adress were found in her wallet. She nodded. Her voice had gone. When she tried to speak it came out in a husky whisper: ' . . . dead?'

They put her mind at rest quickly. Sally had sustained multiple injuries and was in hospital undergoing surgery.

They were kind, considerate. Mrs Sims showed them out leaving Kate, dazed, on the sofa. She was still there when Mrs Sims handed her a cup of tea and said: 'We've got to get weaving.'

There was so much to think about and to do. Kate wanted to go to the hospital but realised she could do no good there.

There were people who must be told; she ran over to Ada who offered to fetch Paul from school and bring him back to her own house. There were the friends in Magnolia Road. They all wanted to rally round. Help of all kinds was offered and accepted. She decided against ringing Guy, time enough to tell him when he came home and he would spare her the unenviable job of breaking the news to Ella.

Kate almost hated the beauty of this day in May and the days, weeks and months that followed were difficult. Hester came and stayed for a week in Sally's house. She looked after Paul and visited her daughter every day with Kate. That was the one blessing in the whole sad affair, being with Hester again for hours every day and talking, talking as they had always done.

The whole summer went by and when Kate looked back on it afterwards it seemed unreal, just as the loss of her parents had seemed unreal. For a long time it was feared that Sally would never walk again but, being Sally − and only those who did not know her were surprised − she got back on her feet, battered, crippled but undefeated.

First she was on crutches, then she could manage with two sticks. Paul grew very important and assured her he was going to keep house and take care of her when she was allowed home.

'Mrs Sims has taught me how to make rock cakes,' he told her the day before she left hospital.

'I can't wait to sample one,' she said.

He produced one from his pocket in a paper bag. It was more like a brick than a cake but she ate it valiantly.

'Delicious,' she said.

Doctors and nurses were amazed at her progress.

'You are a wonder, Mrs Lambert,' one of them told her.

'I have to be. I have a small son to bring up,' she said, but in spite of the lively way she spoke she felt a deep sense of injustice at what had happened. Even in perfect health it was not easy to raise a young son without a father's influence. A boy should have men around him. Of course there was Guy but he did not have a very high place in her estimation. Her name for him was 'the unwilling uncle'. While Tom was alive Guy had been bearable, almost likeable, but now he had reverted to his priggish, superior way and was more like his mother every day.

She did not subside gently and make out she could see a divine purpose in her misfortunes. She did not forgive the cyclist who had crippled her. If I could catch him I'd blow his head off, she said, and she told Kate it was not for her to forgive. Why should she forgive a man who had blighted her life? Did she feel bitter? 'Yes, but I must try not to. Bitterness shows in your face and I don't want any more lines on my homely mug.'

But for the most part she kept her anger to herself, knowing full well it would not help her and might antagonise others. She tried to reckon up her advantages: her father who had invited her to bring Paul to live with him and his young family; her mother in Italy with the warm-hearted, exuberant Morellis. It was comforting to know they were there and that she and Paul were wanted. These were options to think about and consider. In the New Year she would put her mind to it. And yet this house, hers and Tom's, and the rockery they

229

had created, so many memories, such pain in recalling them, almost fancying she could see Tom out there in the garden, knowing she would never hear his voice again, praying she would not forget the sound of it.

Everyone marvelled at the progress Sally made but she jibbed at her forced inactivity. She had always enjoyed going about, bus rides, coach drives, exploring places that were new to her although not very far away. She found plenty to look at in other suburbs and almost always came across curious people, quaint shops, things that enriched her already overflowing life. Now she had to spend a good deal of time sitting.

'Take up dressmaking,' said Kate.

'Not on your life. I remember the larks in The Clearing only too well. That silk shirt your mother nearly made for your father.'

Kate began to laugh. 'Mummy was a wonderful needle-woman but a hopeless dressmaker,' she said. 'She could neither cut nor fit.'

'She was an ace at blouses,' said Sally.

'That's why she thought she could make a shirt. You were there when she nearly came to blows with Daddy over it.'

'He said she stuck more pins in him than ever she stuck in a pincushion.'

'That's when we agreed my parents were more like children than children.'

'So were mine,' said Sally.

'Anyway, Sal, what about petit point? You could make cushion covers.'

'Much too fiddly.'

'Ordinary embroidery then. We can both do it. One each for your sofa.'

'I suppose I might as well while I'm sitting here. Oh, but how I long to sprint round the houses again.'

'You will. In time.'

Summer subsided into autumn and a new school term began. Mrs Allen, Sally's next-door neighbour, offered to drive Paul to school, but first she had to ferry her husband to the station. As there was no entry back into Magnolia Road she stopped at the side gate to pick Paul up. In the

230

afternoons she could take a detour and drop him off at his own front door. The only disadvantage was that Sally had to unbolt the side gate in the mornings and that meant going down the slope.

'It's no bother. I can manage easily with two sticks,' she told Kate who was worried about it.

'It would be much better for you if you had a rail to hang on to,' said Kate. 'Don't you think so, Guy?'

'Good idea. Why didn't you think of it before?'

'Oh, really!'

'I'll find someone to put one up,' Sally said.

'Don't do that. I'll put it up for you,' Guy said.

'Will you? That would be super.'

He took the measurements and ordered iron posts and a wooden rail. He refused Sally's offer to pay, saying it was the least he could do. Rails and posts were delivered in record time and stowed in the garage but by then the evenings had drawn in so outdoor work had to wait for weekends. Guy never seemed to have free time even then. Saturdays were nearly always given over to his own work or to visiting Fiona at school and taking her out. On Sundays he liked to lie in, then there were drinks with Sally, and in the afternoons the weekly visit to his parents.

'I can't see you ever getting that rail up,' Kate remarked more than once.

'Good grief, when have I had a minute? Have a heart!'

Later he said he would do it after Christmas when he would have a few days off but by then the winter had set in. Bitter frosts made digging impossible. 'You couldn't push a pin into the ground,' he said.

'Never mind,' said Sally, but she made up her mind to get a man to do it as soon as conditions improved.

Christmas was as good as could be expected without Tom. There was a family dinner at Kate's as Ella only found herself equal to putting on a tea. 'My health is deteriorating, dears,' she said sadly, but she was spry enough when she was asked out.

Guy had to endure an evening with the Fortunes, paper hats and tinsel all over the place, and then there was the pantomime. Aladdin. The whole family went, pretending they did so for Paul's sake but no one laughed louder than Ernest Lambert. All in all it could have been much worse.

'It'll be the sales now. How I'd love to go,' Sally said.

'Anything special you want?' Kate asked.

'I'd love another Liberty scarf,' said Sally.

Kate immediately said she would go up to town and buy her one. She knew Sally was making a tremendous effort to keep her spirits up though the time of year and wretched weather didn't help so she talked of summer and the projected visit to Santa Carlotta.

'I can't wait to get there,' Sally said. 'Just thinking of it cheers me up.'

Outside the sky was leaden, the fallen snow black and filthy.

'Mind how you go on the way home,' Sally warned Kate.

'The same goes for you ten times over. Look, I'll go as early as I can tomorrow. Promise you won't even step outside.'

'Fusspot.'

'Truly, Sally. I mean it. It isn't safe for you.'

It occurred to Sally that Kate had forgotten Paul started back to school next day and she would be seeing him off. Still, might as well promise. Anything to stop her worrying.

'All right,' she said.

Kate was reassured.

Now her first year without Tom was over and the morning was as cold as her heart but Sally's voice was light and cheerful as she got Paul ready for school.

Yesterday Kate had come and spent hours sweeping the snow away from the path but it lay thick on the rockery. Paul said it would take a week to sweep it all away.

'We'll wait for the thaw. Spring's coming,' she said.

A car hooted by the side gate. 'There's Mrs Allen for you. Time to go,' she said.

He went out of the kitchen door and began to descend the path, looking back anxiously to see she was all right. She moved with caution, step by step, leaning on her two sticks. Hospital tomorrow, she thought. What a drag. But they were so pleased with her. Who would have thought she would be able to see Paul down to the gate so soon after her accident? Yet here she was unbolting it, moving into the road to the stationary car which had three children in the back seat.

'Will Kate be coming to see you today?' Paul asked.

'Not till this evening. She's going to the sales today.'

She waved to the children, Mrs Allen opened the door and Paul got in beside her.

'You'll catch cold without your coat, Sally,' she called.

'I'm going straight in,' said Sally. She waited till the car drove off, then she went back inside, closed and bolted the gate and began to make her way up the path, wishing she was going to the sales with Kate.

As Sally began her upward climb Guy was telling Kate she was crazy to think of going to town in such terrible weather. The snow had been lying thick, hard and frozen for days and there was more to come.

'Here's a nice beginning! 1963 will be the worst winter since records began. It says so here,' he said, rattling the paper at her.

'Yes, but it will all have melted in Regent Street.'

'Take a look at this.'

She glanced over his shoulder at a picture of the moors under six foot drifts. A man in the foreground carried a sheep across his shoulders. There were hundreds more buried up on the hills. Farmers were digging them out.

She shivered. 'Thank heavens we live down here. I wouldn't live up North for anything.'

'It's as bad in Devon.'

She thought of animals starving, foxes desperate for food burrowing into the snow and gnawing the live sheep. The vivid fur of the fox, the grey-white fleece. Blood. She pushed her plate away, not daring to let her mind dwell on the suffering.

They were having breakfast at the little Queen Anne table near the window and watching the few passers-by straggling along to the station. They all walked with their heads down; some wore balaclavas with various types of

233

headgear perched on top. The bank manager from further up the road sported a bowler on top of his. They walked carefully, picking their way.

The branches of the flowering cherries that lined the road were weighed down with snow. Jack Fortune came out with a broom and knocked some off.

'To think those trees will burst into flower before we know where we are,' she said. 'And long before that the snowdrops. Quite soon now. Don't you think it's wonderful?'

'What's wonderful?'

'Why, everything.'

Blank.

Once again she had failed to communicate her sense of rapture. But we must catch at the good things, the promises. She remembered a quotation from school days: 'A man's reach should exceed his grasp or what's a heaven for?' It was given as a subject for an essay and she had tried to express herself with such deep feeling that her effort came to grief. Sally, with extreme simplicity, succeeded brilliantly.

'Sally wants me to get her a silk scarf from Liberty,' she said. 'That's really why I'm going.'

'Sally has enough silk scarves to make a shroud.'

'What a horrid thing to say. Anyhow, she wants another.'

'All right. If you're ready I'll give you a lift to the station,' he said.

'I'll just ring her.'

'Not now.'

'I always ring her at this time.'

'I'm late already,' he said. He had started the Rover up before they sat down and it had been pulsing away outside the garage all through breakfast.

She hesitated a second, then hustled into her coat, dragged on her boots and grabbed a woollen cap.

He opened the front door. 'Got your cheque book? Money?'

She had. He took her hand and they scrunched out to the car and drove out of the gate and down to the main road where sand and salt had turned the ice to filthy black sludge.

'Won't it be lovely when we're home round the fire tonight?' she said.

They had drawn up at the station. He leaned across and kissed her. 'Don't stay out in the cold too long,' he said. Then: 'I like that cap. It suits you.'

She valued any compliment he paid her far beyond its worth; the most casual praise from him meant worlds to her. Although she would not admit it, even to herself, she was rather in awe of Guy, even after sixteen years of marriage. Not afraid. This was different from fear. It might, perhaps, be called diplomacy and meant taking care to avoid conflict, suppressing or toning down opinions that differed from his – in other words, watching her step. She did not like it but she accepted it.

Strangers, meeting her for the first time, said she looked years younger than her age. When she told them what it was they said she must have been snatched from the cradle. She would laugh, pleased to be flattered, glad the sorrows of her life were not reflected in her face.

But now, as she bought her ticket, went up to the platform and boarded the train, she knew she was unlikely to enjoy her jaunt to the shops. It would have been different if Sally had been able to come. Kate found shopping alone an ordeal. She was indecisive and would dither over a bargain so long that someone else snapped it up under her nose. Sally went straight for what she wanted and got it.

Today her luck was in. She found the very scarf Sally would like, bought two pairs of gloves for herself, a cashmere pullover for Guy and three model trains from Hamleys for Paul. Fiona, skiing in Switzerland with a school party, did not need anything new.

She did not like lunching alone and wondering what to order so she had a sandwich and coffee before going along to Orlando Hope's. Her father's shop was situated in a side street between Pall Mall and Jermyn Street. The first thing she saw when she looked in the window was a globe about the size of a small egg made of lapis lazuli with all the countries of the world depicted on it. She stood admiring it for some time. It would be lovely to hold.

John Proctor, who managed the shop, had known her all

her life and came forward, hands outstretched in welcome, as she entered. 'Well, well! It's good to see you on such a gloomy day,' he said. 'What brings you to town this weather?'

'The sales. Sally and I always come together and she wanted a scarf so I wasn't going to let a snowfall stop me.'

'Good for you, Kate. You look blooming anyway. How is Sally going on?'

'Very well. Better than any of us would have believed. She refuses to be beaten. You know what she's like when she sticks her chin out.'

'Indeed I do.'

John Proctor had been a frequent visitor to The Clearing and he knew the Sheridans from those days and had always admired Sally. She had struck him as a game little girl with a good deal more commonsense than either of her parents.

'We must go down to see her soon,' he said. 'Alice is always saying.'

'Wait till the freeze is over,' said Kate. 'You'll be amazed at the progress she's made.'

'That's something to look forward to. Now, is there anything you want? I think I see an acquisitive gleam in your eye.'

'I was admiring the little globe in your window. May I see it?'

'Of course,' he said.

When Guy was away on one of his trips she always followed his route on the large globe in Fiona's room but if she had this she could hold it in her hand and feel she was with him.

'Is it very expensive?' she asked, taking it from him.

He told her the price. 'I *do* like it,' she said. 'I can't resist it. Would you take it off my next month's instalment?'

'My dear, you don't have to ask. You are a partner, after all.'

'A very somnolent one.'

'Any time you feel like waking up – '

'Perhaps, one of these days.'

While he made out the account for her to sign she looked round the shop where she had spent so much time as a child. A framed photograph of her father hung on a wall over a shelf where the most prized acquisition of the day was always displayed. It was a studio portrait by a famous photographer and was still considered one of the best he had ever done. Orlando Hope was in his prime when it was taken and there he was leaning back in his favourite armchair in the act of filling his pipe. Although it was black and white she saw it in colour; she could see the tapestry of the chair and the carved mohogany back and her father's face, quite young, full of humour, with the beginning of a smile. Only the suggestion of a few grey hairs.

Mr Proctor's hair was grey all over. His kindly face lined. I suppose Daddy's hair would be grey by now, she thought. And what about Mummy's? Hers would probably have just faded a bit. Fair hair fades — it wouldn't have gone grey.

'Here you are, my dear.' Mr Proctor's voice almost startled her. He was handing her the package, asking after Guy and if Fiona was back at school yet.

'She's in Switzerland skiing and in no hurry to come home' Kate told him.

'Quite a young woman, I suppose?'

'Between ourselves I sometimes feel she's older than I am. I'm nearly frightened of her.'

'Oh dear, that will never do,' he said but, being acquainted with Fiona, he knew exactly what Kate meant and deplored it. She deserved better.

Outside the sky was darkening though it was only mid-afternoon. It would take at least an hour to get home and she longed to be there.

It was a slow journey. The train kept stopping, starting and jerking in a way she hated. She wanted to get out and push it and was relieved when at last it arrived at her station.

It was colder now. The slush in the road was freezing again and cars crunched along. By the time she reached home it was almost dusk. She let herself in to the warm house, eased off her boots in the hall and went into the drawingroom. In a minute I'll make the tea, she thought.

Mrs Sims had left the fire banked up. She stirred it and it broke into a blaze, flames leapt up the chimney and the

237

heart of the fire glowed red. There was nothing like a coal fire. In a minute she'd throw on some small pieces but first she wanted a few minutes to recuperate before thinking about the evening.

She sank into Guy's chair and stretched out her legs. Luxury. Home. Peace. A ring at the bell disturbed this blissful state. No one was expected. It rang again. She was half inclined to ignore it. It rang for the third time and now the peal was continuous. Someone was keeping a finger on it.

Better go.

Paul, his face white and peaky, stood outside.

'Whatever − ?'

'Mummy's not at home.'

'Not there?' She felt a prickle of alarm.

'I rang and rang and she didn't come.' He was on the verge of tears. 'You didn't come either − not for ages.'

She bent down and hugged him. 'I'm sorry.' She brought him in and over to the fire. 'You're frozen,' she said, taking his cold hands in hers. 'Where are your gloves, ducky diamond, eh? And your coat? And what's all this about Mummy being out?'

'She's not there,' he said.

'I expect she's with one of her friends down the road,' she said, knowing it was unlikely. 'We'll go along and see.' She was drawing on her boots again. There was a muffler of Guy's on the hall stand and she wrapped it around Paul's neck, crossed it over in front and tied it up at the back. He was shivering, trying to stop his teeth chattering. He had on his school uniform, charcoal trousers, Cambridge blue blazer, pullover to match − never an anorak or even a raincoat. In the ordinary way they were unnecessary as he was collected and returned by car each day but it was dangerous to be out without an overcoat in this sub-zero temperature.

'Just a moment − I've something for Mummy.' She picked up the Liberty bag and they set off, walking gingerly because the snow had frozen into hard, ugly knobs that made the road treacherous. The clouds had cleared. In the high, blue-black sky stars were already visible.

Paul told her how he kept calling through the letter box when he got home. He could see the electric fire was not alight in the diningroom where Mummy always sat when she was expecting him after school.

Mrs Allen left him at the front door in the afternoons because it was easy to stop outside. In the morning she had to stop at the side gate and Mummy had let him out that way this morning and waved as the car with him and other children drove off. He looked back and saw her go in, he said.

By this time they had reached Magnolia Road and lights were on in the houses. There were none at Sally's. Kate tried to keep her disquiet at bay. She had a key to the door – no use for Paul to have one, the lock was too high for him to reach. Sally never went out alone. If, by chance, a friend had called to take her out she would have rung Kate to say so. No. She knew Kate was to be out today. Still, she would have arranged for someone to look after Paul till she got back.

It was cold in the house. Kate switched on fires and lights. There was no sign of Sally. The ground floor of the house had been adapted to suit her disabled state and the morning room was now a bedroom for herself and Paul. The beds were not made. Sally was methodical so the unmade beds, cereal stuck to plates on the breakfast table, cups with dregs in the bottom and a teapot half full – what could that mean? A search of the upstairs rooms, just in case, revealed nothing.

Kate was defeated. She knew all Sally's movements. Being disabled – temporarily disabled, Sally always insisted – limited her activities, so thinking herself unbeatable, had she gone out without telling anyone and been unable to get back in time for Paul's return from school? It was just possible.

'Let's go and ask Mrs Allen,' Kate said.

Mrs Allen had not caught a glimpse of Sally since collecting Paul that morning and was concerned to hear she was not at home. Her house was warm and comfortable and her two children, Paul's age, were just sitting down to tea.

'Stay to tea with us, Paul,' she said. 'I'll make you a hot drink to warm you up. How about chocolate?'

'Yes, please.'

Quietly to Kate she said: 'It will be better for him to stay with us while you make some 'phone calls, don't you think?'

Kate agreed although she had no idea who to ring. Paul was pleased to stay: 'Only you'll let me know as soon as Mummy comes, won't you?' he said.

Kate could have felt almost angry with Sally. How could she have had the heart to disappear like this? Back in the house she was just about to dial Guy's number when a freezing draught blew across her legs and a door creaked. Was that Sally coming in? Not at the front. She went to the kitchen and found the back door slightly ajar. She had not noticed it before. It opened a little wider. It could not have been properly shut and the wind was blowing it open, a piercing cold wind.

She must close it. She looked out over the snow covered rockery. What was that, a sack or something on the path halfway down to the side gate? She stared out, her hand to her throat. It was almost dark. People put sacks down to walk on. Had Sally put down a sack?

Fearfully she inched her way down. There should have been a handrail to grasp. Guy had promised to put one up. The posts and rails were in the garage but he had never got round to doing it. Excuses all the time. So why offer in the first place?

It wasn't Sally. It could not be Sally. The beating of her heart smothered her thoughts. She knelt by the dark shape. 'Sally? Sally ...'

And then with fear strangling her voice so only a muffled sound escaped: 'SALLY!'

But Sally was dead.

Late that night Kate could still not bring herself to take in what had happend. She remembered stumbling indoors to the telephone, trying to keep her voice steady as she told Guy. She went out again and tried to raise Sally, tried chafing those frozen hands, tried to believe first aid might yet revive her. She had acted like an automaton, ringing for the ambulance, for the doctor, then that awful crouching

240

at Sally's side, unbolting the gate when the ambulance
flashed. So much fuss and bustle. The ambulance men
out there in the dark with torches. And Doctor Graham
asking so many questions. He knew all the Lamberts. 'There
should be someone with you, Kate?' he said. 'Can you go
next-door?'

'Paul's there. He doesn't know what's happened.' She
was thankful Mrs Allen had her curtains firmly closed.

Dr Graham had known Kate and Sally from their
schooldays, they were almost like his own children. He
thought of Kate as the light hearted one, almost timid,
gentle; Sally was strong with an over-developed sense of
responsibility. He was thankful it had been too dark for
Kate to see Sally clearly.

'What shall I tell Paul?' Kate's teeth were chattering, she
had spasms of shaking. He made tea for her and made her
drink it.

'Say she's been taken ill to begin with. Break it gradually,
my dear. I'm sorry. This is hard for you.' He glanced at
his watch.

'You have evening surgery,' she said.

'Never mind. It can wait.'

'I shall be all right. I have to be. Guy should be here
soon.'

They both heard his car pull up. Dr Graham left her
and she heard him talking to Guy in the hall. She stayed
where she was, glad to be alone for a moment to gather her
strength. No good to sit here shaking. Get on with things.
Do the washing up and then pull up the bedclothes, create
a semblance of order.

She ran the water, holding her hand under the tap till it
was hot. She was filling the bowl when Guy came in. He
was grey-faced, stricken by what the doctor had told him. He
took her in his arms and held her close. They clung together
unable to speak. Her face was against his; having him there
gave her courage. She could feel it flowing in. She was so
thankful to have him she hardly heard the things he said
but she knew he was stunned by Sally's death and would
need her help just as she needed his.

'Your hands are wet,' he said.

'I was just going to wash up.'

'You should be at home. Leave all this. It can be done tomorrow.'

'There will be other things tomorrow.' She began to clear the table; the packet of cornflakes, the marmalade jar with the lid off.

'It won't take a minute.' She replaced the lid and put the jar away. But who would want it now? She folded the red and white checked seersucker cloth and put it in the drawer. Her stomach ached with a griping physical pain.

'Come along, darling. We'll take Paul home and then I must go and break the news to the parents.'

She had forgotten his mother and father. 'Couldn't you ring them?' She wanted him to stay with her.

'It would be worse for Mother hearing it that way,' he said.

'I don't want to be alone.'

'I won't be long, but I must go. Heaven alone knows how this is going to affect her. You do see that, don't you?'

She almost said, 'What about me?' But, of course, Ella must never be upset. 'Mother is so delicate,' Guy had once said, upon which Sally told him he was a clown to let her take him in. 'Your mother is a hypochondriac,' she said. Kate always marvelled at the way Sally could say what she liked and get away with it. If she had been the one to tell Guy his mother was a fake he would have thrown an atmosphere for a week.

But he was splendid with Paul that evening. 'We've got to save our tears,' he told Kate, and he made his voice strong and confident when they called for Paul. 'Come on, old boy, you're coming back with us tonight,' he said, and while Kate told Mrs Allen what had happened she was aware of Guy conning Paul with white lies which apparently satisfied him.

Having to act the lie all the evening put an intolerable strain on her and it hurt to see Paul so trusting and unaware.

At last, when he was blessedly asleep in Fiona's bed and Guy was still not home, she allowed herself to think of Sally, of all she had been and of all she was still to be for, in a strange way, her personality seemed stronger than ever. Guy had said they must save their tears and he was right, for once Kate began to weep she would never stop.

After a long time she heard Guy come in and met him in the hall. 'You look so tired,' she said. 'Come by the fire and I'll get you a drink.' He flopped down in his armchair and she knelt and untied his shoes. His slippers were propped up on the fender.

'It wasn't easy,' he said. 'The doctor came and gave Mother a sedative. Dad was fine.'

'I keep thinking it's a nightmare,' she said.

'I'm the same.'

'It was awful with Paul. He kept saying we must take her some flowers tomorrow and he was sure he had enough in his money box to pay for them. I just let him think she's in hospital. That was right, wasn't it?'

So often when she made a decision without telling him Guy would say she had acted foolishly but her distress had been so overwhelming that evening she could not have done anything else.

'You've been wonderful.' There were tears in his eyes. He stroked her hair, kissed her. This was her own Guy, the one she would go the ends of the earth for.

'I'll tell Paul tomorrow,' she said. 'I dread it. He's been so good with Sally. And there's the funeral.'

'An inquest first, I'm afraid. It's a good thing Fiona's in Switzerland. Let's hope it will all be over by the time she gets home.'

Kate was thankful Fiona was out of the way. It was too much to hope she would have been helpful. The rebellious spell so many teenagers go through had begun the day she was born and gone on ever since, Kate often thought. Even Sally, who got on well with practically everyone, had never been able to strike up a friendship with Fiona.

'Let's go to bed,' said Guy. 'You're whacked and so am I. I'll take time off to make the arrangements.'

'Will you? Will you really?' She had expected him to leave everything to her and felt a wave of relief.

'I'll never sleep,' she said when they were in bed.

'Yes, you will.' He gathered her in his arms. How strange

to want to make love. And yet how wonderful. She didn't
wake till morning.

Later that day Kate told Paul of his mother's death in the
only way she knew how and hoped he would be comforted
by her belief that death is a gateway and when we go
through it we are reunited with those we love. It was too
much to expect him to understand. He was incredulous,
angry, overcome. His terrible grief was awful to witness.
He howled and threw himself down on the sofa, hiding
his face in the cushions. He choked out disjointed words.
'I should have been at home taking care of her,' was what
he tried to say.

'You did take care of her,' said Kate. 'You did, Paul.'

She remembered all the things he had done, running
errands, taking messages, arranging cushions in Sally's
chair. She longed to give way to her own sorrow but
she held it back and prayed to be given some of Sally's
strength. She would need it for the days, weeks, years that
lay ahead.

On the opposite side of the road Ada Fortune found
herself drawn to the diningroom window from which she
had a full view of the Lamberts' house. The milkman had
told her of Sally's tragedy only that morning. 'Frozen to
death on her own garden path,' he said.

'No!'

'True. She'd been seeing her little boy off to school at
the side gate. She must have fallen on the way in. It's a
nasty slope there.'

'Wouldn't someone have seen her from the road?'

'Couldn't. The gate's solid wood six foot high and so's
the fence. And with the traffic noise she could have shouted
herself silly and not been heard.'

'And she couldn't get to her feet?'

'Tried hard enough by the look of it, they say. Finger
nails full of grit where she'd tried to dig in.'

'Who found her?'

'Mrs Lambert. The one who lives opposite you.'

'Oh, the poor girl! They were such friends.'

'Yep. Could have been the boy found her though.'

The milkman left to impart his grisly story to his other customers but Ada put on her coat and hurried across the road, not knowing what she could say but full of compassion for Sally's little boy and for Kate.

Mrs Sims opened the door and shook her head. 'It's the poor little boy that worries me,' she said, expressing Ada's feelings. 'Such a bright little chap and a marvel with his mum. They're in the front.'

Kate, hearing voices, came into the hall. 'Ada! Oh, you don't know how glad I am to see you,' she said.

'Kate love, I just had to come. Jack and I thought so much of your Sally. It's no good me talking now. I want to help.' The warmth of Ada's voice with its homely North Country accent and the touch of her hand brought true consolation and Kate felt better for it.

'Let me take Paul over the road. Jack's in the attic with his precious trains and he's got a new signal. Do you think Paul would like to give him a hand setting it up?'

'I'm sure he would,' said Kate, and she called out to Paul who had been playing with one of the toy cars she bought him on the day she went to town. Only yesterday. Was it really yesterday?

Paul's face was streaked with tears but he brightened a little when Ada told him Jack would be glad of his help.

'You're sure you don't want me, Kate?' he asked.

'Of course I want you, darling, but I can spare you to help Mr Fortune.'

Ada always remembered the trusting way he took her hand as they crossed the road and how enthralled he was when he saw the new equipment Jack had bought. He stayed with the Fortunes the whole afternoon. They had toasted currant buns for tea and iced cake over from Christmas.

Kate collected him later on and he thanked the Fortunes for having him. 'I'd like to come again, please,' he said.

'So you shall,' said Jack. He had been retired from his job as a teacher for some time now and was pleased to find someone to share his enthusiasm for model trains. Paul asked intelligent questions; it would be rewarding to encourage him.

Kate was thankful for Ada and Jack. They told her Paul was welcome any time and they meant it. He spent the day with them when the inquest was held.

Kate never knew how she got through the days before Sally's funeral. She had a great deal to do, letters to write, people to telephone and to see. She went down to Henley to comfort Mrs Sharkey and then to Aunt Josephine and realised how terrible it was for old people to lose someone as important to them as Sally.

'We expect to lose our contemporaries, not our young ones,' Aunt Josephine said. 'I shall be glad when George comes home for good.'

'Won't it be wonderful?' Kate said, and the thought of Uncle George and his family being at Heron House warmed her heart. On her way home in the train she allowed herself the luxury of a little weep, not for Sally this time but for her own dream children, the ones she was denied.

Kate found giving evidence at the inquest even more of an ordeal than she had expected. She said she made a habit of telephoning Sally every morning but on that particular day she didn't as she was going out. Yes, if she had rung up in the morning and got no reply she would have gone round to make sure Sally was all right. Sally always saw Paul off to school. She went with him to unbolt the side gate and then rebolted it after he had gone. She would not have felt safe if it had been left unbolted all the time.

Kate began to feel she was to blame for the accident. She should have telephoned before she went out.

Mrs Allen, who took Paul to school every day, told the coroner she had to stop at the side gate because of traffic regulations. Coming home she could stop at the front of the house. No, she never waited to see him go in as his mother was always there.

She, Kate, and other friends talked this over afterwards when they lunched at the local hotel. Guy, who was host, did not contribute anything to the discussion and soon brought it to an abrupt end.

'For God's sake, don't let's have inquest after inquest,'

he said. 'You've heard the verdict. It does no good to keep chewing it over. Let us put it out of our minds. Now, Mrs Allen, have you chosen your pudding?'

'Vanilla ice,' she said, in a shaky voice.

The others tried to make general conversation with little success and the party soon broke up.

One of the saddest tasks that had fallen to Kate was telling Hester about Sally. It was agony speaking on the telephone, hearing Hester's disembodied voice, her disbelief, when proximity, being together in the same room, would have helped a little. How she longed to see Hester again, to have her to stay for a few days for surely Guy's antipathy would have melted away with this tragedy? Even so she had not yet felt equal to broaching the subject.

Ernest Lambert had taken it upon himself to tell George Sheridan what had happened and now, when they got home from the inquest, Guy said Uncle George would be staying with them. 'Dad arranged it on the 'phone,' he said.

Kate was taken aback. It was extremely cool of her father-in-law to give this invitation without consulting her.

'Can't Uncle George stay with them?' she asked.

'We have to consider Mother's health,' Guy said. 'What's the problem? You can cope, can't you? He can have Fiona's room. I thought you liked George.'

'So I do. I love him. But what about Hester? I've already invited her to stay with us.'

'You've what?' he burst out. 'Without telling me? You know what I think of that woman.'

'Why don't you consider her feelings at a time like this?' she returned, braving his wrath.

'I'm not going to discuss this, Kate. Just drop the idea and tell her to make other arrangements.'

'How can she from Santa Carlotta? She has to stay somewhere.'

'Not with us, thank you very much.'

'Then with your parents.'

The silence that greeted this suggestion was like an icicle stabbing her heart.

'She's Paul's grandmother just as much as Ella is,' she said. 'And Sally is still her daughter.'

'Then let her stay at Sally's house. It's empty.'

Kate was defeated, her inward soul almost screamed for help. Hester alone in that cold, silent house. Oh no! Ridiculous ideas raced round and round in her weary brain. She was alone, completely isolated. Ada would put Hester up, she knew she had only to ask, so would Mrs Allen, but she couldn't ask them. She would have to reveal too much. That afternoon, she went back to the hotel where they had lunched and reserved a room. It was easy for she had already booked a reception room there for the mourners after the funeral.

Paul had been with the Fortunes all day and he was still in the attic with Jack when Kate called for him.

'You must be tired,' Ada said.

'I feel as though I've been flayed. The coroner was sympathetic but it kills you to keep going over it. There's to be a gathering of Sally's friends at the Gate Hotel after the funeral. I do hope you'll come, Ada.'

'Of course I will, love.'

'I'm so afraid of atmospheres developing. Sally's parents are divorced, as you know, and they are both coming.'

'Surely there'll be nothing but sympathy? They must both have loved her.'

'They did. There won't be any trouble with them. It's Guy and his mother. They disapprove of Hester so violently. You'd think no one had ever eloped before. The man she ran away with was a prisoner of war over here so you can't expect them to have any tender feelings towards him, but it's her, it's Hester. They won't allow her a single virtue. Oh dear. I shouldn't be saying all this. It's not fair to Guy.'

'It won't go any further, and it's not good for you to bottle things up. I daresay your husband is very upset and no doubt shocked, as I know you are, love.'

'He is. He'll never get over losing Tom.'

'Grief does strange things to people, especially men,' Ada said. 'Some of them seem to go cold and hard and act as though they don't care. It can be very hurtful to those who do but you just have to tell yourself it's their way of dealing with their pain.'

'You're the most wonderful help to me,' Kate said. 'Ah,

here's Paul. It's time we went home, old boy. We'll wear Mr and Mrs Fortune out between us.'

'Not true,' said Ada, 'and Paul's our adopted nephew now so we're Uncle Jack and Auntie Ada.'

'How splendid,' said Kate, knowing very well that Guy would scorn the idea so it was advisable to keep it quiet.

Paul knew his grandparents were coming to England and was looking forward to seeing them. 'Will Grandpa bring my little uncles?' he asked.

'Not this time. Another time, perhaps,' Kate said.

'And Nonna? I shall be very glad to see her. Will Gianni be coming as well?'

'No. Gianni is staying at home.'

'Who's going to take care of Nonna then?'

Guy, hearing this, said Nonna was quite capable of taking care of herself.

'She's much too old. *I* shall take care of Nonna while she's here,' Paul announced.

'*You* will do as you are told,' said Guy.

Hester Sheridan arrived at London Airport on the eve of her daughter's funeral not expecting anyone to meet her. She knew exactly how she stood with the Lamberts. They had ostracised her when she ran away with Gianni and the intervening years had not softened their attitude so she had not been invited to stay with any of them for the one night of her visit. Kate had arranged accommodation at the Gate Hotel and been most unhappy about it. She had said as much when they spoke on the telephone.

Gianni Morelli could not endure the thought of her meeting this inimical family alone. The news of Sally's death and the manner of it had devastated her. She could not believe it had happened – Sally seemed to be there, so vital, so alive – how could Hester accept that she ceased to be? It was as though Sally had invaded the Hotel Villa Laura. Gianni could feel her presence too. In the long deserted corridors, the shrouded rooms that had echoed with her voice the last time she was with them. Hers and Tom's and Paul's. How well they had been, how happy then.

But this was now.

'It would not be proper for me to come with you but you must not go alone,' Gianni said. 'Aldo will go with you.'

'I'd be so thankful,' she said.

So Aldo Bianchi, who had long been a friend of the Morelli family, accompanied her on the journey. She was at ease with him. He is one of ourselves, the Morellis always said, although he was not a native of Santa Carlotta as they all were. He lived in Genoa and stayed at the Hotel Villa Laura every summer and he had met Sally and her family on their last visit. He intended to protect Hester from the hostile Lamberts as well as he could.

Hester was tall and well-made. Because of her fine bone structure she had retained her good looks – high cheekbones, large grey eyes and a well-set head. She wore a swirling black cape lined with mink which the eldest of the Morelli brothers had lent her from one of his shops, saying it was freezing in England and she would be glad of it.

Aldo carried her overnight case and his own. As they walked towards the exit a tall thin man stepped forward. 'Hester?' he said.

It was George Sheridan.

'George! I never expected to see you!' She was inexpressibly moved. He took her hand and looked at her with compassion. 'I'm only sorry we should meet on such a sad occasion.'

He held her hand for a moment. Then he took her in his arms and kissed her cheek and she could not stop the tears pouring down her face. 'There, there. I know, my dear, I know,' he said.

The crowd streamed round them, shouting greetings to those who had come to meet them; they trundled trolleys full of luggage, men carried small children on their shoulders, women searched in their handbags for car keys and loose change. In the midst of all this George and Hester stood together, their hearts full, unable to speak for neither could find words to express their grief.

Aldo, a few paces away, waited. Then Hester collected herself, turned and held out her hand to him. 'George, this is Aldo Bianchi who very kindly came with me. I'm not used to flying and he's a great traveller.'

'Signor Bianchi.' George shook hands with him. 'It was

good of you to escort – ' He could not finish because he did not know how to refer to his ex-wife. Was she called Signora Morelli in Santa Carlotta? Or was she known as Mrs Sheridan? Any embarrassment at this hiatus was averted by Aldo who simply said: 'I am glad I was able to come with Hester. It is the least I could do for so good a friend.'

George said: 'We'll get a taxi. Kate offered me her car but I'm so used to driving on the right these days I thought I'd better not risk it. We'll go straight to your hotel, Hester.'

'Please,' she said.

He was afraid she might have asked to be taken to Sally's house and was thankful she did not. 'Kate's anxious to see you,' he said. 'She's arranged to dine with you tonight.'

'It may be the only opportunity we'll have to talk,' she said. 'There will be so many people tomorrow.'

In the taxi Hester asked about Paul and George told her he was very brave although he would sometimes burst into tears and cry for his mother. Kate was good with him and would comfort him in the most sensitive and sensible way. George admired her way of handling the whole situation. As far as he could see Guy was either numbed by the tragedy or else he was unfeeling. He appeared to be leaving everything to his wife.

'I've never forgotten him telling me his mother was wondering if we were their kind of people,' Hester said.

'It didn't take long for her to discover we weren't,' said George. 'He hasn't changed. A cold-hearted fellow in my opinion.'

'Poor Kate.'

'Poor Kate indeed.'

Aldo, in his corner of the taxi, was thankful to find Hester and her ex-husband were at ease with each other, and as Kate would be spending the evening with her he could dine in town and meet a friend with whom he wanted to discuss a matter that concerned him deeply.

At the hotel George suggested coffee or a drink in the lounge. 'You will join us, Signor Bianchi?' he asked.

Aldo thanked him but declined, explaining his plan for the evening which he could waive if it meant leaving Hester alone.

'That's fine. I'm staying with her till Kate comes,' George said.

'You mustn't worry about me,' Hester protested, 'I'm perfectly all right.' But she was touched by his concern and later when they were together they talked with each other unreservedly and came to a complete understanding. He felt no bitterness towards her now, only affection and goodwill while she had never wavered in her special kind of love for him.

They were united in their grief for Sally and talked about her for a long time. She had crammed so much into her thirty-three years, never blaming either of them, never losing touch, giving them both such a wealth of love. And in the six years of her marriage to Tom it was as though she concentrated all the years that should have been hers into that short space. Once, almost afraid, when Paul was a toddler she said: 'We're too happy.' She said it to Kate who told Hester.

Paul was bewildered in the chapel. He was in the front row with Grandpa Sheridan on one side and a tall lady in a black cape on the other. She had a piece of black lace over her head. She held his hand and smiled down at him. He tugged at Grandpa's coat. 'Who is she?' he asked.

'Your Nonna. Hush.'

Afterwards, when they left, he went in the same car as this strange lady and Grandpa. She put her arm round him and said, 'You haven't forgotten me, have you, Paul?' Her scent was like the flowers in Santa Carlotta.

'Are you really Nonna?' he asked.

She nodded. 'I really am.'

They reached the hotel and went up the steps just ahead of Ella and Ernest Lambert. Ella studiously ignored Hester and called out to Paul to come with her. He went unwillingly. He did not like her at all and did not want to sit beside her on the sofa she made for. She was always complaining about his noise when he was taken to see her on Sundays. She talked about nothing but dresses and hairstyles, never about anything he liked, so he would escape into the garden and play at lassoing wild horses and he whooped and shouted until Grandpa Lambert came out and told him to be quiet.

Today she kept giving him watery smiles and calling him a poor little lad. 'I'm not little, Grandma,' he said. 'I'm the right size for my age.' She did not like that.

He wished he could be with Nonna, even though she looked so different today. And he was puzzled about Grandfather Sheridan because he knew they were Mummy's mother and father but they didn't seeem to be married to each other. His own mother and father were married to each other and he knew it for certain because they had slept in the same bed. He supposed they were sharing a bed in heaven now. Married people always slept in the same bed. That's how you knew they were married. But Nonna slept with Gianni and Grandpa slept with Monny. Kate had tried to explain when he asked why Monny couldn't sleep with Gianni so Grandpa and Nonna could stay married but she didn't seem to know the answer.

He slipped off the sofa while Granny Lambert was holding her hand out for another glass of brandy and edged his way into the crowd in search of Kate. Lots of people spoke to him in awful put-on voices. They called him a brave boy, a stout little fellow, one of the best, and made him want to say rude words like pong and flea and weasel. Pong was the rudest word in the world. A boy at school had whispered it in his ear and dared him to say it out loud. When he did no one took any notice.

At last he found Kate. She was surviving on aspirin tablets and strong black coffee as this gathering had tried her to the utmost. The Lamberts were behaving disgracefully. There was Ella mopping her eyes and going on like a tragedy queen while Hester was all but abandoned. Uncle George was wonderful, taking care to see Hester had some refreshments, but he had to circulate. She was more than thankful Ada was there as she and Hester had spent a long time in conversation and were obviously getting on well, but as for the family ... only Ernest had muttered a word or two, and Guy scarcely that.

'Nonna's gone up to her room,' she told Paul. 'We'll go and see her, shall we?'

253

Hester was standing by the window when they went in. She looked drained but the moment she saw Paul her face lit up and she held out her arms to him.

'I was afraid you'd forgotten me,' she said.

'You look different,' he said. He had expected her to look as she had done at Santa Carlotta, not like a stately lady in black.

She managed to laugh. 'It's my clothes, darling. Look!'

Her hair was arranged in a French pleat. She took out some pins and shook her head so that it fell loosely over her shoulders. 'There. Better?'

'Much more like Nonna,' he said. 'I like you in colours.'

'I shall be next time.'

'Am I coming to stay with you? Mummy said we'd come.'

'Then we must manage somehow but summer's a long way off yet.' She exchanged glances with Kate. 'What do you say?' she asked.

'It all depends on Guy,' Kate said.

'Then why not let's ask him?' She had recovered her composure and said she was going downstairs again. She pinned up her hair, went on talking to Paul, asking him what he had been doing and hearing about the new aunt and uncle by whom he meant the Fortunes. He told her all about their garden and about Uncle Jack's trains and how he could go there to tea any time he liked.

Hester smoothed down her dress in front of the glass. It was black but the material and cut carried the stamp of high fashion rather than a mourning garb. Kate admired it. 'Rome or Paris?' she asked.

'A little woman round the corner,' Hester said. 'You must let her make you something when you come.'

Paul was beginning to feel comfortable inside. This was his real Nonna, laughing and wonderful. They went down in the lift. Ella was still in the same place and Hester went straight over and sat by her side. 'I can't go away without having a few words with you, Ella,' she said. 'It isn't very long since you were mourning your son. I wrote to you, remember? Can't we console each other a little now?'

254

Ella had seen Hester crossing the room and envied her. That graceful walk, the dress, those long slim legs, the high heels — higher than she would have dared to wear herself. And that necklace! Emeralds. They couldn't be real.

'I have nothing to say to you,' she said.

'Then you should have. You are Paul's grandmother, just as I am. We have plenty in common.'

'Nothing.'

'But there's his future to consider.'

'Don't imagine you will have any say in it. You've put yourself behind the pale and you can stay there.' Ella's voice, always thin and quavering, attracted Guy's attention. He strode over, put his hand on his mother's shoulder and addressed Hester. 'You are upsetting my mother, Signora,' he said.

'I think she is upsetting herself,' replied Hester, but she knew it would be useless to stay there so she rose and addressed Guy directly.

'There is something I want to ask you,' she said.

'Very well.'

Ella was fumbling in her bag for her smelling salts. Her husband had been having a chat with a golfing friend but he saw what had been going on and shot back to his wife's side. Ella in one of her states was not easy to pacify, and the sight of Hester would upset her for days. She would be demanding just such a dress and it would never do to tell her she hadn't the figure for it. As to those emeralds — if they were real they must be worth a mint. He couldn't help admiring Hester. Brazen she might be but attractive she was, and hadn't the time come to let byegones be byegones? But it was more than he dared to suggest such a thing to his wife in her present frame of mind. The best thing would be for Guy to take her home and then, if he was lucky, he might manage to get away for a few hours of relaxation with Mavis. She was his secret strength. A bit on the dowdy side but so comfortable.

On the other side of the room Hester was talking to Guy, asking about Paul, saying it was a great weight off her mind to know he and Kate were looking after him and she felt sure Sally would have approved. He made very guarded responses. It did not do, he said, to rush into decisions, especially after a bereavement when emotions were out of control. Naturally he was concerned with the welfare of his brother's son.

'I am concerned with it, too,' she said. 'Did you know Sally wrote to me every other day? So I knew all about Paul, and about you and Kate, too.'

'Really?' He was not pleased to hear Sally had kept this woman posted with news.

'I do wish you would come to Santa Carlotta, Guy,' she went on. 'It's still undiscovered though it won't stay so much longer. Tom and Sally came every year, as of course you know. It would be lovely if you would bring Paul and Kate – and Fiona, of course.'

'We have no plans for the summer at present,' he said.

'There's no need to stay at the Villa Laura if you'd rather not although you would be most welcome. There are other hotels. Do think about it.'

'We shall see,' he said in a tone that told her he had no intention of taking up her invitation. 'Excuse me. I see my parents are leaving.'

Everyone else was leaving too. She was mortified. It had cost her a great deal to approach the Lamberts and they had not given her any hope of a reconciliation. She dared not give way to tears but the idea of leaving Paul under the control of Guy Lambert made her long to take some desperate action. If only I could kidnap him and whisk him back to Santa Carlotta, she thought. Kate was her first choice for guardian but what chance did she stand with Guy? He dominated her. Anyone could see that.

Here was George coming over to her. 'When do you leave?' he asked.

'Very soon. I shall be thankful to get away. It's been even worse than I feared.'

'Guy hasn't helped. He's a hard nut,' said George. 'Odd to think two brothers could differ so. Tom was such a dear fellow. So right for our Sally.'

'Don't. I wanted to think of Sally all the time but the atmosphere was all wrong. I've felt waves of antipathy washing over me for the Lamberts.'

'They're not worth your notice.'

'But I'm worried about Paul.'

'I'm sure there's no need. Kate will look after him. He'll be perfectly safe with her, and Guy will do his best for him too. If not, my dear, you can rely on me. We *are* his grandparents, you know.'

'So we are.' She paused. What else was there to say? Only goodbye. Goodbye Sally's father. Goodbye dear, good husband I ran away from.

Guy told Kate he would stay with his mother for the evening and that left her free to drive Hester to the airport. She took George home and left him in front of a good fire where he assured her he would be glad to relax.

Hester was in the lounge with Paul and Aldo when she returned to the hotel. They were having tea and talking hard, or rather Paul was talking. Aldo placed a chair for her and signalled to the waiter to bring more tea.

'My other Granny's hair is horrible,' Paul was saying. 'It used to be blue but now its pink, and she has thick black eyelashes and can't keep her eyes open. She squints at you like this.' He gave a creditable imitation of Ella's way of peering at people.

'You're being unkind to Granny,' Kate said, thinking it her place to say so.

Aldo caught her eye and smiled. 'You're going to have your work cut out keeping this young man in order,' he said.

She had only heard him say a word or two so far and was surprised to find an Italian speaking English so fluently and colloquially.

'Are you bilingual?' she asked.

'Not really. I didn't get round to English until I was in my teens.'

'You must have a good ear.'

'He's got two ears,' said Paul, jumping up and down. 'He's got one each side of his head.' He was over-excited, obstreperous, and couldn't sit still.

'If you go on like that you'll be taken home and put to bed,' said Kate.

He stared at her. Something she had said touched a

nerve. His face crumpled. 'Mummy – I want to go home to Mummy!' he sobbed. Hester gathered him in her arms, soothing him. Kate felt her own control giving way. She could have kicked herself. Her sharp reprimand could be harmful. It was no excuse to blame tiredness, the strain of the day, her own grief.

Hester went on consoling Paul in such a soft voice Kate couldn't catch a word but his sobs subsided, he was recovering. Soon he looked round, slid off Hester's lap and went over to Kate, responding to her hug and kiss as though all was forgotten. Aldo suggested taking Paul to the men's room. 'Neither of us has had a lick all day,' he said.

As soon as they were alone Kate told Hester she didn't know why she always said the wrong thing. 'Trust me to put my foot in it. Guy's always ticking me off. I'm afraid to open my mouth when we're out with his friends.'

'Aren't they your friends, too?' Hester asked.

Kate shook her head. 'I'm a fish out of water with them.'

Hester could tell she was very much alone and wondered how she would stand up to the new difficulties she would have to face. She had always been sweet-natured and gentle, just as her parents were. When you were in their house you were aware of a special atmosphere. Orlando and Mary Hope really enjoyed life, every moment of it, and so did Kate in those days. They were the antithesis of the stuck-up Lamberts who seemed to think themselves a cut above everyone else. Tea with the Lamberts was purgatory; with the Hopes it was often hilarious.

There was time for dinner before their flight and Aldo insisted on taking them to a restaurant he knew. Paul's behaviour was exemplary. He imagined himself grown up and Kate was proud of him. He was stoical when they said their goodbyes at the airport; Hester was the one who had to check her tears. She hated leaving her grandson to a life ruled by the Lamberts. Fate had been cruel to rob him of Tom and Sally. And she pitied Kate.

Kate did not pity herself. She would have so much to do in the immediate future there would be no time to indulge in misery. Sally had bounced back after losing Tom and

258

again after her accident. Kate was determined to follow her example. First and foremost she still had Guy, and although they had lost the happiness of their first few years together she convinced herself it was still to be recovered if only she tried hard enough. It was up to her.

Guy was determined to rise to the very peak of his profession and it was her job to help him. If that meant not questioning, not expecting, being ready to fall in with his plans even when she disliked them, she would do so. Her big mistake had been thinking their marriage could be the same as her parents had been. Now she knew it could not. Every case was different and she was determined not to repeat her mistakes.

Guy was in an amiable mood that evening. He sat with Paul on his knee talking to George and the atmosphere was congenial. She made hot chocolate and they sat round the fire drinking it.

George produced snapshots of his family and glowed with pride as they admired them. 'I hope Mrs Sharkey approves,' he said.

'How could she not?' asked Kate.

On the following day he went to see his Aunt Josephine and also Mrs Sharkey, taking Paul with him, and the day after that he left for home. They were sorry to see him go.

The rest of the week went by reasonably well. Kate took Paul to school in the mornings and collected him in the afternoons. She had brought all his clothes, toys and other belongings from Magnolia Road, and with the help of Mrs Sims they were arranged in the little room that was to be his. It was small and cosy and the window looked across the front garden to the road.

'You'll have the best view of the cherry trees when they come out,' Mrs Sims told him.

'We have almonds in our road,' he said.

'Very nice, too.' Dangerous ground, she thought, and went on brightly: 'I wouldn't give a button for those prunus round the corner, would you? All right while the flowers are out but the leaves go nearly black. This is by far the best. You might even see the Queen go by.'

'I'd rather see my Mummy go by,' he said.

Mrs Sims fished a toffee out of her pocket. 'There, unwrap that,' she said.

It was in bright red paper and while the outside was brittle the inside was soft and treacly and tasted of apricots. He put it in his mouth. 'Why do people give me sweets when I say I want to see Mummy?' he asked.

Oh my, he's flummoxed me, she thought, and he was waiting for an answer. 'Because they don't know any better,' she said.

Fiona was due home from Switzerland and a week later, just before lunch, she rang from the airport and asked if she could bring Sandra White home to stay overnight. It would only be for one night as they would be going back to school tomorrow.

'I'm sorry, darling, we haven't a spare room,' Kate said.

'What? We've always had a spare room.'

'Paul's living with us now as Daddy has told you, dear. He's in the room over the front door.'

'Put him in the box room. It's only one night.'

'The box room is packed solid with things from Sally's.'

'Well, really, Mum. I do think it's a bit rough.'

'It's only temporary.'

'It had better be.'

'Don't use that tone, Fiona. I'm sure Sandra will understand when you tell her how things are.'

'Tch. Tch. Tch.'

'What was that?'

'Nothing. Nix. Sod.'

'Fiona!'

An earsplitting noise made Kate replace the receiver hastily. Fiona had blown a raspberry into the mouthpiece.

Just under an hour later a taxi drew up outside and Fiona got out. Kate didn't see her arrive but she heard the front door open and went into the hall. Fiona had just slung her skis down and there was a suitcase and several bags as well.

'You're just in time for tea. The kettle's on,' Kate said.

'Just in time for tea,' Fiona mimicked.

'Don't you want any?' Kate had made up her mind to ignore Fiona's rudeness and guessed there was plenty to follow.

'No, I don't want any. I want Sandra to stay the night. You could easily have done something about it. The little beast could have slept on the sofa.'

'You don't seem to realise we've been through a distressing time at home,' Kate said. 'Daddy was glad you missed it but I'm not so sure. It would have done you good if you'd been here to help.'

'That shows Daddy's got more sense than you have.'

'If you don't want any tea just take all this luggage upstairs.'

'Shan't.'

'And move those skis. Someone will fall over them.'

'Hope it's you.'

'I'm going to fetch Paul. And don't spend hours on the telephone while I'm out.'

Kate was used to Fiona's hostility but she could not understand it. She felt the girl positively prickle when they confronted each other and it was no use appealing to her better nature because she hadn't got one. Compassion seemed to be entirely missing from her make-up. She felt heartsore as she walked to Paul's school that afternoon. It was a relief to mingle with the mothers waiting to collect their children for as soon as they knew who she was they gathered round offering sympathy, eager to help with any problems she was having. They had all known Sally; they had all liked her and wanted to be helpful. Kate was thankful to be among them. After only a few minutes with Fiona this atmosphere of kindliness and understanding helped to restore her equanimity.

Guy was late home that evening and Fiona refused to leave her room till she heard his voice in the hall. Kate was at the door to meet him as he came in, thankful he was home. He hugged and kissed her, laughing at the warmth of her response.

'It's so good to have you home.'

'Good to be here. Hallo, what's this?'

Fiona came whirling downstairs and flung herself at him.

261

'Daddy darling, you don't know how I've missed you.'

'Well, here I am. Anything wrong?'

'Yes. Mum wouldn't let me bring Sandra White home for the night.'

'So what? The heavens haven't fallen, have they?' He had one arm round Kate, the other round Fiona. 'I suppose you sprang it on your mother,' he said.

'I didn't. I rang as soon as we were off the plane.'

'Expected a miracle, did you? Your mother can't get a room ready in half an hour, Fiona. It hasn't been all beer and skittles here, you know.'

'Now you're against me, too.'

'I certainly shall be if you go on in this blockheaded way. Now let me get in. I've had a hard day and I'm tired.'

Kate, who was in the dining room pouring his usual whisky, wanted to run out and hug him for defending her.

'Anything for you, Fiona?' she called. 'A nip of cherry brandy?'

'Nope.'

Fiona sat on the arm of Guy's chair. He sipped his drink, gave a sigh of contentment. 'Well, tell us all about Switzerland,' he said.

She launched into an ecstatic account of the holiday and dwelt on the prowess of Sandra White who had been in charge of the party.

'Oh? I thought she was one of the girls,' he said.

'She's the P.T. teacher. She's super.'

'Are you allowed to call her by her Christian name?'

'Only when we're by ourselves. Otherwise she's Miss White.'

'I'd like to meet her.'

'You would have done if Mum hadn't been such a pig.'

'Fiona!' Kate protested.

'Pig!'

'That's quite enough of that, Fiona,' said Guy. 'I want five minutes' peace so you can take yourself off to bed.'

'Daddy! Let me stay up a bit longer.'

'Off.'

'Please. Please, Daddy.'

'Didn't you hear me say off?'

262

Kate was thankful to see her go without more ado and still more thankful when she left for school in a hired car next morning. With Hester and George both gone and Paul back at school perhaps life would return to normal.

But there was no such thing as normal, she found. Her settled pattern of life had gone forever and she found herself treading warily at every turn. The run up to breakfast was fraught with danger for she had to whisk Paul in and out of the bathroom at speed to leave the way clear for Guy. The meal itself tottered on the edge of disaster because Paul's chatter exasperated his uncle. Guy was always wrestling with problems he might or might not meet in the day ahead and needed quiet.

Kate had always made sure he had it. She understood the exigencies of his job, gauged his mood accurately, responding if he wanted to talk about a problem, or thinking her own thoughts and mentally keeping out of his way if he didn't. Whatever his mood she enjoyed their breakfasts together and looked forward to sitting down at the table and pouring coffee from the silver pot. She was sure the unhurried meal go him off to a good start. Sometimes she would look up and find him watching her, a half-smile on his lips, and he might put his hand over hers and say that seeing her there set him up for the day. When this happened his eyes seemed to have more warmth than usual. She never knew how to describe his eyes: they were a rather light shade of blue, not so pale as to be arresting or the washed-out blue of old seafaring men, but a special blue. Perhaps acquamarine was the right word, a gem-like colour, cold in the way jewels are cold. Sally had had brown eyes with little flecks of gold. Paul's were the same although in other ways he resembled his father and would no doubt grow up good-looking like all the Lamberts.

And now here he was, bouncing with early morning exuberance and full of questions aimed at Guy.

'Hush. Don't bother Uncle now,' Kate said.

'But he hasn't told me. I want to know what keeps aeroplanes up.'

'Ask him on Sunday.'

'Do *you* know?'

'Not really. Ask Mr Fortune. I expect he can tell you.'

Guy was in a mood to grind his teeth. He picked up his empty egg shells and crushed them, one in each hand.

'Guy!' Kate was horrified but Paul thought it funny. He picked up his own egg shell and was about to do the same.

'Oh no you don't,' she said.

'Why not?'

'Because it isn't the thing to do.'

'Uncle did it.'

'Uncle's different. Come along. Time we were on our way.'

Out in the hall he wanted to know why Uncle was so cross.

'He likes quiet in the mornings so you mustn't keep asking him questions.'

'Mummy said if I don't ask, I'll never get to know.'

'That's perfectly true but the first thing you must learn is to choose the right time.'

'I think he's a crab.'

She took no notice because it seemed she was always correcting him and, besides, Guy *was* a crab. Paul followed her out to the car muttering 'Crab' under his breath all the way.

The truth was Guy was most disagreeable these days, and not without reason, she had to admit. The additon of a small boy to the household was bringing problems.

That evening Guy picked on one of them. 'I suppose you realise we'll have to get a sitter for that kid when we want an evening out,' he said.

'Ada said she'll come over any time.'

'I'm not having the Queen of the Mobcaps getting her foot in here,' he snapped.

Kate managed to laugh. 'Darling, how can you? She's a dear. But never mind about her. The mothers have a rota so there will always be someone.'

With this confident assertion came the reminder that she was not on the rota. How could she ask anyone to sit for her when she was unable to reciprocate? Perhaps she could ferry children to school and back? This suggestion was received with enthusiasm so she was soon taking three extra children in her car and could ask their mothers to sit with Paul in return. So that solves that one, she thought, feeling a weight had been lifted.

But without Sally there was a great void in her life. Who could she talk with as she had talked with Sally? They had everything in common: their childhood, the joys, the sorrows, most of all their parents, the quartet, as they had christened them. George and Hester; Orlando and Mary.

In spite of this emptiness, could this be her second chance, she wondered. Life would be different without Sally but it could still be good if she made it so. Again and again she convinced herself that success depended upon her.

The idea gave her energy, hope, optimism. Niggling difficulties could be overcome. They could have another bathroom for a start and do away with the aggravation of the mornings. Her income from Orlando Hope's meant it need not cost Guy a penny. Should she consult a builder first or an architect? Why not ask John Proctor what to do, or even Jack Fortune? Then she could present the whole thing to Guy on a plate.

That evening he came home earlier than usual with tickets for a play they both wanted to see.

'Marvellous!' she exclaimed. Then: 'I'll get someone to sit with Paul.' She had a list of numbers to ring but after half a dozen attempts she was defeated. Willing helpers required longer notice.

Guy was upstairs changing so, without a word to him, she ran over to Ada Fortune who agreed to come in an hour's time. Just long enough for her to get a snack ready and put Paul to bed.

'It isn't my bedtime,' said Paul. 'I shall keep Auntie Ada company.'

'Well, keep out of Uncle's way. You'd better play with your jigsaw quietly.'

Paul gave her a very strange look. 'I shall take it behind the sofa and I shan't come out till you've gone,' he said.

Guy came down in his dinner jacket. He stood in front of the glass adjusting his tie. 'You'd better get into your evening rig, hadn't you?' he said. 'We haven't much time.'

'There's something to eat in the diningroom,' she told him as she went upstairs.

On the stroke of seven the doorbell rang and Guy opened the door to Ada Fortune.

'Here I am,' she announced. 'I told Kate any time and I meant it. Eeh, don't we look grand?' She walked into the drawingroom with a huge bag of knitting and two paper backs.

'Did she ask you?' he enquired, fuming, with his back to the fire.

'I might just as well sit here as over the road,' said Ada, ignoring this question. 'What's the play? Oh, very nice. You'll enjoy that. Make a nice break for you.'

Kate was down, ready to go. 'Make yourself some tea or coffee, Ada,' she said. 'You'll find everything in the kitchen. Biscuits in the tin.'

'Don't worry about me. I'm going to sit here and unwind. We've had a hectic day at the garden centre ordering the peat and everything ...'

'Time we were off,' Guy said.

'Yes, of course. Off you go and don't hurry back,' said Ada.

Outside in the car Guy looked grim. 'Bloody woman. Doing us a real favour, isn't she?'

'She likes it,' Kate said.

'Too bloody true. Just take care you don't get lumbered with her.'

Kate bit back an angry rejoinder and was silent.

It was an excellent play. Guy gradually relaxed and his mood mellowed. He got drinks in the first interval, pushing through the crowd and getting served out of turn as he always did. 'Enjoying it, darling?' he said.

Back in their seats he held her hand. She surrendered to the sheer bliss of it. Guy in a good temper, being with him in this packed auditorium − what more could she ask?

'We'll have some supper now,' he said when the final curtain fell. 'That restaurant in Soho where we used to go when I was in the R.A.F. Remember? The place where the ladies are given a red rose. It's still there, you know.'

Of course she remembered. She could still feel the thrill of being seen with him and now, walking arm-in-arm through the narrow streets off Shaftesbury Avenue, she felt nothing had changed between them. Once again she caught the excitement of Soho at night with the theatre crowds spilling out and making their way to favourite restaurants, prostitutes emerging from doorways or standing on street corners. There was the titillating hint of evil, of danger, but with her hand in his she was safe from it all.

The restaurant proprietor met them as they entered, there was the momentary pause, then recognition flashed.

'Ah! Wing Commander Lambert! After all this time. How good it is to see you. And Mrs Lambert.' The customary red rose. How sweet the scent was − surely out of a bottle? She pinned it to her dress and they followed their host, resplendent in white tie and tails, his greying hair brushed sleekly to his head, his moustache still suspiciously black.

They were being treated as people of supreme importance; the food − would Madame choose? − was on the house, so was the wine − champagne of course for such an occasion. She was dizzy with excitement. Photographs of heroic airmen lined the walls, men who had dined there when they were on leave, famous names, half-forgotten faces. There was a photo of Guy after he had been decorated by the King. She was whisked back in time. How proud she felt, how honoured that this man had married her, loved her, still loved her.

He lifted his glass, touched it against hers. 'Penny for them,' he said.

'They're worth more than that.'

'Come on. Give.'

'I was thinking of you.'

'But I'm here. You don't have to think of me. Drink up.'

'Oh, we're not going!'

'We're going on.'

A perfect meal, vintage champagne and nothing to pay! The proprietor kissed her hand, escorted them to the door, invited them to come again. He had a special feeling for airmen. Anyone whose photograph graced his walls would always be an honoured guest, but alas so few remained, he said. He clasped Guy's hand in both of his.

The doorman stopped a taxi for them. They were going to Ronnie Scott's. It was only a step away but why walk when they were celebrating? Guy gave the driver three times what he asked and that was excessive to start with.

And inside the club, that music, that saxophone, another bottle of champagne. They hadn't had a night like this since − when? The years fell away. Those songs, those solos! Ronnie Scott telling jokes, playing that sax of his. What, more champagne?

The clock had taken them back as far as the beginning. Swooning, falling, the clock. Her watch. Could it be? 'Guy! Guy, look at the time. Can it be − is it really two-thirty in the morning?'

'Where's the car? Can you remember? Do try to walk straight. Guy, you're weaving from side to side. Better get a taxi. Find the car tomorrow. Hang the expense.'

So into another taxi, and a sour taste. Too much champagne. Never mind. It was a wonderful evening. Soon be home. But tomorrow − have to be up early to take Paul to school. Only now − heavens! What about Ada?

'Guy! We should have been home hours ago − Ada will still be there!'

'Bugger Ada.'

And Ada *was* still there. So was Jack. They were at the window pulling back the curtain at the sound of the taxi. They opened the front door while Kate was still fumbling for the key.

'We'll be going.' Jack was indignant.

'Eeh! But we thought you'd had an accident.'

'It's getting on for four o'clock. Play was over by eleven.'

'Eeh! We were that worried.'

'We'll be going.'

'I'm so sorry. We never meant to be away this long.' Kate hardly knew what to say. They had behaved disgustingly. She tried to say so.

Guy pushed past her, making for the lavatory. She heard him being sick.

'Lad's had a drop too much.'

'Lad's had a bucket too much.'

'We'll be going.' Jack and Ada together.

Kate watched them cross the road with the paperbacks, the knitting. What an end to the evening. She dragged herself upstairs, set the alarm, peeped in at Paul who was sleeping peacefully, and fell into bed without even cleaning her teeth. She heard Guy asking if they had any Alka Seltzer but she couldn't remember. She didn't remember anything more until the alarm woke her. It was time to get up, time to get on with the day, and should she wake Guy or shouldn't she? Whichever she did would be wrong.

She was in a bad state of the morning after. Somehow she went through the routine of getting Paul up and making his breakfast. The very sight of a boiled egg made her want to retch but Paul ate his and chatted away about a project his class would be working on that day.

There was no movement from upstairs. When she was ready to take Paul she went up and found Guy still in a heavy sleep. She shook his shoulder gently, spoke to him, told him the time. He didn't even open his eyes. She pulled back the curtains and opened the window, letting in the cool air. Best to leave him. He was in no state to go into the office today.

After leaving Paul at school she stopped at the florist and bought a huge bunch of flowers for Ada. She would take them over later on. First she would have aspirin and lemon and soda for her headache. It always worked.

As she closed the front door there was a shout from above. 'Why the hell didn't you wake me?' Guy came crashing downstairs, livid with rage. 'What the devil's the idea going off and leaving me in bed? You know damn' well I should have been out of the house an hour ago.'

'I tried to wake you — '

'You couldn't have tried very hard.'

'You were in a stupor. Coffee?'

'If you think I've time for coffee you've got another think coming. Where the hell are the car keys?'

'In the pocket of your dinner jacket, I expect.' He crashed back upstairs and came back with the keys. But what about the car? She clapped her hand to her mouth. They had parked the car in a side street near the theatre and he hadn't yet realised.

'We had a taxi home,' she said.

'Oh my God, that's torn it. I should have been in the office hours ago.'

'Better take the day off by the look of you.'

'Can't do that. Ring for a hire car. Do something to help, for heaven's sake, woman.'

This was not the man she had been out with last night. She leafed through the telephone directory, all fingers and thumbs. She rang. She found the Alka Seltzer. He drank it, shuddering.

'You'll have to go up and bring the car back,' he said. 'I don't know when I'll be home. Expect me when you see me.'

He ran out to the hire car that had just drawn up and was off.

She felt as though she had gone down in an express lift and landed with a jolt. Still, time now to pull herself together. Sally would have laughed and told her to snap out of it. She would have told Sally about this disastrous end to a wonderful evening and in no time Sally would have had her laughing too. Dotty old Guy. Always carrying on as though the firm would collapse without him. You should let him rant. Take no notice.

But there was no Sally to make light of things now. She made herself eat a slice of dry toast and began to feel better. She had a bath, put on her favourite two-piece and felt better still. By mid-morning, almost fully restored, she took her peace offering over to Ada.

'Oh, but you shouldn't have!' Ada, in a puce-coloured mob cap, looked drained. She had not had much sleep and would have stayed in bed but that the window cleaner was coming. Freesias, tulips, irises. 'My favourites,' she said. Kate began to apologise but Ada refused to listen to her. 'Never mind, and don't go feeling guilty. And don't think you can never ask again. What about a cup of coffee? Yes? Tell me all about it.'

They talked for a long time. Ada could see Kate was under

a strain for without knowing it she gave the game away all the time. Their supper at the restaurant with the old proprietor so warmly welcoming a war-time hero had obviously gone to Guy's head, and after that the music at Ronnie Scott's and the excitement. The poor girl was ecstatic as she talked about it. She so obviously adored her husband and yet she was not entirely at ease with him. Ada saw the whole picture. It was not a nice, comfortable marriage like hers and Jack's, more a series of highs and lows, an almost manic relationship which the little boy might well complicate still further. As to that girl, Fiona ... why, she wouldn't even deign to say good morning to the Fortunes. A spoilt brat if ever Ada saw one.

Guy approved the idea of an extra bathroom and as it was to be built behind the garage he thought they might as well have another room built on top. They engaged an architect, pored over plans and estimates and found a reliable builder to carry out the work.

At the same time Kate found selling Sally's house had fallen to her lot. Guy made it clear he hadn't the time and said his father would probably help, but Ernest Lambert had no time either.

'You'll manage, m'dear,' he mumbled when she approached him. 'There's nothing to it. Easy as falling off a log.'

She hated disposing of Sally's things. There were hundreds of books nobody seemed to want. Second-hand booksellers turned up their noses so she took them to various charity shops in batches after selecting a few special ones for herself and some she thought Paul might like later on.

Tom had not been well off so the furniture was plain and would fetch very little. She managed to persuade a small second-handshop to cart most of it away for twenty pounds and thought the man was joking when he refused to stump up and asked her to pay him for taking it.

'It's for you to pay me,' she said.

'Nothing doing. The whole lot won't fetch a fiver.'

A slow fire began to burn inside her. 'Twenty pounds,' she said. 'That's what you agreed.'

'Joke over?'

'You offered twenty pounds.'

'Come off it.'

'If you won't pay, you can unload the whole lot and put it back in the house.'

'Oh, yeah?'

The neighbours in Magnolia Road heard the altercation and came out to see what was going on when they realised Kate was being swindled. One ran back home to ring the police.

Seeing himself surrounded by fierce young women, and not wishing to be noticed by the police as his shop was a blind for his real business as a fence, he decided to give in. But not all at once. It became a ding-dong between them as he offered ten pounds and then went up in one pound units as Kate continued to insist. Eventually he produced the largest and dirtiest stack of notes she had ever seen and counted them out grudgingly.

'Good,' she said, and went into the empty house feeling triumphant. She could do it. She could hold her own with the toughest of them.

She kept the house looking as attractive as she could, with the curtains clean and fresh, the brass letter box polished and the carpets hoovered after each horde of prospective buyers left but it was badly in need of redecorating inside.

Ella came to look round and advise. 'It was a mistake to get rid of the furniture, dear,' she said. 'An unfurnished house looks so dreary. It makes the shabbiness that much more obvious.'

Perhaps she was right. The house did not sell till the spring and by then Kate was beginning to feel the strain. There was the constant fear of friction because Paul irritated Guy and she was thankful when the Fortunes took him off her hands as they often did at weekends. They enjoyed giving him treats — taking him to the Round Pond on Sunday mornings, the zoo, a river trip to see Nelson's ship.

Once the sale of the house was completed and the proceeds invested for Paul's benefit — and here Ernest Lambert put himself out to procure the best for his grandson — she felt she could relax a little.

*

The new young postman landed Kate in serious trouble with Guy just as she hoped they were entering a more comfortable phase in their lives, for with the extension completed the early morning hassle was much improved and Paul had a playroom.

The old postman, who knew all about discretion, had retired. The new one came much earlier and often arrived before Guy left in the mornings. Sometimes they met at the gate which was exactly what caused the trouble one day. Kate saw them both studying an envelope, looking over at the Fortunes, then at the envelope again. After a few more words Guy came in holding it.

'What's the meaning of this, Kate?' he demanded, handing it to her. It bore an Italian stamp and was addressed to Mrs Guy Lambert, c/o Mrs Fortune, 35 The Avenue.

Kate didn't read any more. She went cold inside. 'It's from Hester,' she said.

'I know who it's from. You arranged this between the three of you, didn't you? Three sly, scheming women!'

'Don't blame the others. I didn't know how else I could keep in touch with Hester now Sally's gone. You'd only have gone off the deep end if she'd written to me here.'

'I've forbidden you to keep up with her. You know that.'

Kate was seized with an inward trembling she couldn't control. Guy in his present mood was frightening. Those eyes! Cold, cruel, piercing. But she had to stand her ground. She had to. Had to.

'I shall never drop Hester,' she said. 'I was wrong to make Ada a go-between. It was a stupid, feeble thing to do.'

'It must stop. We'll have no more of it.'

'You're right. I shall ask Hester to address her letters here in future.'

'That is not what I mean.'

'As Paul's grandmother, Hester has a right to have news of him. Who else can give it but me?'

'If you'd had the decency to discuss it with me I might have agreed to a limited correspondence between you. As it is I shall never be able to trust you again.' He was white with anger but Kate was angry too.

273

'If you imagine I'm going to let you dictate to me you are very much mistaken,' she said, her voice growing stronger with every word. 'I should never have been such a fool as to kowtow to you the way I have done.' She paused, expecting another vitriolic outburst but he was too surprised to protest.

'You'd better go,' she said. 'You're late already.'

Was it Kate who had spoken like that? Had she really dared? A wave of exultation almost lifted her off her feet but subsided as soon as she was alone. All she knew was that she must hold her own from now on or else become a cypher, and she didn't delude herself into thinking it would be easy.

That afternoon she went over to Ada and told her Hester would be writing to her direct in future.

'I was a fool to deceive Guy,' she said.

'You only did it to avoid trouble. I wouldn't call that deceiving him. It's the same as saving out of the house-keeping,' Ada said.

'He doesn't see it like that,' Kate said.

'He's got a thing about Hester. Anyone could see that at Sally's funeral. Anyway, love, don't you worry about it. He'll come round in time.'

Ada was right about that. Guy did come round and Kate found herself pitying him. She knew how much he missed Tom and was unable to express his feelings. She guessed he was as lonely in their marriage as she was herself and longed to be able to break through the invisible barrier that separated them. If only she could find a way to do it. If only they could have another child! But Fiona was nearly sixteen. It would be a big gap and what would the difficult Fiona think of it if it happened?

Try as she might she could never get through to her daughter. Fiona refused point blank to let her read an essay that had won an inter-school competition.

'Why won't you let me read it?' she asked.

'Because you wouldn't understand,' said Fiona.

'How do you know?'

'Because you're retarded.'

'Is that what you really think I am? Retarded?'

274

'I said so, didn't I?'

'Yes, Fiona. You did.'

After that Kate knew for certain she would never have her daughter's affection. The indestructible bond that had held her to her own mother simply did not exist between them. She gave up and in her anguish even spoke of it to Ella.

'Fiona has never liked me,' she said. 'She adores Guy but there's no room in her heart for me. Please don't think I haven't tried. I'm sure she would have been a different child if she'd had brothers and sisters. It was what I wanted right from the start. I wanted several children. It was my dream.'

'What happened then, dear? Couldn't you have any more?'

'It takes two to tango,' said Kate.

'You're not telling me – '

'No, I'm not. It's simply that Guy doesn't want more than one child and no amount of arguing and pleading will make him change his mind. He's adamant.'

'I see, dear. That *is* distressing for you. And of course after all this time ... Fiona's sixteen, isn't she? Ah, well. And now you have Paul to look after. I'm afraid I can't think of a solution, dear. But I'm very sorry. There's nothing I want more than to see my special little family happy.'

She wiped her eyes on a little embroidered handkerchief. 'You are such a dear daughter to me,' she said. 'I really don't know what I should do without you.'

Although Kate was always slightly suspicious of Ella she knew her sympathy was genuine and was encouraged by it.

It was spring again and that was always a time of hope, renewal, promise. It was warm enough for dinner on the patio. There had been a slight shower and for the first time that year there was the intoxicating smell of warm earth and wallflowers. Seven-thirty. Paul was in bed and she'd had no trouble getting him there. The rest of the night was hers and as soon as she heard Guy's car in the drive she had the door open and was waiting to greet him. She took his briefcase and went on tiptoe to kiss him. He was

275

in an amiable mood, it was almost like one of the old days when all was peace and understanding between them.

When the air cooled and they went inside she watched him bolt the garden doors and pull the curtains across and her heart swelled with gratitude. Her husband!

He opened his briefcase and she was sorry to think he had to work but this time it was not the usual stack of estimates and reports that came out. 'Holidays,' he said, holding up some brochures.

She had visions of France, the Med, long days lounging, swimming, eating, drinking. But that was not what Guy had in mind.

'Iceland,' he said, and the word landed with a thud.

'Iceland?'

'That's right. It's almost undiscovered, no tourists to speak of. Why are you looking so bleak?'

'Nothing. It isn't what I expected.'

'All the better. Have a good look through all this stuff tomorrow and then we'll talk about it.' He yawned, stretched his arms. 'I'm whacked,' he said. 'Let's go to bed.'

He took her hand and rushed her up the stairs, but when they were in bed she found he wasn't tired at all.

In spite of her first reaction to Iceland Kate could see there was a great deal to be said for it. It would be an adventure though not exactly a rest cure. Sometimes they would be sleeping in tents, there would be long treks on foot, there was nothing luxurious about it. She thought of it all day and it was not the disadvantages that made her decide against it.

'Well, what do you think?' Guy asked next evening.

'Fine for adults but no good for children,' she said. 'I think we should defer it for a while and take a less strenuous holiday.'

'What a dud reason.'

'Children like buckets and spades,' she said.

'Which children?' There was the hint of a scowl on his face.

'Ours.'

'What are you on about? Fiona's sixteen and she'd love it.'

'I was thinking of Paul.'

'Who suggested taking him?'

'It goes without saying.'

'Of course it doesn't. We'll park him out somewhere.'

'Who with? Your mother?'

'Don't be absurd. You know perfectly well Mother couldn't have him.'

'But there isn't anyone else.'

'Don't worry. I'll dump him somewhere.' He spoke as though Paul was a dog to be put in kennels.

'Not this year,' she said. 'He thinks we're going to Italy.'

'What gave him that idea?'

'It was spoken of at Sally's funeral. They'd all stayed at the Villa Laura – Tom and Sally and Paul. He remembers it and wants to go again.'

'He can get that idea out of his head and so can you.'

'But it's not six months since Sally died, that on top of losing Tom. It takes a long time to recover from a shock like that. Just think how he'd feel if we went off and left him parked somewhere.'

'I've already told you, it won't be for long.'

'But just try to imagine.'

'Boys of six do as they are told.'

This was not Guy speaking – it was a martinet. She didn't say any more.

Next day something disturbing happened. She never passed Magnolia Road if she could help it but as the Post Office was in that direction there were times when she had to and this was one of them. For the first time since Sally's house was sold the side gate was open. The rockery was unchanged but now there was a handrail from the back door to the gate. Those were the posts and that was the wood Guy had ordered because he was going to erect it.

Seeing it there, so strong and secure, made Kate feel physically sick. Sick and guilty.

'You're very quiet,' Guy said that evening. 'Anything wrong?'

'Only the holiday.'

'It'll be a doddle. I've booked three places so the next

277

thing is to get the suitable gear. Boots and all that. The brochure tells you all about it.'

'I'm sorry you've booked. I hoped you'd think better of it,' she said. 'Let's go somewhere we can all enjoy. I'd love to drive down to the Med. Not Italy if you don't fancy it. Fiona would enjoy France, and I'm sure Paul would too.'

'You know what you're doing, Kate? You're ruining that boy.'

'He'll be ruined if he has another upheaval.'

'We are going to Iceland and I shall make other arrangements for my nephew.'

His tone froze her. My nephew! He was excluding her, reminding her that she was not related to Paul any more than she had been related to Sally. She had no relations of her own at all and no say in any of the Lambert family's decisions.

'You won't make other arrangements,' she said, standing up and holding on to the table because she was shaking. 'You can go to Iceland and I shall take Paul to Santa Carlotta. I'll drive there.'

He threw back his head and laughed. 'That's rich! You'd be in a flat spin before you got to Dover. If you really mean to bugger up the holiday you'd better stay at home and weed the garden.'

'By the way,' she said, 'I passed Sally's today. They've got the handrail up. It looks fine.'

She should have stopped there. He looked stricken and there was still time to stop, but she couldn't.

'If only *you'd* put it up, Sally could still be here.'

She had never seen him with a dead white face before, He looked quite different.

'So you think I'm responsible for her death?'

'It could have been avoided.'

He went out of the room without another word and she heard him moving about upstairs. She was frightened by what she had said but it had been somewhere in her subconscious ever since that awful winter day when she found Sally lying on the path. Perhaps, if she hadn't seen the rail, it would not have surfaced. Or was it better out than in?

All this went through her mind as she stood there gripping

278

her hands together, alone and wretched and searching madly for a way to mend the havoc she had caused for with those few words the structure of her marriage had collapsed. She could cry her heart out, plead with him, beg him to take her hand and set about resurrecting it, rediscover all the good things, blot out the hard words each had said to the other. But she knew none of this would help. Her heart was so gripped with misery it scarcely seemed to beat. She remembered some words she had never understood. 'Be still and listen.' If she kept still and quiet would they be restored to each other? She could only try. But much later, when she went up to bed, she found Guy had moved his things into the box room.

Kate had stopped the papers and the milk and given a date on which deliveries were to be resumed, not forgetting to reduce the amount of milk that would be needed and to cancel her favourite magazines. 'Until further notice,' she told the newsagent. It sounded better than forever.

Now she was checking the windows and the back door for the last time. All safely secured. The refrigerator was defrosted, switched off and empty and stood with the door open, but the freezer, her latest acquisition, was well stocked.

She had loaded her car the previous evening and driven it out to the road first thing this morning. Paul was ready in the front seat with a map he had not yet learned to read spread open on his knees.

All she had to do now was to close the front door behind her. Click. And double lock it. Click. Paul, watching from the car, waved and beckoned, excited. She stood on the step, the keys in her hand, wondering what to do with them. Drop them through the letterbox? No. She could just see Guy picking them up and throwing them into the basket on the hall table without a thought.

She gave the front door a final push and went down to the gate still dithering about the keys. She did not want them adding weight to her already overladen handbag. And what about the keys of Guy's Rover? There was no sense in taking so much ironmongery with her. Of course there was the old tobacco tin in the flowerpot under the azalea but was it really safe?

Before she could resolve the problem Ada Fortune came hurrying over, clad in her outmoded blue wrap. A scalpful of rollers was concealed inside an enormous mob cap. The one she sported this morning had a satin bow on the front. 'I set the alarm for six and it didn't go off,' she said.

'Oh, you shouldn't have troubled − you've spoilt your beauty sleep,' said Kate.

'I'd have worried if I hadn't waved you goodbye,' Ada said. 'There's nothing worse than not being seen off. Have you got your St Christopher? Got your St Christopher, Paul? Of course you have.'

Paul grinned at Ada and pointed to his map. 'I'm the navigator,' he said.

'You'll have to keep your eyes open, Paul. You've a long way to go, and don't forget I'll be following you on the map. Oh, is this the address?' she said as Kate handed her a card. 'Hotel Villa Laura. My! Sounds grand, doesn't it? I can just see it. All white with fluted columns and baskets of trailing flowers. That reminds me. I'll dead head your roses while you're away.'

Ada had made several offers of help when Kate surprised her by announcing she meant to drive to Italy. It seemed quite a hazardous thing to do without a co-driver; it would be the first time she had driven on the continent, and alone. Kate did not strike her as an adventurous young woman, rather the reverse, but Jack reminded her they were in the sixties now and things were very different from when she was a girl.

'I think you're very brave,' she told Kate. 'All on the wrong side of the road, too. They say you have to watch it at the roundabouts. Now is there anything I can do?'

'Yes. Would you look after these keys till Guy comes back? I'd be so grateful.'

'Of course I will. Now off you go, love, and enjoy yourself. Goodness knows, you deserve a real holiday after the strain you've been under.'

Kate had often been on the point of telling Ada more of her troubles than she had done already but she had always resisted. I should only regret it if I did, she thought. People remember things you would rather they forgot.

Paul was getting impatient. 'We're going to see my Nonna and we'll miss the boat if we don't hurry,' he said, his head out of the window.

'That would never do,' said Ada, bending down so her face was level with his. 'Will you bring me back a seashell?'

'If I can find a really nice one,' he said.

On an impulse Kate put her arms round Ada's neck and kissed her. So many emotions filled her heart at that moment she could not speak. She saw The Avenue with its pleasant houses and large front gardens, the immaculate grass verges between pavement and kerb, the air of prosperity, of content, that pervaded the atmosphere. She saw her own house; sixteen years measure of hopes, fears and endless disappointments were shut up inside. Sixteen years of marriage to Guy. But why think of it now on this heavenly morning?

Ada returned her embrace. 'There, love, never mind. It will all come right in the end, never fear,' she said, hardly knowing what she meant by those prosaic words or why she offered them apart from an intuition that comfort was needed. Yet how could things come right for Kate apart from the workings of time? And time doesn't heal. It only blunts, she thought.

'Well!' they both said together, and then they laughed and Kate got into the driver's seat, started up and was away with Paul waving to Ada from the window. As they reached the corner she slowed the car so they could both wave and then they were off towards the Dover Road.

Going back indoors Ada gave a little shiver. It was already very warm so a shiver was unexpected — more of a shudder, perhaps. Very odd, she thought, and made a pot of tea and took it upstairs. Jack, lying on his back with his arms behind his head, sat up as she came in.

'So they've gone,' he said.

'Aye, they're away, and now I come to think of it she never said when they'd be back.'

'When's Guy due home?'

'Not for a fortnight.'

'Funny taking separate holidays.'

'Well, you can understand it. He got his idea of going to Iceland and they couldn't take Paul there.'

They sipped their tea, ruminating. Kate had not said much about her trip to Italy and Ada thought it very strange. A great deal was going on under the surface and as she looked out of the window at the Lamberts' house she wondered just what it had been like there in the past few months. Sally Lambert dying as she did was tragic in itself, but the repercussions ...

'Repercussions, Jack,' she said.

'Now what are you on about?'

'Sally. If she were still alive Kate and Guy would have gone to Iceland together.'

'Instead of which they're lumbered with a six year old.'

'Lumbered? How can you, Jack? Paul's Guy's nephew.'

'I know.'

'What more natural than that they should take him in? You wouldn't expect them to put him out for adoption, would you?'

'I might if he was going to drive a wedge between them. But it's no good speculating about other people's motives. Any more tea in that pot?'

She poured the dregs into his cup.

'Cold,' he said.

'Such a pity.' She was still thinking about Kate and her husband. How handsome he was. And had been. She had seen photographs of him in his R.A.F. uniform. He had certainly kept his looks and so had Kate. She was lovely to look at and there was sweetness in her face. Not sentimental picture postcard put-on sweetness. Perhaps goodness was a better description. And to think I almost used to envy them going off with Sally and Tom at weekends and evenings, the four of them!

The sound of Jack gargling his throat brought her back to earth. What a horrible noise he made. She caught a glimpse of herself in the glass and tut-tutted because her mob cap was all awry. Had it been like that when she was out in the road? If so she hoped none of the neighbours had seen.

A small seersucker cloth on the corner of the diningroom table was good enough for breakfast. She kept looking across

282

the road at number 24 as she put the marmalade down. It looked so well kept, only just repainted. Well, she supposed the grown-ups could take care of themselves but Paul was at their mercy. Poor little fellow, she thought.

If that were true he certainly didn't look an object of pity that morning. He sat beside Kate looking important as they took the road to Dover and arrived there in good time for the cross-channel ferry. Kate drove the car on board without any trouble. First hurdle cleared.

The sea was as flat as her drawingroom floor.

'It's solid,' said Paul.

It looked as though you could walk on it, an expanse of smooth dark rubber rolling away for ever. Seagulls wheeled overhead, men shouted, there was the noise of cranking chains, and they stood watching the boat moving away from the side, the gap growing wider and wider, the people on the quayside diminishing in size as the distance between them grew.

'Let's have breakfast and then we'll look out for the French coast,' she said.

'It's there already,' said Paul, pointing.

'Clouds,' she said.

But he was right. Shapes appeared shimmering against the sky. She had never seen the coast of France so clear. Even the tower of the town hall, insubstantial at first, assumed its firm, unmistakable shape, and when they'd had breakfast and were on deck again they could see the beach and the bathing huts and the bathers. There was a holiday atmosphere even before they docked. There were men on the harbour walls fishing and flags flying everywhere.

Of course, it was the 14th of July. Bastille Day! She heard the sounds of France, the cadences of French voices, an accordion playing, shouted greetings, laughter. She was concentrating on the directions, following the line of cars in front. She drove cautiously towards the town centre in the procession that had disembarked from the boat and soon they were through Calais and on the road to St Omer and she began to feel confident, taking the right hand side with an ease that surprised her.

There was a roundabout in every little village and men were fishing wherever there was so much as a puddle. The atmosphere was a tonic. She suddenly felt free and didn't bother to wonder why. This was a spontaneous happiness such as she hadn't known since her schooldays. She had been prone to most glorious upliftings then and if Sally was with her would say: 'I'm so happy!' It happened when the most mundane things were touched by magic and it was happening to Paul now. It was a roundabout churning out its harsh mechanical music in the middle of a gravelled square. She couldn't resist his plea to ride on it and watched as he went round, waving every time he passed.

'I'm thinking of an icecream cornet,' he said after his second turn. They had a large one each, vanilla and strawberry. They walked round the square blissfully licking them.

'We're on our holidays,' said Paul.

The day went by without a hitch. She found a pleasant hotel for the night but next morning it was cooler and the sky was overcast. By eleven o'clock it rained. At first it was a light shower but by midday it had grown heavier and before long it was pouring. Kate drove slowly wishing she had stopped for lunch at Bethune. Her reduced speed annoyed other motorists; they sounded their horns at her but the rain was dancing in the road, the sky was black and visibility so bad she pulled into the side and stopped.

The rain beat on the roof, the windows steamed up and passing cars threw up sheets of water. She felt a twinge of anxiety.

'I'm thinking of a cup of tea,' said Paul.

It was good to be reminded of something as homely as tea.

'I'm afraid you'll have to wait. And we can't have tea till we've had lunch.'

He was not at all perturbed by the odd flash of lightning or the roar of distant thunder and before long saw a patch of blue in the sky and watched it getting larger. As soon as the rain eased off she started up but the windscreen wipers had stuck and wouldn't restart. She didn't know why and had no idea what to do about it. A little longer and the rain stopped completely, the sun came out and the road dried so quickly it was as though a heavenly charwoman had wiped it up. They were on their way again and presently came to Vitry which Kate thought so attractive she decided to stay there till she could get the windscreen wipers repaired.

All the lamp posts were festooned with flowers, there were tubs of them in the streets and the feeling of holiday persisted. She cruised round looking for a hotel and very soon found one. It was in a secluded square so she booked in and then asked about a garage at reception.

A man had just moved away from the desk but he lingered nearby and seemed to be listening. When she went out for the cases he was standing beside a large Jaguar with GB plates. He gave her a wave. Fellow countryman, she thought without enthusiasm. He was square, sandy-haired and wore the kind of clothes she hated. Shorts, rubber shoes and a shirt open to the waist, revealing a hairy chest.

She had one more try to set the windscreen wipers in motion.

'Are you having some trouble?' The man was beside her. 'Can I help?'

'The wipers gave up on me a little way back,' she said.

'Not in the middle of that cloudburst. I hope?'

'I stopped while that was on and afterwards they wouldn't move. I expect the garage will put them right.'

'I might be able to do it,' he said. 'Would you like me to try? Cars are my line.'

'That's really very kind,' said Kate.

'Not a bit. We British must stick together.' She shuddered inwardly and noticed the hair on his chest was going grey.

'My name's Green,' he said. 'The wife and I are going down to the Med. Ah, here she is.'

The wife of Green was coming out of the hotel and didn't look as though she deserved to be referred to as the wife, thought Kate, who liked her on sight.

'Ah, here you are, Stella,' said Green. 'Our friend,' indicating Kate who cringed, 'is having a spot of bother with the wipers.'

'They've bust,' said Paul.

'Oh dear.' Mrs Green had a pleasant smile for Paul. 'Well, I daresay you can fix them, can't you, Fred?' And then to Kate, 'Are you staying here? It's a good little hotel and the food's delicious.'

'I've just booked in and now we're going to have lunch,' Kate said.

'Do you mind if I join you while Fred mends the wipers?' Mrs Green asked. 'We've had lunch but I'd like another cup of coffee. It's really so good here.' Kate went back into the hotel with Mrs Green. 'Come along, Paul,' she called over her shoulder.

'Your son?' asked Mrs Green.

Kate explained the relationship and said they were going to stay with his maternal grandmother who lived in Italy at Santa Carlotta.

'I've never been there before,' Kate said.

'Neither have I. We go camping and it isn't always easy to find a site. I wonder if there are any at Santa Carlotta?'

'I don't know. It's a very small place from what I've heard. It isn't even on the map.'

'Well, we may come across it. As a matter of fact this holiday is mine to plan. A special treat. I've always longed to go to Italy but Fred simply isn't interested. It's Spain every time for him, and I do not like Spain. It gives me the willies. I think it's the bull fights − not that I've ever seen one − or else because they had the Inquisition. Do you get feelings about places?'

Kate got feelings about people but she didn't say so. She agreed about places and said she knew she was going to love Santa Carlotta.

The first course was brought and Paul was pleased to see sardines with the hors d'oeuvres. He told Mrs Green he could eat a whole tin and one day he was going to.

'You'd never get the tin open,' Kate said.

'Bet I would.'

The lunch proceeded at a leisurely pace and they talked about the choice of routes and the best places to stay until Fred Green came back.

'All fixed,' he said.

'Marvellous.' Kate was thankful to be spared leaving the car at a garage. 'You're a genius,' she said.

'I'm an engineer as matter of fact. I've a garage on

the North West Road and we do all kinds of repairs and servicing as well as sales. We're agents for your little bus so I know it very well.'

'All the same, it's very kind of you and I'm most grateful,' said Kate, and thinking that something more than words were required she added: 'Perhaps you'd have dinner with me tonight?'

They thanked her but they were going on, as they were making several overnight stops on the way down.

'I expect we'll spend a night at Nice before striking left for Italy,' Mrs Green said.

'Or right for Spain,' remarked her husband.

'Oh, Fred you wouldn't!' Mrs Green looked worried. Mr Green winked at Kate over his wife's head, put his hand on her shoulder and twisted her towards the door. His hand looked strong, beefy, with ginger hairs.

Kate and Paul went out to see them off. Their car was loaded with camping equipment, all meticulously packed. Mrs Green got in and spread a map out on her knees. 'What was the name of that place you're staying at?' she asked Kate.

'Santa Carlotta.'

'We'll look out for it.'

Mr Green held out his hand. Kate had to take it. 'It's only just struck me. Are you doing all the driving?' he asked.

She laughed. 'Paul's too young yet though I wouldn't put it past him,' she said. 'It's my first taste of continental driving and I'm enjoying it.'

'I take my hat off to you,' he said. He squeezed her hand and gave her an admiring look which she didn't like. 'Take care of her,' he told Paul, and got in and drove out of the square.

She appreciated his help but she didn't like him though she had taken to his wife and would have been pleased to see her again. All the same, she hoped they wouldn't turn up at Santa Carlotta.

Kate never drove for more than two hours at a stretch and limited herself to five hours a day in all. She thought that enough for a six year old. She didn't tire easily herself and

287

exulted in the feeling of freedom. As they cruised along to Martigny she felt she was making for home rather than leaving it.

The day was almost too perfect, too beautiful, with fields of ripe corn on either side. And the flowers along the wayside! Dark mauve clover, small red poppies and clumps of yellow and purple flowers that looked like miniature snapdragons. They got out to look at them and then sat on the grass eating the cherries she'd bought and listening to the buzz of countless insects.

This time last week Kate would never have believed she would have the nerve to tackle this journey without a co-driver, although she had told Guy she would. He had said she'd never get as far as Dover. That taunting voice of his! And weeks later the way he had said: 'This is your last chance, Kate. Will you or won't you come to Iceland with me?'

'I can't leave Paul,' she had said.

'Very well, then. Sandra White can come in your place. Fiona will like that.'

She felt dead inside.

And after he left, without one kind word, the way she had wandered from room to room, lost. It was not until the following day when she went to cash a cheque at the bank that she found herself asking for French and Italian currency. It was as though a powerful spirit had taken her over. Petrol coupons, green card, all the arrangements Guy made for their holidays — she managed it all quite competently and now here they were, she and Paul, eating cherries on their way to Aosta.

Now she knew the thrill of free-wheeling on the descent from the Great St Bernard with the road to themselves and the sun on the mountain peaks and it was glorious. They had spent three nights at comfortable little hotels and very soon now they would be in Santa Carlotta.

'We'll be there in time for tea,' she said.

They were on a narrow, twisting road and there was no other traffic. She had bought a picnic lunch from a delicatessen in Turin and they stopped to eat it as soon as she found a place to pull off the road.

It was extraordinarily quiet. Odd that not a single motorist passed them. It was so quiet she was almost afraid to speak but Paul chattered away. He was insect spotting and kept calling to her to come and look at strange creatures he had found.

'It's a grasshopper,' she said, but then she thought it was a cicada and the noise of the insects was part of the quiet. It was the absence of humanity that made this loud, frightening silence. No cars, no aeroplanes, no voices except for Paul's and her own.

It seemed a long time since they had passed a petrol station and she was running low. There must be one soon, she thought.

Paul had stopped eating. He was sitting on the grass clutching half a ham roll in his hand and he didn't look at all well.

'Come on, let's get going,' she said. 'You'd better break up that roll for the birds if you can't eat it.'

'I feel sick,' he said.

Oh no, she thought. Don't be ill, for goodness' sake. He was looking at her with eyes open to their fullest extent. He was beginning to heave and suddenly clapped his hand over his mouth. He vomited. She knelt beside him and held him hard, trying to absorb the violence of the paroxysms into her own body. He had three bouts of sickness and was exhausted when they were over. Tears ran down his face, his forehead was clammy and he was trembling. She laid him down on the grass and covered him with a rug from the car, cleaning him up as well as she could with a damp flannel from her sponge bag.

He looked a wretched little creature and seemed to have shrunk to half size. She decided it would be better to push on rather than to stay where they were so as soon as she dared she packed him up in the back seat where he could lie quite comfortably.

There was no way of knowing whether the switchback road or the food had upset him, probably a combination of both. Now she drove slowly, taking the sharp turns as slowly as possible and praying civilisation would be round the next bend, but it never was.

She realised now that she had misread a signpost, taken the wrong road and was in the Ligurian Alps. Mile after mile of twisting, tortuous road. She dared not think of brake failure, tyre damage or the petrol running out, but they were all at the back of her mind. The screech of the tyres on the road, pebbles flying ...

She began to feel desperate, her mouth was dry, she was breathing much too fast. And then ahead, in the distance, she caught her first glimpse of the sea and her hopes rose. The road must lead to it but there were many more twists before suddenly, and without warning, she was there, at the Autostrada, with the petrol guage on reserve.

The sight and sound of the roaring traffic had never been so wonderful to see and hear. Juggernauts, cars, lorries − how beautiful they looked, how friendly and familiar and safe.

Paul was awake now, face streaked with dirt but obviously safe from further attacks. She filled up with petrol and stopped at the first trattoria to wash and clean up. There was a patio with rustic seats and tables, and there was the Ligurian Sea.

'What are you thinking of?' she asked Paul.

'I'm thinking of something to drink with a sparkle.'

He had fresh lemonade without any sparkle and she had strong black coffee with four spoonsful of sugar.

'I was no good as a pilot,' he said. 'It was horrid, wasn't it?'

'I think we'll forget the last bit,' she said. 'We've still quite a long way to go so I'll ring your Nonna or she'll be worrying.'

A man's voice answered her call. 'Kate Lambert here,' she said.

'Kate! Where on earth are you? Oh, Aldo here. Aldo Bianchi, remember?'

Of course she did. The man who had escorted Hester and taken them to dinner. She told him she was near Savona and would he tell Hester they would soon be there?

She was very tired, much too tired to go any further, but it was less than fifty miles now and she didn't want to spend another night on the road.

The light was fading by the time they reached Santa

Carlotta. The town had a narrow main street with buildings on either side that hid the sea. She knew the hotel would be on her right and there it was, in the dusk, waiting for them. It stood back from the road and a lamp near the front door swung in the warm breeze and shed a flickering light.

Paul had been asleep but he began to stir. She got out, stiff from sitting so long, and leaned against the car finding it hard to focus.

'That's Nonna's house! We're here!' Why don't we go in?'

Because I'm not sure it's real. Yet it's as Sally described — the iron gates, the gravel paths, the huge old acacia trees leaning down and the lawn. There's the pool in the middle, the fountain. And there's the house. Magnificent at a distance, Sally always said, and it is. Shallow marble steps sweeping down from the door and the balustrade invisible beneath that unbelievable bougainvillaea.

Kate remembered laughing at bougainvillaea and saying it sounded like a prop from an old film, and Sally laughed too. Exactly like that, she had said,. You'd know it by the bougainvillaea even if the name wore off.

But the name was still there. 'Hotel Villa Laura' on a plaque fixed to the gatepost. Kate traced it with her finger. Then she got back in the car and drove in, over the gravel path that was thick with weeds, past the tangled lawn, the empty pool and the dry fountain that was thick with moss. Not a bit like Sally had said.

There was no one in the hall and only one low-powered lamp in a pink glass shade on a side table. She stood uncertainly holding Paul's hand, gradually seeing things as her eyes adjusted to the light. The floor was marble; there was a small untidy desk that didn't look as though anyone ever sat there to write, and several ornately carved chairs upholstered in faded rose tapestry. The dark glass of a massive mirror in an ornate gilt frame lent their reflections a softened appearance. Their pallor after the long journey and their crumpled clothes were reflected kindly.

'Where's Nonna?'

She couldn't see a bell anywhere but as though in answer to a summons a man appeared at the top of the stairs and flicked a switch so the hall was flooded with light from a great chandelier.

'Aldo, Aldo, where's Nonna?' shouted Paul, running to the stairs.

Aldo Bianchi, in casual clothes, did not look anything like the man in a dark suit who had come to Sally's funeral.

'Nonna was called away not a minute ago,' he said. He took Paul's hand and then Kate's. 'We've been worried about you, it's good to see you.'

'It's good to be here.' She sat on one of the carved chairs.

'How long were you driving?' he asked.

'Seven hours.'

'Much too long. I'll find Hester.'

A boy and girl scampered in at the front door, paused to stare and ran halfway up the stairs, calling for Signor Aldo. They ran down again as he reappeared in the hall and grabbed a hand each.

'Hold on. Not so fast,' he told them, and to Kate: 'Hester's on her way. One of the Albini kids pushed a bean up his nose and his mother all but blew her top. Hester was called to the rescue.'

While he was speaking the children were trying to drag him away. 'We're going to the Piazza to see the illuminations and these kids think the lights will go out if we don't run all the way.'

A door slammed. 'Here she is,' he said, and went out with the jabbering children as Hester came running towards them with outstretched arms.

Paul ran to her. 'I thought you'd got lost,' he said.

'As if I would, my darling.' She dropped on one knee and Paul flung his arms round her neck and nuzzled his face against hers.

Seeing them together Kate knew how right she had been to bring him. Hester was hugging him and looking at Kate over his head, smiling, welcoming her. 'To think you arrived just as I was called away,' she said. Kate was crying and saying, 'It's so wonderful to see you. Oh, you don't know!'

'I know how I've longed for you to come. My dear, dear

darlings. You're exhausted, both of you, and you must be famished as well.'

'Not really,' Kate was too tired to eat but Hester was leading the way to a small comfortable sitting room where a table was laid for supper. Paul had orange juice in a tall crystal glass; Kate was thankful for tea. 'I was gasping for this,' she said. 'I'm just beginning to realise how frightened I've been. We were lost in the Alps. I took the wrong road.'

'So that was it! It can be horrendous.'

'It was. But I'll tell you tomorrow.'

Paul had fallen asleep and looked like a very tired little old man with his pasty face and spiky hair.

'Shame to wake him,' Hester said. 'Can you carry him?'

Kate could and did. He woke momentarily, looked at Hester and said: 'Nonna, my other granny has blue hair now,' and was off again.

The room to which Hester took them was cool and rather bare. Their luggage had been brought in but Kate couldn't think of unpacking. 'I could sleep forever and a day,' she said.

'Bath first?'

'No. Just sleep.'

Hester hugged her. 'You don't know what it means to me having you here,' she said.

Kate eased off Paul's jeans and T-shirt without waking him, pulled the sheet over him and then collapsed on her own bed. She didn't even hear Hester go.

Hester closed the door quietly and leaned her back against it. She fought back tears and controlled the sob that was filling her throat. She mustn't cry but it was hard work not to when she recalled that not much more than a year ago Sally and Tom and Paul had spent their summer holiday with her.

She went slowly down the corridor of the empty hotel Gianni had recently sold to Aldo Bianchi, retaining the annexe at the back and the peach orchard which was now a holiday camp. Sally would have applauded that. The Villa

Laura could not compete with the modern purpose-built hotels the tourists favoured but the camp had a future. Aldo's plans for the Villa had not materialised yet and until they did she organised what work had to be done and could use the rooms as she wished.

She went outside to the camp where some of the tents were in darkness while in others lamps shone through the red, yellow and tan canvas walls. There were cooking smells. A lot of chatter came from the Albini tent; from another she heard the drone of an old voice reciting the rosary and a young one joining in; there were transistors, the sound of cicadas in the trees, then a sudden overpowering burst of pop music from the dance hall at the restaurant up the hill. That meant it was nine-thirty and Gianni would be shutting the shop.

She went down the dusty lane under the olive trees and into the road. The shop was on the corner and stocked a bewildering variety of goods, tinned, dried and fresh. Gianni was at the counter checking invoices when she went in and he looked up, eyes questioning. His eyes were beautiful, large and clear for all his forty-five years.

'They've arrived. Tired out and sound asleep by now,' she said.

She sank down on a sack of grain and he came round the counter, locked the shop door and sat on the next sack while she told him.

'Time you came home,' she said at last.

'You look worn out yourself,' he said. 'Have you had a tough day? Is the camp full?'

'Pretty well. Lots of Germans with lovely cars and swish tents. One English couple by the name of Green, some French, two Dutch, and our usual Italians.'

'And what about our own couple?'

'Too travel weary for words but Kate looks beautiful even so. She'll take your breath away, Gianni. Terribly thin, though.'

'She won't stay that way on your food,' he said. 'Did she say what decided her to come so suddenly?'

'No, but she will. I know there's something wrong. She looks so strained.'

'Can you wonder, driving from London? Come on, let's go.'

He went to the door at the back of the shop and shouted up the stairs: 'Mama, Papa, we are going now. Back early tomorrow.'

'Right, Gianni,' came Papa Morelli's deep voice, and Mama joined in with her blessing: 'Goodnight, sleep well,' which took rather a long time as her children were still children to her.

Hester followed Gianni into his kitchen garden where she could just discern row upon row of beans growing, ranks of raspberry canes, plantations of red and white currants, sturdy tomato plants where the sun shone hottest, fig trees close by the old brick wall, and hard against it the espaliered nectarines.

It was peaceful and delightfully warm; everything seemed to hold the heat of the sun and there was the smell of wet earth from the sprinkler hose. She liked to hear the soft clucking from the chicken runs at the far side.

She put her arm through Gianni's and happiness flowed into her. He was hoping Kate and Paul were not going to upset her although she was bound to find them disturbing. Her little grandson – she worried about him. Gianni remembered Kate as Sally's schoolgirl friend but that was years ago and since then she had married a snobbish Englishman and produced a child called Fiona who was far from amiable. Sally used to tell them unbelievable things about this cold-hearted girl who seemed to delight in spiting her mother.

They were home in the annexe of the hotel where they lived blissfully together.

'I'll pop the lasagne in the oven while we have a drink,' Hester said.

Gianni produced a bottle of wine; he laid the table, wandered into the kitchen for bread and cheese and arranged a large bowl of fruit from his garden. The peaches were prime, still warm from the sun, he had some dessert gooseberries, their thin green skins tinged with yellow and absolute perfection, and a few bunches of white currants.

Hester came back and put out his cigars ready for

afterwards and then sat opposite him at the table. He was a thin man in spite of the deliciously fattening food he liked, and extraordinarily handsome, like all his family. She enjoyed looking at him, not so much for his fine features and the set of his head as the goodness in his face. Sometimes she was quite frightened by it, she was afraid he would die. She knew she was crazy but happiness was rather frightening and she sometimes thought she had had more than her fair share of it with Gianni.

He poured the wine. They clinked glasses. She had felt tense all day thinking of Kate driving from home but now she could relax. The wine was good, the red glow of his cigar made her feel peaceful and secure, their enormous double bed was turned down ready to get into. Would we be as happy if we were married? she wondered, and knew they could never be more so.

Gianni always slept soundly but Hester lay awake for hours that night. Making love was the best sedative on earth but it hadn't worked this time and she could only put her wakefulness down to the stress of the day. But now it was morning and with the sun rising her natural optimism reasserted itself.

'Gianni, time to get up. Gianni!' She kissed the tip of his nose, pulled his ear, and he stirred lazily and was awake. He gave her a huge hug. Lucky she'd woken early. He was in no mood to get up yet.

'Coffee,' she said at last. She wore a flimsy see-through nightdress which flattered her. Her skin was good, she had slim arms and legs and beautiful feet, and she had always taken care of her neck so she looked very well. Gianni never tired of watching her but she didn't stay. She would give him coffee now and he would go down and collect the eggs and work in the kitchen garden gathering fruit and vegetables till it was time to open up shop. Then he would breakfast with his mother. Hester often joined them but this morning she would stay at the Villa with Kate and her grandson.

Morning was heaven with the sun coming out and the hills sloping up and away at the back of the Villa Laura to a

296

gently undulating skyline. In the hills a cottage window took fire from the sun and sparkled like an enormous diamond. There were groups of tiny half-primitive houses up there, each with its piece of land to cultivate, and the tall spire of a church at the top glittered in the early light.

Soon the camp began to stir. In a little while it would present a bustling scene with people packing up to leave, others arriving and those already settled going about their various employments at whatever pace suited them.

Kate woke to a chorus of voices — strident, assertive, shrill, but eminently cheerful. She stirred lazily. The room was dark but a thread of light on the floor beside her bed struck the polished floor, the faded rug, and a sandal which lay sole uppermost on top of its fellow. She made out a greenish stain on the instep from the grass she had cut after the rain a few days ago.

But that was at home and she wasn't going back.

She kicked the sandals out of her way and pushed the shuttered window open. A lizard on the sill whisked away. She scarcely saw it as she turned to look at the sun pouring over the bed from which she had just risen. The crumpled sheet was thin as butter muslin and the striped ticking of the mattress showed through.

Paul's bed was near the window. He stirred in his sleep, his face pudgy and pale as wholemeal bread, his hair spiky but with a silken gleam. She remembered being fascinated by a Japanese boy's hair standing up straight in its black silken spikes. She had been tempted to touch it and see if it would lie flat under her fingers or spring up again. Paul's was like that only not so dark.

He sat up, wide awake. 'Hallo, Kate,' he said. 'What's this place?'

'As if you didn't know! We're at your Nonna's. Don't you remember arriving last night?'

He frowned, put his arms behind his head. 'Of course I do. But I don't remember this room. Its a bit grotty-looking, isn't it?'

'It isn't grotty outside. Come and look out of the window.'

He padded across in his skin. The lizard was back on the sill, green, with eyes like tiny glinting stones.

'Look at all the tents!' he exclaimed.

They ranged beneath groves of peaches. People were going in and out, shouting to one another, carrying buckets of water, bags full of rolls, packets of cereal, bottles of milk. The hubbub must have woken her but she hadn't expected to see a camp under Hester's window.

'Can we have a tent?'

'I shouldn't think so. We didn't bring one.'

Aldo Bianchi was walking towards the house along the central path between the peach trees. She saw his hair had flecks of grey in it. He looked up. 'Coming for a swim?' he shouted.

'Yes,' said Paul. 'Wait for us.'

'Not till after breakfast. We're starving,' said Kate.

'We'll be on the beach all the morning. It's pebble and grit with chunks of oil. You need shoes.'

The boy and girl who had been with him the night before were tagging along with towels over their shoulders. They both wore little round linen hats. She wondered what had happened to his wife. He waved and disappeared from view. Paul was excited by all the people and the activity. He was also very dirty, and said what did it matter as he would be going in the sea, but she insisted on a bath. They were both ready when Hester knocked at the door.

'Good. You're up. Feeling better?' she asked.

'Marvellous,' Kate said.

'Nonna, I want a tent. I want to go on the beach with Aldo —'

'You want your breakfast,' said Hester, giving him a hug and kiss. 'What would you like to eat?'

'Egg,' he replied.

Kate shook her head. 'Say an egg and please,' she reproved.

'Egg please,' he responded.

'You shall have one of Gianni's,' Hester told him.

Kate asked if the hotel was full as they went along the corridor.

'There's no one here except you two and Aldo,' said

298

Hester. 'It's not a hotel any more. We sold it to Aldo but the annexe is still ours and so is the orchard. Camping is all the go these days and the orchard is just right for it.'

The annexe was a long building extending along the back of the hotel. It consisted of a large sitting room, two bedrooms, kitchen, all the usual facilities and it gave on to the verandah where Hester spent most of her time. A straggly old vine grew up the side and smothered the roof and the trendrils looped down to the iron railings. Wooden steps led down to the ground. There was a large table and an assortment of chairs, both upright and for lounging. Shelves on either side of the door were stacked with crockery, paperbacks, magazines, sandals and sun hats. Directly under the verandah was the camp shop which was doing a brisk trade judging from the noise.

The coffee was ready and Hester brought it out in a large brown jug with another one of milk. There was a basket of rolls, a slab of butter and some assorted preserves, and by the time it was all ready the eggs were boiled. Kate fell on them. They were rather small but better flavoured than any she had tasted for years. Hester cut little slivers of buttered roll for Paul and he dipped them into the yolk till it was all gone and then spooned out the white. She didn't eat herself but drank several cups of coffee.

'It all tastes so good,' said Kate, helping herself to another egg. 'I was a punctured balloon last night but I'm blowing up nicely now.'

'That's what Santa Carlotta does for you,' said Hester, pleased to see them eating so well.

'We saw Aldo crossing the camp when we got up,' Kate said. 'Heaven knows what he thought of me still thick with dirt and looking quite blotto. He had his two kids with him and invited us to bathe.'

'They're not his kids,' Hester said. 'He's not married.'

'They seem very attached to him,' said Kate.

'They're the underprivileged from the big towns round here. They come in droves in the summer and stay at local schools and convents. Aldo helps the nuns by looking after them, and there are usually one or two tagging on to him as a special treat.'

'I'm surprised he's not married,' said Kate.

'So am I. He'll settle down one day, I suppose. Sometimes he'll bring a girl here with him but not many girls are prepared to share him with the children so love's mostly a winter pastime with him.'

Kate laughed. 'He sounds quite a character,' she said.

Paul had finished eating and Hester asked him what he thought of the camp. 'You'll find plenty of people of your age down there,' she said.

He went and looked through the railings, enthralled by the tents and the people. There was a huge marble sink in front of the camp shop and half a dozen women were washing their dishes and carrying on conversations in loud lively voices. Most of them were in beach wear regardless of suitability, all seemed good-humoured. Small children were entrusted with piles of plastic tableware to carry back to their tents. One dropped a mountain of plates and the ensuing hubbub brought Hester to the rail.

'It's Cesare Albini, the one who got the bean stuck up his nose last night,' she said. Cesare, undismayed, stacked up the plates and took them back to be re-washed.

'Do you see that big blue tent with the cat sitting outside?' Hester asked Paul. 'That's the Albinis'. They'll be going to the beach soon.'

'I can swim,' Paul said.

'I daresay they'll take you with them if you'd like to go.'

'He won't understand a word they say,' Kate protested.

'I will, I will!' shouted Paul.

Hester was sure he would fall in with them easily enough. 'Then you and I can talk a bit,' she said.

'That's what I'm busting for,' said Kate.

'Rosa!' shouted Hester, leaning over the rail and addressing a short square woman who had just emerged from the blue tent in a bikini over which she wore a hip-length smock. Her head was swathed in a scarf and she wore a triangular nose protector. She came and stood in front of the verandah, large feet planted apart, a child by each hand and others at the rear.

Hester was asking her if she would take Paul with them as

Kate was not yet ready. Rosa saw Paul peeping at her through the railings and her face expanded in a huge smile.

Yes, of course she would take him and she would see he didn't come to any harm. Certainly she was going to paddle and she wouldn't let go of his hand.

They all went down, Paul shy but eager.

'You'll come soon, won't you?' he asked Kate.

'Yes. Now don't swim till I get there. Just paddle with Signora Albini. Understand?'

'Yes,' he said.

The little brown Albini children gathered round all smiles and wonder. A small girl took Paul's hand, giggling. He knew a word or two of greeting. '*Buon giorno*,' he said politely. They all came back with it in a chorus, they laughed so much that Cesare fell over. Wasn't it comical to find a little foreign boy speaking their words? Rosa took Paul's hand and the whole party trooped off carolling '*buon giorno*' at the tops of their voices.

'He looks so small and puny beside those children,' Kate said.

'You won't know him after a week or two here,' said Hester cheerfully.

He breaks my heart, thought Kate.

A camper came by and stopped to talk to Hester and Kate turned away and wandered aimlessly towards the Albinis' tent where the little cat was sitting outside. It had unusual markings, broad dark stripes on much lighter fur and huge yellow eyes. It rolled over on its back when she tickled it and clawed at her hand pushing with all four feet.

Hester was beside her. 'Isn't it pretty,' she said. 'I wonder if they'll take it home with them.'

'Are they staying long?'

'Rosa and the kids are here for the summer. Her husband comes at weekends. A good many families do that.'

They went back to the verandah and Hester poured more coffee. She lit a cigarette. It's no good beating about the bush, she thought, and came straight out with what was on her mind.

'You don't have to tell me if you'd rather not, Kate, but why did you make such a snap decision to come?'

301

She could see Kate felt desperate and soon realised there were much worse problems for her to solve than Hester had even guessed at. Fiona actually disliked her mother and had told her so more than once. She hero worshipped Sandra White and would have liked to live with her. Then there were all the minor irritations. Kate always did the wrong thing, said the wrong thing and upset Guy. He had begun to see her through Fiona's eyes. She was a drip. She made friends with the wrong people. She was odd man out in their family of three.

'I've been in love with Guy all my life,' she told Hester. 'I tried to help him in his career every way I could except the way he wanted. I was simply not one of his crowd. But it was bliss at first, when he was still in the RAF, and when he first started this job. But I did so want more children – a large family. But please don't think he's to blame for everything. I've been a weak kneed fool. And then, when I make a stand, it's the wrong one.'

Hester pitied Kate with all her heart. Knowing how sensitive she was it was easy to understand how deeply she had been hurt. She knew how she had cringed from Fiona's offensive remarks and Guy's disdain. Sally had told her as much as she knew of the Lamberts' uneasy family life but Hester had never heard it from Kate's own lips and now it was coming out in an uninterupted flow. How to advise, how to help this girl she loved as much as if she had been her own – what could she say?

She was surprised to find how far Kate had gone in her plan for the future. Working at Orlando Hope's – well, that was feasible – but living alone with Paul, arranging for his education, being entirely responsible ... it was a tall order. And would the elder Lamberts permit it? Surely something could be done to salvage her wreck of a marriage? She tried her best to suggest alternatives.

'No,' said Kate to everyone. 'I'm never going back to him.' She twisted her hands and tossed her head to shake away the tears as she recalled what Guy had been to her and how she had loved him. Oh, for one embrace, one kind word, one assurance that he still wanted her.

'Kate darling, this separate holiday may change everything.

302

He'll realise how much he needs you. Don't believe it's all over.'

'But it is. I told him Sally would still be alive if he'd put up the handrail he promised. I blamed him for her death and I still do.'

Hester felt a chill at this. She could almost see Guy's cold eyes turned on Kate and feel his fury. His was not the hot anger that burns itself out but an icy one that grows thicker and deeper.

'Even so,' she said.

Kate was so ashamed of the situation she had created for herself that she didn't know how to tell Hester about it. She didn't know how to get it out. At last she said: 'He hasn't slept with me since. He sleeps in another room.'

What was the answer to that? Hester put her arms round Kate just as though she were a child. She had never been hurt like this herself, rejected, humiliated, but she knew the pain must be deep and all pervading.

At last she said: 'This is all too much for you to solve alone, my dear. I think you should write to Guy, just a short letter telling him where you are, and perhaps it would be wise to let George know, too? Don't tell Guy you've left him. After that try to treat this as a real holiday. Live for each day and enjoy it. Later on you may feel quite differently, so don't burn your boats. There's nothing like a good rest, lots to eat and drink and being with people who really love you to work wonders. How's that?'

Kate was still recovering from the ordeal of reliving her experiences but the sobs were beginning to subside. Presently she was in control of herself.

'You've time for a dip before lunch,' Hester said. 'Why not go down to the beach?'

'I think I will,' Kate said.

A row of shops opposite the Villa Laura obscured the sea from view. It was reached by way of an alley. Kate soon discovered that Aldo had been right about the oil. It lay on the gravelly beach like pieces of coal and the people who flocked there every day accepted an occasional plastering as a minor inconvenience.

No rows of umbrellas in brilliant colours blossomed on this strand but there were a few dilapidated ones looking like survivors from a storm. Some rather tattered deckchairs lay about for anyone to use. It was a free beach in no way related to those with manicured sands and high prices not half a mile away, and the bathers who basked in sea or sun here were of a different order too.

A cheerful atmosphere prevailed. Family parties had no pretensions to anything higher than their own comfortable state and although the children might squabble among themselves there was no doubting their affection.

Kate had never been anywhere like it. The colourful scene lay before her when she emerged from the alley in all its blatant vulgarity, and she loved it. She saw fat jolly women bulging out of their bikinis, surrounded by clamorous children. She longed to join them. Old women, grotesque in swimsuits, their legs hideously veined, their feet mishapen by corns and bunions, lay on bright straw mats for the sun to shine on them. They anointed themselves with sun tan oil and kept bottles of spirit and cotton-wool ready so they could clean off any smears of tar-like oil.

The children ran in and out of the sea screaming with excitement, young men with splendid torsos preened themselves and swam out to a raft for the pleasure of diving off it over and over again while others paddled themselves out on air mattresses or in little inflatable dinghies.

Next to the free beach was a section roped off for the holiday children, the underprivileged from the towns and cities. They were even more vocal than the family children but their behaviour was exemplary. There were so many of them that they bathed in batches. Kate saw them splashing about in the water, splashing, swimming and throwing rubber balls, but one sharp blast on a whistle blown by a nun sitting in a deckchair brought them all out. There were no stragglers, they obeyed instantly, picked their barefoot way to where she was sitting and donned their round cotton hats while another blast sent the next batch hurtling in. They raced down with whoops of joy and flung themselves into the water. A safety boat, plying from one side of their roped off strip to the other, prevented them from going out too far. Near it, sometimes holding on to the side, sometimes swimming strongly, was Aldo. He came back to the shallows and swam among the children, tossing the ball when it was thrown to him, shouting commands in his harsh voice. He seemed to persuade the more timid ones to venture in up to their necks and was obviously teaching them to swim.

She was fascinated but wanted to find Paul and began to look for the Albinis. She found them close to the sea. Rosa had reserved their pitch with towels and was paddling close to the shore with the children. The water was up to Paul's thighs and he was splashing his free hand in it and sending cascades of drips over one of the girls who returned it with interest. He spotted Kate. 'Come on,' he yelled. 'I want to go deeper.'

She waded in, glad of her beach shoes as the stones were sharp. The tide was ebbing. Waves purled up to the shore foaming as they broke with a sibilant sound, and then receded, dragging the loose pebbles with them.

Rosa extended her hand and Kate gripped it. She liked this friendly handshake and the way Rosa raised her arm in an expansive gesture as though to embrace the sea and sky and indicate her pleasure in them. Kate thanked her for looking after Paul.

'He's enjoying himself – the more the merrier,' Rosa said, or something very like it. Paul was calling her Mama Rosa, he knew the names of all her children, and although he longed to swim he didn't want to lose sight of them.

Kate took him out a little way but she was careful not to go out of her depth, especially as most of the swimmers had left. Rosa, on shore now, was collecting her things and calling for Massimo, Mariella, Luigi, Cesare, Luisa in an ear-shattering voice. Not one of them could pretend they didn't hear her.

The last of the holiday children were out of the sea and lining up in a crocodile. They began to move off in single file, their white hats bobbing as they passed the nun in charge who was counting them.

'Everyone's going home to lunch. Perhaps we should go too,' Kate said.

'Not yet, Kate, not yet.' Paul had been able to swim from

infancy and he slid free of her and made off, to be caught by Aldo who had dived under the dividing rope. Paul stopped, treading water.

'Never swim out on a falling tide,' said Aldo.

'Why?'

'Because you'll be swept out to sea.'

'Oh. Then I'll swim back to shore,' Paul said.

'You'd have to be some swimmer to do that,' Aldo told him.

'He's been paddling with the Albinis all the morning,' Kate said. 'I was late coming down.'

'Then you've seen nothing of Santa Carlotta yet?'

'No. Hester and I have been catching up with our news.'

They waded towards the shore together. She picked up her beach bag and put a towel over her shoulders and one for Paul whose skin was reddening slightly.

'That's right. You don't want to fry,' Aldo said.

She was conscious of her pale skin. It made her feel undercooked. Aldo's tan probably never left him; he shone with an animal gleam and the muscles rippled in his arms and back. He had a powerful look.

'Are you coming home?' he asked. 'I'm eating with Hester today. I was wondering if you'd like me to show you the town afterwards so you'll know your way around?'

'I'd like that very much.'

'Good. We'll buy you a straw hat. Now, if you'll excuse me, I'll go on. I have to pick up some wine on the way.'

She watched him walk up the beach and wondered how much she was going to like him. He seemed to be part of the Villa Laura scene, completely at home there.

Only a few stragglers remained on the beach now. A couple who had been sunbathing were just getting to their feet; the woman had her back to them and was shaking the loose sand from a towel. The man, stockily built, looked round, saw Kate and said loudly, 'Well, I'll be darned! Mrs Lambert!' He was over, grasping her hand. 'Of all the beaches in Italy,' he said.

'You couldn't call it the smartest,' said Kate. She was not at all pleased to see Fred Green.

'It must be the oiliest. But Stella likes it.'

His wife had turned at the sound of their voices and immediately joined in with exclamations of surprise and pleasure. 'Why, it is nice to see you, Mrs Lambert. And Paul. But it's not really a surprise. I liked the sound of Santa Carlotta when you mentioned it, and as soon as we drove in I said, "this is it, Fred. This is where we'll stay." And then we found the Villa Laura camp site and that's where we are so I guessed we'd run into you sooner or later.'

'That camp's the best we've struck in all our travels,' her husband said. 'Such a situation! You've had no more trouble with the windscreen wipers, I hope?'

'No more rain but plenty more trouble, though not with the car. I'll tell you sometime,' said Kate. 'I'm still indebted to you, Mr Green. Without your help we'd probably still be at Vitry.'

'I doubt it. With your looks help wouldn't have been long coming.'

She turned off the compliment with a laugh. She simply did not like him. He had helped her. She was grateful, but she didn't like him.

'Call us Fred and Stella,' he said. He ruffled Paul's hair and was met with a cool stare.

'I bet your tent's not nearly as big as the Albinis',' Paul said, neatly putting Fred in his place. Kate chuckled inwardly. He resented people treating him as a pet. 'We'll be late for lunch,' she said.

They strolled back together. Fred walked with her and Paul with Stella whom he obviously liked as he talked all the way.

Hester was on the verandah when they arrived and the Greens stopped to tell her how pleased they were to meet Kate again. She left them talking and went with Paul to take a shower. There were showers in the washrooms but Paul was smitten with the one in the open where campers were splashing off the dirt and the salt of the sea. There was plenty of chatter and calling out. The Albinis, dripping with fresh clear water, were just departing.

'*Giorno*,' they said when they saw Paul. '*Spaghetti*.'

'*Spaghetti*!' he shouted, dancing about. '*Spaghetti, spaghetti*!'

The shower was cold. Kate stood underneath and let it stream over her while Paul streaked in and out. He took off his trunks and put them over his head, he sloshed Cesare with them and they both rolled in the dust.

'Get up at once!' shouted Kate and Mama Rosa dived in and separated them and then held them under the shower till they shrieked for mercy but were not in the least abashed.

The Greens had left when they returned to the verandah. Aldo was mixing a green salad. Hester was in the kitchen so Kate went to their room, combed her wet hair straight back and put on her lime green linen dress. It was sleeveless with a large square neck and patch pockets.

Paul was at the table with his knife and fork at the ready when she went back. He was telling Aldo how far he could swim and that he went to the baths every day when they were at home.

'Here's Gianni,' called Hester. 'Now we can begin.'

Kate's memories of Giovanni Morelli belonged to her teenage years. Now here he was, a highly respected middle-aged man who gave her an enormous hug and made her feel at ease with him. Who, seeing him now, would guess at all the trouble he had caused?

A harmonious atmosphere prevailed on the verandah. They ate anchovies with a tomato salad, and the flavour of the firm-fleshed, sun-ripened fruit sprinkled with garlic and parsley sent Kate into ecstasies.

'Only Hester can make a salad like this,' Aldo said, and Kate listened while he and Gianni argued about the exact proportions of oil and vinegar that should be used, and Hester told Kate in an undertone that she never measured anything.

Ham was served next with a dish of green beans swimming in butter and potatoes sliced and fried a mouthwatering brown. They ate contentedly. The talk desultory. They drank the local wine. Hester was telling Gianni about the Greens and their meeting with Kate at Vitry and how Stella Green had liked the sound of Santa Carlotta.

Kate was puzzled by her instinctive recoil from Fred Green.

She had felt exactly the same at their second meeting on the beach this morning and began thinking about likes and dislikes. She liked Gianni, she had felt a positive glow of warmth for Signora Albini, and she was pretty sure she would like Aldo when she knew him better.

Quietness fell in the afternoons. Dogs snoozed in the sun, campers reclined on loungers under the shade of the peach trees or inside their tents. Traffic chugging past the Villa Laura was reduced in volume and there were not many pedestrians on the street. Kate paused to look back at the Villa Laura.

'It's really beautiful,' she said.

'It's no good as a hotel now,' Aldo told her. 'Too far from the good beaches and the wrong end of town. You'll see the new hotels further on. The Morellis did well to give up and go in for camping. Here's the convent where the holiday children are staying. There's another up the hill and several more further on.'

'I saw crocodiles of them this morning,' said Kate. 'They reminded me of ants on the march.'

'Ants on the march are ruthless. They go through anything. I'd rather think of them as individuals,' said Aldo. 'Here's the hat shop.'

The shop sold everything for the beach and most things a camper would need as well as innumerable hats. They came in straw or linen. Most of the straws had enormous brims and Kate tried on several while Aldo watched critically. Wrong colour. Not that one, no good. Yes, that's the one.

It was a coolie hat of finely woven straw and a brim that seemed to be made of ears of wheat. It was most becoming. She opened her purse but Aldo forestalled her.

'Oh no,' she protested. The assistant beamed, looking from one to the other, a little man like a stage Italian waiter, all shrugs and smiles. 'It is the gentleman's privilege,' he murmured.

'It was my idea. I chose it,' Aldo said.

'But I can't let you pay,' she said.

'Next time the treat's on you.'

'O.K.' She was pleased with her hat and didn't want to argue.

'Here's Gianni's shop and you can see a bit of his garden,' Aldo said. 'His parents live over the shop and his brother Antonio has that house just up the hill. Antonio has many children. One of the girls is getting married to a friend of mine soon. Now, here's the level crossing.'

The pole had been lowered and a procession of cars was waiting to cross. A woman ducked under the barrier and ran across the lines with a dog at her heels.

'I don't like this kind of crossing,' said Kate. 'What's to stop a child walking under? We have gates at home. They're much safer.'

'It's custom. We are used to this kind.'

She could hear the train approaching and a moment later it roared past, then the poles went up and they continued on their way. Aldo pointed out the station and the bank and presently they came to the Piazza. One side formed part of the promenade by the sea, shops lined the two others, and a church occupied most of the fourth side. They had reached it by way of a narrow lane making a gloomy approach to the piazza which seemed to burst into radiance like a lily. The light was dazzling and the church gleamed like an edifice of gold. Palm trees lined the promenade and there was well-watered grass beneath them and beds of brilliantly coloured flowers: zinnias, salvia, begonias, marigolds.

The shops attracted Kate. They were small and elegant, their windows protected by canopies, bead curtains at the open doorways. Oleanders grew outside and scented the air.

'They have such lovely things,' Kate said, and they dawdled to look at richly coloured leather goods — embossed book covers, smooth handbags, and then there were shoes, all kinds of shoes, the fine leather dyed delicate shades of lavender, pink, grey; sandals were made of multi-coloured thongs; shoes of brightly woven straw. Aldo was admiring them too.

'I was a barefoot boy,' he said. 'Shoes fascinate me.'

Kate laughed. She had noticed his shoes of cream-coloured leather that looked as soft as kid and were obviously

310

expensive. She thought he was joking. 'You barefoot? I suppose you were in tatters too?'

'All but. If it hadn't been for my mother's mending we'd have been a crew of raggamuffins.'

'I didn't realise you meant it,' she said apologetically.

'It doesn't matter. We were so happy we didn't mind being poor. A happy childhood lasts for life, don't you think?'

'I hadn't thought about it. Perhaps so. I had a lovely childhood myself.'

'So did I. See that lingerie? My mother's darns were as good as any of that lace.'

She couldn't help laughing. He was so proud of his mother and she liked him for it. He obviously had deep feelings about families, his own in particular, and before long she had a picture of them. It was rather blurred because his way of painting people and their surroundings was impressionistic rather than clearcut but he made her see the countryside of Tuscany, parched, brown and dusty in summer, green when the September rains came. His village was little more than a hamlet, his father made shoes and cobbled but there were not many customers.

'We were barefoot, I told you. O.K. in summer, agony in winter. We wrapped our feet in paper and then tied rags round. We had awful chilblains. In the spring, when the river filled, we'd dabble our feet in the stream. Feet have a special meaning for me. Shall I tell you something? I've got two dozen pairs of shoes. I suppose you'd say I'm compensating myself.'

'Are they all as good as those you're wearing?'

'Some are better. My father was an artist in his trade, but there weren't the opportunities then. Mostly he cobbled.'

There he was, Aldo's father, at his work bench in an old check shirt, sleeves cut off at the elbow, hands grimed and horny. His spectacles had very small lenses and steel frames and he wore them on the tip of his nose. He sang while he worked. He talked politics with his friends; there was going to be war. He shook his head over it and hoped they could keep out. All he wanted − all any of them wanted − was a quiet life, enough to eat and wood to burn. He hoped

311

to see his children grow up, and if they couldn't do better than he had done, he'd thank God if they did no worse.

'Do you know what I do, Kate? I make shoes − but on a large scale. You can buy my shoes in London, Paris, New York − everywhere. See that range? The slender, high heeled shoes over there? They're from my factory.'

'I had no idea,' she said. 'Your father must be more than pleased with you.'

'Perhaps,' he said, and they went on, but now she felt she knew his family and was beginning to know him. He thought about children a great deal and was concerned for those who had to live in the worst parts of industrial towns, mostly in high rise blocks or tenement houses that often swarmed with rats.

'I've seen babies with rat bitten faces,' he said. 'So many kids live in squalor. It wasn't like that at home. We didn't have much and yet we had everything. We weren't overcrowded and we had fresh air and miles of country all round. These children − my God! Their mothers go out to work. What kind of life is that for a child? To come home from school and find no mother there? I'd have thought the sky had fallen in. My mother was *always* there.'

And there she was in the kitchen-living-sittingroom. There was a wooden table scrubbed white and she was rolling spaghetti on it. Her hands were so light, so deft, although she worked them hard. She chopped wood for the fire, pumped water from the well down the road, took her washing to the river and rubbed it on the flat stones. She dug their bit of garden and grew beans and tomatoes, garlic, onions, carrots. Not an inch was wasted.

'When the *padre* came she'd spread a cloth over the table. It had been in her family for years and was all lace. I used to sit under the table and hold the edges up to the light to see the patterns.'

The last shop they passed was a baker's but besides the plain loaves and buns there were lavish fruit and cream confections. These were almost too tempting to pass but Aldo's eyes were on a basket of iced sugar buns. 'We used to have those on Saturdays for a treat,' he said. 'They were sold singly but if you bought four there was a reduction so

312

that's what my mother always did. Trouble was there were five of us. They had to be divided up so we never had a whole one each.'

He was laughing as he told her and she imagined the scene in the kitchen with the buns laid out on the table and his mother carefully measuring while the children looked on. Aldo, Manuela, Francesca. She cut them in halves — that made eight pieces — half each and three halves over, so the three were halved again making six quarters. A half and a quarter each but what of the odd quarter? They had to take it in turns for that.

'So when it was your turn you actually had a whole bun,' said Kate. 'If she'd given you a whole one in turns and divided the other three between four it would have been easier.'

'It wouldn't have seemed right however she did it. We could never have a whole one each — not altogether,' he said.

They passed in front of the church and were on the promenade.

'You haven't seen much so far,' he told her. 'There's a maze of streets behind the shops so you can wander for hours.'

Ahead were the luxury hotels, the beaches in front of them artificially designed with sands raked night and morning, free from oil and litter. There were rows of bathing huts at the back and lines of deckchairs in front and uniformly coloured umbrellas, red, blue or yellow.

'Let's have an ice,' Kate said as they came to a cafe. 'You must let me buy you one.'

'Fine. If it's to be a treat I'll have a black cherry.'

'So will I.'

They sat outside and were immediately attended by a dark-haired man of the same age and type as Aldo. His name was Giorgio and he was introduced as the owner of the cafe and an old friend. He shook hands with Kate and his look was approving.

'What a beautiful 'at,' he said.

'Yes, isn't it? I shall live in it,' she said.

Giorgio wouldn't allow her to pay for the ices, not even to settle her debt. These were on him and he'd have one

313

with them if they didn't mind. A waitress served them and Kate gasped at the delicious confections in tall glasses — the masses of whipped cream, the delicious ice and the cherries swimming in thick syrup flavoured with maraschino.

'I shall get so fat,' she said.

'You can do with it,' said Aldo. 'You could take another ten kilo.'

'Oh, Aldo! I've only just lost it.'

She didn't tell him how. Anxiety and misery accounted for her weight loss for she hadn't been dieting, but she wasn't going to think about that now. It was pleasant to be enjoying an ice with two attentive men; it was nice to be flattered by Giorgio's admiring looks. It was good being with Aldo. Now he was talking with Giorgio, saying he had not had any news from Bruno and for a few minutes their talk was unintelligible to her. She didn't feel left out but she was pleased when he recollected himself and apologised.

'Are you staying in Santa Carlotta long, *Signora*?' Giorgio asked.

'I don't really know. It depends.' A shadow crossed her face; Aldo perceived it.

The hottest part of the day had passed and the promenade gradually became crowded. The tables at the cafe filled and presently people were waiting for seats. Giorgio said he had to work now but he hoped the *Signora* would come again. She had no doubt she would.

'I *have* enjoyed it all so,' she told Aldo as they strolled back the way they had come. 'I don't know when I've felt so light-hearted.'

'It must be the air. It couldn't be all the nonsense I've talked.'

They were back at the Villa Laura, in the dim, mysterious hall with its enormous dark mirror. They were reflected in it just before they separated, she to go to the annexe, he to his own part of the house. She saw the mirrored man saying: 'It couldn't be all the nonsense I've talked.' There was something unfathomable about that man now, the dark glass made him seem remote. The woman he addressed seemed far away too.

'But it wasn't nonsense and I loved it,' she said.

Was his smile sardonic? Was it a smile at all? She turned from the glass and faced the real Aldo. She had been mistaken; he looked tired, almost drained, but his expression was kind.

'Aldo do you ever go back to your village?' she asked.

'No,' he said.

He went up the stairs and she watched him go. He did not look back.

Something in the way he had said 'no' disturbed her. It was the tone. Was it a snub, a rebuff? Was hers an impertinent question? It seemed a natural enough one after the easy way he had talked all the afternoon. Not worth thinking about, she told herself, but she couldn't help going back to it.

Hester was coming out of the office where the campers booked in and out. 'That's a lovely hat you're wearing,' she said.

'Aldo chose it.'

'You must have made a hit, my dear.'

'Nothing like that but it was nice walking round with him. He told me all about his family just as though he'd known me for years.'

Hester was astonished. 'You *did* make a hit then,' she said. 'I've known him for years and he's never mentioned them.'

'Not his parents — how they lived?'

'No.' Hester knew all about his factory, his workforce, his flat in Genoa. She knew about his interest in deprived children. She knew about his girl friends. No more.

'You're honoured,' she said.

'I think it's because I'm a stranger. The kind you meet on a train. You know the way someone you've never met in your life will pour out their life story and get off at the next stop, don't you?'

'I know what you mean,' Hester said, and thought no more about it as she wanted to show Kate round the camp.

There were tents all round the perimeter and two rows down the middle with ample space between them. Some tents were enormous and Kate was surprised to see they were like chalets with summer furnishing, full-size stoves and refrigerators. It was early evening and tempting smells of food issued from several of them.

'That must be the Greens'. That's their car,' Kate said. Then she saw Fred and Stella talking with their neighbours who were German. Stella waved to them. She was obviously out of the conversation but as they passed Kate could hear Fred talking fluently. She had heard him speak French at Vitry. So he's good at languages, too, she thought.

The Albinis' tent was nearest to the Villa and Paul was playing some kind of hide and seek game with the children. They seemed to get on very well together apart from the fights he had with Cesare, but as neither of them got hurt this didn't matter.

'Did Aldo tell you Giorgio's going to marry the eldest Morelli girl?' Hester asked. 'The wedding's on Monday week and we'll all be going — you too of course.'

'But I don't know the Morellis, and anyway I've nothing to wear,' protested Kate.

'There's a girl over the road I told you about. She'll run you up something in no time. That'll be no problem.'

Hester went on to tell Kate that Fiorella had been engaged to Giorgio for years and was getting on for forty. She had no idea why they had delayed their wedding for so long. Giorgio was doing very well, Antonio was making them a present of another ice cream parlour, and it was all very mysterious.

Kate was finding it hard to believe she had only been in Santa Carlotta for one whole day. She felt as though she had no connection with the Kate Lambert who had left home four days ago, she was not the same woman and wasn't going to think of her or of her arrogant husband and disdainful daughter. They belonged, all three of them, firmly imprisoned in the past and she meant them to stay there. This was now and now was what counted.

She sat in one of the deckchairs near the shop leaving Hester to go and prepare the supper. Her feeling of freedom was such a new experience that she wanted to be alone to exult in it but Stella Green came by with a basket of ripe peaches on her arm. She offered one and Kate took it; they both bit into them and the juice flowed.

'Did you ever dream of a place like this?' Stella said. 'Come and have a drink with us. Fred goes for chianti but I like a nice dry Martini. What about you?'

Kate couldn't refuse. Fred Geen had a table set out with a large array of bottles and a bucket of ice. He was all set to pour drinks and Kate was surprised to find a party going on. There were four Germans and a Spanish couple.

Fred greeted her effusively, shook hands and held her by the arm as he steered her round the circle, introducing her to his guests and then placing a chair for her next to Stella who had been hovering about looking slightly de trop. 'I don't understand German or Spanish and I do feel out of it,' she said in an undertone.

'I'm the same,' said Kate, though it was not a language problem that made her feel out of things at home.

'Never too late to learn,' said Fred, pouring wine for Kate, and he translated the phrase into German and Spanish for the benefit of his guests who all raised their glasses to Kate.

'It must make it much easier for you when you're on the continent,' she said.

'It does, my dear. I'm fluent in French, German and Spanish as well as my native tongue. By the time we go home I expect to be halfway there in Italian.'

'He catches languages the way some people pick up dialects,' Stella said.

Fred, having filled everyone's glass, had settled down to talk to the Germans who were all very well dressed.

'They may have lost the war but they're much better off than we are,' Stella whispered, 'They change their clothes three times a day, and I'd like you to see inside their tent. The equipment they have! The quality of it all! Honestly, it beats me.'

Aldo came walking along the path with Paul. They stopped when they saw Kate.

'There she is,' said Paul.

Kate realised she had not told Hester where she was going and it was their supper time. 'I'm just coming,' she said, and to Stella, 'You will excuse me, won't you?'

But Fred was on his feet greeting Paul, telling the Germans this was his young friend whom Kate had driven from London

317

and how they had met on the way. He insisted on Paul shaking hands with everyone, and then he asked Aldo to join them in a drink.

'We saw you helping the nuns out with the kids,' he said. 'Splendid work.'

Aldo inclined his head. 'Hester is waiting for us,' he said.

'Won't you meet my friends?'

The Germans nodded and smiled. They raised their glasses. Aldo bowed. 'You will kindly excuse me,' he said.

Kate, beside him now, with Paul's hand in hers, felt a decided chill. 'Thank you very much, Fred. I have to go now,' she said.

'Goodnight,' they all chorused as she hurried to join Aldo who had walked on. He took her arm. 'We'll have a much better drink with Hester,' he said.

'Don't you like the Greens?'

'I don't know them. I do not like Germans. I would not drink with a German.'

Oh dear, she thought. But there was no need to be upset by the drop in temperature at the Greens'. They had a delicious drink with Hester followed by a very good supper, and after Paul was in bed Kate rejoined the others on the verandah and they sat talking and enjoying themselves until well after midnight.

On Friday more campers arrived and Hester was busy booking them in and allocating sites. In the late afternoon the husbands of the long-stay campers drove in. Kate had been wondering why so many of the women had worn their hairs in rollers all day and spent more time than usual cleaning their tents.

Uncle Bernardo, a gaunt, taciturn Morelli, came to help Hester with the newcomers. Kate had noticed him hosing down the outbuildings each morning and evening, and pausing to swig from a flask of chianti every now and then.

As soon as Hester was free she took Kate to see Flora, the dressmaker, and left her to choose material and look over designs. Flora had bales of stuff, plain and patterned. Kate decided on a plain honey-coloured silk but Flora disagreed, shook her head, and produced a far more dramatic length in a rich dark blue splashed all over with crimson and green. Kate demurred. Flora insisted. She sniffed at the plain silk. It was too quiet, too drab. She talked at a great rate, throwing French and English phrases into her voluble Italian. Kate with her fair hair needed colour. She must not lose herself in dullness. What was she trying to hide?

Flora draped the blue silk around her, pinching and gathering it to give an idea of how the dress would look. Kate was astonished to see how well it became her, and submitted. 'And when you have the shoes, gloves, maybe a handbag!' She found herself laughing at the dressmaker's enthusiasm and went back to tell Hester.

'You can trust that one,' Hester said.

Sunday was always an extra special day. In the evenings all the Morellis gathered at Antonio's. He was Gianni's brother and senior by ten years. He was a large expansive man, devoted to Gianetta, his wife, and to their children. he owned a chain of supermarkets and had the Midas touch. Kate was looking forward to meeting the family she thought of as Hester's in-laws. Once again Uncle Bernardo took charge of the camp. He disliked large gatherings and preferred meeting his relations in twos and threes. This left Gianni and Hester free to go to church and then take his mother and father to lunch at a hilltop restaurant. Mama and Papa Morelli were both enormous so Kate said she would follow in her car with Paul. It would be too much of a squash in Gianni's.

'Come in mine,' Aldo offered. He had a super Alfa Romeo.

'I'd like that,' she said.

He was taking a contingent of ants to the beach first. She had been afraid he might avoid her after their walk round Santa Carlotta; his abrupt 'no' when she'd asked if he ever went back to his village still troubled her and she couldn't understand why she kept thinking of it. What did it matter anyway? He was nothing more to her than a friend of the Morellis but it troubled her to think she had presumed on their slight aquaintance. Still, wasn't it a natural question to ask? And yet

319

again, why had he told her so much and told Hester nothing?

It was beyond her. He had been stiff with Fred Green, but he had taken her arm as they walked back to Hester's. Perhaps he was touchy, unpredictable, the kind of person who tells all and then freezes and becomes almost resentful towards the one he has confided in. It didn't matter anyway. She didn't care.

But thinking, as she kept thinking, she decided not to ask questions, to try to suppress her wish to know all about everyone although it was hard when she was interested in people. She had cultivated curiosity at Sally's instigation. It was Sally who began it when they were in a Lyon's Corner House waiting to be served after an excursion to the British Museum.

'What a bore this is,' Kate complained as the minutes dragged by.

'No, it isn't. It's like being at a play. Look – see that man and woman sitting two tables away? They came in together but they haven't said a word to each other since they sat down. She read the menu and then put it on the next table. He had to reach over for it. Why do you think they're like that with each other? She hasn't got a wedding ring. Perhaps she's his sister.'

'Or his mistress,' Kate said.

'With a hat like that?'

Kate began to study the couple minutely. She noted their clothes – his bowler was under his chair, her umbrella hung from her wrist by a leather strap. He had steak and chips. She had a Welsh rarebit. Perhaps she would have liked steak too. She saw the woman as a downtrodden drudge, the man as greedy and domineering. She began to discuss the possibilities with Sally and the restaurant became a stage. It was fun to be an onlooker; one could make endless permutations with such a large cast.

She never lost the urge to enquire, to imagine, to find reasons for people's behaviour. Guy was never the least interested. He couldn't see why she wanted to weave fantasies round people she didn't know. So she never fantasised with him as she had done with Sally.

320

And now here she was speculating about Aldo, wondering why he never went home. As if it meant anything to her! She watched a procession of ants returning to the convent next-door. Two nuns led the way and Aldo brought up the rear accompanied by a Benedictine monk whose head was protected by a peaked cloth cap of loud coloured check. They were talking volubly, the special timbre of their voices fascinated her, they were laughing.

She felt nervous, rootless, full of a vague longing without being able to pinpoint what she longed for. Not home if that meant the house she had lived in with Guy and Fiona so long. Not her old home that had vanished as though it had never been. It must be a state of mind, she supposed, something inside.

Paul came and tugged at her hand. 'They're all going to church. There won't be anyone to play with,' he said.

'Never mind. Aldo's going to take us out in his car.'

He joined them as she spoke. 'Aldo is going to High Mass first. Why not come too?'

'Could we?'

'Of course. Ten minutes on the verandah.'

Mama Rosa, unrecognisable in her Sunday best, emerged from her tent followed by the children. The girls wore pretty cotton dresses sprigged with a flower pattern, the boys were in white shirts and blue trousers. Their hair was brushed flat. They carried prayer books. Signor Albini came last, a tall, strikingly handsome man in a white linen suit. They all walked along the path past the verandah pausing to say '*Giorno*'. Cesare managed to stick his tongue out at Paul without anyone noticing and Mariella gave him a wink.

'Yah,' he shouted mockingly.

'That's very rude,' said Kate, but Mariella's wink amused her so much she almost laughed out loud. She went up on the verandah and found Hester sitting there transformed by her Sunday attire. She was in apricot silk with a large hat and high-heeled shoes.

'Hester, you look stunning!'

'I try to make an effort for the Morellis,' Hester said.

'Then I should make an effort, too. Have I time?'

'Hurry up then.'

321

Kate scuttled off with Paul and got him into his best blue shirt and shorts. That was easy. Her own clothes were more of a problem as she had simply thrown things into cases not knowing what she would need. She had a swirling black skirt and the treasured chiffon blouse. That would have to do.

Gianni, Hester and Aldo were sitting on the verandah. The two men were in lightweight suits. Hester looked at the blouse and recognised it. She kissed Kate. 'Dear Kate,' she said softly, and then: 'All ready?'

She went first with Gianni, Kate and Aldo followed, Paul walked beside her. They went along the road, over the level crossing and through the narrow street to the Piazza where the church looked dazzling in the sunlight. The interior was ablaze with candles and the air heavy with the scent of flowers and incense. She held Paul's hand and Aldo guided them up the aisle to the benches marked with the Morelli name.

Afterwards she remembered the intense atmosphere inside the church, the sense of unity, the coming together of the whole congregation in this act of worship. She was almost bemused by the colour — the rich vestments, the stained glass made even more glorious by the sun outside, and then the singing. The organ filled the church with its pulsing, powerful sound making her feel she was an instrument and the notes were beating inside her. She was overwhelmed by it, fainting, sinking. She had to lower her head in her hands and felt Aldo pushing her head even lower down. The organ stopped and she began to revive. She looked up at him and saw his anxiety. 'I'm all right,' she whispered.

The Mass was over, the congregation filing out. She took Paul's hand again and Aldo held her arm. Gianni and Hester were waiting outside, unaware of her faintness. They were going to pick up Gianni's parents. 'We'll meet at the restaurant,' they said.

Aldo still held her arm. 'What was it?' he asked.

'Nothing. I don't know.'

'Can we have an ice?' Paul asked.

'Why not?'

Giorgio's ice cream parlour was only a little way off. 'Go and find us a table,' Aldo told him, and then asked Kate if she disliked being in the church.

'I loved it, but it was overpowering,' she said. 'So many things came crowding in. My head was full and so was my heart. It was so much, and the feel of it. It was like and yet so unlike the little church we used to go to years ago. I can't tell you what it did to me. It was a wonderful experience. It couldn't happen a second time.'

Although he didn't say anything she felt he understood as the silence between them was soothing and he had taken her hand again. Paul was waving from the table he had secured. Giorgio spotted them and paused beside them. 'I shall see you at Antonio's this evening,' he said. 'This will be my last Sunday there as a bachelor. The next wedding, my dear Aldo, must be yours.'

'I'm not like you. I haven't got a Fiorella waiting for me,' Aldo said. 'Yours has been more than patient.'

'Your time will come,' Giorgio said and moved on. Paul had finished his ice and was eating the cone.

'May I go and look at the sea?' he asked.

'Yes, but we'll be going soon.' Kate watched him squeeze between the tables and go over to the stone coping. There were families all round, seemingly happy, parents with their children enjoying the special pleasure of a Sunday morning interval between church and the midday meal. She envied them. People might easily suppose that she, Aldo and Paul were a family. She was fond of Paul and hoped she would be able to bring him up. And Aldo? She scarcely knew him but he would make an ideal father. A man who devoted so much of his time to poor children, who was treating her as a friend, a man Gianni and Hester had known for years, a man she found herself liking more and more ... She must put the brakes on her feelings before they ran away with her.

'You're married, aren't you?' His question startled her out of her reverie.

'You know I am,' she said.

Silence. His and hers. Did hers tell him anything? Could he know how it felt to be repulsed, scorned, made to feel of no account? She raised her eyes and saw in his a look of deep compassion. She had never felt with any human being as she felt with him then.

He put his hands over hers. 'We're two of a kind,' he said.

Afterwards she looked back on that Sunday as a day ringed in gold. The drive to the restaurant, and they went the long way round, was uphill over roads that were little more than tracks, past small cabin-like dwelling places with gardens that blazed with flowers, glowed with fruit. She absorbed the sights and scents of the country, watched Aldo's hands on the steering wheel, shared Paul's excitement as they twisted round bends, scattering pebbles as they went.

Hester and Gianni were already there with Mama and Papa Morelli who held out their arms in welcome, greeting her and Paul as though they were long lost children. The food was delicious, so was the wine, the pace leisurely, the sense of companionship heart-warming. There was laughter and gentle teasing. When the coffee came and there was a lull, she felt she was home.

It was the same later on when they went to Antonio Morelli's and met his large family. Paul was in his element at once because there were many children of his age and he fell in with them as easily as he had done with the Albinis.

Giorgio was there looking proud and happy and Fiorella, his bride-to-be, wanted to try out her English on the visitors. As Hester had said she was not young — in her late-thirties, Kate guessed. She wasn't beautiful either but when she spoke and her face lit up she immediately became so.

She took Hester and Kate to her room to show them her wedding dress which was displayed on a stand with the veil, the shoes and all the accessories. She was so pleased with it and with the prospect before her. 'It will be strange leaving home after all these years, but very exciting,' she said. 'Papa has given us a new ice cream parlour so there will be a lot to do.'

They admired the dress and asked about the honeymoon but that was not to be till much later, she told them. They couldn't leave in the middle of the tourist season, could they?

There was a burst of sound from the enormous sitting

324

room. Someone struck chords on the piano. Verdi. The Morelli family were at their favourite pastime – they were all singing, and singing remarkably well. All the famous arias and choruses were trotted out. 'How they love to sing,' Hester whispered to Kate, and there was no doubt they enjoyed it. Giorgio, Aldo, Gianni, Antonio and his sons.

The wine flowed, there was supper, there was endless talk, and whenever there was a lull one or other of the men would burst into song. The party didn't break up until the early hours and Paul had to be carried out to the car as he was sound asleep. There seemed to be no question of sending children off to bed early in the Morelli house. It would mean they'd miss the singing and that, as Mama Morelli said every Sunday night, would do them more harm than good.

Next day Kate went to buy shoes to match her new dress. Aldo was leaving the convent as she passed so he went with her as he wanted to see Giorgio. He insisted on going into the shoe shop with her and then took charge. She tried on two pairs of shoes and would have decided on one but he rejected them and asked to see more. Eventually it seemed as though the whole stock of the shop was out on the floor.

'I wish you wouldn't,' she protested.

'Shoes must be right,' he responded, on his knees, taking them on and off her feet while the assistant stood by helplessly. Eventually his choice was for shoes that matched the design on the dress material, not the background. They were expensive and he went over to the cash desk and paid.

'Now we'll have an ice,' he said.

'And we'll settle up,' she said, but when they sat down at Giorgio's he refused to let her. She was angry with herself and with him.

'First you buy me a hat and now these shoes. I'm not having it,' she said.

'Please.'

'No.'

'Indulge me.'

'I won't. If you refuse the money I shall put it in the poorbox,' she said.

'You do that,' he said.

'And you were so overbearing in that shop!'

'That assistant would have sold you cripplers. Be glad I was with you.' He was so serious, and after all why not? Shoes were his business. 'They are beautiful,' she said, writing out a cheque for the church.

'Two white currant ices,' he ordered from the waitress who came to their table.

'You didn't even ask me what I wanted,' she said.

'I knew what you would choose.'

He was right. She had been wanting to try a white currant ice and when it came it was even better than she expected.

'It's heaven,' she said. 'This ice and – oh, everything.'

'So you'll think of all this, the beach and the ants and the Villa Laura and perhaps of me when you go home?'

She didn't answer at once. His question provoked so many thoughts. She would not describe her stay at Santa Carlotta as a holiday, more as a breathing space between her past and her future, whatever that might be. At present it was unplanned but there were aspects she would soon have to think about. When summer was over she must leave Santa Carlotta, take Paul back to England, find a small house for them and see about his schooling. All these things were for her to decide and so far there was only one thing she was absolutely sure about.

'I'm not going home,' she said. 'Not ever.'

There. She had said it aloud, in words that could not be misunderstood. She had committed herself.

He said nothing. The remains of the ices melted.

'Let us go,' he said. As they walked away he took her hand and they strolled slowly along the promenade, hand in hand, with the fountains playing, the flowers brilliant in the ornamental beds, and such sadness in her heart she could have wept.

Sometimes she thought, I've only known him a little while and he's in my mind all the time. What is it about him? He's not stunningly good-looking. His eyes are kind, his voice can be gentle – but it can be harsh too. His laugh – that's good. It's catching. Children run to him. He's like the Pied Piper. Oh, but I must begin to think, it's no use dwelling on him or on the Villa Laura or Santa Carlotta. Soon Guy will be home. He'll expect us back. It'll never dawn on him that I've left.

They had fallen into a routine: beach in the morning, siesta and writing postcards after lunch, and then a stroll to Giorgio's in the early evening. Paul had not yet found a shell that was good enough for Ada so he sent her a card to say he was still looking. Kate sent her a card, one for Ella, and one for Uncle George. She also wrote him a long letter telling him of her dilemma over Paul, and her resolve not to return to Guy. She hated doing it but Hester advised it.

Aldo was with her when she posted it. It was evening. Everything sparkled. Fountains on the promenade threw up glittering cascades which turned into rainbows, her hand was in Aldo's, the flower beds were planted with zinnias and marigolds, her least favourite flowers but now she was enchanted. The palm trees, the stone seats, all of it was magical, nothing could change it. For her it would always be there.

Giorgio sat with them for a while at the cafe.

'I would like time to stand still,' she said.

Giorgio told her it had. 'Time spent at table eating with friends is time captured,' he said. 'You get no older when you eat with friends, even if it's only a cornet.'

As a child she had lived for Saturdays and the cornet her father bought her when he paid the paper bill. She remembered the smell of the shop and the fascinating array of sweets on the shelves, tall jars of toffees and fruit drops wrapped in twists of paper and the chest in the corner that held the ice cream, strawberry or vanilla measured and pressed down into the cornet. Which to have was always a tantalising choice.

Giorgio went to serve new customers and she found herself telling Aldo about it and feeling happy as she recalled scraps of her life she thought she had forgotten. It was wonderful to say out loud the things she had never said to herself. The safe feeling of having her father beside her and the disappointment of never being allowed two cornets. One is enough, her father told her.

Aldo was watching her across the table, listening to what

she said as though it mattered. It was a long time since anyone had paid her such attention.

'We're two of a kind,' he said.

'You said that before.'

'It's true. You with your cornet, me with my sugar bun. Our Saturday treat.'

'Paul always had a comic. I don't think that's such fun as something to eat, do you? Will he remember his comics as we remember our treats?'

'I doubt it,' he said.

That evening after dinner, and when Paul had consented to go to bed, Aldo suggested going to the Piazza. There would be dancing to the music of the town band. 'Come on, Hester, take an evening off,' he said, but she declined.

'I like to be here when Gianni comes home, but don't let that stop you two going,' she said.

So Kate and Aldo went by themselves. They could hear the band long before they got there. The area set aside for dancing was packed but they managed to find enough floor space to join in and soon they were moving in time to a Strauss waltz. Because of the crowd Aldo held her close and she liked it. She could smell his aftershave and saw he had shaved for a second time that day. Some couples were dancing cheek to cheek, others gazed dreamily into each other's eyes. Aldo looked down at her, smiling. 'This is good,' he said, and found enough space to whirl her round. He was a good dancer, she was not. 'I'm so clumsy,' she said.

'So you are. I shall teach you better. We'll come every night.'

Oh, the bliss of it. It was like something out of a story: the setting, the delightful evening with the soft warm air, the incongruous brass band – it should have been strings – a rather mysterious man and an escaping girl. All the right ingredients except that we're both too old. I should be eighteen and he twenty-five.

'What are you laughing at?' he asked.

'Just an idea.'

'Tell me.'

'I couldn't.'

The band stopped playing, he squeezed her hard and she

thought he was going to kiss her. His lips just touched her cheek as a hand gripped her shoulder and a hearty voice told them to break it up. It was Fred Green exuding bonhomie, declaring he had never seen a couple so well matched in a waltz but it was his turn now and Aldo could push poor old Stella round the floor.

Kate had as much as she could do to contain her annoyance and Aldo was plainly furious. Fred was too thick-skinned to notice but Stella, standing awkwardly by, didn't look happy. 'Fred, you shouldn't ...' She protested, but he had already danced Kate away.

'Why's that fellow so snooty?' he asked her. 'He looks at me as though I smell.'

Kate wanted to say, 'No wonder – you stink,' for Fred had a strong sweaty smell made more objectionable by some kind of lotion he used. Instead she said, 'I don't find him standoffish.'

'Of course not. Anyone can see he's got no eyes for anyone else. You've made a right conquest there.'

'Oh, don't be silly,' she said.

'He's not the only one you've bowled over,' he went on, and held her much too tightly, pressing the lower part of his body against her while the hand that should have been resting on her shoulder slid down her back and gripped her bottom. She brought her stiletto heel down on his foot so smartly he yelped. He let go of her and hopped about nursing his foot in his hands, his face contorted with pain.

The band had stopped, the floor was clearing. She spotted Stella and Aldo at the side and went over to them. 'I trod on your husband's foot,' she told Stella.

'Oh dear.' Stella hurried over to Fred and put her arm round his middle to help him to the side. His face was crimson, his eyes watering. 'Those damn' heels are dangerous weapons. They ought to be banned,' he said.

'I'm not a good dancer,' Kate said.

'You're a menace,' he returned, but he was beginning to laugh the incident off, to pretend it was an accident and that they were the best of friends. 'Here come our Germans. Let's all go and have a beer, eh?'

'Thank you, but we have another engagement,' Aldo said, and took Kate's arm.

'Can't you have just one drink,' asked Stella. Kate guessed she knew her husband had behaved badly and was trying to compensate.

'No. We really have to go,' she said as Aldo urged her away. 'See you back at the camp.'

She was sorry to leave the Piazza, it was so lively there, but she certainly didn't want to be with Fred and his party and it was pleasant strolling along the promenade with Aldo. She wondered if he would suggest stopping at a bar on the way but he didn't and she was disappointed when they reached the Villa Laura and went in at the front door and out to the verandah where Hester and Gianni were sitting.

'You're home early,' Hester said.

'It was very hot, very crowded, the band was vile, Kate can't dance, and to crown it all the Germans turned up!' said Aldo.

Kate was shattered. 'Oh, I thought it was super!'

So hadn't he enjoyed dancing with her, hadn't he been on the point of kissing her?

'So I thought we'd have a ball here. Is that all right, Hester? In the drawingroom.'

Kate had never been in the drawingroom. She knew it was on the ground floor and that it must be large. Now Hester was leading the way there. She threw open the double doors, switched on the lights and there it was, empty except for a few little gilt chairs and an occasional table. There was a grand piano on a dais with a shawl thrown over it, cobwebs hung from the glittering chandeliers. Kate saw how splendid it must have been, what ravishing balls might have been held there – it was the kind of place she and Sally would have woven into their fantasies as girls.

The air was musty but how sweet it could be with masses of flowers, how it would quiver with the sound of violins, how the dancers would whirl to the music of Strauss.

And there was music for Gianni had records and before she knew what was happening she was in Aldo's arms waltzing. She thought they were alone on the floor and so they were till the middle of the waltz and then she saw

Hester and Gianni and even more surprisingly Mama Rosa with Signor Albini. She suspected they had retired for the night because Mama Rosa looked surprisingly elegant in a long nightgown that could have passed for an evening dress. Her hair, done up in rollers, was swathed in fold after fold of chiffon and this gave her height.

Just the three couples dancing there yet it seemed the room was full. Kate closed her eyes. She felt she was moving gracefully now, no longer gauche as she had been at the Piazza, and the way Aldo held her, the way he kept his arm round her when the waltz ended, was all in keeping with that dreamlike ballroom.

They changed partners. Signor Albini was a wonderful dancer, he made her feel light as a dandelion puff. Gianni, too, excelled. She felt she could dance forever and it was Mama Rosa who saw Mariella and Paul watching them from the doorway. Neither of them had a stitch on.

Such sharp cries from Mama Rosa, such a torrent of words, but Signor Albini laughed and whipped Mariella up in his arms and continued to waltz, singing as he went.

Hester, down on one knee, held out her arms to Paul and he ran to her, exclaiming, 'Nonna, Nonna, dance with me.'

Kate laughed to see him watching Hester's feet and trying to follow her steps. There was something more than magic in the ballroom now. There was innocence. She had laughed but now she wanted to cry, in the same way as a junior school choir moved her to tears. Aldo caught her eye and she was sure he knew how she felt. There was Mariella, secure in her father's arms, with her good mother and her brothers and sisters, and there was Paul, orphaned, alone.

But I won't have comparisons, she thought. Who knows — who knows? And as the music stopped she said, 'There. You'll have to be bathed all over again. Just look at your feet.'

'Don't scold,' said Aldo, but he was laughing. 'Who's for a midnight swim?'

Gianni whooped at the idea, so did Signor Albini, but Mama Rosa said she would wash the children and put them back to bed and Hester said she would bring the towels.

Kate was between Aldo and Gianni. They had a hand

each and were running her through the garden, down to the beach.

'My swimsuit,' she gasped.

'Who wants swimsuits in the dark?' laughed Gianni.

'My beach shoes.'

'I'll carry you,' Aldo said. But she picked her way down to the sea in her pants and bra and waded in, only to be seized and swum out to the raft on her back. She knew it was Aldo who held her as Gianni and Signor Albini were swimming round her and splashing her, trying to duck Aldo. When he hauled her up on the raft they tried tipping it up and, not succeeding, climbed up themselves. They sat there, back to back, gasping and exclaiming till they heard Hester shouting from the shore and there she was with her arms full of towels.

They dived in, swam back. 'It was wonderful, wonderful,' said Kate, and to Hester she confided: 'I feel as though I'm just beginning to live.'

Next day Aldo took her into the surrounding countryside. He drove his sleek, wicked Alfa Romeo like the devil. She adored speed. 'I've always wanted a sports car,' she said.

'I'll give you one.' He had to shout because the wind was carrying their voices away.

She kept saying, 'Faster! Faster!' Her hair got tangled, her face tanned, her nose peeled.

'What a fright I am!' As if she cared.

'I'll buy you a nose shield.'

'Just now it was a sports car.'

'It's still a sports car.'

Can he mean it. She wondered.

Paul could never be persuaded to accompany them. He was in his element with the Albinis, bathing with them in the mornings, taking his siesta with them in the afternoons and joining in their games afterwards.

'He might as well make the most of it,' Hester said.

Her words gave Kate a sharp reminder. This stay in Santa Carlotta would have to end before long. But till it did why not make the most of it, as Hester said. Enjoy being at the Villa Laura, enjoy driving with Aldo, talking with him, walking with him, getting to know him.

'What do you want to do most?' she asked him one day.

'I have two aims in life. The convent's always packed out so I'm going to convert the Villa Laura into a holiday home for the ants.'

'What a super idea. That's real generosity, Aldo.'

'Not a bit. I owe it.'

'How do you mean?'

'For my own happy childhood.'

'Better still,' she said. 'It never occurred to me to pay for mine. What's your other aim?'

'I can't tell you that. You wouldn't like it and I doubt if you'd believe me. But I will tell you one thing — I'm beginning to hope I'll never achieve it.'

'If that's how you feel, why not forget it?'

'I wish I could, Kate.'

Remembering her resolution not to indulge her curiosity she did not say any more, but she wondered. There had been something in the way he had looked at her; it was as though he wanted to say more but was restrained by a force over which he had no control.

Next morning Hester said Gianni would be back for mid-morning coffee. He was having the weekend off before Fiorella's wedding.

Aldo was on the beach with the ants, Kate was in the kitchen topping and tailing beans while Hester made coffee and got out the biscuits they always had.

'Don't let's have those,' Kate said. 'I'd like to get something special. A surprise. Shan't be long.'

As she went out of the gate she saw Aldo marshalling the ants into the convent yard and gave him a wave. She hurried to the baker's, bought the sugar buns he liked so much and was back in the kitchen as Hester was taking the coffee out. Gianni was already on the verandah, Aldo was coming up the steps. She heard them greet each other, loved the sound of their deep voices. Hester was pouring the coffee, they were all talking.

She piled the buns on to a dish. Aldo smiled at her as she came out. How could I have thought him anything but handsome? He's stunning, she thought. She put the dish down. 'It isn't Saturday but it's still a treat,' she said. 'Here you are, Aldo. You can have a whole bun all to yourself. Two if you like.'

His face, his whole demeanour, changed. He sat staring at the dish. It was unnerving to see him so still. His hands gripped the table. She saw the hairs on his arms, the muscles in his neck, his open shirt and the gold crucifix gleaming on his chest, and she knew that what she had done was terrible. She was still, Hester was still, Gianni didn't move. Then Aldo stood, made Hester a little bow, murmured some words — '*Mi scusi*' perhaps — and left the verandah.

They heard him run down the steps, heard his car start up, heard the engine roar as he drove off and up the hill. They listened till the sound died away.

'What have I done?' Kate asked out of her dry throat.

Hester was perplexed. She had never known Aldo behave so strangely in all the years of their friendship.

Kate told them the story of the buns as Aldo had told it to her, and about his village, his parents, his sisters.

Gianni leaned back in his chair watching her as she spoke. Then he said: 'Aldo has no family, Kate. His village was wiped out by the Nazis and the villagers were all lined up and shot.'

She couldn't believe him. She was cold in that burning sun. The colour went out of the sky. This did not match with what Aldo had related with such obvious pleasure and yet how could she doubt Gianni either?

'Oh God,' she said.

'Why did you never tell me this, Gianni?' asked Hester.

He took her hand. 'There was no need. Aldo was a boy when it happened. There are many like him. They merge in with the rest of us and live ordinary lives. But sometimes a word, a sound, even a scent, resurrects the private hell that's never far away. Then, for a moment, the mask falls.'

Kate couldn't speak, she couldn't take her eyes from Gianni's face. She had unleashed evil and now it was spreading out, pervading the air like a filthy smell. It grew more overpowering every second and she felt it envelop her in its suffocating mist.

She could hear the noises of the camp going on as

334

though nothing had happened: children playing together were unaware of it, there was the click of balls from some French campers playing boules not far away, the clatter of dishes, a dog barking excitedly. These ordinary things emphasised the horror Gianni spoke of and she blamed herself entirely. How stupid she had been, how unperceptive. It was impertinent to do what she had done, to intrude into Aldo's life, and she could imagine his resentment. She would have been affronted if someone she scarcely knew had behaved in such a way with her. She would have seen it as familiarity of the most objectionable kind, and now didn't know how she could ever face him again. Apologies would make it worse. A green lizard streaked across the verandah close to her foot. The swift movement, the flicking tail and tiny glittering eyes repelled her. She was finding it hard to swallow.

Gianni patted her shoulder. 'It will be all right,' he said. 'He'll come back recovered. You'll see.'

Hester tried to console her, told her Aldo was much too big-hearted to hold it against her. 'He will understand,' she said. 'You were not to know.' But she knew how sensitive Kate was and how she would suffer for inflicting pain on Aldo. With Fiorella's wedding so close any disharmony could cast a shadow.

'I'm going to see Fiorella,' she said. 'Would you like to come with me, Kate?'

'I don't think so,' she said. 'I'll go for a little wander round the camp if you don't mind.'

She went down the steps and strolled around the camp. People greeted her. Mama Rosa, in the doorway of her tent, was rolling spaghetti as usual. The children were playing some game of their own but Paul detached himself and walked by her side. He slipped his hand into hers. They stopped to watch the men playing boules. An old woman dozed in a deckchair; her clothes were black and she had a rosary wound round her hands.

'Is she in mourning?' Paul asked.

'You can't tell. They go in for black,' she said, and felt heavy-hearted enough to be in mourning herself.

Stella Green was at a communal sink washing a lettuce

under running water. She did it a leaf at a time, back and front, rinsing and rinsing. She called out to Kate, making her stop. She looked happy, her eyes shining. 'We're staying on another fortnight,' she said. 'I was afraid two weeks would be enough for Fred but he loves it here as much as I do. Isn't it marvellous?'

'I'm so glad,' said Kate, trying to put some enthusiasm into her voice.

'What about you?' Stella asked. 'Are you staying on?'

'For a time,' Kate said. 'We haven't a settled plan.'

'We're not tied, either. Fred left the business in capable hands so that's all right. Will your husband be joining you?'

'He's used up his holiday for this year,' Kate said. He hadn't. He had at least fourteen days to come.

'I'd like to live here,' announced Paul.

'So would I,' Stella agreed. 'There, I don't think there's a single grain of grit left.' She piled the lettuce into a colander and covered it with a tea towel. 'Tea time. Would you like a cup?'

Kate thanked her and declined. She felt too restless to sip tea and exchange small talk today. She wanted action. If she'd had a fast car she would have driven it madly, recklessly. As it was she could only think of swimming, making for the raft and diving off it.

Paul wanted to go too.

'No, darling,' she said.

'Please, Kate. Please.'

'No,' she said. He looked disappointed and made her feel mean. 'We'll do something special this evening,' she said. 'I'll only be gone half an hour anyway. Go back with Cesare.'

There were only three or four people dozing in the shabby old deckchairs on the beach and two men lying on straw mats lazily tossing pebbles. She had forgotten her beach shoes in her haste to get to the sea. She went down as close to the water as she could, kicked off her sandals and made her way painfully to the edge.

The sea was rougher than she had seen it; large waves hurled themselves at the beach and went purling back again.

She paddled in and it was soon deep enough to swim. She wanted to reach the anchored raft but after she had taken a few strokes she realised the strength of the tide. It was carrying her out so fast she would have to turn now or she would never get back. She swam with strong, measured strokes and thought she was making headway. She could measure her progress against a breakwater but soon found she had scarcely gone forward at all. She tried harder but it was useless. If she could get to the breakwater there might be something to cling to and help herself along so she made in that direction and reached it after a struggle but the wood was too slimy to hold. If she could only pull herself up on top someone might see her.

She dug her nails into the wood and then felt the ground under her feet. She was up to her neck but she could stand and thought, Well, it's all right. The tide's going out, the sea will leave me. She took a step forward, another and another, stood and was only waist deep. Then, without warning, a wave picked her up, broke over her, hurled her into the shallows with such force all her breath was knocked out of her. When she tried to struggle up the wave dragged her back with it. It was like a wild animal, tossing her forward, dragging her back, pounding her on the stones.

She couldn't breathe, she couldn't see, and each time the sea went purling back she got to her knees only to be dashed down again before she could rise. It happened again and again. If she could only get her breath, open her eyes. She did open them and saw the wave, terrible and strong, saw cascades of drops and the grey light under the grey water, and then the stones cutting into her. She had no strength left. She lay flopped like a stranded whale, drowning in the dregs of the sea.

Hands grabbed her. She heard voices. She was lifted, carried up the beach half conscious. The voices were angry and when she managed to open her sore, smarting eyes for a second she saw the two men who had been sunbathing. They had seen what was happening and hauled her out and they were angry. She was too shocked to understand them but they went ranting on at her, not attempting to help any more. She lay with her eyes shut and heard another voice. Aldo's.

337

They were talking to him, telling him what had happened. That fool of a woman! They had such loud indignant voices.

She sat up, clasped her arms round her knees and bent her head.

'How could you be such a fool as to go in on a falling tide?' His voice had a rough edge to it. He was angry.

She was shivering; her legs were grazed and bleeding. 'What does it matter? They dragged me out. I shall be all right.' She struggled to her knees. He left her to fetch her sandals and towel, came back, lifted her up and carried her up the beach. When he put her down he kept his arm around her.

'I'm sorry,' he said.

'For what?'

'Talking to you the way I did. I was indulging myself, telling you all that nonsense about my family.'

'It wasn't nonsense. It was a blessing,' she said.

The thud of those relentless waves, dragging back the stones, tossing helpless bodies, throwing them backwards and forwards, cruelly playing with stones, pebbles, toys, people. With her. Trying to kill her.

'Suppose I'd lost you?'

She turned to look at him. 'Suppose?'

'We would miss each other,' he said.

For one of those moments, those fragments, those periods of time that have no name she was looking into his eyes and she knew everything. Loss. Hers, his.

She put her arms round his neck. She said softly: 'I love you.'

It was late afternoon in the quiet that always preceded the activity of early evening when the camp bestirred itself, the aperitifs were brought out and the cooking began.

'You'll stay with me?' Aldo said.

They sat side by side on his bed. Towels and shoes littered the floor; her bikini, his slacks, a jar of the arnica cream he had used to soothe her scratches.

'Yes, I'll stay.'

She knew now that he could revert to that other life. It was preserved intact in his memory but he had never spoken of it till the day he told her. There were others who knew.

Gianni knew though not from him; Gianni knew because Giorgio knew. The Benedictine monk with the incongruous cloth cap, he knew. Now she knew, too.

Aldo wanted her to see the country of his boyhood, to smell the scented air, the jasmine – how it grew there! And then the summer evenings, especially when there was no moon and fireflies, myriads of them, filled the world with their enchanted light. Such a small world. Such a little village with the woods all round, those woods where wild violets grew thick and cyclamens flowered in clumps, so many flowers hidden away.

But the time came when men hid in the woods. There was an armistice when Mussolini fell but Aldo's father was soon shaking his head over the news and saying things would be worse now for the Germans were masters and they were everywhere.

Often the children picking up kindling amongst the trees would come on a man lying in the bracken, a man with startled eyes who put his finger to his lips. They would run home frightened, trying to hear what their elders made of it. One of the villagers would wait until dark, then make his way carrying half a loaf, a little wine and water, to where the man had been seen. Gradually the children came to realise the man and others like him were Allied soldiers who had been liberated when the armistice was signed but not repatriated. If they were not to be captured by the Germans their only hope was to rejoin their own armies.

They lived like hunted animals evading the Germans, seeking remote farms where they might be given food and allowed to take shelter till they were warned of approaching Germans. Many times Aldo's father mended broken army boots brought to him by night. Sometimes they were bloodstained.

Aldo told her all this. He told her about an English soldier with a poisoned foot. His name was Captain Bradley and they hid him for weeks, resorting to all kinds of subterfuges. The Germans came several times but they never found Captain Bradley and when his foot was well enough for him to go on his way he left them.

'Did he get home?' Kate asked.

339

'Oh, yes. He got home.'

Aldo was reliving those times, seeing himself as he was then.

'We were always hungry, always short of food,' he said. 'Our priest, Father Pietro, used to take us boys into the woods to collect chestnuts. We never knew when we would meet a friend or an enemy. It was exciting. We were out of the war and when English soldiers came our way we hid them. It was a game to us boys — I can't tell you the hair's breadth escapes we had. My father helped many like Captain Bradley. There were no more after him.

'The last time we went to gather chestnuts was a glorious day. There were ten of us boys from the village and we picked baskets of chestnuts. Then, late in the afternoon, we saw smoke from the direction of the village. Father Pietro must have had a premonition of trouble there because he made us keep quiet. We stayed there a long time and then we heard shots and we were scared. When the shooting stopped Father Pietro told us to stay where we were, he was going down to see what was happening. There was a lot of smoke now, and flames. He was gone a long time and it was dark when he came back. He told us the Germans had come and some were still there but he had managed to evade them. They had shot every man, woman and child in the place and set fire to the houses. That was not all but it was as much as he told us then.

'He made us kneel and pray for our families. Some of us wept, but we were dazed. He took absolute control of us. He was so calm. We followed him through the woods all that night and in the early morning we came to a monastery and the monks took us in and kept us there. But we couldn't really believe what had happened — we wanted to go back and see for ourselves. We thought well, perhaps they didn't all die. Perhaps they just lay still feigning death and when the Germans went they would hide in the woods. They might still be there. Some of them. They would be anxious about us, their sons. Sometimes, even now, I wake up thinking I hear them calling. I know it can't be so because they were all accounted for and now they lie together in the little cemetery by our old church.'

340

There was nothing she could say but she would stay with him. He needed her, wanted her. She dared not look too far ahead but somehow she would overcome whatever obstacles were waiting for her.

Later she asked if he had ever seen Captain Bradley again.

'But of course! He came back after the war to find us. He took me home with him. I went to school in Norwich and then I learned my trade in his shoe factory. He was such a good man, Kate. He had no children so he made me his heir. Imagine that!'

'I expect you were fond of him?'

'We were buddies,' he said.

These days Paul had taken to charging into Aldo's room first thing in the morning to wake him up. Kate, lying in bed, would hear them talking and smile to herself. She would hear Aldo protest at this early awakening. Most days Paul would tell Aldo he wanted to live in Santa Carlotta for ever: 'With you, Aldo, and Nonna and Gianni.'

'What about Kate?'

'I shall always live with Kate,' said Paul.

Before long they would both appear in her doorway, argue over who should have the first shower, and if Aldo went first Paul would climb on her bed for a cuddle. That was when she hinted they would soon have to be thinking about school. 'Pooh to school!' was his response.

On Fiorella's wedding day Aldo went to the beach as usual with the ants and was back by midday. He came on the verandah for a snack before going to Giorgio's house. He wore the traditional full evening dress and it changed his appearance considerably, Kate, having learned his face by heart, felt as though she was seeing him for the first time. This was love at first sight. It amazed her to realise he loved her and that they would be together all their lives. Somehow. She wanted everyone to know. Hester was polishing her nails, Gianni was reading the morning paper, Paul was drinking orange juice. Aldo smiled down at her.

He stood behind her chair with his hands on her shoulders

and she turned her head. He bent and kissed her full on the lips.

Hester looked up and knew the way things were. 'You two?' she said.

'We are staying together,' Aldo said.

'Oh, I'm so glad!' Hester dropped her polishing pad and embraced Kate, hugged and kissed her and then kissed Aldo too. Gianni shook hands with him and kissed Kate.

Paul took in the scene. 'I knew we'd all stay in Santa Carlotta forever,' he said contentedly.

The wedding that day far exceeded anything Kate had ever imagined. Antonio Morelli spared nothing to make his eldest daughter's wedding an occasion no one would ever forget. The church was full to the doors. The scent from the superb flower arrangements mingled with the incense. The nuptial mass, the singing, the organ, made Kate feel this marriage was a celebration of her own with Aldo. In spirit they were together at the altar, they were taking those vows, and everything that was happening now cancelled the past. His misery, her heartbreaks and disappointments were in another life. We can never be hurt again, Aldo and I, she thought.

The church bells rang out.

Crowds packed the Piazza when they came out and cheered when Fiorella and Giorgio drove away in their flower-lined car to the Morelli house up the hill where a sumptuous feast had been prepared. Everyone ate, drank, laughed, cried — there was toasts, speeches, and late in the evening there was singing. How the Morellis sang!

Fiorella and Giorgio began to leave at midnight, but by the time they had taken leave of all the relations and friends it was almost morning.

'Why shouldn't we have a honeymoon now?' said Aldo. 'I want you to see where I live in Genoa. That's where we'll live when the season's over unless you'd prefer somewhere else?'

'What about Paul?' She hated to raise an obstacle but she had no choice.

'Hester will look after him.'

And Hester said of course she would. Much later the same day Kate asked Paul how he liked Fiorella's six little bridesmaids. 'They were very nice but not such fun as the Albinis,' he said. 'Mariella's prettier than any of them. Can I go to the beach with them this morning?'

She was afraid he might be upset over her projected few days in Genoa but he didn't mind at all. 'I can't afford to miss a day with Mariella,' he said. 'They won't be here all the time, you see. Not like us.'

Kate hugged him and almost cried. She had a flash of fear. She had no doubts about Aldo but when Paul said things like that it was impossible to pretend there were no other influences, no obstacles to overcome.

'What's the matter?' asked Paul. 'Why have you put on that long face?'

'Oh dear, have I? Sorry!' she said, and she laughed and told him to take care of Nonna till she came back.

Aldo lived in a first-floor flat overlooking the bay of Genoa. The rooms were large, high-ceilinged, well-proportioned and comfortably furnished. There were books everywhere and a baby grand. He sat at it and played jazz. He liked Louis Armstrong, so did she. He sang: 'It's a Wonderful World'. It was her favourite. It was her turn to play — she improvised, found they could play duets.

He showed her his bedroom. 'Ours,' he said.

The bed was enormous, the white carpet inches thick underfoot.

'You do yourself proud,' she said. Then she saw a bra hanging on the back of a chair and couldn't help laughing. There was something homely about it, it saved the room from being too perfect. 'I'm shocked,' she laughed, pointing at it. He picked it up and threw it in the waste basket, opened a drawer and took out jars and boxes of make-up, tights and lacy pants and tossed them after it.

'Did you think I was an angel?' he asked. 'Down the chute with this lot.' He went to the kitchen and disposed of them.

'Oh, how mean!' she exclaimed, following him.

343

'Not a bit. I've seen her all right. She knew it wasn't permanent.'

'That brand of make-up costs a bomb.'

'You're not cross, are you? Should I have told you about my mistresses? You must have guessed I had a few.'

'Of course. But it's just so funny to see you clearing up.'

'It's the last time I'll ever have to do it,' he said. 'There won't be anyone after you.'

'After?' The word had an ominous sound.

He took her in his arms. 'There will never be anyone but you, silly,' he said, and she knew he meant it.

'Siesta time,' he said.

'How clever you are to have the siesta,' she said. Hours had gone by. 'It's so quiet, so drowsy,' she said.

'And it gives us the energy to extend the night,' he told her.

'Wonderful!'

Those few days, just the inside of a week, how magical they were, how far removed from any previous experience. She had complete confidence in Aldo; every moment of the day she loved him more till she sometimes felt overpowered by the strength of her feelings. It made her inarticulate, and though she longed to tell him what he meant to her she could only say his name over and over, she could only learn every line of his face, every muscle of his body, listen to his breathing when he slept, feel the texture of his skin against hers, put her hand on his heart to feel it beat.

What did I ever do to be so blessed? she asked herself, and the thought didn't only come when they made love, it was there all the time, especially when he teased her, made her laugh at his nonsense, donned a chef's apron and cooked lunch or dinner as he sometimes surprised her by doing. She thought it when she saw his strong hands on the steering wheel of his car or when they dined at exclusive restaurants, their feet locked together under the table. She thought of it when they danced and when he told her he'd make a passable dancer of her yet. She thought of it especially when she saw him kneel to pray as he did every night, his head bowed on

344

his hands. That was when she loved him most, when she longed to stretch out her hand and touch him, when she wanted time to stand still.

She concentrated on him, willing herself to keep every aspect of him imprinted on her mind so that nothing else would ever blur the perfection of what must inevitably become a memory, for their glorious days and nights were spent. She had laid down her responsibilities while they were away but soon she would have to take them up again. Aldo knew all about her life, her parents, her loss and her marriage. He knew about Sally, not only from her but from Hester, and he knew of her commitment to Paul and the difficulties that beset her.

As they approached Santa Carlotta she felt a knot of anxiety tighten inside, and as though he sensed it Aldo took a hand off the wheel and patted hers.

'It will be all right,' he said. 'You are not alone any more.'

She knew it but feared the Lamberts. Paul was their blood relation, she was not. Already she had received affectionate letters from Ella saying how much she longed to see her home and how she missed her. There had been a rather stilted one from Guy reminding her that the September term was not far off and Paul would need to be kitted out for school as he must have grown out of his uniform. She had not replied to either and though she tried not to think of what they meant she wouldn't be able to ignore them forever.

'Let's stop at Giorgio's,' Aldo said.

As they sat at their usual table he began telling her how much they would have to do in order to convert the Villa Laura into a proper holiday home for the ants without spoiling its outer appearance. By this time next year, earlier if possible, it should be ready. She tried to give him her full attention and found it difficult because a thin, swarthy-looking man was staring at her. Aldo had his back to him so didn't notice. The mouth had a cigarette drooping from the side of his mouth.

She tried to ignore him but her eyes were drawn back and this irritated her. Why did she have to keep looking? Just to see if he was still staring. Well, she wouldn't look again and then he'd stop. She ate her ice and didn't allow her gaze to wander from the immediate vicinity. Aldo had taken a cigarette from his gold case and was tapping it on the table. He lit it with a match. She would give him a lighter. He was leaning back, looking up at the sky. She loved his looks, his smooth skin and hazel eyes. She would concentrate on him and then she wouldn't be distracted by the stranger. Only the man was by her side now, standing by her chair. Aldo saw him.

'Bruno!'

'Hallo, Aldo. We didn't think it would ever happen, did we?'

'Has it?' Aldo said.

'At last.'

Kate moved her chair a little and the man called Bruno stood between them.

'I'm sorry. I've interrupted you,' he said. 'I'll see you some other time.' He ignored her, spoke as though she wasn't there.

Kate addressed Aldo. 'I'm going back to the Villa,' she said.

'I'll come with you.' And to Bruno he said: 'Wait for me. I'll be back in half an hour.'

She had a strong sense of apprehension. Aldo took her arm but said nothing and that made her more uneasy still.

'Who was that?' she asked when they were in the car.

'A friend from old times,' he said.

'From your village?'

'A neighbouring one. He had uncles and cousins in ours.'

She felt as though Bruno had created a rift between them. It was ridiculous. She wouldn't allow it. 'I expect you have a great deal to talk about?' she said, trying to sound easy.

'I don't know what he may tell me. He has a mission.'

'Goodness! I hope it's a good one.'

'I haven't seen him since we met in London when I came with Hester for Sally's funeral.'

'There's something wrong, isn't there? Don't go back — don't see him again.'

346

They were back at the Villa now. 'Don't see him again,' she repeated.

Aldo laughed and took her hand. 'There's no need to be upset,' he said, but he didn't convince her.

'I've a premonition. He's come to tell you something. What is it?'

'I don't know. You'll have to wait, and so will I.' He hugged her, tried to cheer her up. 'Come on, the heavens haven't fallen yet. Go in and see Hester. I shan't be all that long.'

She didn't want to let go of his hand but she had to. She walked past the bending acacias, up the shallow steps and into the hall where she had seen him when she and Paul arrived. Reckoned in days and weeks it was not long ago but in her life it was all that counted now. Guy had gone, vanished. She never thought of him. Her house, her garden, her sorrows, disappointments and hopes might have belonged to some other woman, one she didn't really know and could brush aside without a qualm.

The hall was dim as it always was but there was someone running down the stairs. Paul.

'I've been looking for you,' he said, and he clasped her round the middle, his face full of the relief he felt.

'I've missed you.'

'I've missed you too.' But honestly she hadn't, and felt mean and miserable for telling him a lie. Her exhilaration and joy had begun to seep away as soon as Bruno appeared and now it was diminishing fast and leaving a vacuum that would fill with anxiety. She knew it so well, the depression that made her feel dragged down, impervious to joy.

'What have you been doing?' she asked.

'I've made Cesare cross.'

'Oh dear. Why?'

'Because I'm going to marry Mariella when she grows up.'

'How lovely. She'll be just right for you by then.'

They went to the verandah and found Hester drinking iced Cinzano with Stella Green. They looked so comfortable and contented they made her think there could be nothing

347

to fear. Why had she felt threatened just now? No reason at all. Just the appearance of Aldo's old friend.

'I don't want to go home,' Stella was saying. 'This has been the best holiday I've ever had. There's something about this camp you don't find anywhere else. It must be your influence, Hester.'

'Nonsense. It's the wine and the weather.'

'It's much more than that,' Stella said.

Hester asked where Aldo was and Kate told her he had met a friend at Giorgio's. She shivered.

'Are you cold?' Hester asked.

'Not a bit. It's hot.'

'The sun is. I hope you're not getting a chill.'

'Of course not. I feel fine.'

But she didn't feel as fine as she pretended. She was on edge and kept going to the gate to see if Aldo was coming.

Stella went back to her tent and Hester began to prepare vegetables for supper. Paul was making a fortress out of pebbles and Mariella was collecting stones for him. She trotted backwards and forwards and each time he accepted her offering she squatted down to see how his work was getting on.

Kate fidgeted about and eventually joined Hester in the kitchen.

'Did you like Aldo's flat?' Hester asked.

'It's super. We had such a lovely time and we're so right together, Hester. The only thing that troubles me is Paul. He really thinks we're going to live here, but what about his school?'

'That worries me, too,' Hester said.

'You know my original plan? Find a house or flat for us in London and have him with me?'

'It's not really for you to decide though, Kate. That sounds hard. It *is* hard, but it's true. As for me, I may be his grandmother but I'm beyond the pale.'

'So we're both excluded.'

'And now there's Aldo and you're in love with him. Oh, my darling Kate, what a pickle we're in!'

They came up with various ideas, none of them satisfactory, and all the time Kate was thinking of Aldo. Why didn't he come? At supper time he had still not returned so they ate without him to suit Gianni who only took an hour off from the shop. He said Aldo and his old friend might well yarn all night.

Kate resisted her impulse to stroll into town on the offchance of meeting him. At dark the Albini children were all put to bed, Paul came up on to the verandah and presently she said he had better go too and he didn't object. He slept peacefully every night the whole night through and she sat by the window of their room for a little while, listening to the camp noises. The voices and the lighted tents fascinated her. She could hear Gianni talking to Hester. Aldo was not with them.

She felt too restless to sleep and knew she would lie awake for hours if she went to bed so she had better rejoin the others, have a nightcap and wait.

There was a light under Aldo's door. He must have just come in. She hurried along the corridor, heart beating, and knocked.

'You don't have to knock,' he said.

She clung to him. 'I've been so worried. What did Bruno tell you?'

'Let's sit down.'

They sat on his bed; she was afraid of what she was to hear and he did not want to tell her.

'It only concerns *me*,' he told her. 'It's much better that you don't know.'

'How can you say that when we belong to each other? Don't you trust me?'

She had an unnerving sense of foreboding yet she had to know. The idea that either should keep anything from the other could threaten the bond that held them together, and if it weakened and broke she would be destroyed.

'Knowing won't help either of us,' he said. 'Can't you let me keep it to myself?'

'Whatever it is won't make me love you any less,' she said.

'It might even make you love me more. I love you more this last hour, Kate.'

She thought of what this could mean. They had been sad,

349

serious, light-hearted together. She felt secure in him and believed he did in her but now he spoke as though they were threatened.

'What can happen to harm us?' she asked.

'Something I have to do,' he replied. He put his head on her shoulder and she felt him trembling and held him hard. It took time for him to regain his composure.

'You know what happened to my family,' he said. 'I've waited years to find out who raped my little sisters then killed them, but since we've been together, Kate, I almost hoped I wouldn't. I was beginning to think we could be ordinary, like other people.'

'Why can't we?'

'Not now I know who murdered them,' he said. 'That's what Bruno came to tell me.'

'Bruno!' she exclaimed angrily. 'Why did he have to come? It won't do you any good knowing!'

'But I do know and it alters everything. There's no going back now.'

'Why? What are you going to do?'

'I'm going to kill him,' he said.

She froze. The tone of his voice appalled her. It was hard to believe they were sitting side by side on his bed talking of a thing she could never have imagined. People don't kill people in cold blood just like that. Aldo had reason enough to want to do so but actually to do it – that was another thing. In hot blood, yes. But now, years after ...

Would she want to kill the man who had demolished her parents' house with them in it? If she met that man now, and she might without knowing it, he would probably strike her as any ordinary man of his age would. Most likely he would have a wife and family. Would she want to ruin their lives by killing him?

But this was different. An air raid was somehow impersonal. Aldo's story was an entirely different matter. It was sheer brutality – the raping of his sisters, the end of his mother and father, lined up against the church wall and shot.

'I don't care what you do. I love you every minute of

the day and night and I always shall. Only I'm afraid for you now. I couldn't bear to lose you.'

'Or I you.'

'I suppose you'll be going away — to wherever this man is,' she said.

'The man is here. In this camp.'

'Here?' It was hard to credit this.

'In this camp,' he said.

'One of the Germans?'

'There are all kinds of people camping here. Germans, French, Spanish. Don't ask me any more.'

But she had to know. It was not curiosity. It was the certainty that she should know the identity of the man who had caused him immeasurable grief, set him apart and sentenced him to bear it alone while he waited the chance to avenge himself.

When she heard the name she thought her brain was playing a trick.

Fred Green.

Fred Green? She didn't like him but that was no reason for anyone to kill him. It was a joke. Yet she knew Aldo would never say what he had just said unless he believed it.

'I don't understand,' she said at last.

'I've told you what was done. I've waited years to find out who did it. Bruno has spent as long tracking him down.'

'He must have made a mistake. You can't really believe that an Englishman ravaged your village and killed everyone in it? It doesn't make sense. Fred was in the Tank Corps — Stella said so.'

'She didn't say it was the German Corps, did she? And do you know why? It's because she doesn't know. *She doesn't know, Kate.* They didn't meet till long after the war. You don't suppose he told her about his part in it, do you?'

'How could he have been with the Germans? He's as English as I am!'

'He had English parents but he was born in Hamburg. His father worked there for years. Fred's bi-lingual, hadn't you noticed? He lived in Hamburg till he was twelve — went to school there. The family had many German friends. No harm in that.'

351

'Aldo, none of this proves anything.'

'Listen. They went home to England and went back at least once every year to keep up with friends. Green senior died leaving Fred the garage and engineering business he had built up. Fred had a German passport and never bothered to get an English one although he has one now. He happened to be in Hamburg when war was declared and when he tried to get home he was prevented and conscripted into the German Army.'

'That was pretty bad luck, wasn't it?'

'Don't you believe it! He was always pro-German. He was with the Mosley lot at home so he went down very well with the German authorities. He joined the Nazis.'

'And Bruno discovered all this?'

'Everything.'

'But your family ...?'

'He commanded the unit that came to our part of the world seeking out allied soldiers on the run. We had hidden so many, fed, clothed, helped them on their way. Well, we were betrayed.'

Kate was holding his hands, bewildered and shocked by what he was telling her and forced to believe it because Bruno had incontrovertible proof. Every shred of evidence had been tested, every argument in Fred Green's defence considered and refuted. Other Germans responsible for atrocities like this had been tracked down and were frequently found to be leading ordinary blameless lives, respected members of the community, upright citizens held in high esteem, as was Fred Green. These same men were often found murdered. Executed, as Aldo said. There was a network of men like Bruno who spent their lives searching them out.

'It's all past and done,' she said.

But to Aldo this was not so. Neither was it so to others whose families had been slaughtered.

'It's revenge,' she said because she was afraid for him.

'It's justice.'

'Then let justice be done by the law.'

'Kate, haven't you any idea how I feel? How other men like me feel? I can never be free while the man who murdered my family lives. Don't you see that? I'm a prisoner. I've been in

352

bondage ever since the day we heard the shots ring out.'

She was not so much calm as dazed but as the truth of what he had told her sank in she saw their new happiness threatened. She knew Fred Green would be killed and Stella widowed. She saw Aldo charged with murder and could not endure it. She began to plead with him passionately, she begged him to forswear his oath so they could go on with their lives together.

'I can't break my vow,' he said.

'Why not? I've broken mine — my marriage vow.'

She couldn't move him. Nothing she said carried any weight. Tears poured down her face. She buried her head in the pillows and sobbed her heart out and all he said was: 'You'll make yourself look a fright. People will want to know what you've been crying for. Are you going to tell them?'

She forced herself to stop. Look at me with my mediocre little suburban life, she thought. I've never known anguish like this. Sorrow, yes. Loss. Never anything like this. How can I understand it? How dare I blame him? No. I don't blame him. And she thought of that sunlit village, of the boys gathering up chestnuts on the hillside, of the cobbler and his wife and their pretty daughters. And then the rumble of tanks, the shouting, allied prisoners dragged from their hiding places. Then the screams of terror, the whimpering, and soon the splattering of blood on the churchyard wall, the bodies on the ground, the awful quiet.

She sat up, looked at him. He was watching her. He took her hands in his. 'My dear, you can go home. This needn't touch you. You are no part of it. Forget it all. Go back to your husband, pick up your life. It isn't too late for you.'

She put her arms round his neck. 'Don't ever say that again,' she said.

From that moment Kate began to know herself. A strength she didn't think she possessed seemed to grow inside her. She realised the difficulty of the part she would have to play. Knowing so much, she must behave as though she knew nothing. She imagined meeting Stella, talking with her, seeing her enjoy life at the camp, knowing all the time that she would soon be widowed. Was it treachery?

353

Then she remembered seeing Fred loitering near the Albinis' tent one day. She saw him watching Mariella, saying something to her, and Mama Rosa coming out, picking up the child and saying something far from pleasant. She didn't hear the words but the tone was enough. So no matter how deeply she felt for Stella, she must leave her out of it.

'Go on as though nothing has changed,' Aldo told her. And he told her other things as well. He explained the reason for Giorgio's long engagement to Fiorella. Giorgio's parents had been murdered by the Nazis and he had sworn not to marry until he avenged them.

'And did he?' she asked.

'Six months ago.'

'Does Fiorella know?'

'Of course. The Morellis know. Gianni knows.'

'Hester?'

'There is no need for her to know.'

There was to be a festa in Santa Carlotta. Placards announced the attractions in store: a children's bicycle race round the Piazza in the afternoon, then a dog show, a grand concert performed by the local orchestra and chorus, competitions for the best soprano, tenor, baritone and bass. Finally a huge balloon would be launched and the day would end with a firework display.

'Do you realise it's September?' Stella remarked. 'We've never been away from home so long before. I don't think I shall have any trouble getting Fred to come here again.'

Kate had to force her smile and Hester said: 'We'll save you a pitch, Stella.'

'Fred wanted to leave this week but we simply must stay for the festa,' Stella went on. 'We'd like you all to come for a barbecue before setting off for the celebrations.'

'Me too?' asked Paul.

'Of course you too,' Stella said.

'We're going to see the balloon launched, aren't we, Kate?' said Paul.

'I expect everyone will be going to see that,' she said.

'If I had my bike here I could go in for the race.

Cesare's going in for it and I bet he can't ride nearly as well as I can.'

Aldo looked up from reading the paper. 'Would you like a bike, Paul?'

'Yes.'

'I daresay we could find you one. May Paul and I go to the bicycle shop, Kate?'

How on earth does he manage to behave as though he has nothing more important on his mind, she wondered, and agreed to the expedition and said Paul would have to get some practice in if he were to stand a chance.

'Those two get on like a house on fire,' said Stella. 'Paul will miss Aldo when you go home. A friendship like that is a great benefit even if it has to end with the holiday. But perhaps this one won't?'

Kate thought Stella was fishing. 'Who knows?' she said airily.

'I do hope you and I will keep up, Kate.'

'There's no reason why not,' she said, thinking there would be a very strong one when Aldo killed Stella's husband, unless he could manage it without her knowing.

'I certainly intend to keep in touch with Hester so she'll be a link between us,' Stella said. 'Oh dear, do you dread going home and getting back into the old routine?'

'Don't let's think of it. Let's have another Martini,' said Kate, but Stella couldn't stop. Fred would be champing for the evening meal and, as she said, he would expect her to join him in an aperitif first and she didn't want to get tiddly.

Bruno had taken to visiting the camp. Kate saw him strolling around with Giorgio one evening. Most of the campers knew Giorgio as his ice cream establishment was so popular and consequently he was greeted on all sides. Kate saw him chatting to Stella and apparently introducing Bruno to her and then Fred joined them. The four of them were laughing. Fred, with a bottle in his hand, was obviously inviting them to have a drink but they declined and moved on.

How dreadful it is to have foreknowledge, she thought. How innocuous that little scene. Who but I would see anything sinister in it? And she began to offer up fatuous little prayers in the hope divine intervention would prevent a tragedy. Only it was not a tragedy, but justice. And even the Almighty had never changed the past. What happened on that Spetember day in 1943 happened for ever.

But Aldo meant even more to her now. She watched him escorting the ants to the beach every day and then back again. Rewards were given for good conduct; the most popular was a drive along the coast road in his car, or to see the illuminations in the next town.

She would see the children clamouring round him, grabbing his hands, fighting for his attention, and it seemed to her that he was doing even more for them now that he knew the secret of his past.

Paul had a bicycle. He raced Cesare along the camp paths, furiously ringing his bell, and campers stood back and cheered the rivals on. Kate felt drained of energy. She was no nearer to solving the problem of Paul's future.

Saturday. Even before it was light and before anyone stirred there was the same feeling of a day apart just as there is at Christmas. It was the festa. Aldo was sleeping peacefully. Kate slid out of bed and tiptoed back to her own room without disturbing Paul. She opened the shutters and felt the cool air on her face, heard the rustle of the vine leaves and saw the first tinge of colour in the sky. It was a rare and beautiful colour, a strange pale magical green. She held her breath as she watched it. Soon the sun would rise, it woud be a cloudless brilliant day and the camp would be astir.

Nothing bad will happen today, she thought.

Paul woke up, remembered the bicycle race and before she could stop him had charged into Aldo and was shouting at him to wake up.

'What a littel beast you are,' growled Aldo.

But there was no peace. Judging by the noise from the Albini tent an almighty quarrel was going on between the children and presently Cesare was forcibly ejected and sat on the ground howling. Paul ran out to see what was going on, Mariella emerged and put her arms round his neck, whereupon Cesare stood up and hit her and in no time all three were locked in combat, kicking and punching and making a hullaballoo.

'Come back here at once!' shouted Kate. She ran down the verandah steps, caught hold of Paul and dragged him away. 'Any more of that and you won't be allowed to enter the race this afternoon. Go and take a shower.'

'Aldo's having one.'

'Then you go next.'

Aldo emerged towelling his hair. 'Time's running on. The ants will be rampaging,' he said. He gave her a kiss and hurried away. She knew a moment of pure happiness. We could be a family, she thought, my family, the ideal family I always dreamed of.

At breakfast Hester said Uncle Bernardo would take charge of the camp that evening so she would be free to go to the festa.

'I don't know if Gianni will come to everything but I'm sure Aldo will and all the Morellis. The camp's usually empty as there's so much going on in town.'

'What about the ants?'

'There's a special place reserved for them so they can see the balloon go up and the fireworks,' Hester said.

Nothing awful is likely to happen tonight, Kate thought, and she accompanied Mama Rosa and the Albini children to the bicycle race.

Paul's bike, being brand new, outshone Cesare's. The competitors were lined up, their bicycles checked, their names entered, and a large number pinned to the back of their shirt. Paul was full of confidence, he knew he could win. Cesare, more subdued, ignored him. Going through the preliminaries took an unconscionable time as the officials argued with one another in excitable tones thus increasing the tension of the children but at last all was ready. The signal was given and off they went, twenty-four boys and girls pedalling away as though their lives depended on it. Once, twice round the square. In the third lap two children fell off and were snatched up by anxious mothers while fathers retrieved their bicycles.

Paul was ahead to begin with but by the third lap he was nowhere; he was twelfth past the winning post, Cesare third.

Prizes were given, Cesare's was a T shirt. Paul shook his hands with him. 'Congratulations. The best man won,' he said, referring to the contest between the two of them.

There were stalls selling all kinds of goods along the side wall of the church — jewellery, gloves, blouses, jumpers, straw hats, parasols, cakes, sweets, soft drinks. Mama Rosa treated all the children to sticky bars of toffee stuffed with nuts which were soon plastered all round their mouths. Kate came to the rescue with her box of moistened wipes and then they all made for the fairground where they went on the roundabouts, the swings, the dodgems. Mama Rosa and Kate took it in turns to look after the bicycles.

Screams of delight from the children as the swings rose higher and higher. Kate took a turn and thrilled to the sensation forgotten since childhood — the lift, the fall, higher. Oh, to go right over the top. Mama Rosa shared a dodgem with Paul. It was all noise and excitement, the pleasure tempered now and then by the woebegone howls of a child who had lost its mother.

At last, having sampled all the delights, Mama Rosa rounded up her brood and they headed for home because, as she said, they must eat and rest now or they wouldn't enjoy the events still in store.

Fred and Stella were keeping open house inside and outside their tent. Barbecues were still something of a novelty and Fred was proud of his new apparatus. He cooked innumerable chicken joints seasoned with garlic, pieces of steak, lamb, red peppers and mushroom kebabs, sausages. Stella made bowls of salad. Campers they scarcely knew came to partake. The Germans stuffed themselves.

Stella hurried over to the verandah. Only Kate, Hester and Paul were there. 'Do come. We're having a lovely party,' she said.

On the way back to the tent she walked between Kate and Hester. 'I'm worried. Fred's drinking too much,' she said. 'He's unpredictable when he's drunk.'

Fred, with a bottle in one hand, clasped Hester to his chest, gave her a smacking kiss and told the assembled company that she was his dearest friend, a game old girl and one of the best. Kate managed to elude him and saw he took it badly. He gripped her arm so hard it hurt. 'Stamped on my foot on purpose,' he said in an undertone. 'Just you wait, my girl I'll have your skirt over your head before this night's over.'

'You're hurting my arm,' she said loudly.

'Serve you right if you can't take a joke.' As he said this he gave her a horrible leering smile which Stella saw. She was pressing food on everyone. 'Come and help, Fred,' she said, giving him a platter full of chicken joints to hand round.

The evening was going on and people didn't want to miss the fun in the Piazza. They were drifting away. Hester ate a little for politeness' sake. She said the singing competitions would be first and they were usually worth hearing. This year one of Gianni's nephews had entered so she mustn't miss it.

'Soon it will be dusk,' she said. 'The evenings draw in so quickly.'

'Why don't we go now?' Stella suggested. 'Nearly everyone else has gone.'

'Come on, Nonna,' urged Paul. 'Mama Rosa's gone. Come on, Kate.'

'You go on, Hester,' Kate said. 'I'll follow soon.'

So Hester and Stella went off with Paul dancing ahead and Kate went back to the Villa and found Aldo in the hall.

'The others have gone on. Fred's drunk and the camp's all but empty. Shall we go?' she asked.

'You go,' he replied. 'I'll see you there.'

'Can't you come now?'

'Not just yet.'

'I'll wait till you're ready.'

'Please,' he said. 'Go now. I'll see you on your way.'

She noticed his car engine was running but didn't remark on it. The road was deserted; everyone was at the festa. He kissed her, his face was rough as it was hours since his early morning shave. 'Sorry,' he said.

'I like it.' She rubbed her cheek against his, enjoying the prickly feel of it. The harsh noise of the roundabout was just audible and was soon drowned by the brass band which was that much nearer to them.

It was almost dark. She began to walk towards the

Piazza, turned to see him still at the gate. She waved, walked on, looked back and he was no longer there but she heard voices. Aldo's, Bruno's, Giorgio's. She stood still. The night was delightfully warm but she felt cold. She hesitated, then began to walk back. There was no one in the hall or on the verandah. There was light inside Fred's tent. She approached it stealthily, passing the tent where an old woman's voice was droning the rosary.

She heard Fred greet Aldo. His speech was slurred. He was offering food and wine. Bruno was there talking in a conversational tone. She crept as close to the tent as she dared. Bruno was talking about the war. She thought she heard him say he had been in the tank corps.

'Shake hands. I was in the tanks corps too,' said Fred.

'Here in Italy, I'm informed.' Bruno's tone had changed.

'Informed? What's this? An inquisition?'

'A statement of fact.'

'We're having a party. Help yourself to a drink.'

'Mr Green, you were born in Hamburg of English parents. You grew up there, went to school there. Your parents returned to England and you continued your education there. As a very young man you joined the party of Oswald Mosley − the Blackshirts. Correct?'

'What's all this in aid of?'

'You'll be told in good time. In 1939 you went to Germany on holiday. War broke out. You had a German passport and were prevented from leaving.'

'So were plenty of others.'

'You joined the Nazi party and the army.'

'Didn't have much choice, did I?'

'Perhaps not. You had a good record.'

'Thank you very much. Won't you have a drink now?'

'You were in Italy in 1943. The occupying force. You scoured the countryside rounding up allied soldiers.'

'That was my job.'

'And the country people, the peasants who succoured them. How did you treat them?'

'Look here, I'm fed up with all this. What's it got to do

360

with you? All right, I was here. It was fate sent me. And now I'm off to the Piazza.'

'Not just yet. Do you recall a village where a cobbler lived with his family? A boy and two girls?'

'There were plenty of cobblers and plenty of girls.'

'This cobbler sheltered an English Captain. Captain Bradley. He'd been wounded and the family looked after him. They were not the only ones to succour allied soldiers. Practically everyone in the village did. So you ordered them all out. You lined them up against the church wall. The cobbler's little girls ran into the church and you went in and raped them. Both of them. Then you dragged them out and shot them in front of their parents. And after that you shot the villagers. Men, women and children.'

'Quite finished?'

'Not yet. Do you remember the cobbler's name? It was painted over his shop.'

'What do I care? This is just a lot of balls. Anyway, I'm off to the fair. Coming?'

The bravado in his tone made Kate's teeth chatter. Crouching beside the tent, straining her ears to catch every word and yet not being certain she heard everything, she had no doubt of Fred Green's guilt. He had not denied anything, he was brazening it out.

'The cobbler's name, Mr Green?' Bruno persisted.

'How do I now and what do I care?'

'There was a press photographer with your unit, Mr Green. He took a photo of those villagers as they were shot. Then he took one of you standing in front of the cobbler's shop. They were never published but he kept them. I have them here. You may see them for yourself.'

'Stuff your photos!'

'The cobbler's name is perfectly clear. Read it.'

Fred Green refused. He began to bluster and shout; he ordered them out of his tent, threatened to fetch the police.

'It has taken us a long time to catch up with you, Mr Green. Years to find the photographer and get these prints. The cobbler's name, as you see, was Bianchi.'

Fred Green began to make gibbering noises. It was

sickening to hear him. Kate hugged herself there in the dark. She ached with crouching, with keeping still. Then Aldo spoke.

'You raped my sisters. You murdered my family. My name is Aldo Bianchi. I have a car waiting to take you away.'

'No, I'm not going,' screamed Fred. 'It was war. I was under orders. Please, listen. I'll do anything – '

Kate heard his disgusting, grovelling pleas for mercy. She could imagine him on his knees, trying to clutch Aldo's hands, begging to be spared. He must have been near the opening for he made a dash for it. She saw him running from the tent past the villa and into the road, calling for help in a strangulated voice.

Aldo was after him. Bruno drove the car out to the road. Giorgio was with him. She followed. Fred was running in the direction of the Piazza and Aldo was not far behind. The poles of the level crossing were down so they would have to stop. She could hear the noise of the express. Fred had reached the barriers, he was under it. There was a single shot. She saw him pitch forward and go under the train.

Aldo was standing there, the gun in his hand. She took it and slid it into the pocket of her dress. There was a path to the beach. She went down it slowly. A pleasure boat which ran trips along the coast was berthed a little way back and it was there now with a queue waiting to go on board. She had promised Paul they would take a trip one day; now she would take one by herself. She joined the queue. People were saying they would be able to see the balloon launched from the boat and have a much better view than from the crowded Piazza. No one was aware of what had happened. The street had been deserted when she left it. Everyone was at the Piazza.

She went on board with the others. It was a small boat with a noisy engine and as soon as all the seats were taken they set off and went chugging out to sea. There was a warm breeze. She could trail her hand in the water.

When they were some way out the boat turned and cruised gently along the coast. Sounds came over the water, the town band playing and the noise of excited voices for the balloon was about to be launched. They had a clear view of it from the boat. Then there was a triumphant roll of drums and loud cheering as it rose and began to gain height. All the passengers were craning their necks and shouting as the balloon floated over their heads. It had the name 'Santa Carlotta' in bold letters all round it. How they cheered and shouted and stood up, and how the boatman bellowed at them to sit down. Noise, confusion, high spirits. Kate quietly dropped the gun into the sea.

The boat went on. Those who wished could disembark at the Piazza. They tied up and nearly everyone, including Kate, got off. The balloon was high up now and drifting along in the direction of the next resort. Everyone lost interest in it.

Kate walked about hoping to see Hester but the first person she ran into was Stella wearing a comic hat and licking a cornet.

'My dear, it's been such fun,' she said. 'They couldn't get the balloon of the ground at first and the officials were all going mad. Did you see it?'

'I wasn't near enough but I certainly saw it go up. Where's Hester?'

'In the fairground with Paul.'

They walked along together. 'There! There's Hester on the roundabout,' Stella said.

Kate just caught sight of her on a horse with Paul in front. Then she saw the swings and there was Aldo at one end of a boat with Signor Albini at the other. She felt very odd. How on earth had he got there? He couldn't have crossed the railway line. But Bruno could have driven round over the bridge a mile or so further on. It was not necessary to cross the level crossing to reach the Piazza from the camp – it took longer, that was all.

Mama Rosa was at the hoop-la stall, she had just won a china dog. She seemed delighted with it and was showing it to the man next to her. It was Bruno.

Kate felt her legs would give way under her. Only a few hours ago I was here with Paul for the bicycle race. Now I'm accessory to an act of murder. But it's not murder – it's justice.

'Are you all right, dear?' It was Stella, looking anxious. 'Let's find a seat.'

She led Kate to a stone seat still warm from the sun. 'It's wonderful but a bit wearing,' Stella said. 'I'll get you a lemonade.'

She was off and back again with a glass of ice cold lemonade and Kate drank it thankfully. Whatever happened she mustn't give way now.

'That's lovely — a real reviver,' she said.

'Good. You know, I wouldn't have missed this for anything,' Stella said. 'There's nothing like seeing people enjoy themselves.'

The roundabout had stopped. Paul saw them and came running. 'It's the fireworks now,' he shouted. He tugged at Kate's hands and Stella laughed to see his excitement.

Looking down at him Kate thought: If anyone were to treat him as Fred treated those little girls, I'd kill them without a second thought.

'All right. We'll go and find a good place,' she said. Hester was with them now.

'Aldo said we can go on the stand with the ants,' said Paul. 'They've got the best place.'

Privileged for once, Kate thought.

Gianni was pushing his way through the crowd. Stella said, 'I wish Fred would come. Gianni, did you see him?'

Gianni had not seen Fred. 'I expect he's here somewhere,' Hester said. 'He'll want to see the fireworks.'

Aldo was with the ants. They pushed up along the benches to make room and Paul, Kate and Hester sat down. Stella hesitated. 'I think I'll just wander about and see if I can spot Fred,' she said. Aldo squeezed in between Kate and Paul. She took his hand and held it. The first rocket went up and then the display began in earnest. The sky, a black cavern without a single star, was soon full of fire, fountains, cascades and showers in every conceivable colour. They seemed to come from nowhere and burst out in glory from the darkness.

Kate saw the look of wonder on the children's faces; they were overwhelmed by the magic, clutching one another's hands, jumping out of their seats, flinging their arms round one another. The nuns looked on, serene and benevolent.

But even before the display was over Kate sensed unease in the crowd. There had been a disaster at the level crossing.

364

Word spread quickly. Someone tried to run across in front of the train. What a fool! There's enough warning. Blind? Deaf perhaps? They ought to have gates there, not bars.

The display went on. Kate was gripping Aldo's hand now. How was she to stay calm? Keep her wits about her? It was easy enough. She had simply not seen. She would have been here, at the Piazza, when it happened if she had gone when Aldo told her to. She almost wished she had. But then she wouldn't have been able to dispose of the gun. Well, she had wanted to share everything with him and if she was to share the best she mustn't try to escape the worst.

The display was ending. High up in the sky the name of Santa Carlotta appeared in letters of fire embellished with sparkling lights, there was a final burst of rockets and then it was dark. People cheered, clapped and stamped their feet, the band played a final march and then put their instruments away and mingled with the crowd.

Time to go home. Aldo was helping the nuns to marshal the children into line. Kate slipped her arm through Hester's and held Paul's hand. They kept together in the crowd shuffling out of the Piazza and made their way to the road. Hester was saying the festa was almost better than last year's and she hated it ending because it always seemed the season was over afterwards. They would still have fine weather but the holiday people would soon go home. The ants would go back to Milan on Monday and very soon the Albinis would be packing up too.

Kate managed to make suitable rejoinders. She could see the level crossing ahead; the poles were up and people were going over and as far as she could make out there was no sign of an accident.

'It was probably a rumour, or maybe a dog, though that's bad enough,' Hester said.

The air was soft and scented with oleanders and the cicadas were chirping away. They went on to the verandah and sat there watching the campers trailing back to their tents, laughing, talking and calling out their goodnights.

'Too late for coffee,' Hester said. 'Warm milk for Paul and a nip of brandy for us, Kate.'

She felt she could do with it. Gianni came up the steps

and sat down, saying he was thankful tomorrow was Sunday. Kate took Paul off to his bed and then came back. She sipped her brandy. Chatter from the Albinis' tent ceased, they could be heard reciting the Ave Maria, and then their light went out. Soon all the other lights were out too with the exception of the Greens'.

Kate could not keep her eyes off it. Presently Stella came out and crossed over to the verandah.

'I can't imagine what's become of Fred,' she said, and her voice was tight with anxiety. Hester, knowing nothing, began suggesting where he might be — having a last drink with friends, perhaps, or probably with the Germans. Or on a midnight boat trip.

'He's not with the Germans. They're back and they haven't seen him,' Stella said.

'Come and have a drop of brandy. He'll be back soon,' said Hester.

'I think I'll go back to the tent and wait. He'd had too much to drink and I only hope he hasn't got into trouble somewhere and been arrested.'

Hester offered to keep her company and went with her.

'Gianni?' Kate said.

He put his arm around her. 'It's hard, this part,' he said.

'I feel such a snake.'

'You should have been kept in ignorance as Hester is,' he said.

'I made Aldo tell me.'

'Then you have to live with what you know. Think of it as the settling of a score. You see, for a lot of us the war still goes on even though it's supposed to be over. It will be hard for Stella but she'll never know the truth about her husband.'

'You mean about what's happened to him?'

'That and everything else. She'll never know what he was. He wouldn't have told her and neither will we. You may be sure of that.'

Aldo came on to the verandah and poured himself a large brandy. 'The children leave by coach on Monday,' he said. 'After that I must go to Genoa for a few days. Are you coming with me, Kate?'

'And Paul?'

'Naturally Paul.'

'I think it would be better for us to stay here,' she said. 'I have to ring Guy and tell him not to expect us back. I've put it off too long already.'

'Then the sooner it's all settled the better,' he said. He pulled her to her feet.

'Say goodnight to Hester for us,' he said to Gianni.

She looked in on Paul who was sound asleep. Aldo was kneeling by the side of the bed when she went in. She got into bed and presently he got in beside her and took her in his arms. 'At last I am free,' he said.

The next few days were worse than she expected. It was wonderful to see Aldo serene, released from the oath that had hung over him so long. He told her it was like being let out of prison from a life sentence and now they could look forward together.

'I'll soon be back,' he said as he took off for Genoa.

Hester had stayed with Stella all night and was as mystified as she was over Fred. Instead of going to church in the morning she went with her to the police station to report Fred missing and Stella, hearing about the rail accident for the first time, began to tremble uncontrollably. She knew he must have been in an accident of some kind, but not that, please not that. The police rang the local hospitals but the identities of the few who had been admitted on Saturday night were known.

'Perhaps he's lost his memory,' said Hester, recollecting that people sometimes suffered temporary amnesia.

'I know it was Fred went under that train,' Stella said.

Hester left her sitting on a bench and went to speak to the policeman whom she knew very well. He was a kind fatherly sort of man. He told Hester that it was true that a man had gone under the train and was horribly mutilated. The body, what was left of it, was in the mortuary but he wouldn't like the poor lady to see it. Perhaps someone else would be reported missing. Had the lady a relation who could identify the body? Not here, Hester told him. In England. Well, mustn't jump to conclusions. If her

367

husband had too much to drink he might be sleeping it off somewhere.

Hester clutched at every shred of hope but Stella seemed to have accepted that her husband had met with a fatal accident of some kind. 'What am I to do?' she kept asking. Hester took it upon herself to supply an answer. They would close the tent and Stella must come and stay with them until they had positive news of Fred. If nothing was known by Monday they would ring home and ask one of her brothers to come out to be with her.

By that night the victim of the rail disaster was identified. Some personal items were brought to the Villa Laura and Stella was asked if she recognised them. A shoe, the back scuffed through driving, a thick gold chain with a charm, a signet ring.

'They are Fred's.' Her voice was a hoarse whisper. 'Those are Fred's things.'

She picked them up and held them. 'I must see him,' she said.

The official shook his head. 'It will not be necessary. When your brother comes.'

'Take me to see him.'

Hester tried to dissuade her but she was intractable.

Gianni said, 'This is not a thing for you, Stella.'

'I'm his wife. I can't leave him here. I have to be sure.'

'I shall come with you,' said Gianni.

They were driven away in the official's car. Afterwards Gianni said the mortuary attendants had done as much as could possibly be done to spare Stella pain. The body was sheeted over. They drew back the cover to reveal the face. The head — Gianni doubted if it was there — was thickly bandaged but the centre part of the face, eyes, nose and mouth, appeared to be undamaged. It was Fred without a doubt. Stella stood looking down at him for what seemed a very long time. Then she bent and kissed him on the lips. 'My husband,' she said, calm, upright, in command of herself.

Gianni led her away but outside her control snapped. She began moaning and crying out for Fred. 'Cry,' Gianni said. 'Cry your heart out, my dear.' He held her in his arms sitting on a bench outside the mortuary. He tried to soothe and comfort her but her agony was for a man she had never really known. The real man, the real Fred Green, was ruthless and cruel and had done unspeakable things. Gianni was thankful Stella would never know this any more than she would ever know he had fought with the Germans throughout the war.

Kate found the next few days intolerable. Stella, looking stricken, made futile attempts to pack her belongings but every time she picked up something of Fred's she would sit down and hold it, staring into space.

'Don't try to do anything till your brother arrives,' Hester said. 'He should be here tonight.'

'There's the inquest, there's the funeral. Arthur won't be able to stay here long.'

'You must let him take you home as soon as possible.'

'But I can't leave Fred here. I can't bear to think of him being buried away from his own home, Hester. There's a lovely little cemetery near where we live. I've always thought we'd both lie there when our time came.'

'I'm sure everything can be arranged as you wish it, my dear, and you may count on Gianni and me to help you. Leave all the details to your brother and to us.'

'You're such a good friend, Hester.'

Gianni, overhearing most of this, was more than ever thankful that Hester knew nothing of the events that had led up to Fred's death. Her ignorance was a blessing and enabled her to behave with complete sincerity. It was much worse for Kate. He knew she was suffering and was afraid her love for Aldo might weaken. She was at a crossroads and had the responsibility of Paul to complicate matters.

Paul too was in trouble. The Albinis were leaving and he was desolate. He might fight with Cesare but he had never had such a friend, and he loved Mariella. Parting with them struck at the foundations of his life. Mama Rosa tried to console him. 'We shall be back next year,' she said. 'You will be here, too. Time soon goes.'

'It doesn't, it doesn't,' he sobbed.

'You can write to Mariella and she can write to you,' said Kate.

'Letters aren't people.' He was so distressed he choked the words out. Mariella cried too.

Mama Rosa looked different in a dark dress with stockings and shoes. Signor Albini wore a suit. They were returning to their flat in Milan where they had no garden. Worse still, it was back to school for the children.

School. The word hit Kate hard. Paul must go to school. Her head ached. Her body ached. She longed for Aldo. She wanted his support, his encouragement, and yet she knew he would not try to influence her in a matter as important as Paul's future. She was so tired and so frightened. Suppose they found the bullet in Fred's body? Suppose, after all, there had been witnesses? Suppose, suppose.

She went to see Giorgio. There were not so many people at the ice cream parlour now and the weather was cooler. Giorgio and Fiorella came and sat with her and she poured out her fears to them because she could not confide them to Hester. They assured her there was nothing to fear. Giorgio had acted as Aldo had done; the Benedictine monk had settled his score long ago. 'But how can he be a priest?' she asked. 'With that on his conscience.'

'He did it before he was ordained,' said Giorgio. 'And what's all this about conscience? None of us has a conscience. We'd have one if we *didn't* settle our affairs.'

Fiorella knew how Kate felt as her experience had been the same. She knew all about the doubts and fears, the heartsearching, the agony. It had to be endured but it passed and one came out into the daylight again. 'Giorgio and I waited for years,' she said. 'Now it may be too late for me to have children.'

It was not too late for Kate. She was long overdue and realised the sensations she had dismissed as pre-menstrual tension might well be something different altogether. Oh, if only! Was she to have another chance – was her dream family to become a reality?

How different the camp looked now all the tents had gone! How quiet it was, how dull for Paul without the Albinis and all the other campers. But there was plenty of noise inside the Villa Laura for the work of reconstruction had begun. Building materials were stacked up outside and Aldo was busy with the contractors. Bricklayers, carpenters, plumbers, electricians and painters sang and whistled all day. There were pats on the head for Paul and wolf whistles for Kate who took them as compliments, which they were.

The exterior of the Villa was not to be changed, only restored to its original splendour. The fountain was to play and the tangled grass would be replaced by velvet lawns.

'What about a peacock?' Kate asked. She was amused and touched by Aldo's extravagance. He had been able to buy the adjoining peach orchard and part of it would be laid out as a playground for the ants. He discussed every detail with Kate, valued her opinion, and was so in love and so happy his world was heaven and so was hers except for the threatening letters from Guy. She literally cringed when she saw his tiny neat writing on an envelope and was terrified of what he could do. She was to bring Paul home without further delay and he and his parents would decide where and with whom the boy was to live. He reminded her she had no rights over his nephew and hoped she would comply with his request within the next ten days as he did not wish to take legal action.

'I've no choice,' she told Aldo.

She broke the news to Paul and he didn't believe her. He hated Uncle Guy and didn't like Granny Boodle either. He was going to live with Kate and Nonna for ever. They wanted him, didn't they?

The Morellis found it hard to believe people could be so cruel. The poor little boy had lost his father and mother — wasn't that enough? Antonio Morelli offered to pay lawyers to fight the unspeakable Lamberts, no matter what the cost. Aldo offered the same, but money didn't come into it. Wasn't Hester the boy's grandmother? Surely no one with a heart would send him away from those who loved him?

'Let him go to boarding school in England and come back here for the holidays,' said Aldo.

Kate doubted that this would meet with a favourable reaction but she wrote to suggest it, trying to make the offer sound as reasonable and attractive as in effect it was.

'Now we must wait,' she said.

Days passed by. The interior of the villa was taking shape as a holiday home for the ants and she was consulted about suitable curtains, bedspreads, carpeting, wall paper. She and Aldo often went to the big stores in Genoa to make choices and also for other necessities. There would be a nursery at Aldo's flat and also at the Villa Laura for now she knew for certain she was pregnant. Aldo was so pleased he could hardly contain himself. He sang, he made her teach him nursery rhymes, he said his heart was swelling with pride and contentment and happiness and he owed it all to her.

Sometimes Gianni told him to take the grin off his face.

One day Kate returned laden with shopping for Hester and was met at the gate by Paul who looked full of mischief. 'There's someone to see you in Nonna's sittingroom,' he said, dancing up and down.

'It's not Uncle Guy, is it?' she asked for she lived in fear of him descending on them.

'Nonna wouldn't let Uncle Crab through the door,' said Paul.

'How many times have I told you not to say horrid things about Uncle Guy?'

'Nine hundred and ninety-nine,' he said, and danced away round the back of the house, leaving her to dump her shopping in the hall.

Could it be Ada Fortune, she wondered, as she opened the sittingroom door rather gingerly for she had no idea who to expect.

It was Uncle George. He was rising from an easy chair and holding out his arms to her.

'My dear, dear little Kate!'

Her eyes went misty as she stumbled towards him half-crying with relief, thankful to be safe in his embrace as she felt the sheer power of his goodness envelop her. 'How wonderful to see you!' That was all she could say to begin with, how glad she was, how glad, and it dawned on her that she had never expected to see him again and now of all times this was the best.

'I've come to take the weight off your shoulders, Kate, my dear,' he said.

She was too bewildered to realise what this meant so he had to explain that he had brought his family home to Heron House and they would be living there from now on. He had already decided to retire when news of the crisis in the Lambert family reached him. From Ernest, of all people. As grandfathers, Ernest said, it was up to them to arrange for their grandson's future between them and he would like to know what ideas George had.

George didn't have to think twice. Paul must live with him and his young family. No question of it. He made that abundantly clear.

Ernest jumped at the idea. Anything to let him off the hook. 'Splendid, splendid,' he rumbled when he met George to discuss the subject. 'Just the job,' he said.

This solution had never occurred to Kate but it was so right and she was so thankful. George and his family were staying at one of the large new hotels on the seafront and when she went there to meet them the whole weight of anxiety fell from her shoulders and bounced away out of sight. Paul, as the senior child, looked very important as he introduced them to her. 'My new Granny, my Uncle Jamie, my Uncle Charles and my Aunt Sarah. She's very little but she'll grow.'

Kate was enchanted with them. How fitting it was that Sally's father, Sally's son and Sally's little brothers and sister would all be at Heron House together. Uncle George told her that Mrs Sharkey had supervised the work of getting ready for them. She was very old now but very much in charge and she had a helper.

'Do you remember that evacuee called Puss?' he asked. Kate remembered her well. 'She's called Jackie now. A very capable young lady. She's Mrs Sharkey's right hand assistant. How about that?'

'Super,' said Kate.

Paul had a worry on his mind. 'I'm troubled,' he told Kate. 'I was going to live here with you and

373

Aldo and Nonna. Does that mean I'm deserting you now?'

'No, it doesn't,' she assured him. She had her arm round him as they walked along the promenade with the family. 'I think you're being very sensible and you'll come here for the holidays. Grandpa will see to that.'

'I can trust Grandpa, can't I?'

'Implicitly,' she said.

They were all on their way to Giorgio's for ices, Nonna and Aldo, too, for they were having a few days' holiday, the last before winter and they were making the most of it.

On his last morning Paul found a shell for Auntie Ada and Kate slipped it in with his things. One day soon she would write to Ada.

Time to go.

An enormous car brought the Sheridans from their hotel to the Villa Laura to collect Paul.

Hester, Kate and Aldo took leave of George, Monny, and the children with much talk, some laughter and a few tears.

There was an enormous pool of love in that little group for Sally was not forgotten and any trace of bitterness there might have been had vanished long ago.

When it came to the last goodbye Paul cried heartbrokenly. He hugged and kissed Hester and then clung to Kate. 'You will always be my best friend,' he sobbed.

'That I will,' she said.

He mastered his tears and stood to attention as he shook hands with Aldo. 'You will take great care of Kate for me, won't you?'

Aldo had a lump in his throat and had to swallow hard before he could speak.

'Upon my honour I will,' he replied.

And he did.